June Tate was born in Southampton and spent the early years of her childhood in the Cotswolds before returning to Southampton after the start of the Second World War. After leaving school she became a hairdresser and spent several years working on cruise ships, first on the *Queen Mary* and then on the *Mauritania*, meeting many Hollywood film stars and VIPs on her travels. After her marriage to an airline pilot, she lived in Sussex and Hampshire before moving to Estoril in Portugal. June, who has two adult daughters, now lives in Sussex.

To Be A Lady

June Tate

headline

First published in 2005
by HEADLINE BOOK PUBLISHING

First published in paperback in 2006
by HEADLINE BOOK PUBLISHING

A HEADLINE paperback

1

ISBN 0 7553 2111 1

Typeset in Sabon by Palimpsest Book Production Limited,
Polmont, Stirlingshire

Printed and bound in Great Britain by
Clays Ltd, St Ives plc

Headline's policy is to use papers that are natural, renewable and
recyclable products and made from wood grown in sustainable
forests. The logging and manufacturing processes are expected
to conform to the environmental regulations of the country of origin.

HEADLINE BOOK PUBLISHING
A division of Hodder Headline
338 Euston Road
London NW1 3BH

www.headline.co.uk
www.hodderheadline.com

To my friend and fellow writer, Jan Henley, with whom, over the years, I have shared the highs and lows of being a published author.

With thanks to my editor, Sherise Hobbs: the girl with the beautiful eyes! And to Yvonne Holland, my copy editor, for her sharp eye for detail. As always, love to my two daughters, Beverley and Maxine, who keep me on my toes!

CHAPTER ONE

Bryony Travis adored her father, Dan, but she also despised him for his crudeness. She had read copies of *Tatler*, the society magazine, and dreamed of belonging to the world where she could grace the Royal Enclosure on Ladies' Day at Royal Ascot, and swan around Henley, mixing with the toffs; of being part of a world that was cultured, and the men, suave, well-mannered and sophisticated, unlike her father's social circle. Certainly many of the men he knew were wealthy, but not one had any class. Most of them earned their money by devious means, sailing close to the law and, often, beyond it.

Big Dan Travis was one of the hardest men in Southampton. He was scheming, ruthless and without sentiment, except for his devotion to Bryony. In some ways her father shared her ambitions of bettering herself. She was educated privately at the local convent school, where it had been her greatest delight to shock the nuns at every opportunity.

Reverend Mother had been heard to exclaim, 'You have more of the devil in you, Bryony Travis, than Satan himself.' The nun would cross herself quickly afterwards as if to ward off the wickedness evoked by this troublesome child.

Bryony was never intimidated by the nuns, and when she was sent for, she always argued fiercely for her rights.

'Sister Mary Geraldine was rude to me,' she accused on one occasion as she stood defiantly before the head of the convent.

'You are but a child and in no position to question your superiors! And I am sure in no way was she rude to you.'

Bryony was not so easily admonished. 'Excuse me, Reverend Mother; she said if I didn't study I would end up on the end of the pier telling fortunes. That was very rude of her!'

The gypsy connection in Bryony's family was well known among the staff, but Reverend Mother was loyal to her teachers. 'That's enough! I believe you have been given extra homework as a punishment. I suggest you do it well, then Sister Mary Geraldine will have no need to comment about a dubious future for you. You may go.'

Thus dismissed, Bryony stomped back to her classroom, glared at her teacher and took her seat, fuming at what she thought to be an injustice.

Whenever Dan had been summoned to the convent to listen to yet another list of misdemeanours perpetrated by his daughter, he would make the necessary noises, promising that Bryony's behaviour would improve, and

2

then hand over a substantial amount of money in the form of a cheque, 'for the church funds, Reverend Mother'. It suited him that Bryony should continue to attend the convent school.

Big Dan's wealth was made in various ways. He had a huge car lot, with second-hand cars for sale, and a repair shop on the site, plus a hand in every dirty deal that happened in and around the town. His father was originally a costermonger, who had started with a fruit and veg barrow, but who also bought and sold anything and everything as a sideline. Young Dan learned from an expert how to wheel and deal.

'Supply and demand,' his father had explained. 'You can't beat it. People want things, you get them and then you make them pay through the nose!'

Dan senior saved and bought a shop, then later a bigger one and eventually others. So his empire grew. But as a boy, young Dan had an obsession with engines. He saved his money and bought broken-down vehicles, did them up and sold them on. That was the start of *his* empire.

Leila, his wife, could be as ruthless as her husband. She came from a gypsy background. Her family had made their pile from horse-trading and fairgrounds. She was a beautiful woman, with almost blue-black hair, olive skin and smouldering amber-coloured eyes, and a figure that was voluptuous and enviable. She and Dan both had fiery tempers, so their marriage had always been volatile. It was like a clash of the Titans when they rowed, which they did often.

3

Leila was a jealous woman and not without cause. Dan was a big chap, over six foot tall and handsome, with shoulders that could shatter a door if the need arose – and on occasion he had been known to do so, to gain access to a someone who owed him money, but his wide smile and twinkling eyes could charm the pants off any female.

They made a striking couple. Dan's hair was thick and dark, worn a little longer than was fashionable for 1955, but kept sleek with Brylcreem. He dressed well, but although Leila, too, paid a lot of money for her clothes, she was inclined to be flashy, lacking finesse, proving very clearly that money didn't necessarily produce good taste.

From the moment Bryony was born, Dan was besotted with his daughter. She was his 'little princess', and he indulged her. She, in turn, adored him.

'She'll have everything I didn't,' he declared when first he held her. 'She won't have to scrimp for anything.'

'Then you'll ruin her!' warned Leila. But Dan ignored her.

'I'll send her to the best schools to make sure she has a good education, not like me. I was working in Kingsland Market when I was twelve. I'll send her to the convent.'

Leila protested, 'We're not Catholics, for goodness' sake. The nuns will fill her head with religious nonsense.'

'They take non-Catholics, and I can assure you my daughter won't be taken in by a load of black crows,

4

not if she has my blood running through her veins.'

And because of his plans for her, Bryony was different from her parents. Education had made the difference. She spoke in cultured tones, had been taught her manners by the sternest of teachers, and was definitely a cut above her parents, which didn't always sit well with her mother.

'You can't make a silk purse out of a sow's ear!' she would snap. 'You don't fool me with all your posh talk and your long words. Education didn't make the money your father earned to send you to a decent school. It was know-how.' She jabbed at her head. 'It was what he had up here, not what some sanctimonious old nun taught him!'

'I know that, Mum. Good heavens, I should – you shove it down my throat often enough! But what I don't understand is why my education makes you angry. I would have thought it would have made you proud of me.'

Leila looked at the beautiful girl standing before her and smiled. 'I am proud of you, of course I am, but I'm worried that you will be out of your depth mixing with people from different backgrounds to us. People who may think you are someone other than who you really are. The same people who will despise you when they learn of your ordinary roots.'

'But I do mix with those kind already and it hasn't been a problem.' Which was true. At the convent, Bryony sat with the daughters of lawyers, doctors and big businessmen from the middle classes, men who were held in high esteem in the town and who lived in large houses in the Chilworth or Bassett areas, salubrious places inhabited only by the wealthy and influential.

She lived with her parents in a large house in Westwood Road, opposite the Common, a huge expanse devoid of houses, with lakes and wide stretches of untouched land, kept neat and tidy by the town council. Westwood Road wasn't quite the upper bracket but was wholly respectable and way above the means of *hoi polloi* in Southampton. Dan had furnished his house with some priceless antiques and therefore it was a home that Bryony could invite her friends to with pride. They came with the dubious blessings of their parents, who didn't want to upset Dan Travis. With his influence in the town through his wealth and contacts on both sides of the law, he was not a man to cross.

Theresa Kerrigan was Bryony's closest friend. She was the daughter of a general practitioner who held one surgery in an unfashionable area near the town's docklands to help the poor, which, as a good Catholic he felt was his duty, whilst holding another surgery in the more exclusive area of The Avenue, for his private, paying patients. It was whilst dealing with the poor that he was party to some of the local scandal, much of it about Dan Travis – his business dealings and his women.

This was a dilemma for him. Theresa was fond of Bryony and they visited each other's homes. He liked Bryony. She was a sparky girl with a great sense of humour, and as far as he could ascertain from their conversations, she was also intelligent. But did he really want his daughter mixing with a girl whose family background was suspect, to say the least?

He came to the decision that there was little he could do about it, as the girls were friends at school anyway, and at least he and his wife didn't mix socially with the Travises. Once Theresa left school, she and Bryony would go their own ways. And so he let things be.

The good doctor may not have been so happy with his decision had he heard the girls' conversations at school.

'Do you think Sister Mary Joseph has breasts?' Bryony asked her friend.

'Of course she does! Every woman has breasts.'

'Do nuns wear brassieres then?'

'How the devil do I know?' snapped Theresa. 'And anyway, that's no way to talk about the nuns. Where's your respect?'

'Oh, stop being so stuffy and so Catholic. They're not saints, you know. They're just women dressed in black, like old crows! You have this notion that they are all virginal, and pure; well, I definitely smelled wine on the breath of Sister Agnes after she'd taken delivery of the Communion wine the other day.'

'I don't believe you!'

'Why would I lie? You have no idea what sort of people they were before they took the veil.'

'Whatever do you mean?' asked Theresa.

'It's like the French Foreign Legion,' Bryony stated. 'Men join the Foreign Legion, take on new identities and no one asks questions. We could have a mass murderess among us and who would know? I heard the other day that in an earlier life, Sister Luke had been engaged to someone who was killed in the First World War, and she became a nun after because her heart was broken.'

Theresa looked thoughtful. 'Well, she is about the right age. I think that's so romantic, don't you?'

'No I don't! Fancy shutting herself away in a nunnery when she could be out in the world, having a good time and maybe meeting another man to marry. What a waste. I mean, even now as an old woman she's not bad-looking; as a young girl I expect she was beautiful.'

'Well, she is married,' protested Theresa. 'She's a bride of Christ!'

'A lot of good that is. He can't take her dancing at the Savoy.'

'Don't be so blasphemous! What are you talking about, anyway?'

Bryony took a copy of *Tatler* from her school satchel. 'Just look at these pictures,' she said, opening the magazine. 'This was a dance held at the Savoy. Look at the elegant women in their gowns – and the men, don't they look handsome? I would love to be able to do that.'

'Fat chance!' scoffed her friend. 'They are all society women.'

Letting out a sigh, Bryony said, 'I know. Life isn't fair, is it?'

At that moment one of the younger nuns appeared.

'What are you girls doing? Shouldn't you be in your classroom? And what are you looking at?' She took the magazine from Bryony.

'Doesn't the Savoy look a glorious place?' Bryony said.

The nun looked at the pictures. 'Yes, indeed, and it is quite magnificent, especially when they decorate the ballroom for an occasion.'

'You've been there?' Bryony asked eagerly.

The nun realised she'd been indiscreet and immediately moved them on. 'Come along; stop wasting time here with your idle chatter. Be on your way now.'

'I told you so!' said Bryony with a triumphant smile as they walked along the corridor to the classroom. 'You never know who lurks beneath a nun's habit! I bet she comes from a titled family. She does have an air about her, don't you think?'

'Then why would she take the veil and give it all up?'

'Who knows? Maybe she disgraced her family in some way and they disowned her!'

'Really?' Then, looking at the mischievous grin on her friend's face, Theresa exclaimed, 'Oh, but you have a wicked mind!'

Bryony just laughed. 'But for one moment you thought I may be right. You'll have something to confess now when you next go to church, won't you?'

'It's you who should take the confessional, you with your wicked thoughts! I don't know where you'll end up.'

'I shall work in a smart office for a wealthy man where I'll meet someone who can take me to the Savoy.' And Bryony walked away, laughing.

At seventeen, Bryony left the convent, to her relief and that of the nuns who taught her, and took a course in typing and shorthand, but at the weekends, she worked in the office of her father's car lot. It was some way from her dream.

Dan was not so besotted with his daughter that he forgot his upbringing and the hard times. 'You need to learn the value of money,' he told her. 'To understand it doesn't grow on trees, but has to be earned.'

'I could always marry a rich man,' she said quietly. 'Then I wouldn't have to worry about it.'

He looked askance at her. 'Even rich men have to earn their cash, my girl!' he snapped.

'Not if it is inherited.'

He started laughing. 'You've been stuffing your head with those society magazines,' he said. 'You have no chance of marrying into the aristocracy, princess. That kind only marries their own. A girl has to be from the right stock, be a brood mare, bear sons to carry on the line. And let me tell you, Bryony, my dear, many of the nobility are in debt up to their ears. The upkeep of large estates and country houses takes up all the money, there is little left to indulge the wife.'

'Many of them have houses in the South of France, so they can't be doing too badly,' she argued. 'And what about the débutantes? It must cost a fortune for their coming out.'

'Yes it does, but it's looked on as an investment.' Seeing her puzzled expression he explained, 'The London Season is a marriage market, with young girls being sold to the highest bidder.'

'What rubbish!'

'That's putting it a bit crudely, I suppose, but it's true all the same. Mothers are on the lookout for suitable husbands, preferably with a title.'

'What's the point of that,' she scoffed, 'if they are in debt, as you say?'

He grinned at her. 'Don't you see, the girl will come with a dowry of sorts. She will get a title and her dosh will help to pay off the debts.'

'It sounds more like a cattle market to me.'

'Now you're getting the picture.'

When, one evening after dinner, her father first told her she was to work for him in the office of the car lot, Bryony was less than enthusiastic.

'What's the point of giving me a good education and then wasting it?' she demanded angrily.

He glared at her. 'What do you mean, wasted? You need to know how to run the business so that when I retire, you can take over.'

'What? I certainly don't want to do that!'

'And why not?'

Seeing the anger smouldering in his eyes, she tried to humour him. 'Look, Dad, if I were your son, then I could understand you wanting the business to carry on through the family, but I'm your daughter, for God's sake.'

'What had you in mind, may I ask?'

'Well, I thought I might work in the office of a solicitor, or be someone's private secretary when I finish my course.'

Taking out a cigar from a box in front of him, Dan said, 'By working for me, you'll be paying me back for the money I invested in your education.'

'That's totally unfair! You never ever told me that this was what you had in mind.'

'There is always a price to be paid for everything, princess; you'll learn that as you grow up. You'll be a great help; you'll be able to make my life a bit easier – isn't that a good enough reason?' He rose from his chair and called upstairs to Leila, 'I'm going out. I'll be late back, so don't wait up.'

Bryony was still angry when her mother came downstairs. 'Can't you talk to Dad?'

'What about?'

'Working for him. He wants me to learn the business.'

'And what's so wrong about that? When I was younger than you I was helping my father at the Appleby Horse Fair, and after, on various fairground rides around the country, learning the business, so why can't *you* help your father?'

'But, Mum, I've been given an education; that makes a difference.'

'And the car lot made the money to give it to you. The least you can do is show your father a bit of respect and do as he asks.'

Working for Dan at the weekends was not as bad as Bryony had envisaged. She shared her father's love of cars and enjoyed being shown the intricacies of an engine, was thrilled to sit in the driver's seat, turn on the ignition and listen to the purr of the motor, longing to take one out on the road.

Such was her enthusiasm for the automobiles that one day on the forecourt she saw a prospective customer looking at a new car and, seeing the salesmen were busy, she walked up to the man and started talking.

'Nice motor, isn't it?' she remarked as she ran her hands over the slope of the bonnet. 'The Riley is one of my favourite cars. The lines of the chassis are so classy.' And before long they had lifted the bonnet and were discussing the engine.

Dan walked over and stood unobserved, listening to Bryony, smiling as he did so, thinking, she's definitely a chip off the old block.

'Can I help you, sir?' Dan asked eventually.

The man looked up and said, 'I like the look of this motor – any chance I could test-drive it?'

'Of course, sir. I'll get one of my men to go with you.'

As he looked around, Bryony said quickly, 'I'm free. I could go with the gentleman.'

'Very well,' said Dan. Turning to the customer, he said, 'You drive carefully; this young lady is my daughter.'

The man looked surprised. 'Oh, right. I'll certainly take care of her,' he said.

Dan watched them drive away and wondered if he'd done the right thing, but he really wanted Bryony to be interested in the business, and if selling cars appealed to her – and from what he'd heard, she was good at it – then that was fine with him. He had to give her the chance to prove herself.

Half an hour later, the Riley pulled into the car lot. Dan watched from the office window and saw Bryony and the driver laughing together. He walked out on to the forecourt.

'How did you like the car?' he asked.

'It drove well, and your daughter gave me the car's history. If you and I can come to an agreement over the price – I might buy it.'

Whilst her father was in the office with the man, Bryony was on pins, but when they came back on to the forecourt together, she casually strolled over, hiding her impatience, and waited.

Turning to her, the customer said, 'You made a sale today, miss.'

She wanted to cry out with triumph but just smiled sweetly and said, 'I'm sure the car will give you many hours of enjoyment, sir.'

'It's for my son; he'll pick it up tomorrow. I'm sure he'll be pleased.'

When Dan walked back to the office, Bryony was just behind him.

'You did well today, princess. Congratulations, you made your first sale.'

'Great! How much commission do I get?'

Dan burst out laughing.

Bryony made her point. 'The salesmen get commission, don't they?'

'Yes, of course.'

'Then so should I if I sell a car, shouldn't I? It's only fair, Dad.'

Putting an arm around her shoulders, he said, 'Yes it is. You did well today. Would you like to work on the forecourt when we are busy as well as helping me in the office?'

'Yes! Could I? Could I really?'

Her enthusiasm delighted him. 'Yes, if that's what you want. Besides, you need to learn about that side of the business too, but there will be no favouritism. You take your chances like all the others out there.'

'There is just one more thing.'

'And what's that?'

'Don't you think if I am to sell cars, I should learn how to drive one? I mean, it's a bit ridiculous not being able to, isn't it?'

Shaking his head, Dan couldn't help but smile. 'All right, but when you pass your test, don't expect me to buy you one. You'll have to save your money yourself.'

Tossing her head, she said, 'Fine. I'll do that with my commission!'

CHAPTER TWO

The following day, Dan announced to his salesmen that Bryony would be joining them on the forecourt at week-ends when they were busy, as well as helping him in the office.

Seeing a few of the men looking less than pleased at the news, he told them, 'There will be no special treat-ment just because she's my daughter. She'll have to take her chances just like you. Now let's get to work; there are a lot of motors to be moved.'

As they dispersed, Bryony saw the customer who had bought the Riley drive in with a young man in the passenger seat. As the senior salesman started to walk forward, Bryony said, 'Sorry, but he's mine. I sold him the Riley yesterday.' He turned away, cursing under his breath.

As she moved towards the car, smiling at her customer, a young man got out of the passenger seat. He was tall and as blond as Bryony was dark. He smiled at her.

'This is my son,' the older man said. 'He is the one I bought the car for.'

'Have you insured it?' she asked.

'Yes, I rang my insurance company when I got home yesterday. It's covered and they'll send me all the papers.'

'Excellent,' she said. Then, turning to the young man, she held out her hand. 'Bryony Travis. You are lucky; this car is one of my favourites.'

Taking her hand he answered, 'James Hargreaves. Why don't you show me the car, Miss Travis?'

'Bryony, please. Come this way.' And she led him over to the other side of the car lot and removed the sold sign stuck to the windscreen. 'Isn't she a beauty?'

He looked it over and said, 'Indeed it is. Get in and show me where everything is. Then we can really get the feel of it.'

They sat side by side as Bryony went over all the controls, then told him about the engine – the fuel consumption and oil changes.

He gazed at her with admiring eyes. 'How unusual to meet a girl with such an interest in mechanics. You are very different from most girls, but I expect you know that?'

'No I don't, but thank you.' She felt her cheeks flush at his flattery. She hadn't had a lot to do with boys – her parents had seen to that – and for once she was a little out of her depth.

'Perhaps one day in the near future you'd let me take you for a run?'

'That would be lovely,' she said without hesitation. 'Meanwhile, why don't you back her out and drive over to where your father is?'

James reversed the car adroitly and pulled up in front of his father. 'She's lovely, Dad. Thanks.' He got out of the car, walked round to the passenger seat and opened the door for Bryony. He held out his hand to her and gently squeezed it as he helped her from the vehicle. 'I'll give you a call very soon,' he said quietly.

As she watched them drive away, Jack Saunders, the salesman whom she had thwarted, said to her, 'You watch that young bugger, Bry. He'll be quite a handful, mark my words.'

'You don't know anything about him and my name is Bryony.'

'All right, *Bryony*! I may not know anything about that young man but I know his type. He'll have your knickers off you before you can say "knife".'

'Don't be so disgusting!'

He walked away laughing.

Her father was sitting at his desk when she walked into the office. 'Everything go all right?'

'Yes, no trouble. Do you know the people who bought the car?'

Shaking his head, he said, 'No, love. But they are pretty well-heeled, I would have thought. Why?'

'No reason.' She wasn't going to tell Dan the young man had asked for a date. Her father was inclined to be a bit possessive and she didn't want to upset him. Besides, whatever he said, nothing was going to stop her going out with James Hargreaves.

*   *   *

Business was brisk that day. At mid-afternoon, Bryony saw her mother drive in. Dan was talking to a tall leggy woman who was looking at a small sports car. He was working his usual charm, and Bryony could see her mother fuming as she sat watching. Bryony made herself scarce, not wanting to be a part of the confrontation that was surely going to happen.

The woman left the car lot, laughing up at Dan as he made some remark, wagging her finger at him as she did so. When he walked back to the office, Leila got out of her vehicle and followed him. Flinging open the door, she stormed in.

'I saw you, you bastard!'

Dan, used to her outbursts, very quietly asked, 'And what did you see?'

'I saw you flirting with that bit of skirt.'

'You saw me flirting with a potential buyer.'

'So you don't deny it then?'

'No, my dear wife. That bloody sports car has been sitting on my forecourt for three months and I want rid of it. I'll use any means to sell it.'

'I suppose you'd sleep with her too, if necessary!'

'Now you're being ridiculous.'

She looked at him and said, 'Well, it wouldn't be the first time, would it?'

'Now don't start that nonsense, Leila. I haven't time for your histrionics.' He rose from his chair saying, 'There is another customer. I've got work to do.'

As she went to open her mouth to continue her tirade he grabbed her wrist and threatened, 'Don't you dare cause a scene here in front of my staff, because if you do I promise you won't be able to walk for a month! Now go home.'

Leila sat in one of the chairs and lit a cigarette. Her fingers trembled as she held it; what Dan had said was no idle threat, she knew that. It wouldn't be the first time that he had raised his hand to her. She did have a temper, and she was aware that at times she was uncontrollable, but she loved Dan Travis and had done so from the first moment she'd seen him. He was dynamic, charismatic and he knew about women. He also knew exactly how to press her buttons. In their own way they had a good marriage. She wasn't a fool – she knew he was unfaithful to her – but she also knew his dalliances were temporary. He always came back to her bed.

Her mother had warned her before her marriage. 'You marry him, girl, he'll always be looking at other women, but it ain't serious. You keep your temper and you'll keep him; but if you don't, one day you'll drive him away.' And that was Leila's one fear: that one day she would drive him into the arms of another, for good.

Bryony had never wondered much about her father's business and means of making the money to pay for her education and clothes. She'd assumed it was from the car lot, but helping him in the office had opened her eyes. A lot of shifty dealing was going on behind her back as she was sent on various errands when strange men would call to see her father. One day she returned to see several pieces of expensive jewellery laid out on

Dan's desk. He covered them with papers and casually sent her to mail some letters at the main post office, telling her to send Jack, the senior salesman, to him.

Bryony didn't like Jack and since he heard she was to be allowed on the forecourt, he'd been curt with her. She thought he was shifty, but at the same time her instinct was not to get on the wrong side of him. Beneath his smooth sales talk and ready smile, there was something she couldn't fathom but which made her a tad nervous of him. Not that he ever knew or would have guessed by her demeanour.

With her growing knowledge of engines, Bryony was gradually made aware of the fact that on occasion, the mileage of the cars bought in was being tampered with in the repair shop and she confronted her father about it.

He was dismissive. 'Of course we do it, everybody in the trade does it, and it sells cars.'

'But it's dishonest!'

'No, love, it's business. A few thousand knocked off the clock isn't going to harm the buyer. They go away pleased with their buy and I am delighted with the sale. If you are going to nit-pick about such details, you won't succeed in this business, I can tell you.'

She wondered what else went on in the repair shop, as it was the one place that she wasn't allowed to linger. Dan made the excuse that she could get covered in oil if she stayed there and that wouldn't look good for the customers to see her like that, but she knew he was hiding something.

* * *

21

It was Dan's fortieth birthday and there was to be a big celebration. A party was to be held at the Bridge Tavern at the Six Dials. Dan had hired the large room on the first floor. A pianist had been employed, and outside catering to supply the food. At one end of the room was a bar stocked to the gunwales with spirits on optics, and barrels of beer. Leila had wanted to go to the Polygon or one of the more fashionable hotels, but Dan had been adamant.

'My friends want to have a proper knees-up, let their hair down and enjoy themselves,' he said, 'not worry about poncy waiters and management. When Bryony gets married, then we'll go to the Polygon, but not for my birthday.'

Bryony had been allowed to ask Theresa to the party, an invitation that was not met with any great enthusiasm by Dr Kerrigan.

'I'd rather you didn't accept,' he had said, but Theresa had persisted.

'Bryony is my friend. You are always spouting off about loyalty, and she wants me to be with her. If I don't like it, I'll leave.'

And he had given in.

The large room looked splendid. Along one wall was a table bedecked with pristine white cloths, on which was laid a very attractive buffet. Around the room, small tables had been placed for the convenience of the partygoers, a pianist playing softly in the background.

Leila was dressed in a sleek black dress with a plunging neckline, over which she wore a gold lamé jacket, and with matching gold shoes. Dan looked very handsome in a dark grey suit and silk tie. Bryony was rather more sedate in her choice of dress. It was pale green with a round neckline, a fitted bodice, which showed her shapely bosom, and a full skirt. The contrast between mother and daughter was marked. Leila looked common and Bryony untouched and pure, but because of her dark hair, wide eyes and slim figure, she also looked enticing to the male eyes that beheld her.

One young blade from the motor trade turned to his male companion and nodded in Bryony's direction.

'I'd like a bit of that!'

'You best keep clear,' he was warned. 'You muck about with Dan's daughter and he'll bloody kill you!'

'It might be worth it,' was the answer, and the young man went to try his luck.

'Hello, darlin', you look beautiful, if I may say so. Good enough to eat.'

Bryony took an instant dislike to him. 'Thank you. I don't believe we've been introduced.'

He was quite startled by her educated tones. 'Er, well, no we ain't. I'm Lenny Marks of Marks and Son. I'm in the same business as your father.'

'Well, Mr Marks, if you are hungry there is plenty to eat here. I'm sure you won't have long to wait.' And she walked away.

'Stuck-up bitch,' Lenny muttered angrily as he made his way back to his mate, who had been watching.

'Sent you off with a flea in your ear, did she?' he laughed.

'Toffee-nosed cow!' exclaimed Lenny. 'Talks very posh, not like her parents.'

'She's been educated,' explained his companion. 'Dan sent her to the convent. She wouldn't look twice at you, Lenny! Come and have a drink, drown your sorrows. Come on, it's all free.'

Theresa Kerrigan, who arrived shortly after, had never seen quite such a gathering in her life. Her parents gave parties, of course, but they were usually very sedate affairs, whereas this was quite the opposite. After a couple of glasses of champagne, Theresa began to lose her inhibitions and relax.

She sat with Bryony at a table with a plate full of food: sandwiches, bagels with smoked salmon, sausage rolls, and miniature vol-au-vents with delicious fillings. She gazed around at the strange collection of people. The women, she noticed, wore a lot of gold jewellery, and there were a few serious diamond rings to be seen, but it was the men who fascinated her. This was no dour collection of males such as those who frequented her home; these men, though reasonably well-dressed, had features that were less refined, and if she was honest, many of them looked quite common and spoke badly. She even heard a few swearing, which shocked her. But they were interesting, exciting even.

'Let's have another glass of bubbly,' said Bryony.

'I shouldn't,' said Theresa. 'To be honest, my head's beginning to feel a bit swimmy.' And she giggled.

Bryony grinned at her. 'Have another sandwich,' she said. 'It's bad to drink on an empty stomach. Besides, when will we get another chance like this?' And before Theresa could argue, she was gone.

Lenny Marks ambled over and sat beside her. 'Hello, darlin', how are you enjoying the party?'

'I'm having a lovely time,' answered the slightly inebriated Theresa. 'Who are you?'

'Lenny Marks. I'm in the motor trade, like big Dan. What do you do?'

'I'm a receptionist at the Court Royal Hotel.'

'Are you now? I sometimes go in there for lunch with clients.'

'I don't remember ever seeing you.'

'Look what you've missed,' he laughed. 'Next time I'll look out for you.' He saw Bryony making her way back and rose to his feet. 'Be seeing you,' he said, and winked.

I might not make it with Miss toffee-nosed Travis, he thought, but I bet I could have fun with her friend. It was obvious to him she wasn't used to drinking. A few gin and tonics and he'd be away, he reckoned.

Bryony had seen Lenny chatting to her friend and as she sat beside her with two more glasses of champagne, she asked, 'What did that twerp want?'

'I thought he was rather nice,' argued Theresa.

'You keep away from him,' warned Bryony. 'I wouldn't trust him with our cat.'

'You don't have a cat!' giggled Theresa.

'Don't get stupid. You know what I mean.'

Gazing around the room, Theresa said, 'You know some very interesting people. All my parents' friends are so boring. I mean, look over there. That tall blonde woman in the very high heels with the trousers and cowboy hat. Who on earth is she?'

'That's my Auntie Rosa. Mother's sister.'

'Her sister! But they look so different.'

'The blonde is out of a bottle,' laughed Bryony. 'That's her husband, my Uncle Barney, standing next to her.'

Theresa looked at the man, who was as flamboyant in his dress as was his wife. He was wearing riding breeches and boots, with a suede jacket. His hair was fair and worn long at the collar.

'He reminds me of pictures of General Custer. Remember when we did the American Civil War at school?'

Laughing, Bryony said, 'You're right. I've never thought of that. They work in a circus. He's the lion tamer and my aunt is his assistant.'

Theresa nearly choked on her drink. 'Are you serious?'

'Of course. Come on, I'll introduce you.' And, taking Theresa by the hand, she marched her across the room. 'Uncle Barney, meet my friend Theresa.'

The tall man beamed at her. 'Hello, my dear.'

'Do you really tame lions?' asked Theresa with bated breath.

'Oh, yes,' he said nonchalantly. 'And tigers.'

'But isn't that dangerous?'

'Very. I never turn my back on any of my cats.' He

started to chuckle. 'But then neither do I turn my back on my wife.'

Theresa wasn't sure if he was making a joke. Seeing her consternation he explained, 'She's also a knife thrower, and very accurate.'

'I suppose she would have to be, wouldn't she?'

He thought that highly amusing. 'Indeed. When the circus comes to Southampton you'll have to come along with Bryony.'

'I'd love to. Thank you.' As they walked back to the table, Theresa said, 'What an exciting family you have, Bryony. My mother's sister is a nun, and her brother a priest.'

'Never mind, Theresa. Just think, when you die they will have kept you a place in heaven!'

'Oh, Bryony, you really are dreadful!' But she laughed just the same.

Towards the end of the evening several of the guests had had more than their share of alcohol, and two men got into a serious argument. Theresa became frightened and caught hold of Bryony's hand.

'It's nothing to worry about,' her friend assured her. 'Dad will soon sort them out.'

Dan Travis intervened just as the two were about to exchange blows. He caught one by the front of his jacket and lifted him two feet off the ground. 'Behave yourself or I'll put you through the window,' he threatened, at the same time shoving the other backwards with such force, the man lost his footing and tumbled to the ground. There was a deadly hush in the room.

Nodding to one of his men he said, 'Pick that stupid bastard up and show him the door.' He glared at the man and said, 'I'll see to you later. This is my birthday party and you are not being respectful.'

Although drunk, the man recognised the threat. 'Sorry, sorry, Dan,' he stuttered.

Dan just glared at him and very softly said, 'Get out, now.'

The man almost ran out of the room. Dan lowered the other to the ground and looked at him expectantly. 'Sorry, Dan,' the man said. 'Didn't mean to upset the party. I apologise.'

Travis smoothed the man's jacket, setting it back in place on his shoulders, removing imaginary dust from the revers with the back of his hand, and said, 'Fine, but remember, you owe me now.'

'Yes, any time. Just say the word.' And he scuttled away.

Bryony was overcome with embarrassment. 'I am sorry about this, Theresa,' she said, 'but drink can be a problem. Perhaps it would be best if we left them all to it. Dad's parties can become a bit rowdy, and frankly I've had enough. I'll tell Mum we're going home. She'll give me the money for a taxi. He can drop you off first.'

As they made their way to the door, Lenny Marks looked over and, catching Theresa's gaze, smiled, winked and blew a kiss in her direction.

CHAPTER THREE

Once outside the Bridge Tavern, it wasn't long before the girls hailed a passing taxi. Sitting in the back, Theresa said, 'I really enjoyed myself. In all the years I've known you, you have never told me about your relatives in the circus.'

'I never gave it a thought. We don't see Uncle Barney very often; the circus is always on the move. My mum's parents used to work the fairgrounds, you know.'

'You never told me that!'

'You never asked, as I recall.'

This was true, thought Theresa. As school friends their backgrounds hadn't been discussed. Everyone knew that her father was a doctor and that Dan Travis sold cars – what else was there to know?

When the taxi eventually stopped Theresa got out and staggered slightly. Giggling, she said to Bryony, 'Whoops! Best be careful when I go inside. If Dad thinks I've been drinking, he'll have a fit.'

'Thanks for coming,' said Bryony. 'I'll phone you tomorrow evening.'

As she was driven home, she smiled to herself, wondering if her friend would be able to sneak up to her room without being seen. Dr Kerrigan was a nice man, but he was very strict, with a strong sense of what was right – as he saw it – and Bryony had wondered on several occasions if he ever harboured a single thought that could have been deemed as wicked. She chuckled as she realised that as he had three children he must have had at least three naughty thoughts, and this amused her highly. The more she pondered this, the more it tickled her sense of humour. Did he confess to the priest that he had lustful leanings towards his wife? But then, she reasoned, probably a wife didn't count in this context, as the Catholics were all for procreation, and she couldn't imagine he would have looked at another woman. Now that would have *had* to be told in the confessional!

Over their school years, surrounded by nuns in a Catholic convent, Bryony and Theresa had often had heated rows over religion. Bryony could never accept that going to confession was a good thing.

'What's the point of it?' she would ask. 'You go one Sunday and confess, you're given so many Hail Marys to say, your sins are forgiven and you can go out on Monday, do the same thing all over again, to be forgiven on the following Sunday. It's a load of rubbish, as far as I can see!'

Yet despite their differences on this subject, they remained good friends, and when Bryony left the convent to study typewriting and shorthand and Theresa got her job as receptionist at the Court Royal Hotel, they had continued their friendship, which wasn't what the good doctor had envisaged at all.

As Dan Travis finally left the Bridge Tavern with the few of his friends who'd stayed until the very end, he put an arm around Leila's shoulders and said, 'That was a good party.'

'Except for those two stupid bastards who wanted to fight.'

Laughing, he said, 'Now you know why I didn't want to go to the Polygon. Can you imagine the scene that would have caused? No, it was better this way. I could sort it myself without any aggravation from anyone else.'

'One thing it did prove to me,' said Leila firmly, 'is that when eventually Bryony does get married, we'll be very careful who we invite as guests. That is one day that will not be spoiled by your so-called friends!'

'You don't understand, do you? Many of those men who were there tonight were business associates. I did a few deals during the evening, but my daughter's wedding will be a different matter.'

His wife sighed. 'Couldn't you just have enjoyed your party without bringing business into it?'

'Don't be stupid, Leila! When have I ever turned down an opportunity to make a few bob? The fact that it was my party was irrelevant.'

How could she argue with him? It was because of this sort of thinking that they were able to live in comfort where money was not a problem. Dan was very generous, as far as she was concerned, but for once it would have been nice to see him enjoy such an occasion for what it was.

'It was nice to see Barney and Rosa, though,' Dan remarked. 'It was good of them to take the trouble to come. They looked well, both of them, don't you think?'

'Yes, but Rosa wants Barney to retire. She's worried that he is getting older and isn't so agile as he used to be, and he's in one job that is definitely not for an older man. After all, he's almost fifty and slowing down.'

Dan shivered. 'I don't know how he does it. Being inside a cage every night with those big cats would give me nightmares. One mistake could be fatal.'

'That's what she's worried about.'

As they drove home, Dan was feeling very pleased with himself. Tonight he'd clinched a deal to take in a two-year-old Rolls-Royce. He knew it was stolen, but by the time it had gone through his workshop, been resprayed, and the number rubbed off the engine and replaced with another by his man the ex-engraver, plus the chassis number changed and new number plates put on, it would be a different car. He would send it over to France, where it would bring him a pretty penny. It was a good night's work. He frowned. He'd have to make sure that, at the weekend, Bryony didn't enter the workshop. She was so keen to learn about engines, she was inclined to wander in and watch the men working, questioning them as to what they were doing and why. This was one motor he didn't wish her to see.

* * *

Theresa Kerrigan was facing the wrath of her father. As she had entered her home, he had emerged unexpectedly from his study and taken her so by surprise, she'd started to giggle stupidly.

'Have you been drinking?' he demanded.

'Yes, Dad. I had two glasses of champagne to celebrate Mr Travis's birthday.'

'You're drunk!'

'No I'm not!' she declared, but she staggered on the stairs as she said it.

'Nuala!' He summoned his wife, who came hurrying into the hallway. 'Your daughter is inebriated. See to her, please.'

Theresa was taken by the arm and led upstairs.

'What were you thinking of?' asked her mother as Theresa was helped to undress.

'Good Lord, Mother, I only had two glasses of champagne, and I had such a wonderful time. Bryony's family are *so* interesting, not like our stuffy sanctimonious lot!'

'Theresa!'

Looking at her mother through slightly bleary eyes she said, 'We don't have a lion tamer and a knife thrower in our family!'

'What?'

'There you go!' continued Theresa, not making a great deal of sense by now. 'I think I'll run away and join the circus.'

Nuala chose to ignore this and, tucking her daughter up in bed, said, 'I'll get you a glass of water. You'll be dehydrated after drinking so I want you to drink it all.'

'How do you know so much about being drunk?'

Nuala grinned and said, 'Before I married your father, I used to sink a few glasses of the black stuff when I was studying to be a nurse.'

'Guinness?'

'That's right. It's full of iron – at least that was my excuse.'

'Dad would make a good lion tamer, you know. He wouldn't need a whip. All he'd have to do was look at them.'

Laughing, Nuala said, 'I doubt that would really be enough but, thank God, he's a doctor. The only cats he has to deal with have two legs and bother him in the surgery!'

Giggling softly, Theresa said, 'You'd better not let him hear you.'

'Now go to sleep,' said her mother. 'I'll wake you in the morning in time to get ready for Mass.'

Sean Kerrigan looked up from his book as his wife returned to the drawing room. 'Well?'

'She's safely tucked up in bed and, before you say anything, she's only had two glasses of champagne. It's not as if she has really been on the razzle.'

'I know that, but she's only seventeen.'

'And growing up. For God's sake, Sean, you're not that old that you can't remember being seventeen and having your first drink, surely?'

'That's not the point!'

'That's exactly the point. Now I don't want to hear any more.'

She looked at him thoughtfully and, seeing her gaze, he asked, 'What?'

'I was beginning to wonder what happened to that wild Irishman I married.'

'He grew up,' he said quietly.

'Just make sure you don't grow old and miserable, that's all.' And before he could reply, she went into the kitchen.

A few days later, under cover of darkness, Dan took delivery of the Rolls-Royce. As it was driven into the workshop, he and his men looked it over. Dan walked round it slowly and then sat in the driver's seat. The cream upholstery smelled of leather . . . and class. He put his hands lovingly on the steering wheel. 'One day I'll buy one of these for myself,' he said.

'In that case the one you buy had better be kosher,' laughed the foreman. 'We'll start on this tomorrow. I've got everything ready.'

'Good,' said Dan. 'I want it out of here as soon as possible.'

'No trouble,' he was told.

The papers were full of the great tragedy at Le Mans, where eighty people had died after three cars crashed and ploughed into the spectators' stand. Bryony and Theresa saw the newsreels in the cinema when they went to see Marilyn Monroe in *The Seven Year Itch*.

As they stared at the screen at the horrific consequences, Bryony said, 'What a dreadful way to die.'

'There's no good way,' said Theresa quietly, 'unless you are very old, ill and in pain; then it is acceptable.'

And later that month, when Ruth Ellis was found guilty of murdering her boyfriend and was sentenced to hang, the girls once again discussed death.

'Well, I wouldn't swing for any man!' Bryony declared.

'She must have really loved him to do such a thing,' argued her friend.

'Listen, if a man didn't want me, I certainly wouldn't chase after him. Where's the dignity in that?'

'But if you *really* loved him, you might.'

'I very much doubt it! The trouble with you, Theresa, is you are a romantic. You think with your heart, not your head!'

'I wonder when you do fall in love, if you won't be the same?'

'My heart will never rule my head,' Bryony declared. 'I take after my father too much for that.'

'He must have loved your mother to ask her to marry him, and he certainly loves you.'

'And I love him, but that's different. I will only marry a man who can give me what I want.'

'Which is?'

'A lovely home, car and a good life, mixing with nice people.'

'Thanks very much!' exclaimed her friend.

'Don't be daft, I don't mean you. I just want to get away from the crowd my parents mix with. I want a bit of class in my life – sophistication. I don't want tawdry.'

'Your home isn't tawdry, it's lovely, and beautifully furnished.'

'Yes, it is, but you saw the people my parents mix with. I don't like most of them and I don't want that type in my life.'

'I thought they were interesting,' Theresa insisted.

'Only because they are so different from your parents' friends.'

'Well, you certainly wouldn't want them. They'd bore you to death in five minutes!'

It was soon after their conversation that young James Hargreaves turned up at the garage one Saturday morning, driving his Riley. When Bryony saw him, she walked over and, smiling, asked, 'Something wrong with the car?'

'No, it runs like a dream. I wanted to know if you would let me take you out to dinner one evening?'

Bryony was aware of the salesmen watching and felt her cheeks flush with embarrassment. 'Thank you, I'd like that very much.'

'How about Wednesday evening?'

'That's fine.'

'Right, where shall I pick you up?'

Bryony, not wanting Dan to know her plans, suggested in front of the Avenue Hall, which was just down the road from where she lived.

'I'll see you there around seven thirty,' said James, and swept out of the parking lot.

Jack Saunders, the senior salesman, strolled over.

'What did young Lochinvar want then?'

'He came to say how pleased he was with the car, that's all.'

'And to ask you out on a date, I suppose.' As Bryony went to dispute his remark, he gave a sly smile and said, 'Don't try and pull the wool over my eyes, girl. It was obvious to any man why he was here. I don't know what your father will say about it.'

'It's none of his business!' snapped Bryony.

'I'm not sure he'll see it like that.'

'Are you going to tell him then?'

Jack just grinned at her and walked away, leaving Bryony with a dilemma. If her father heard about her date from someone else, he would be furious, and if she told him, would he tell her she couldn't go? She felt he was overprotective and sometimes she felt smothered by this. He was inclined to run her life for her and as she grew older, she wanted her independence.

Her typing course was due to finish in a month, and Bryony was sure that he expected her to work for him full time, but that was not her wish and she was damned if she was going to be bullied into it. She had already had a word with the head of the typing school, who was sure she could find Bryony a job as she was good at her work. This was her plan, and her father would just have to accept she had a life of her own.

Dan Travis had other things on his mind. That evening he was meeting a few cronies at the Silver Dollar Club just off East Street, above a hardware store. It was a large room with a bar at one end, with subdued lighting and tables set around the room on which were small lamps. The atmosphere was supposed to be intimate and sophisticated, but it just looked cheap and tacky, yet it was the favourite meeting place of the criminal world of Southampton.

Dan arrived with Jack Saunders from the car lot. He was greeted warmly by Sophie Johnson, real name Derek who, being a homosexual with a fondness for young men, was known to all his friends as Sophie. He was one of the best fences in the South of England.

'Dan, you beautiful man, come and have a drink!'

'Hello, Soph, how the devil are you?' Looking around he asked, 'All alone tonight?'

'You know me better than that, Dan.' Sophie gazed towards the door of the gents as a tall, good-looking boy of about seventeen walked out and joined them. 'This is Giles,' he said. 'My latest favourite friend.' He tapped the boy's bottom. 'Great arse.'

Giles looked embarrassed and angry. 'Don't talk like that, I don't like it.'

Sophie raised an eyebrow and with a soft smile said quietly, 'He's very sensitive.'

Looking at the lad, Dan thought what a shame it was to see such a good-looking boy in such a situation. And what a waste, because girls would fall over themselves to know him if they were ignorant of his sexuality.

'Quite right,' said Dan. 'Don't you let this old queen treat you with anything other than respect.' Turning to

Sophie, Dan said, 'I don't know how you find such attractive boys – after all, you're no oil painting!'

And it was true. The man was in his fifties and slightly bloated from too much drinking, yet he was not without a certain charm and a quiet, sometimes deadly, sense of humour.

Sophie smiled. 'How true, darling, but I'm a good lover and, let's face it, Dan, I'm bloody loaded! Money, as you know, dear fellow, is a great aphrodisiac. Otherwise how would you get women falling at your feet?'

'Ah, but then I'm bloody handsome, Soph, so with me women get both looks and lucre!'

Their conversation was cut short as others joined them, but Dan leaned over and said in the fence's ear, 'I need a word later, all right?'

Sophie winked at him and said, 'Fine. We'll meet in the gents.' And added with twinkling eyes, 'Don't worry, I'll keep my flies closed.'

'If you don't I'll twist the bloody thing off, then where will you be?'

Sophie winced at the thought, then grinned. 'I might like it!'

'With a knot in it you'd be buggered.'

'Poor choice of words, darling boy.' And he walked away chuckling.

Later that evening, the two men were alone in the gents' toilet. Dan took a small soft leather bag out of his pocket and showed Sophie various pieces of diamond jewellery.

From his pocket the fence took out an eyeglass and peered at the stones. 'Nice bit of gear,' he said.

'And I want a decent price for them. You know me, Soph: I'm not one of your punters you can screw for a few quid.'

'Now don't threaten me, dear boy. You and I have done business before; you know I wouldn't rob you.'

'Maybe, but a warning won't go amiss in case you forgot who you're dealing with.'

Putting the eyeglass and gems in his pocket, he grinned broadly at Dan. 'As if I could. Come on, I'll buy you a drink.'

'I should bloody well hope so . . . and be good to that lad. He's too pretty to be cruel to.'

Sophie's expression hardened and he snapped, 'Now *that* is out of order. You got something to sell and you want my help, that's your business, but my boys are *my* business. I hope you understand, Dan. Let's get the ground rules straight.'

'All right, keep your hair on. Let's get this drink.'

Walking back to the bar, Dan had to admire the man. He liked ground rules himself. There were always lines in every business that had to be adhered to, and it was safer for all concerned to know what they were.

CHAPTER FOUR

James Hargreaves drew up in front of the Avenue Hall just as Bryony arrived for their date. Leaping out of the driver's seat, he hurried round to the other side of the car and opened the door for her.

'Hello there, I'm so glad you came. Please get in.'

He looked very handsome, she thought, casually glancing at him. He was dressed in a pair of light-coloured slacks, white shirt, tie, and a navy blazer, on the pocket of which was an imposing-looking badge. How presentable he was, she thought, and such impeccable manners.

'As it is such a beautiful evening,' said James, 'I thought we'd drive out to the White Swan. We can eat outside overlooking the river. What do you say?'

Not knowing the venue, Bryony said, 'It sounds lovely.'

He drove with confidence, and Bryony relaxed as he chatted to her about inconsequential things until they arrived at their destination. The warm summer evening had tempted other people along to the picturesque place, but James had booked in advance.

They sat at a table by the banks of the River Itchen,

studying the menu, and both decided on the hors-d'
oeuvres to start with and halibut to follow. 'As we're
having fish, perhaps we should have white wine. Do
you prefer it dry or sweet?' he asked.

'Medium dry, please,' she said, used to having wine
at home, and sat back watching a family of ducks glid-
ing along.

When the waitress had departed, Bryony asked, 'What
do you do for a living, James?'

'I'm studying law,' he told her. 'My father is a barris-
ter, so I suppose I'm following in his footsteps, but I
do love the work. It's so interesting. I'll probably
specialise in criminal law.'

So her father was right when he said they were a
well-heeled family, she thought. 'What do you do for
fun?' she asked.

His eyes twinkled. 'Lots of things. I like riding point
to point, watching polo, I play a bit of rugby and I like
dancing, when the occasion arises.'

'I've never been on a horse,' she said. 'They look
such big animals and so strong.' Frowning, she said.
'They look like trouble.'

'You must come with me to watch a polo match,
then you'll see that they are nothing to be frightened
of but to be admired.'

'Do you play polo?'

'Good heavens, no. For one thing you need your own
polo ponies to do it seriously and that's very expensive.
Besides, I don't have the time with my studies. Watching
is great fun, though. And you, Bryony, what do you do?'

'In comparison, I lead a very dull life. I have one more month at college then I'll be looking for a job.'

'Does that mean working for your father?'

'No it does not!'

'Oh dear, have I hit upon a sore point?'

'Not really. Dad expects me to work full time for him, but I have other plans. I'm sure it won't please him, but I must be able to lead my own life.'

'Quite right! Life is to be enjoyed.'

'I'll drink to that,' she said, raising her glass.

As they ate their first course, James said, 'I'm absolutely amazed to meet a girl with an interest in cars and who knows what goes on under the bonnet.'

'Why? Women are allowed to enter a man's world, you know. Good heavens, during the war they worked in factories, on the buses, they drove ambulances and . . . even flew planes!'

Chuckling, he said, 'Don't sound so defensive. I'm all for the female sex stepping outside the usual parameters. I like independent women.'

After their meal, they strolled along the riverbank, holding hands. 'Next Sunday there is a polo match at Cowdray Park. Would you like to go?'

'Oh, yes, I'd love to,' said Bryony with enthusiasm.

'Good,' said James. 'I'll get Mother to prepare a picnic for us. You'll really enjoy it. I'll pick you up about ten thirty.'

'I'll be ready. Come to the house,' she said, deciding that it was better to let her family know she was going out with him than to have to lie. After all, what could they say? James was a decent type and she fervently hoped they would continue to see each other. Her father had better get used to the idea of her being her own person, she determined, and she gave James the address.

'Do you want me to drop you there tonight or would you prefer the Avenue Hall?'

'If you take me to the door you'll know where to come on Sunday,' she said.

It wasn't late when they arrived in Westwood Road, and as James stopped the car he said, 'Thanks for coming. I enjoyed your company,' and he leaned across and kissed her softly. Then, getting out of the car, he opened her door and helped her out.

'I'll see you on Sunday.'

She watched him drive away and walked up to the front door, unaware that her father had been watching from the window of his study.

'Bloody hell,' he said as he observed them kissing. Then he recognised young James as the owner of the Riley he'd sold. 'What *is* going on here?' he exclaimed, and went into the hallway as Bryony came in through the front door.

'Where have you been with that young man?' he demanded.

'I've been out to dinner at the White Swan. We had a lovely meal,' she said.

'You never asked my permission,' he stormed.

'For goodness' sake, Dad, I'm nearly eighteen, not eleven. You may not have noticed but I've grown up!'

'That's what worries me!'

Her mother came to her rescue. 'For God's sake, Dan, leave her be. She's been out on a date with a young man. If you had your way you'd lock her up with your bloody cars.'

Putting her arm through Bryony's, she asked, 'Did you have a good time?'

'I did, and he's taking me to a polo match on Sunday.'

'That should make you happy,' her father said sarcastically. 'You'll be mixing with the toffs.'

Walking towards the stairs, Bryony turned and retorted, 'That will make a nice change then, won't it?'

'Don't you get arsey with me, girl,' he snapped. And stomped back into his study, muttering under his breath about people with ideas above their station.

Bryony pulled her bedroom curtains closed with a feeling of satisfaction. Tonight she'd made her first strike towards freedom and it felt good . . . as had the kiss that James had given her. She remembered Jack's warning at the car lot about James's behaviour, but tonight he'd been the perfect gentleman and she felt quite safe accepting his invitation. She'd seen pictures of polo matches in *Tatler* magazine and couldn't wait to be a part of the spectators.

Whilst Bryony had been enjoying her first proper date with a man, her friend Theresa had been approached by Lenny Marks. He'd arrived at the Court Royal Hotel with a friend to have lunch. There, he'd sought out Theresa and presented her with a bunch of flowers.

'I wondered if you would be on duty,' he said as he gave them to her.

Blushing with embarrassment, Theresa said, 'I'm surprised you remembered me.'

'Why would you think that? You are the best-looking girl I've met in a long time.' He began to walk towards the dining room. Turning he said, 'I'll see you later, sweetheart.'

'Sweetheart is it?' remarked the head receptionist. 'A friend of yours, Theresa?'

'I only met him once at a party,' she confessed.

'Well, it seems you made a conquest. You'd better put those flowers in water or they'll be dead before you get home.'

Secretly thrilled by the encounter, Theresa hurried away to find a receptacle. She remembered Bryony's tirade about Lenny, but he seemed very nice . . . and he'd called her 'sweetheart'!

Two hours later, Lenny walked out of the dining room and saw his companion off the premises before returning to the reception desk.

Theresa watched his approach, her heart beating with excitement.

'What time do you finish?' he asked.

'Six o'clock,' she told him.

'I'll be back to pick you up,' he said, and turned and left the building before she could say anything.

Theresa could hardly contain her elation. She'd led a very sheltered life. She'd been a member of St

Bernadette's Youth Club, which met in St Anne's School hall in Bedford Place once a week, and was run by the nuns, but it had been for girls only. Her father hadn't allowed her to go dancing, saying she was too young, so her experience of boys had been only at the odd barn dance, organised by her parents four times a year. She was a complete innocent. Had she realised what plans Lenny Marks had for her, she would have run a mile.

At six o'clock on the dot, Lenny pulled up outside the Court Royal Hotel, and waited. He'd handle this girl with kid gloves, he'd decided. It was obvious to him that she was naïve and he didn't want to scare her off, but if he were careful, he would take her virginity, eventually. A slow smile crossed his countenance as he imagined it. It would be his first one. He laughed to himself as he thought of the women he'd had in the past. None of them could have been called virginal, that's for sure. It would be a new and highly delightful experience – one to savour.

As he saw Theresa walk down the front steps of the hotel, he got out and opened the car door on the passenger side.

'Your carriage awaits, my lady,' he said with a bow. She was quite overcome.

Getting into the vehicle he asked, 'Where to?'

When she said The Avenue, he thought, very nice too.

'My father has his surgery downstairs,' she said, 'so we should stop outside as there may be patients who have parked in the driveway.'

As they drew up outside the house, Lenny let out a slow whistle. 'Blimey,' he said. 'It's big enough.'

The house was set back off the road, with a sweeping driveway to the door. He saw a brass plaque outside by the gate.

'How many of you live in this mansion?' he asked.

'There are five of us; I have a brother and sister who are at university, and of course my parents. Dad has one of the reception rooms as his surgery.'

'How many reception rooms are there, for goodness' sake?'

'Three. Isn't your house like this?'

He had to laugh. 'Theresa, not everyone lives like this, you know,' thinking how, as small children, three of them had had to share a room. Now, of course, they had a bigger house, but Northam was not a salubrious area, to say the least, and his home would fit inside the downstairs of this one, easily.

'I shall know where to come if I get sick,' Lenny said.

'Dad has a surgery in Bernard Street also,' she said, 'for those who don't go private.'

'Don't you worry about me, sweetheart. I can afford to go private.'

Poor Theresa was deeply embarrassed. 'I didn't mean it that way,' she began.

'I know. No offence taken. How about coming to the flicks with me sometime this week? Glenn Ford is on at the Odeon in *Blackboard Jungle*. I hear it's very good.'

She was delighted by the invitation. Her first real date! 'Thank you. I would like to.'

They arranged for Lenny to pick her up from the hotel when she finished at six thirty the following Thursday.

He leaned across her and opened the door. 'There you go, Theresa; I'll see you, then. Take care now.'

As she walked up the path Theresa wondered what all the fuss had been about when Bryony warned her about this man. He'd been perfectly polite and nice. But she decided to keep her date to herself. She didn't want Bryony pouring scorn on her and spoiling things.

And when Thursday came, Lenny was the perfect gentleman. He bought two of the most expensive seats in the front circle; he presented her with a small box of chocolates and insisted on buying her an ice cream during the interval. Apart from casually draping his arm around her shoulders during the second half of the programme, he didn't do anything wrong. And when he drove her home, he helped her from the car and kissed her gently.

'I hope you enjoyed yourself?' he asked.

'Yes, I did, thank you . . . and thank you so much for the chocolates.'

'My pleasure,' he said. 'I'll be seeing you.' Then he got into the car and drove away, chuckling to himself, thinking: that'll keep her wondering if she'll hear from me again. Now if I wait another week, that should be long enough to keep her on her toes. Then we move into phase two.

CHAPTER FIVE

Sophie Johnson was really pissed off. His latest boyfriend was getting above himself, just because he was educated and Sophie wasn't. He felt that young Giles was throwing his weight about unnecessarily. They were now in the East End of London where Sophie was dealing with a broker for the diamonds that Dan Travis had asked him to sell, as well as some other goods acquired through his contacts in the underworld, and here was Giles, moaning that he wanted to be taken up West to go shopping. Whinging away like a woman!

'Shut your bleeding cake-hole or I'll shut it for you,' snapped Sophie. 'Sit down and be quiet.'

The broker looked up for a moment at this outburst, then returned to studying the gems through his eyeglass. He eventually laid out all the goods for sale and said, 'Well, times are hard, you know . . .'

He didn't get any further before Sophie grabbed him by the throat. 'Now listen to me, you little bastard. I know the worth of these, so don't try and pull a fast one. You should know better than that. Christ, we've done business for too long for you to make a mistake. Remember what happened all those years ago when you didn't know me very well and tried to pull a flanker?'

The man unconsciously put his hand to the scar on his cheek. 'I haven't forgotten. I'm just telling you it will take time to move the rocks, that's all.'

'Well, don't take too long. I'll call you in a week.' Turning to Giles, he said, 'Come on, you little bastard, let's go shopping.'

The young man leaped to his feet. 'Oh, Sophie, you are so good to me.'

Sophie glowered at him and snarled, '*You* had better remember who you're with too.' He caressed the side of Giles's cheek and said menacingly, 'It would be a great pity to spoil such good looks.'

An expression of fear clouded the boy's eyes for just a moment, but then he gave Sophie one of his glorious smiles and whispered, 'How could I forget I was with you, you silly old fart.' He ran his hand across the backside of the older man. 'Come along then, let's go.'

'You play me for a fool, you little bleeder, and you will surely live to regret it, that I promise you.'

'Come along, darling,' coaxed his young lover, 'don't be an old grumps. Come on and make me happy, and when we get home I'll do the same for you.'

Sophie listened to the cultured tones, looked at the smile and, taking the hand that was held out to him, he said, 'Of course you will – that's what you're there for!' As he walked out of the shop with Giles behind him, Sophie missed the look of hatred in the eyes of the young man.

In the very expensive men's shop, Giles picked out a sports jacket of the finest Harris Tweed and tried it on, posing in front of the mirror. Turning to the shop assistant he said, 'I need a pair of trousers to go with it.' And in a very imperious manner said, 'Show me what you have, and you'd better take my measurements in case I've gained any weight.'

As the man measured his inside leg, Giles looked over his shoulder and raised his eyebrows at Sophie and pursed his lips, making his benefactor laugh.

Sophie sat back and watched the performance. Truth to tell, he envied young Giles his polish. The boy had class, and his breeding was obvious. He insisted they eat at decent restaurants, and Sophie fancied that some of Giles's polish was rubbing off on himself. When he was at home with Sophie, Giles laid the table properly and used linen napkins, objecting strongly to Sophie's paper ones, tossing them aside with contempt. 'How very common! Now, Sophie, I'm not prepared to lower my standards. We will do things the right way or not at all!'

And the older man had lapped it up. For too long the dregs of society had surrounded him and this indeed was a pleasant change. Certainly on occasion, his business took him to the kind of exclusive places that were exquisitely furnished and catered for his particular tastes.

There were many clients from the upper classes who sometimes needed to raise some money very quickly and Sophie's net of clients was spread wide, but his visits to such places were fleeting. He was an outsider and he knew it.

After purchasing the jacket and trousers, the two men went to a club that was frequented by homosexuals, where at last they could indulge each other: dancing to the music from a jukebox, laughing and drinking, eating and relaxing among others with similar preferences, before returning to Southampton on a late train.

As they prepared for bed, Giles said, 'I'll have to go home this weekend.'

'But I had plans,' protested Sophie.

'Sorry, but Father has arranged a family get-together. My brother is home from Oxford and we're having a party. I have to be there, you know that. After all, I come to see you from school most weekends.'

'Oh, very well. When will you be back?'

'Don't know for sure. It depends what Hugo intends to do. I'll let you know.' Seeing the angry look on Sophie's face, he said, 'Now come along, you knew from the beginning I have to go home when my father asks me, otherwise he'll start asking questions and I don't want him to stop my allowance.'

'I give you plenty of money!'

'You are more than generous, darling Sophie, but I certainly don't want to jeopardise my inheritance, do I, my dear man? Being such a good businessman you will appreciate that.'

'You make sure you behave yourself, that's all.'

'What, with my parents there – are you joking? I will be the perfect son, and the perfect brother. What trouble can I get into, for God's sake? It's not as if I'll be chasing the housemaids, is it?' And he laughed loudly. 'Come to bed, you silly old man.'

As Sophie slept beside him, Giles lay back, his hand behind his head, smoking a cigarette, wondering just how much longer he could stomach the old man whose life he shared at the moment. He knew that if his parents discovered his sexuality, they would disown him. His father, Sir Douglas Sinclair, was an eminent High Court judge with a country estate and a position to uphold. He could trace his family lineage back to Thomas Cranmer, and any scandal would be looked upon as a disaster to the fine name of Sinclair.

Despite the money that Sophie gave him and the generous allowance from his father – on the understanding he worked at his studies – Giles had a predilection for gambling, mainly on the horses or at cards, and was always running out of cash. He would tell his father from time to time that he needed more money for books, which swelled his funds and, of course, he took his studies in physics and mathematics very lightly, thinking to cram before exams. But his biggest problem was ahead of him when he became the age to marry. Then he knew he would have to be clever and hide his penchant for men – mostly older and wealthy.

When he was at a party, he flirted with all the good-looking girls, to allay all suspicions, and even took some home and kissed them good night, but that was as far as it went. It was enough, however, to cover himself. Not even his own brother, Hugo, suspected he had a secret. This weekend, they planned to go to the polo match at Cowdray Park together. Giles was fond of his brother, even if he was a little dour and dedicated to his study of politics and social history. It was Hugo's intention to become a politician, eventually, which delighted the judge, his father. Although he had little in common with his brother, they both enjoyed a game of polo and this one at the weekend should be good.

It was Saturday morning and Bryony was sitting next to James in his car, driving through the Sussex countryside towards Cowdray Park. He was trying to explain to her the rules of the game, and she was fascinated.

When they arrived at the polo grounds, James drove the Riley on to grass lined with cars, and parked. He said 'hello' to the people parked either side and then, opening the boot of the car, took out a picnic hamper, followed by a small foldaway table and two chairs. Bryony was intrigued as he began to unpack the most delicious food. There were two dressed lobsters, smoked salmon and prawns, with a bowl of salad, cold new potatoes and all the condiments, which he carefully laid out.

'You've done this before,' remarked Bryony with a grin.

'Polo is my weakness,' James explained. 'I try to go to as many matches as I can.' He then produced a cold box with two bottles of champagne. He deftly opened one and poured some into the glasses he had supplied.

'Sit down, Bryony, and make yourself comfortable. We have some time yet before the first chukka.'

As they tucked into their fare, Bryony looked at the people around her. The women were wearing summer dresses that looked expensive, straw hats to keep off the sun, and the men were in casual but smart trousers, with ties or cravats in the necks of their shirts. There were many with blazers, others with lightweight jackets, and glancing around at the make of the parked cars, Bryony knew she was surrounded by class and wealth.

One or two people walked by and greeted James, who introduced her as his friend. They greeted her politely, passed a few words with him, and moved on.

Looking up as she sipped her champagne, Bryony saw a tall blond young man heading towards them, smiling. She thought him the most beautiful man she'd ever seen – much too pretty for a boy.

'Hello, sport,' he greeted James. 'I wondered if I'd find you here.' He smiled at Bryony and asked, 'Aren't you going to introduce me to this beauty?'

'Bryony, this is Giles Sinclair. Giles, this is Bryony Travis.'

'James always knows how to pick them,' Giles said, shaking her hand, 'but this time, old man, you've surpassed yourself.'

Bryony beamed at him.

'Would you like to join us, Giles?' invited James.

'That's jolly nice of you, but I'm with my brother

and we are about to eat with some friends. Perhaps see you both later?'

'Who's that?' Bryony enquired as he left.

'Giles's father is a judge, so he and my father socialise quite a bit. I've known him for years, he and his brother.'

'Is his brother as good-looking?'

Laughing, James said, 'No, not really. Old Hugo is a bit of a stick in the mud, rather like his father. Strait-laced. Giles looks like his mother.'

The match eventually began and Bryony was thrilled as she watched the two teams of four riders each, charge around the field, swinging their sticks, controlling their horses at a gallop, and was in awe of the players as they pushed their horses into their opponents' mounts, riding them off the ball. It was done so ferociously she looked horrified and asked, 'Are they allowed to do that?'

'Yes,' said James, 'it's all in the rules of the game, I assure you.'

Halfway through the match, when the commentator invited the spectators to tread in the divots, she giggled as she and James walked on to the pitch, stamping on the sods of grass that had been removed by the exuberance of the ponies.

'This is great fun!' she exclaimed.

'I knew you'd enjoy it,' he said. 'After the match we'll go over and look at the horses.' Seeing her look of consternation, he said, 'Don't worry, they won't bite you.'

'Can I have that in writing?'

*　　*　　*

As it was, James proved to be right. He walked Bryony over to where the horses from the final chukka were being attended, and introduced her to a tall young man, unsaddling his mount.

'Hello, Toby. Good match. Congratulations on a fine win.' As the man turned towards him, James added, 'This is Bryony Travis, a friend of mine. Bryony, this is Toby Beckford, a merchant banker pal of mine. But he never makes any money for me!'

Toby shook hands and said, 'Hello, Bryony. I hope you enjoyed the match.'

'It was great,' she said. 'This was my first time. I couldn't believe how you all managed to control these animals.'

He stroked the nose of his horse and said, 'It takes a lot of practice, but Napoleon here always sees me through, don't you, old boy?'

'Stroke him,' James urged Bryony. 'Just rub his nose.'

Somewhat gingerly she did so and then more bravely stroked his neck. With eyes shining she looked at Toby and said, 'He's lovely!'

'My dear girl, I've been looking for a woman who can love my horse as much as me. If you get fed up with James, give me a call.'

'Now that is not playing the game!' retorted James with a grin. 'You find your own women.'

Bryony lapped up the conversation, and as Toby left them she waved and said, 'I'll remember what you said.'

* * *

Later, as they drove home, Bryony was still chatting about the game and then she said, 'James, that was such a lovely day, I don't know how to thank you enough.'

'I'm at Cowes next week. Come over. Dad has a yacht moored there, and we can stay on board.'

'I would love to, but I'm a working girl.'

'What about Saturday? Couldn't you come over, then stay the night? I'm sure we can find you a berth; then we can sail back on Sunday night.'

She didn't hesitate. 'I'd love to.'

'Good. I'll arrange it and give you a call. Give me your telephone number. We'll stop off at the Cowherds for a drink on the way home and you can write it down then.'

As they left the Cowherds sometime later that evening and walked to the car, James took Bryony into his arms and said, 'Thanks for being such good company. I'm looking forward to this coming weekend so much,' and he kissed her.

Bryony snuggled in his arms and returned his kisses. And although he kissed her with great ardour, he didn't forget that he was a gentleman and try to fondle her, which pleased her after the remark Jack the salesman had made about James when he'd come to the car lot to collect the Riley.

James released her, helped her into the car and drove her home.

Once home, Bryony ran into the kitchen where her father and mother were drinking tea. 'I've had the most exciting day!' she cried. 'I met a merchant banker who was playing in the match, and the son of a High Court judge. Many of the cars were Rolls-Royces and Bentleys, Dad! I have spent the day with the rich and famous!'

'You be careful it isn't the rich and infamous!' was his tart reply.

She turned on him, quick as a flash. 'Don't you dare spoil my day!'

Leila agreed. 'No, you shut up, Dan.' Looking at Bryony, she asked, 'Are you seeing the young man again?'

'Yes, I'm going to Cowes next weekend.' Glaring at her father, she said, 'Cowes is about yachts, not cattle, you know.'

'That's enough! Don't try and treat me like an imbecile, Bryony. I'm well aware what happens at Cowes. Don't you get above yourself, girl, because if you do you will fall on your backside very heavily one day.' He rose from the table and marched out of the room.

'Now, Bryony,' chided her mother, 'that was quite uncalled for.'

'I'm sorry but he always pours cold water over me when I'm really thrilled about something.'

'He's your father, what can I tell you? You know what he's like; just don't upset him, that's all.'

Bryony filled a glass with water. 'I know,' she said to Leila. 'He just makes me so cross at times. I'm off to bed. See you in the morning.'

* * *

As Leila got into bed that night she said to Dan, 'Don't spoil things for Bryony. This is her first boyfriend. He's a nice boy from a good family – what more can you ask?'

'It's not that, but she has such great expectations, and I can see she is going to get hurt. She thinks that rich and influential means without fault, and you know as well as I do that isn't the case. She'll learn the hard way and that's what worries me.'

Cuddling into her husband, Leila said, 'I know, but we can't live her life for her. We'll just keep an eye on her, but you must let her grow up.'

'I know, I know. But if anyone does hurt her they'll have me to deal with!'

But that worried Leila much more than her daughter becoming a young woman.

CHAPTER SIX

Bryony was thrilled to receive a telephone call from James the following Thursday evening. 'Where are you calling from?' she asked.

'I'm in Cowes. I thought I'd get in touch to tell you to bring some casual clothes for the yacht as we may go for a sail, and a pretty frock for the evening as we will probably go to the Yacht Club for a drink or dinner. And please, Bryony, wear shoes with rubber soles for when we're on board as my father has a fit when a woman wears high heels. It spoils the deck, you see.'

'Right,' she said, thinking it was just as well to be told, as she had already chosen her prettiest shoes, none of which were flat or had soles of rubber.

'Are you having a good time?' she enquired.

'Yes, the racing is excellent. My father and I sailed the *Beatrice* – that's the yacht's name – in a race yesterday and won.'

'Congratulations,' she said, and then with some trepidation asked, 'Will your father be there when I come?'

'Sadly no. He has to prepare for a case he's taking in court next week.'

She was greatly relieved. She had met Mr Hargreaves when he bought the Riley, of course, but being in such close proximity to him so early in her friendship with James was more than she felt she could face. She was also a trifle worried about the sleeping arrangements, and she wondered if they sailed out of the harbour whether she would be seasick. How embarrassing that would be!

They arranged which ferry she was to take so that he could meet her, and then James said, 'I'm really looking forward to seeing you again, Bryony.'

'Me too,' she said, and hung up, delighted James had taken the time to call.

When the ferry docked in Cowes on the Saturday morning, Bryony walked up the jetty with what seemed like the world's population. Cowes was very popular with the yachting fraternity, and there were also holiday-makers on the boat. Many of the wealthy and well connected arrived by yacht, but as berthing was at a premium, some came to stay on board various crafts of friends; others to crew for those who owned racing yachts.

Bryony saw James before he saw her, and she marvelled that such a good-looking young man should choose her company rather than that of the young women from his own social standing. She waved frantically and he saw her and walked forward.

'Come here,' he said, and enveloped her in his arms, kissing her briefly on the mouth. 'I have so looked forward

64

to you coming.' Picking up her small case, he looked at her, trim in pale blue linen trousers, navy and white striped top and yachting shoes, which she had rushed out to buy.

'You look wonderful. Come on, I'll take you to the *Beatrice* and you can meet my chums.'

The *Beatrice* was a beautiful yacht, forty foot long, with sleeping quarters for eight. James helped Bryony on board, led her below and showed her a small single cabin. 'This is used usually by the captain who crews for my father, but he's crewing on another yacht this weekend, so we can use it in his absence. Dump your case and come and meet my friends.'

As they made their way along, a cabin door opened and Toby Beckford emerged. 'Hello, Bryony, this is a pleasant surprise.'

She was delighted to think he remembered her. 'Where's your horse?' she asked with a grin.

'At home. Here I ride the waves – much more dangerous!'

'Oh dear! Is it?'

James laughed and said, 'Don't you listen to that old reprobate. The wind isn't that strong today. You'll be perfectly safe, I promise.'

Up on deck, several of James's friends, whom Bryony had glimpsed briefly as she came aboard, were laid out beneath the mast, sunbathing. James made the introductions.

'This is Davinia.' A long-limbed, languid blonde girl, clad in shorts and top, glanced casually at Bryony. She waved, then lay back with closed eyes.

A tall dark young man, seeing to various ropes, smiled at her and said, 'Hello. I'm Sebastian.' He pushed a prone body at his feet, whose face was covered by a hat. 'Giles, come on, you lazy devil, give me a hand, will you?'

Giles, whom Bryony had met at the polo match, uncurled himself and, getting to his feet, smiled at her. 'Hello, there. How very nice to see you again.'

'We thought we'd sail over to the Hamble River and have lunch at either the Yacht Club or The Bugle,' said James.

'That sounds lovely,' said Bryony with a smile. 'Hamble is so pretty.'

'Come and sit by me in the cockpit. We'll have to go out on the engine to start with, until we find the wind.' They went to the stern and then, yelling to Sebastian, James asked, 'All set up there?'

Sebastian gave him the thumbs-up. Giles leaped ashore and untied the ropes before jumping back on board, then pulled the fenders in over the side. Suddenly they were moving.

Just as they were approaching the moorings in Hamble, a girl emerged from below. She was stunning. She had long red hair that tumbled down her back, and wore the briefest of bikinis, which barely covered her voluptuous body. She cast a bored glance in Bryony's direction, then made her way to the prow of the yacht where she stood poised as if to say to the world, look at me!

James was too busy negotiating the mooring to notice her and Bryony wondered who she was.

* * *

Whilst Bryony was enjoying herself, her friend Theresa was also on the river, but in not quite such a classy craft. Lenny had called her at home and invited her to go to Botley, where they could go out on the river in a punt. She, of course, accepted without hesitation.

And here they were, pulled in beneath the trees, a punt tied up and a rug laid out on the bank. Lenny had produced some fresh rolls and cheese to be washed down with white wine, which he had put into the water on the end of some twine, to cool.

'Lovely here, isn't it?' he said.

Theresa nodded. 'I've never been here before. It's so peaceful, and everything is so lush and green. Oh, do look,' she said, pointing. Three swans glided by.

'You have to be careful with those buggers,' said Lenny. 'Did you know that their wings could really cause you a lot of damage if they attack you?'

'So I believe.'

'Of course, I keep forgetting, I'm with an educated lady . . . and a beautiful one.'

Theresa blushed.

Lenny laid out paper plates and they buttered the rolls, cut the cheese, sliced some tomatoes and ate, Lenny retrieving the bottle of wine and pouring it into two glasses. 'Drink up,' he said, 'the wine is cooled enough now.'

He had thought of everything. He produced a portable radio and, switching it on, found a programme playing popular music. 'There you are, my lady, what else could you want?'

Munching away on her rolls, Theresa said, 'It's perfect, thank you so much.'

After eating, they both relaxed. Lenny had brought a couple of Sunday papers to read and they discussed various articles, until he folded them away and, putting his hands behind his head, stretched out and said, 'Come and lay down, Theresa. It's so warm in the sun, we'll wait awhile before we row any further.' He patted the empty space beside him.

Somewhat nervously she did so.

'There you are,' he said. 'Isn't that better?' He made no move to touch her.

'Yes, it is. It's so quiet. I've often thought I would like to live in the country. I fancy a thatched cottage with a nice garden . . . with a stream running by the garden.'

Lenny thought it would be the last thing he wanted. He liked city life, with the buzz that went with it. He liked to be on the move all the time. London would suit him. But today, the quiet and peace of the countryside were part of his ploy to get to Theresa.

'I suppose you'd want chickens too,' he teased.

'Oh, no. But maybe a couple of cats.'

He hated cats! 'No, sweetheart. A couple of dogs, maybe. I like dogs.'

He sat propped up on one elbow and gazed at her. 'You have the longest eyelashes I've ever seen on a girl,' he said, 'and lovely eyes.'

He gently swept her eyelashes upwards with his finger, then caressed her cheek. 'You are quite beautiful,' he said softly, 'but I expect you've been told that many times.'

Quite overcome by so much flattery, Theresa said, 'No, I haven't.'

He pretended to look surprised. 'I can hardly believe it. You'll be telling me next you've never been kissed!'

Her cheeks flushed with embarrassment. 'Well, it's the truth. I never have, not properly.'

'We can't have that, can we?' he said in a very quiet voice and, leaning over, he placed his lips on hers and kissed her gently.

Theresa closed her eyes and let the experience of a man's mouth on hers sweep over her. She found that she liked it.

'When a man kisses you, sweetheart, you have to kiss him back or he'll feel a fool. Shall we try it again?'

She nodded and closed her eyes.

It's like taking candy from a baby, Lenny thought as he lowered his head to kiss her again. This time she responded and as she did, he slid his arm beneath her and drew her to him, his kiss becoming just a little bit more passionate, but not enough to frighten someone who was so vulnerable. Knowing he was holding such a pure and innocent creature made his pulse race. It took all his concentration to stop himself from taking her on the spot.

Theresa lay back against the rug, her senses swimming. This must be what it was like to be in love! She gazed across at Lenny, who, seeing the wonderment in her eyes, thought, I've done it. Next time, she's mine!

'Come along,' he said. 'We'd best make our way back down the river.'

Theresa was disappointed. This was so new to her, this closeness, this intimacy; she didn't want it to end. 'Do we have to?' she pleaded.

With a sly smile of satisfaction, Lenny said, 'Yes, I'm afraid we do. Never mind, we'll do it again another day.'

'Soon?'

'Yes, my sweetheart, very soon. I promise.'

He punted them back to the jetty, tied up the punt and took their belongings into the car. Then he drove her home, stopping outside the house.

'Thanks, darling, for a lovely day.' He pulled her to him and kissed her, and was delighted when she returned his overture with some enthusiasm. This girl was ripe for the picking and how he was going to enjoy himself when the time came. 'I'll call you soon,' he said as he opened the car door for her.

As she walked into the house, Theresa felt she was walking on air. She went straight to her room, threw herself on the bed and tried to remember just how wonderful it felt when Lenny kissed her. She couldn't wait to see him again.

James and his friends, on arriving in Hamble, walked up the jetty towards the Yacht Club but, seeing it was packed inside, decided to go across the road to The Bugle. They found a large empty table in the garden where they all sat and drank beer to quench their thirst whilst looking at the menu.

The redhead was called Cassandra Felton-Browne, and was the daughter of a baron. Bryony was thrilled when James told her. She was mixing with the aristocracy! Not that Cassandra had a great deal to say to anyone.

'Don't take any notice of Cassy,' James told her. 'She doesn't come to life until after dark.'

'Like Dracula, you mean,' quipped Bryony.

James thought this quite hilarious.

The blonde girl, Davinia, was very friendly in a laid-back sort of way. 'Do you sail often?' she asked Bryony.

'No, this is my first time, but it's great – not that I think I'd be very good in a rough sea, though.'

'You'd love it!' Davinia exclaimed. 'It is truly exciting pitting the boat against the elements. Especially when the wind takes you and we all have to sit out on the trapeze to balance the yacht.'

Bryony couldn't think of anything more scary.

Toby came to sit beside her. 'When are you coming to my stables to look at my horses, and renew your aquaintance with Napoleon?'

'How many horses to you have?' she asked.

'In all we have about eight.'

'Eight! Good heavens.'

'Well, Dad has a couple of hunters. He likes to ride to hounds whenever he can. You must get James to bring you along sometime.'

'Thanks, Toby, I'd really like that.'

*　　*　　*

The day went well. After lunch they sailed along to Beaulieu and eventually back across the Solent to Cowes. There they went to the Yacht Club for dinner and then walked back to the boat where they sat on deck, drinking champagne until the early hours.

It was heady stuff, this life of the privileged, thought Bryony. She also thought she could get used to it very easily.

One by one, the others went to bed, leaving Bryony and James together on deck.

'Thank you for a lovely day,' she said. 'It was such a change for me.'

James put on arm around her shoulder and kissed her. 'I hope it will be one of many in the future,' he said softly as he ran his fingers through her hair.

'I hope so too.'

Pulling her to her feet, James once again took her in his arms and kissed her long and hard. 'Come along,' he said, 'a yacht moored in the moonlight can do funny things to a man and a woman. Whilst you are still safe, you had better go below to your cabin, or I might forget I am a gentleman.'

The gentle swaying of the boat as the tide moved soon lulled Bryony to sleep, as she half wished that James hadn't been quite such a gentleman.

The following day, after a leisurely lunch, James sailed the yacht back to Hamble where it was moored and, after seeing that everything was in order, he drove Bryony home.

Once parked outside her house, he kissed her and

said, 'I'll call you in a couple of days. I may not be able to see you next week, as I have a lot on with my work, but keep the weekend after free for me.'

'I certainly will,' she said, 'and thanks for a lovely time.'

Walking into the kitchen, where her mother was drying up the dishes from lunchtime, Bryony said to her father, who was sitting at the kitchen table, 'I had a great time, Dad. We sailed over to Hamble, later up to Beaulieu, and watched some racing from the harbour in Cowes.'

'That's nice,' he said. 'We were rushed off our feet and could have done with an extra hand.'

She was furious. 'Can't you be pleased for me? Does everything have to revolve around you? Do you know what, I'm only just beginning to realise just how selfish you are!' And she walked out of the room.

Leila turned on her husband. 'For goodness' sake! You had to spoil it for her, didn't you?'

'I don't know what you mean.'

'You're jealous! That's the root of it all – jealousy.'

'Don't be so bloody ridiculous!'

'Your little princess is growing up and you can't stand it. You, who have always been the centre of her universe, can't stand the competition. It's bloody pathetic.' And throwing down the tea towel, she left him alone.

Dan scowled. Jealous! What a bloody stupid thing to say about his own daughter. He was just looking after her welfare, that was all. It was his duty as a father. And he would continue to do so.

CHAPTER SEVEN

Dan Travis left the house, got into his car and drove towards the Silver Dollar Club, knowing if he stayed at home Leila would only continue to rage against him about Bryony. As he journeyed he questioned the truth of his wife's accusations. It wasn't that he was jealous, he reasoned, but it was difficult for a father to see his daughter growing up. It would be different if she were a boy. Being a womaniser himself, he knew about men's desires and this worried him. And he supposed it did hurt a bit to see her so interested in young James, be excited when he rang, when usually he had been the one to bring such a look of happiness to her countenance. Letting out a deep sigh, he wondered if all fathers went through this kind of thing.

At the club, Sophie Johnson was the first person he saw sitting at the bar, looking utterly dejected.

'What's up, me old mucker?' Dan asked. As soon as Sophie spoke, Dan could tell he'd been drinking heavily.

'I'm down in the dumps and pissed off. To be honest

with you, Dan, I'm feeling my age and, at this moment, I'm bloody lonely.'

As he ordered them both a drink, Dan said, 'That's not at all like you, Sophie. What's brought this on?'

'It's that little bleeder Giles.' He swayed on the stool and Dan put out a steadying hand. 'I'd got such plans for this weekend, but he had to go rushing off to see Daddy.'

'We all have family commitments, you know,' said Dan, trying to placate him.

'I don't bloody well have none, not me. I've no brothers or sisters and my parents are long gone. I'm just a lonely old man.' He leaned towards Dan and, slurring his words, confessed, 'You see, my dear, the trouble is . . . I really love that little bleeder.'

'Then that should make you happy, you daft old queen.'

'No, Dan, it doesn't. Don't you see? Giles ain't in love with me. He's like them all – he uses me to get money; they all do. I ain't daft, you know. I know I pay dearly for my pleasures, and normally I don't mind . . . but this young boy has touched my heart.'

For Sophie, normally a hard man, to unburden himself so only proved to Dan just how much alcohol he'd consumed, 'And what are you going to do about it?'

'What can I do, Dan? I'll go along with him. Mind you, I don't let him take me for a fool. Oh, no.' He placed his hand on Dan's shoulder and, leaning forward, whispered, 'It's what I'll do if he wants to leave me that bothers me.'

Dan Travis became immediately wary. Sophie Johnson

had a formidable reputation. He'd been inside for grievous bodily harm before now and it was well known that he was not averse to using his cutthroat razor at times.

'Now don't you go doing anything stupid, Sophie. No one is worth doing time for.'

Sophie looked suddenly very sober as he said, 'Time? I'm not worried about time, darling Dan. It's the rope I'm more concerned with.'

'Now stop that kind of talk! There is no one on this earth worth swinging for!'

'You're probably right.' Sophie straightened his shoulders, emptied his glass and said, 'Let's have another.'

'Come along, Sophie, I'll drive you home,' said Dan firmly. 'Sitting here and getting drunk and maudlin isn't good for anyone.' And easing him off the bar stool, he helped to get him down the stairs and into his car.

'I've got some money for you, Danny boy,' said Sophie when they arrived at his house. 'You can come inside and get it if you like.'

'Another time will do, thanks,' said Dan, not wanting to become involved in more drinking, which he knew would happen if he entered Sophie's house. 'You get your head down. I'll see you tomorrow. I'll meet you at the Star Hotel at noon. OK?'

'Yes, all right.'

As he drove home, Dan wondered if the other man would remember. But one thing he did know, he wouldn't want to be in young Giles's shoes. Oh, dear me, no!

* * *

Giles, unaware of Sophie Johnson's thoughts, had returned from Cowes, which he had not mentioned to Sophie, to his father's London house in Chelsea, where he sat and had dinner with his family. The party at his parents' house had been an invention to give him the freedom to go to Cowes with his friends without inciting Sophie's jealousy.

'You've caught the sun, my boy,' said his father, the judge.

'I've been over at Cowes, Father. It was great. James Hargreaves invited a few of us on to his father's yacht.'

'The *Beatrice*, I know it. Lovely craft. I shall be seeing Oliver soon, I'm hearing one of his cases in court next week. So, how are your studies going?'

'Fine, thanks.'

'Good. I'm expecting good results from you, Giles. Make sure you don't disappoint me.'

'No, sir.'

'I know that Hugo is more academically gifted than you, but with a little perseverance, you too could do well and uphold the family tradition.'

Giles stifled his anger. He was sick to death of his father always shoving his older brother down his throat. Hugo himself never put him down, but their father always managed to do so. Giles had had such a good time this weekend at Cowes with his friends, away from Sophie Johnson, and now his father had spoiled it. It was too much.

'I'm well aware, Father, that I am not your blue-eyed boy, but must you always make it quite so apparent?'

'Giles!' admonished his mother.

Sir Douglas glared at him and for a moment Giles could see how his father could put the fear of God into the barristers appearing before him.

'That's enough! You have a privileged position in life, remember that. Just make sure that you are worthy of it. There are many young men who appear in my court who would willingly change places with you if they had the chance. Many of whom, I might say, would make a much greater effort than you!'

'Let's not spoil my time at home with an argument, Father, please,' said Hugo intervening. 'Giles will work hard, I'm sure.'

The judge just grunted, glared across the table at his younger son and cut into his steak.

Hugo looked at Giles and gave a shake of his head to shut him up.

After dinner Hugo took Giles into the library and, pouring two brandies from the decanter on the sideboard, said to his brother, 'Don't take it to heart, old thing. You know how Father goes on. He doesn't mean it.'

Letting out a sigh Giles said, 'It's decent of you to say so, Hugo, but unfortunately he does. Every bloody word!'

'Then get your own back and get good results. Then you can hold up two fingers to him!'

'Metaphorically speaking, of course,' Giles quipped. And both the brothers laughed, knowing that neither of them would dare to show such disrespect to their parent.

As he sipped his brandy Giles wondered what the

judge would say if he knew his younger son was a queer. That would upset his applecart! In his spiteful mood it gave him a certain satisfaction. How shocked the old man would be if he told him.

In his mind he conjured the picture of father and son together in the study sometime in the future. 'Isn't it time you thought of settling down, my boy?' his father would say, and he, Giles, would smile and say, 'No, I don't think so. I don't see myself as any woman's husband.' His father would ask why and he would say . . . what would he say?

'No, thanks, I prefer to fuck men!' He began to laugh. How crude? How wonderful! It would almost be worth losing his allowance just to see the look on his father's face.

'What's so funny?' asked his brother.

Shaking his head, Giles said, 'Nothing really, just something that tickled me. A childish thought.'

Hugo picked out a book on law from the extensive collection and sat down. Within seconds he was immersed in his reading. Giles looked fondly at him. Hugo was a good sort, so dedicated to his work. Giles liked and admired his older brother, but he wondered how *he* would behave towards him if he discovered the secret of his sexuality. Would he be disgusted? The thought that he might be was upsetting. Giles would be really hurt to lose his brother's respect. He sighed. Next weekend he would have to return to Southampton and pacify Sophie for his absence. Now *he* himself found that disgusting!

He had become involved with Sophie when they met at a party in London given by Tarquin, a designer friend who had in the past been one of Sophie's boys. Indeed, Sophie had invested money in his new venture. Tarquin had spoken warmly about his benefactor and had recommended him to Giles.

'He's a bit of an old fart,' he explained, 'but he looks after you well.' And with a knowing look added, 'Financially, I mean. If you treat him right, he's a generous man.'

Giles, whose run on the horses had left him in a dangerous situation moneywise, had chatted to the man – and it had gone on from there. Sophie was good company, with his acerbic wit, and Giles had been fascinated by his links to the underworld. It had been exciting to start with, but Sophie was becoming increasingly possessive and Giles was worried as to how he would get out of this relationship when the time came.

At noon the following day, Dan Travis parked his car and walked into the bar of the Star Hotel in the High Street, wondering if he would be drinking alone. But sitting at a table reading the paper, was Sophie Johnson. He looked up as Dan entered.

'Hello, Dan, old boy. Bet you're surprised to see me,' he said with a smirk. 'I'm having a hair of the dog!'

'Want another?'

'Why not?'

Dan took their drinks over to the table and sat down. 'You all right, Soph?'

'Fine!' he declared. 'Haven't hung one on like that in an age. Felt bloody awful when I woke up. I told the cat to stop stamping on the carpet!'

'I'm glad you're feeling better.' Dan made no further comment on what had passed the evening before, knowing that Sophie wouldn't welcome it.

Putting his hand inside his jacket pocket, Sophie produced a large envelope and passed it over. 'Best price I could get, but you haven't done bad.'

Dan put away the envelope without looking inside it, saying, 'That's fine. I know you won't do me down.'

'My man knows better than to try,' said the fence. 'He only tried to screw me once. He still carries the scar on his face.' Rubbing his chin, he said quietly, 'I know of a very nice house full of antique furniture that's going to be empty over the next weekend. You interested?'

'Could be,' said Dan.

'You got the man power?'

'Yes, I can manage that for you. No trouble. What about burglar alarms?

'They'll be short-circuited before your boys arrive. I've got an address in London who'll take delivery.'

'And my percentage?' asked Dan.

'Thirty.'

'You're having a laugh. Forty-five and not a penny less.'

'Well, you've got to try, haven't you?' said Sophie with a broad grin, and they shook hands. 'I'll have all the details tomorrow. I'll pop them into your office.'

* * *

The following day, Sophie arrived at the car lot with a set of plans of the house to be burgled, and a list of goods to be lifted and their placement within the house.

Dan read the paper before him, studied it carefully and eventually said, 'Very thorough.'

'I don't want anything else taken other than what I've marked, Dan. I've got a home for all the items, so they will disappear very quickly once you've delivered the stuff up west, leaving no trails, so don't let your boys get grab happy.'

'They'll do exactly as I tell them. Do you think four men will be enough?'

'Yes,' said Sophie. 'Any less will take too much time. Four men can handle the furniture as some of it weighs a bloody ton.'

'When do the owners leave the property?'

'Friday afternoon. They're going over to France. If your boys arrive on Saturday morning . . . I'll leave the rest to you.' They shook hands and Sophie left.

Dan sat silently reading the list once again. He knew about antique furniture; it was a love of his and he had many superb pieces in his house in Westwood Road, all bought fair and square. He never took chances with his home. You never knew when the filth were likely to call. So far all his dirty dealings had been well camouflaged and, apart from sometimes looking at the motors on the forecourt, the police had no reason to bother him, although they carried a file on him in the station. You couldn't mix with the villains that Dan Travis did and not be noticed.

He scratched his chin and thought of the best way to go about this. His men could empty the house of the wanted items in the dead of night and probably get away with it as the house stood in its own grounds, but he always thought it was better to be blatant. Bluff was a wonderful thing in his world, if you were smart enough. He would get a furniture delivery van from one of his mates and the men would arrive in broad daylight. Should there be any queries from nosy neighbours, they would be told very politely that the furniture was being shipped to a new house in France. That was the way to do it. Sophie could get the alarm cut during Friday night. Dan picked up the telephone.

On Saturday morning, a smart furniture removal van arrived at the Chilworth house and four men dressed in brown overalls removed the listed contents, closed the front door, climbed into the back of the van and drove away without raising suspicion. They were well pleased with themselves, as was the owner of a very exclusive antique furniture shop in London's West End, where the goods were delivered. They were due to be shipped out to America the next morning, where they would earn a small fortune.

Bryony was coming to the end of her course at the typing school and so far had passed her exams very competently. She had been asked to go to the head's office.

'You've done well, Bryony,' the woman told her. 'What are your plans for the future?'

'As you know, I want to work for a firm with a sound reputation.'

The head smiled. She liked this girl. She had a good grasp of business, and ambition, unlike some of her pupils. 'It so happens that I might have the right job for you,' she said. 'They want somebody competent, someone with a bit of personality, able to meet their clients, sometimes to take notes.'

Bryony was intrigued. 'Where is this situation?' she asked.

'It's an advertising company with some very important clients. I think you would find it more interesting than a solicitor's office or accountant's. It has been going for only about five years, but it has already made a name for itself and I could see you fitting in well. Are you interested?'

'Of course.'

'Then I'll set up an interview for you. It so happens that the managing director is a friend of my husband's and we have met socially. He's a nice man. I think you'd get on well together.'

'Thank you, Mrs Hall. I really appreciate it.'

Bryony returned to the classroom, thrilled at the news. She would wait and see if she was successful at the interview before breaking the news to her father that she wouldn't be working for him full time. That she wasn't looking forward to. And she wondered if her mother would support her. Leila was very much of the 'working for the family' school. Well, anyway, if she got the job, she would take it whatever her parents said.

She would be eighteen in a few weeks' time. She'd already been having driving lessons as a start to being independent. Her father, who was paying for them, would just have to accept she was wanting independence in other aspects of her life. And she would help him out now and again just to keep him happy.

CHAPTER EIGHT

Bryony chose her clothes carefully on the day of her interview. She picked a costume with a plain dark grey skirt, and a jacket that was fitted with a slight basque at the back in a small grey and black check, beneath which she wore a plain white blouse. She eyed her reflection carefully. The style of the jacket, she felt, showed a bit of flair. She didn't want to appear sedate and prim because she was neither of these things and she felt she needed to fly under her own colours.

The receptionist showed her into the waiting room of Langdon and Associates. The room was not that big, but was bright, with a large window overlooking London Road. Two doors led off the room. On the walls were posters advertising various products, and she assumed correctly that these were some of the results of advertising campaigns. Studying them, she thought they showed perceptiveness and originality.

A door opened and a tall man of about forty-five, in his shirtsleeves, with a bow tie, a colourful waistcoat and grey trousers, peered over his glasses and said, 'Miss Travis? Please come this way.'

She followed him into his office and sat in the chair that he indicated. He was completely informal. 'Right. I'm Richard Langdon, the director of the company. Mrs Hall has said encouraging things about your progress and I need someone who is efficient.' He smiled at her. 'We're all a bit mad here, I'm afraid. It's the kind of business that we're in, I suppose. Sometimes the workload is frantic, and the other times it's exceedingly boring. How does that sound to you?'

Laughing, Bryony said, 'Different.'

Grinning, he said, 'That just about sums us up. Your duties would be very varied. Sometimes I need you to take letters; others, to take notes of meetings, and occasionally to look after my clients if I'm busy. Would you like to give us a go?'

'I would,' she said. 'I would like that very much. I have another week before I finish at the typing school, but then I'm free.'

'Excellent. The hours are from nine to five but on occasion when we have to meet a deadline things can be a bit behind and we have to work late.'

'That's not a problem.'

They discussed her salary and when everything was agreed, Richard Langdon rose to his feet and shook hands with her. 'See you in a week's time, Bryony.'

As she walked back to the school, she was in seventh heaven. A job on her own merit! She instinctively liked her new boss. She was taken by his lack of formality and felt that although when it was required she would have to work hard, if the rest of the staff were of the same disposition, the company could be fun to be a part of. Later that day she would have to tell her father, but first she had to report back to her head teacher.

Mrs Hall was delighted. 'Well done, Bryony. I'm sure you'll enjoy working with Richard. He might appear a bit of a scatterbrain and a little eccentric, but he and his son are very clever.'

'His son?' said Bryony.

'Yes, Nick. He and his father work together. Nick is twenty-five and very bright. They make a great team.'

That evening, when she sat down to dinner with her mother and father, Bryony waited until they were eating dessert before she made her announcement.

'I've got some good news,' she said.

'Oh, that sounds interesting,' remarked Leila.

Dan looked up and asked, 'What is it?'

Taking a deep breath, Bryony said, 'Today I went for an interview for a job and I start in a week's time.'

'You what?' Dan looked angrily at her. 'What job? Where?'

'Langdon's in London Road. They do advertising.'

Dan's face was like thunder. 'I thought you were going to be working for me full time!'

'No, Dad,' Bryony said quietly. 'I did tell you that I didn't want to do that, remember. I said if I was a boy I could understand you wanting me to eventually take over the business in years to come. I don't want to do that . . . I did tell you,' she added defiantly.

'You might have consulted me before you went ahead with this!' he exclaimed.

Now she was getting angry. 'Why? If I had done, you would have tried to stop me. I want to find my own way in life. For God's sake! You gave me an education, now let me make use of it!'

'So my car lot isn't good enough, is that what you're saying?'

'No, of course not. But don't you see, although I enjoy being on the forecourt, it is like a hobby. I don't want to make it my life's work, that's all I'm saying.'

At this point her mother intervened. 'You've got to give her a chance to prove herself, Dan.'

'It's not how I planned things!' he said petulantly.

'It's time you learned, Dan Travis, that not everyone wants to dance to your tune!' Turning to Bryony, Leila said, 'Well done, love. Don't you take any notice of your father; he has to learn that you have your own life to lead. Give him time, he'll get used to it.'

'Will you stop talking about me as if I wasn't here, woman! I don't know what's got into you two lately.'

'Bryony's growing up and spreading her wings, and I'm her mother so I'm encouraging her, that's all.' Leila glared at her husband. 'You did the same at her age . . . and sometimes you still do!' she said sarcastically. '*You* often seem to forget that you are already grown up!'

Getting up, Dan threw his napkin on the table. 'I

don't have to listen to this,' he said, and swept out of the room.

Leila pulled a face. 'Your father just has to get used to the fact that you are no longer a child, that's all.'

Bryony rose from her seat and hugged Leila. 'Thanks, Mum. What would I do without you?'

Dan was in a vile mood as he drove down to Southampton's docklands where he had a warehouse. It was used to store cars and many other bits and pieces that might be part of some deal or other. It was also the headquarters of his motley crew of men, who gathered there regularly.

As he entered he saw them sitting round a table eating fish and chips. This was the crew who had done the robbery in Chilworth.

He spoke quietly to his head man. 'Everything go all right? Any hitches?'

The man hesitated just a moment too long before answering, 'Yes, fine.'

Glowering at him, Dan asked, 'But what?'

The man scratched his head. 'Well, it was Sam. I told the boys that nothing else was supposed to be lifted other than what was on the list and I saw him pick up a silver salver, which was engraved. I made him put it back, though; otherwise it went like a dream. It was all safely delivered and unloaded.'

Dan walked over to the table and sat beside Sam, who looked up at him and smiled. 'All right, guv?'

Picking up a knife that was on the table, Dad said,

'Fine.' But as Sam reached over for the tomato ketchup, Dan speared his hand to the table with it.

Sam let out a scream of agony and tried to move his hand away, but Dan pressed his weapon even deeper.

'When you work for me, my son, you *never* get light-fingered!' He removed the knife. 'Do I make myself clear?'

There was a deadly silence around the table.

'Yes, guv,' sobbed Sam, trying to stem the blood with a handkerchief. 'I'm sorry.'

'Now you have two choices,' Dan said in a quiet voice. 'You either follow my rules or you take a swim in the docks . . . with something heavy tied to your feet. What's it to be?'

'Sorry, sorry, it'll never happen again, honest.'

Rising to his feet, Dan said, 'Good night, gents. Nice job. You'll be paid shortly.' And he walked away.

'Fucking lunatic!' cried Sam. 'I need to go to the hospital. Look at what he did to me.'

The others were unimpressed. 'What did you expect, you stupid bastard?' said one. 'You should have known better. That salver could have been traced. You just got greedy; well, you've paid for it. You're bloody lucky you're still breathing!' And he continued with his dinner.

'If you go to the hospital, you'd better have a good story as to how you received that injury,' another warned. 'You want to live to a ripe old age, you'd better tell it right.'

Sam staggered out of the warehouse, swearing at the others, saying they were heartless and no friends of his.

'You don't have any friends in this game, mate,' one called, 'but you drop us in it at the hospital, Dan Travis won't need to sort you out. I'll bloody well do it for him!'

Bryony picked up the telephone and rang Theresa, wanting to give her friend her news, but she was told that Theresa was out for the evening. Disappointed, Bryony replaced the receiver, wondering where she'd gone and with whom.

In the back row of the cinema, Theresa Kerrigan was sitting with Lenny Marks watching *Love Me or Leave Me* with Doris Day and James Cagney. Cagney's portrayal of a gangster filled Theresa with loathing, but Lenny was in admiration of him. He would like to be a hard man like him, or like Dan Travis. Now there was a man to admire. No one messed with him, and he, Lenny, aspired to such a position. He put his arm around Theresa.

Feeling somewhat intimidated by the storyline of the film, she snuggled into her companion for comfort, but she was a little shocked to feel his hand upon her breast and brushed it aside.

Lenny smiled to himself. You'll get used to it in time, girl, he thought, and when they left the cinema, he drove to The Avenue and turned into the quiet road of the Common. When he stopped the car, trees on either side surrounded them, with not a soul in sight. He switched off the headlights and plunged the car into darkness.

'What are you doing?' asked Theresa nervously.

'I just wanted to be alone with my girl, that's all,' he said as he gathered her in his arms and kissed her.

Theresa kissed him back.

'You're learning,' he said. He kissed her again and caressed her cheek, her neck, then running his fingers down the front of her blouse; he undid the buttons and slid his hand inside, gently cupping her soft breast.

She began to protest.

'Relax, darling,' he coaxed. 'Your skin is so soft, I just want to hold you,' and he kissed her more passionately.

Theresa moaned softly, carried away with his ardour, which was awakening feelings she had never ever experienced before. Her senses were swimming and she was slowly sinking into oblivion, as her sexual awareness overcame her caution.

Sensing this, Lenny became more adventurous and lowered his mouth to encompass the pink nipple now standing proud. At the same time, he lifted the edge of her skirt and, slipping his hand inside her knickers, he softly stroked her womanhood.

'Theresa, Theresa, I love you,' he said as he felt himself harden. Women were more pliable when he declared his love, he had found, and it certainly seemed to be working this time.

'I love you too, Lenny,' she whispered as he spread her legs, and slipped his fingers inside her.

'Oh, Lenny, Lenny,' she cried, before he kissed her again.

'Let's get into the back of the car,' he said. 'This bloody gear stick is in my way.'

Theresa, carried away with this new-found passion, didn't argue.

He laid her down on the back seat, and undid her blouse and bra, loosening her soft breasts. Then he slipped off her knickers, and climbed on top of her.

There was a moment of panic in her voice as Theresa asked, 'What are you doing?'

'I'm loving my girl,' Lenny said huskily as he entered her. He closed his eyes as his rhythm increased. 'Christ! You're wonderful,' he cried as he drove himself into her.

Theresa let out a cry of pain, which she quickly forgot as she was overcome with his lovemaking. She moaned softly.

When he reached the zenith of his desire, Lenny trembled and cried out as he came. Then he collapsed on top of her, sweating and breathless.

Theresa lay still, silent and stunned, hardly able to believe what had just taken place. 'You do love me, Lenny, don't you?' she asked in a small frightened voice.

'Didn't I tell you I did?' he said as he straightened his clothes. 'You'd best get yourself together before I take you home,' he added.

Once they were sitting in the front of the car again, Theresa glanced across at Lenny, who was lighting a cigarette. The enormity of her indiscretion began to dawn.

He patted her knee. 'That was your first time, wasn't it?' he asked.

With downcast eyes she nodded.

Putting out his hand, he tilted her chin upwards. 'It's nothing to be ashamed of, baby. It's what people in love do.' He wiped away two tears rolling down her cheeks. 'Come on now. You enjoyed it, didn't you?'

She looked into his eyes and had to admit that she did. 'Yes,' she said.

'There then.' He kissed her gently.

Theresa threw her arms around his neck and clung to him.

As he patted her back and made comforting noises he thought, bloody women – why do they have to be so emotional all the time? Why can't they be like men? If you felt like a good screw you had one and that was that!

He released her hold on him and said, 'Best get you home. We don't want your father telling me off for keeping you out late.'

Theresa paled when she thought of her father. He would kill her if he ever found out she'd lost her virginity!

Lenny pulled up outside the house. 'I'll call you,' he said as he pecked her on the cheek.

Letting herself into the house, Theresa was greatly relieved when she found her parents ensconced in the drawing room. 'I'm home!' she called as she went upstairs to her room. Once there, she opened the wardrobe door and looked at her reflection in the mirror. She didn't look any different. This surprised her. She was now a woman, so why didn't it show? But then if it did, her parents would notice.

In the bathroom she was horrified to see her underwear stained with blood. She very quickly rinsed them out in the sink. With a bit of luck, if she draped them over the chair, they would be dry in the morning. If not, she would stuff the articles in a drawer, away from prying eyes.

As she lay in bed, she went over everything that had happened in her mind. Lenny Marks loved her . . . and had made love to her. It was exciting really, but she couldn't tell a soul, not even her great friend Bryony. But deep down she had a feeling of pride. She was a woman now! Being made love to in the back of a car was not exactly how she'd envisaged losing her virginity. She'd always thought it would be in bed on her wedding night but, nevertheless, there was a certain thrill to be gained by the enormity of being deflowered without marriage. Bryony couldn't say the same. She would hug her secret to herself.

Turning over, Theresa closed her eyes and slept.

CHAPTER NINE

Bryony was thrilled when James rang her after her job offer. She told him about her successful interview and was delighted when he suggested they celebrate. It appeared that Toby Beckford was having a house party the following weekend and had invited James, and told him to bring Bryony.

'Can you get away?' he asked.

'Of course I can,' she told him. 'Where does Toby live?'

'In Gloucestershire. We'll leave in the morning on Saturday and get there for lunch. The party's in the evening and on Sunday we'll go clay pigeon shooting—'

'Shooting? I've never done that in my life!' Bryony interrupted.

She could hear his laughter down the phone. 'That doesn't matter. It's mainly the men who do the shooting. You can sit and watch and look pretty.'

'What shall I wear?'

'Bring warm clothes for the shoot and some Wellington boots in case it rains,' he told her, 'and something glamorous for the party. It'll be great fun – Toby's parties always are. By the way, he said he would renew your acquaintance with Napoleon!'

This intrigued Bryony and she wondered what Toby's house was like. Gloucestershire was a popular county for the rich and noble. She wondered also who else would be there. She would tell her mother first about her plans; she couldn't face another grilling from her father.

Leila looked concerned when Bryony told her about her proposed weekend. 'Who is this Toby Beckford?' she asked.

'He's a friend of James's. I met him at the polo match. He has a beautiful horse called Napoleon and I'll be visiting the stables to see him.'

'Stables? Does Toby play polo then?'

'Yes, he was playing in the match. Oh, Mum, you should see the way they ride, these men. It's so exciting!'

'And so expensive,' said Leila drily. 'He sounds as if he comes from a wealthy background.'

With a shrug, Bryony said, 'Yes, I imagine he does. He's a merchant banker, I believe. But he's really nice, and he's a friend of James's.'

'And what about the sleeping arrangements?'

'Oh, Mum!'

'Never mind "Oh, Mum!". I'm not letting you go away unless I know that everything is above board. Can you imagine what your father will have to say?'

'I was hoping that you would smooth the way for me,' Bryony pleaded. 'I really want to go so much, and I can assure you that Toby is a gentleman; there won't be any funny business. I wouldn't put up with it anyway – you should know that!'

Wrapping an arm around her daughter, Leila said, 'It isn't that I don't trust you, darling, it's the others. But I know you want to go, so all right, as long as you promise to be careful.'

Flinging her arms around her mother, Bryony said, 'Thank you so much. There is one thing, though. I need a really nice dress for the party in the evening.'

'Then let's go shopping!' said Leila. 'I can't have you going to such a posh do without being dressed for the part.'

They spent the afternoon combing the dress shops in Southampton, ending up in Chanel, where Leila bought a cocktail dress for Bryony, in deep burgundy chiffon, which complemented her colouring to perfection. The bodice was softly draped, with narrow shoulder straps, the skirt falling straight to just below the knee. It was sophisticated and classy.

Standing back and looking at Bryony, Leila felt a knot in her chest as she saw before her a young and desirable woman, not a young girl who was almost eighteen.

'I think maybe it's a bit old for you, Bryony.'

'Oh, no, please say I can have it. I absolutely love it. And just think, all the other girls will be dressed to the nines!'

Seeing the look of happiness in her daughter's eyes, Leila couldn't refuse. 'All right, we'll take it.'

Once outside the shop, clutching her large white bag with her dress inside, Bryony said, 'I need a pair of Wellington boots.'

'Wellingtons?'

'Yes. James said I will need a pair as we're going on a shoot on the Sunday morning.' Seeing the look of horror on the face of her mother she quickly added, 'I'm only there to watch, I'm told.'

Leila started laughing. 'I don't know. Wellington boots and a chiffon dress, it doesn't quite sound right, does it?'

'I'm not wearing them together, Mother!' Then she started laughing. 'Imagine! If I walked in wearing both to the party, it might start a new fashion. You know, how to be ready for anything in the country!'

Early that evening, Bryony walked alone to The Avenue and knocked on the door of her friend's house. Theresa opened the door, and Bryony walked straight in, saying, 'I've got so much to tell you!'

The girls went up to Theresa's bedroom. Bryony flung herself on the bed and started, 'I've got a job in an advertising agency. I start in a week's time. Isn't that great?'

'Yes, wonderful. Congratulations.'

'And I'm going to Gloucestershire with James next weekend to a house party.' She hugged her knees. 'Isn't life exciting?'

'Yes,' said Theresa.

Bryony looked at her and asked, 'Whatever is the matter with you? Is something wrong?'

Theresa was feeling uncomfortable before her friend, knowing how much Bryony disliked Lenny Marks, and she was also feeling guilty. 'No, nothing.'

'What have you been up to then?'

'What do you mean – "been up to"? I haven't been up to anything!'

Suddenly Bryony stopped her happy chatter. She knew Theresa inside out and there was definitely something bugging her. 'What's wrong?'

'There's nothing wrong, honestly.' Desperate to change the subject, Theresa said, 'Tell me about this weekend with James.'

And so the danger passed as Bryony gave her all the details, and of the shopping trip with her mother. 'You should see the dress, it's wonderful. I feel just like a film star,' she declared.

And so the girls chattered on as young women do until Bryony left to go home. 'I'll give you a call soon,' she said.

Theresa closed the door with a sigh of relief. She had dreaded seeing Bryony, with whom she had shared so many secrets. She did feel a bit of a traitor, but there was no way she could confess that she had let Lenny Marks make love to her. She hadn't even been able to do so when she was in the confessional. And that was a great sin in her eyes. So consumed with guilt was she that she had decided she would refuse any further advances from Lenny when he took her out the next time. The fact that her parents may discover that she was no longer a virgin terrified her.

Giles had come down to Southampton on the Friday evening to stay with Sophie. He needed to make a fuss of him because he was going to be at Toby Beckford's party the following weekend, which he knew would not please his benefactor one bit, but he decided not to tell him until the last moment.

Sophie was so happy to see him, and kissed him, smiling with delight. 'I thought you were coming tomorrow.'

'Well, I missed you, you old queen, so here I am.'

'Darling boy! Let's do something special. We can go out to dinner and go on somewhere after, what do you say?'

'It sounds great,' said Giles, trying to sound enthusiastic.

After a meal, the two men finished up at the Silver Dollar. The club held a fascination for young Giles. He knew that many of the members had connections in the local criminal world and was aware of Sophie's part in all of this. He found it exciting. Dangerously so.

They sat at a quiet table in the corner, where Sophie held court as various men who looked as if they were sure to have their mug shots at some police station or other approached him about business.

One vicious-looking individual came over and sat

himself beside Sophie. In a low voice he said, 'Need some money laundering, Soph.'

'How much?'

'Several thou. Bank job up north.'

The men put their heads closely together and spoke quietly so that Giles was unable to hear the conversation. Then they shook hands. Sophie called to the barman to send over two large brandies.

The villain looked across Sophie and gazed admiringly at Giles. To the fence he said, 'Nice looker. Classy. When you've finished with him, I'll take him over.'

Giles felt the blood in his veins freeze as he glanced into the cruel eyes of the man. He wondered what would be the reaction of his benefactor.

With a slow smile, Sophie said, 'Back off, Harry. He's special, and frankly I wouldn't hand my cat over to you.'

Harry was furious. 'What do you mean by that, you bloody old shirt-lifter?'

Giles noticed the tightening of Sophie's jaw. 'Don't get lairy. Show a little respect. You want to do business with me, then watch your mouth. Now apologise . . . then fuck off!'

For one moment, Giles thought the man was going to cause a scene, but when Harry looked at Sophie, who was no longer smiling, he hesitated. 'Sorry, just a slip of the tongue.'

'Your mouth was always bigger than your brain, Harry boy. One day it will be the death of you.' There was such a note of menace in Sophie's voice, Giles wondered if it was a personal threat.

It was obvious that Harry thought so because he rose quickly from his seat. 'I'll see you later, Sophie, and thanks,' he said, and walked over to the bar.

'Who the hell was that?' Giles asked, pleased and relieved that the man had left them.

'A very nasty sadistic bugger. He likes to torture people, especially young men, when he's finished with them. The last one was castrated, or so rumour has it.'

Giles felt sick. Especially when he looked up and saw Harry staring at him. The man grinned and raised his glass. Giles quickly turned away. What the hell am I doing here? he asked himself. No longer did this seem to be an exciting world. For the very first time he realised just how dangerous was the crowd he was mixing with.

'Let's go home, Sophie. This place gives me the creeps.'

But at that moment, Dan Travis arrived and, seeing the two of them, came over.

'What can I get you gents?'

To Giles's horror, Sophie asked for two more drinks. He watched Dan walk over to the bar. But he observed in fascinated silence as Dan gruffly told Harry to get out of his way. The villain turned, ready to hurl abuse until he saw who had spoken, and without a word, he moved.

'Did you see that?' Giles declared. 'That dreadful man just moved without a word.'

'That's Dan Travis,' said Sophie. 'No one with any sense crosses him. He's the king pin in Southampton. Been top of the heap for many a year. Even I respect him.'

Giles studied the two men at the bar. Whereas Harry looked rough and ready, Dan had an air about him. He looked a powerful man, and there was something about his demeanour that courted respect.

Dan returned with the drinks and sat down. Smiling across at Giles, he asked, 'How was your weekend at home?' At Giles's look of surprise, he added, 'Sophie was like a fish out of water without you.'

'Oh, I see. It was fine. My brother was down from Cambridge, so it was a family get-together. You know what they're like. But duty called.'

'I sometimes think it would have been easier to have a son than a daughter,' Dan said. 'My Bryony is grow-ing up far too quickly and I don't like it one bit!'

Laughing, Sophie said, 'I've heard many a father say that, my boy. But you have to let them fly the nest sometime, you know.'

'Yes, but it's harder than you think. Do you have any sisters, young man?'

'No, sir, only a brother.'

'Your father's a lucky man then.' Turning to Sophie, he said, 'Don't see Harry Burgess in here very often. God, I can't stand the man. Someone ought to do us all a favour and get rid of him – permanently. He's the scum of the earth.'

'He wanted me to do a bit of business for him,' said Sophie. 'Cheeky bugger took a fancy to young Giles here. I told him where to go.'

With a frown Dan looked at the young man and said, 'You keep well away from him. He's dangerous.

He should be locked away in some mental institute instead of walking around among decent people. You have any trouble, you let me know.'

Now Giles was beginning to panic. At least he had Sophie and now Dan looking after his interests, but he asked himself if all this was worth his friendship with the fence. Whereas before the danger had been because of the people Sophie mixed with, now it seemed Giles himself was personally implicated and he was scared.

'Can we go?' he asked Sophie. 'I really feel uncomfortable here.'

Sophie downed his drink. 'Yes, come on. See you, Dan,' he said as he rose to his feet.

Giles didn't look at Harry Burgess as he left, but Harry watched him with a sly smile spreading across his face. Nice, very nice, he thought as Giles walked by him to the exit.

Giles may have missed the look on Harry's face, but Dan Travis saw it. Picking up his drink, he went to the bar and stood beside Harry.

'Don't get any funny ideas about that young man, if you know what's good for you, Burgess.'

'Or what?' he asked with a show of defiance.

'Or they will be arranging your funeral. All I need is a good excuse. Do I make myself clear?'

'Perfectly.' Harry downed his pint and left the club, anger coursing through him. 'Fucking Dan Travis! Thinks he owns everybody,' he muttered. 'Well, he bloody well don't own me!'

*   *   *

As Giles was getting ready to return home on Sunday evening, he told Sophie he wouldn't be down the following weekend, and the older man flew into a rage.

'What's the bloody excuse this time?'

Deciding it was better to be truthful this time, he said, 'I'm going to a house party in Gloucestershire.'

'You'd rather be with your poncy friends than with me, is that it?'

'Not at all,' said Giles quietly, 'but you must realise, Sophie, that I do have a life that requires my presence now and then. I have to keep up appearances, you know I do.'

'I was good enough for you the other day when I took you to the races and gave you money . . . which you bloody well lost.'

It was true. Giles had persuaded Sophie to take him to Goodwood, and he'd lost the best part of a hundred pounds. 'But I thought you enjoyed yourself! At least you won money, so it wasn't a complete loss.'

'Now you listen to me, you little shit. Don't think that I'm just your bank balance, because I won't be taken for a fool by you or anyone.' Sophie was now striding angrily up and down the room. Turning suddenly, he pointed a finger at Giles and shouted, 'Don't think you can bleed me dry and get away with it. Better men have tried, and paid the price!'

Giles became very wary. Sophie in a temper could be a dangerous thing. 'Don't be silly, you old tart. I'm here because of you, not because of your money.'

In a quiet menacing voice that sounded far more

deadly than when he shouted, Sophie said, 'Don't take the piss, boy. I may not be educated but don't think I'm not intelligent. If you hadn't known I had plenty of dosh, you wouldn't have touched me with a barge pole in the beginning.'

To deny it would have been foolish, and Giles wasn't stupid. 'Money is a great aphrodisiac, Sophie darling, you know that, but I could have walked away at any time. I'm still around, aren't I?'

Sophie stared at the young man and Giles held his gaze. 'If you want me to leave for good, Sophie, you only have to say.'

The fence knew that his lover was calling his bluff, and although it angered him, he had to admire the effrontery of it.

'You are such a little bleeder, you know that, don't you?'

'But I'm lovely with it,' grinned Giles, knowing that the danger had passed.

'All right, go to your poncy friend's house for all I care.'

'Shall I come back the following weekend?'

'Now don't push your luck, you little bastard. Go on, fuck off.'

Giles walked over to his benefactor, gave him a hug and kissed his cheek. 'You keep out of trouble now. I'll see you soon.'

Giles breathed a sigh of relief when he reached the street and hailed a taxi to take him to the station. Sitting in the back of the vehicle he thought, I must find someone else.

Sophie Johnson was too hard to handle and the consequences of upsetting him could be dire. Giles wiped the side of his cheek, remembering the long scar on the face of the jeweller who had once crossed Sophie. He didn't want to end up disfigured. His face was his fortune.

CHAPTER TEN

When Leila told Dan about Bryony going to Gloucestershine for the weekend, he went spare. 'Going away! Staying with strangers – and her boyfriend! Over my dead body.'

'I've had enough of you, Dan. You sound just like Bluebeard, and I won't have it. James Hargeaves comes from a good family, as do his friends. You want your daughter to mix with the right people, don't you?' At his hesitation she added, 'Well, it's better than her mixing with the likes of your cronies.'

'They were good enough for you,' he stormed.

'I don't mind them because I'm used to them and I can handle them. At one time, Bryony moving up in the world used to worry me, I don't deny it. Now I think if she's really going to get on, it's no bad thing. We have educated her for better things, so now we don't have the right to hold her back.'

'Don't tell me you're turning into a snob, my darling.'

Leila ignored his caustic tone. 'It will do her good; after all, she starts work next week. She won't have the spare time then.' She sighed and said, 'If you are that concerned, have a word with young James when he collects her.'

'I'll certainly do that, make no mistake.'

He was waiting at the front door for James the following Saturday, and hustled the young man into his study.

'Let's get one thing straight,' said Dan, coming to the point. 'You are responsible for my daughter's well-being this weekend.'

'I know, sir. She's in safe hands, don't you worry.'

'You keep your bloody hands off her, do I make myself clear?'

'Mr Travis, you forget I was brought up a gentleman.'

'And don't you forget that or you will have me to answer to.'

Bryony was coming down the stairs with her suitcase when James emerged from Dan's room. Seeing the look of anger on her father's face and the flushed look on James's, she was immediately embarrassed.

'I'm ready,' she said quickly, kissing Dan, and her mother, who had emerged from the living room. 'I'll see you sometime on Sunday,' she said, and headed for the front door to prevent any further discussion.

Once in the car she turned to James and said, 'What was all that about?'

'Your father was being protective. He was making sure I would behave like a gentleman and take care of you.'

She was furious. 'He has no right to interfere.'

'He has every right, Bryony,' James said gently. 'Don't be angry with him; be grateful that he cares.'

'I am grateful, but he stifles me. I won't let him control my life!'

'Forget him,' he suggested. 'Come on, we're together, aren't we, and we're off for the weekend. Let's just enjoy it.'

The day was fine and the journey through the English countryside was more than enjoyable. They left Hampshire, crossed Salisbury Plain and on through Marlborough, with its old buildings, then northwards. From Cirencester, James pointed out the Cotswold stone, which adorned the walls and houses.

'Whenever I get to this place I know exactly where I am because of that particular stone. I think it's beautiful.'

They stopped to look at a cottage with a thatched roof. 'Isn't it lovely!' exclaimed Bryony. 'The garden is so pretty. It looks just like a chocolate-box picture.'

Just outside of Winchcombe, James slowed the car and turned in through tall wrought-iron gates. Carved in the stone pillars was the name 'Wallbourne Manor'. Ahead of them was an elm-lined avenue, with vast grounds either side where sheep grazed. In the far distance James pointed out a small herd of deer sheltering beneath a cloister of trees. Bryony sat silent and breathless from the beauty of it all.

112

Eventually she said, 'It's like a calendar that you buy full of photographs of the English countryside. Can you imagine how wonderful it would look, covered in snow?' Then she held her breath as beyond them she saw the house. It seemed vast. In front of the building was a huge lawn with a fountain surrounded by a rose garden, which gave the drive a deep sweep up to the front door.

As James parked the car, a footman came down the steps. 'Good morning, sir,' he said, as he took the luggage from him. 'Mr Toby is in the drawing room and wishes you to join him there.'

'Thank you, Baines,' said James. Turning to Bryony, he took her arm and said, 'Come on. Toby's waiting for us.'

She was absolutely speechless.

They entered the huge front door into a vast baronial hall. There were suits of armour standing like sentinels around the walls. In one corner were three flags on tall poles. Bryony recognised the Union Flag but neither of the other two. In the centre stood a huge circular oak table with a magnificent display of summer flowers. It reminded her of the tale of King Arthur and the Knights of the Round Table. The smell of wood smoke emanated from the open fire on one side, beside which were two comfortable-looking armchairs. On a mat in front lay two Labradors, who lifted their heads and looked up at the visitors with bored indifference, then lay back down. The staircase looked like a film set, thought Bryony. It swept upwards in a single rise, with family portraits against the walls, then branched into two elegant landings.

Bryony wondered just who Toby Beckford really was. Was he a member of the gentry, or just from a very wealthy family? She was intrigued.

Despite its size and grandeur, the drawing room felt cosy. It had settees covered in chintz at either side of the open fireplace. Other comfortable chairs were placed around the room, with tables of different sizes between them. Over the fireplace was a huge mirror in a heavily carved golden frame.

Toby rose from the depths of a chair and walked over to greet them. 'Bryony, my dear. I'm so glad you could come.' He kissed her on both cheeks. Shaking hands, he said to James, 'Good of you to come. Sit down. I'll send for some drinks now. I was waiting for some company as I do hate to drink alone and the others haven't arrived yet.' He walked over to the wall and pulled an embroidered bell pull.

A servant appeared. 'You rang, sir?'

'Bring the champagne in, Jarvis, there's a good chap.'

Bryony had regained her equilibrium. 'What a lovely place you have, Toby. I saw the deer as we drove in.'

'Wonderful, aren't they?' he said. 'Sometimes in the winter I stand at the window there,' he indicated the huge casement window overlooking the grounds, 'and I watch them for hours. They are such graceful creatures. Mind you, the gardeners curse them if they get into the vegetable garden.'

'How's Napoleon?' she asked.

'Fine. After lunch I'll take you to the stables and you can see for yourself.'

The butler reappeared with a tray of glasses and a bottle of champagne in an ice bucket, and proceeded to open the bottle and pour the contents into the glasses. 'Will there be anything else, sir?'

'Not until the others arrive, thank you.'

As Bryony sat beside James on one of the settees and sipped her champagne in her elegant surroundings, she thought, if only Theresa could see me now!

In complete contrast to her friend, Theresa was sitting in the front room of Lenny Marks's parents' house. The furniture was old and dowdy. The room was dark, with a damp, musty smell and in need of a good dust. She thought it was awful. Lenny had invited her there, as he had to pick up some papers belonging to a car he was selling.

'Want a cup of tea, love?' he asked.

'No, thank you,' said Theresa, who was anxious to leave these depressing surroundings as soon as possible.

Lenny sat beside her and, putting an arm around her, said, 'Mum and Dad are out at the pub, so we have the place to ourselves.' He went to kiss her, placing one hand on her breast as he did so.

Theresa shrank back from him, pushing his hand away.

'What the hell's the matter with you?' he asked angrily.

She was a little frightened of him and his brusqueness but she said, 'Look, Lenny, I'm sorry, but I don't want this. I want to go.'

A look of fury crossed his features. He'd planned to have a little love session with her this afternoon. 'You didn't mind the other night in the car. You enjoyed it, if my memory serves me right. A little bit of a raver you were.'

She suddenly felt cheap and dirty. 'I was carried away. It was my first time, but if my parents found out, they'd kill me.'

He grinned at her and said, 'Well, who's going to tell them? You certainly won't; neither will I.'

'But I'll know. I'll feel so guilty it'll show and I know it will all come out if I don't stop now.'

He stroked her hair. 'My poor little virgin,' he said, trying to coax her. 'There's nothing to worry about. You just have to learn to relax about it all.' He leaned forward and kissed her. Whilst his mouth covered hers, denying her the ability to complain, he again caressed her breast. She struggled but he was stronger than she was, and her reluctance only served to fire his basic instincts.

'Come on, love, you want it really, you know you do.'

'I don't!' exclaimed Theresa, now frightened and alone. 'I want to go home. Please take me home.'

He laughed at her. 'Now that's the last thing I want. Feel this and you'll understand.' Taking her hand he placed it on his trousers, over his swollen manhood. 'See what you do to me, you little vixen.'

116

Theresa struggled to stand but he pulled her back on to the settee, trapping her beneath him. Pushing up the skirt of her dress, tearing at her underwear, he spread her legs, ignoring her cries, and drove himself mercilessly into her, again and again until his passion was spent.

Looking at her tear-stained face he said, 'Oh, for God's sake! Stop behaving like a bloody child. You're my girl and I can do what I like to you, when I like!'

She screamed at him, 'No! No, I'm not your girl. I hate you! I hate you! I wish I'd never met you!'

Lenny stood up and straightened his clothes. 'Pick your stuff up,' he said, 'and I'll take you home. You hate me so much I won't bother you again. I've got what I wanted from you, anyway.'

Sobbing, Theresa followed him out to the car and crawled into the passenger seat.

'For goodness' sake, stop your snivelling, can't you?' he said as he made his way towards The Avenue.

When they drew up outside her house, Lenny leaned over her and opened the car door. 'Now go on, go running to your parents. You accuse me of anything I'll tell them you were willing.' And he pushed her out of the vehicle, then drove away.

Theresa, in complete disarray, leaned against the wall of her house. Whatever was she to do? She couldn't go inside in this state. She started running and only stopped when she reached Bryony's house, where she hammered on the door.

It was Leila who answered it. She took one look at

Theresa, said, 'Bloody hell, whatever has happened?' and she led her into the kitchen, closing the door. Taking the sobbing girl into her arms, she just held her tight until Theresa, gasping for breath, eventually stopped crying.

'Sit there,' said Leila, pointing to a chair. Getting a clean glass cloth from a drawer, she soaked it in cold water and gave it to the girl. 'Here, hold this over your face whilst I make a cup of tea.'

Pouring the tea into two cups, she slipped a couple of drops of brandy in Theresa's. 'Drink this,' she said, 'it will help to calm you down.'

Letting the girl settle for a while, Leila lit a cigarette and eventually said, 'Now tell me what has happened.'

Theresa looked at her with wide eyes full of fear.

'Darling, whatever you say to me here in this room, now, will remain a secret between just the two of us. I promise.' Reaching out, she took Theresa's hand and said, 'Now, start at the beginning.'

It was such a relief to tell someone at last that Theresa told Leila the whole story – how she met Lenny at Dan's party, had been flattered by his attention, when she lost her virginity and now . . . how she'd been raped.

As Leila listened to the sorry tale, her anger grew. Bloody Lenny Marks! Conniving little bastard! She had never liked him and now he'd taken advantage of a decent girl whose knowledge of men and the hardships of life were negligible.

'My parents will kill me if they find out!' Theresa cried.

'Now pull yourself together, dear. I'm not going to tell them and you can believe that Lenny Marks will keep his mouth shut.' But one thing bothered Leila. 'Did Lenny use any means of contraception, Theresa?'

The enormity of the question suddenly hit the girl. After all, she was the daughter of a doctor, and although Catholics didn't believe in contraception, she was aware of the consequences of not using any.

'No, he didn't,' she whispered. 'Oh my God, I could get pregnant. Oh, Mrs Travis, I have been so stupid. After the first time I was so excited about being a woman . . .' She couldn't continue.

'There's no need to worry yet. It may be all right. It doesn't happen every time you have sex. Some people try to make a baby and don't manage to do so for ages, and some never do. When is your next period due?'

'In a week's time.'

'Then we'll have to wait and see. Try not to worry too much, because if you do, that can sometimes make it late.'

Theresa dissolved into tears once again.

'Come along,' said Leila. 'I'll give you an aspirin and you try to sleep on Bryony's bed. We'll have to make you look decent before you can go home.'

'You won't tell Bryony, will you?'

'No, of course not.'

Once she'd settled the young girl and made her comfortable, Leila came back downstairs. She could just imagine the shock to the Kerrigans if they knew what had befallen their youngest. Kerrigan may well be a good doctor but Leila had always found him a bit pious. She didn't know his wife, but they were devout Catholics and this would shock them especially deeply. Whatever was she to do? She wouldn't betray the girl's confidence, but she would wait and hope that all was well. In another ten days or so, they would know. If Theresa had become pregnant, then she would have to make a few decisions. Leila could arrange an abortion for her if necessary, but would that be the right thing? Would Theresa be able to handle the situation if she did? She doubted it. And if she did this and then the parents found out . . . it didn't bear thinking about.

If the tables were turned and this was her daughter, she thought, would she welcome the intervention of another? She knew she would not. She would want to know. But one thing she was certain about, she would make sure that Lenny Marks got his comeuppance. She certainly had the means to do so, and she wouldn't let him get away with this. He needed to be taught a lesson.

CHAPTER ELEVEN

Theresa slept for an hour. When she awoke, she was confused for a moment, then, realising where she was, and why, she made her way tentatively downstairs, relieved that Bryony's father didn't seem to be around. She found Leila in the kitchen.

'Hello, love. Feel any better?'

'A bit.'

'Well, we can't send you home looking all tear-stained, can we? You come upstairs with me. You can have a bath, then you'll feel better. After, we'll comb your hair, and you can put on a bit of make-up. That ought to do the trick.'

Sitting in the soothing water of the bath, Theresa scrubbed herself viciously, trying to get the smell of Lenny Marks off her, and wondering if she would ever feel clean again.

Leila brushed her hair afterwards and helped her apply a light make-up, before declaring, 'There. You look lovely.'

'I don't know how to thank you, Mrs Travis. I didn't know where else to go.'

'You did the right thing, darling.' Putting her arm around the girl, she led her downstairs. At the front door she paused.

'You come here or phone me at any time, you hear?'

Theresa nodded.

'And let me know about your next period.'

Fearfully Theresa asked, 'What will I do if it's late?'

'Let's wait and see, shall we? It's no good looking for trouble which might not be there.' She hugged and kissed her. Then, opening the door, she said, 'Now try not to worry.' As she watched Theresa walk away, her heart went out to her. Poor child. So naïve, so vulnerable. God, she hoped she would be all right.

Unaware of her friend's traumas, Bryony was enjoying herself. Several of the other guests had arrived at Wallbourne Manor. Sebastian Wallace swept up to the front door in an old Lagonda, wearing a leather helmet and goggles. He was followed soon after by Davinia and Giles, who had driven down together, and there were others who arrived at varying intervals. It was a merry bunch who gathered in the drawing room, quaffing champagne.

Bryony was in her element. James introduced her to those she hadn't met as 'my friend Bryony'.

With her cultured voice, she seemed to the others to be their equal, and they chatted about the Season.

'Royal Ascot was marvellous,' said one. 'Daddy's horse won the King George VI and Queen Elizabeth Diamond Stakes. It was frightfully exciting.' Another spoke of Henley and, of course, the polo match that Bryony had attended.

Cassandra Felton-Browne arrived late, accompanied by an older, rather portly, slightly balding gentleman, who although smartly dressed, looked very out of place.

Davinia sidled over to Bryony. 'Oh my God, she's bought that dreadful man with her!'

'Who is he?' asked Bryony.

'He's her lover, darling. Of course, he's rolling in it. Something to do with the steel industry. Trade, you know.'

'But Cassy is beautiful. I would have thought she could have the choice of any young man.'

'But this one pays so well,' stated Davinia before she walked away, calling to someone, 'Darling. Haven't seen you in ages.'

Bryony was very puzzled. Whatever did she mean, pays so well? Pays for what?

The butler announced that luncheon was served and they all trooped in to the dining room, with its wood panelling and stags' heads adorning the walls. Bryony thought caustically that this was not the room for such trophies. What if they were served venison? How could anyone eat it with the deer's ancestors staring down on them? However, the main course was rack of lamb, so she was able to tuck into this without a feeling of guilt.

She found she was seated beside Cassy's gentleman friend, who was very easy to talk to. His flat vowels revealed his northern roots.

'Have you been here before?' he asked Bryony.

'No, this is my first visit . . . and you?'

'Mine too. To be honest with you, love, I didn't want to come. This isn't my cup of tea all, but Cassandra insisted.'

'What is your scene, Mr Bamforth?'

'George, please. I'm from the north, Sheffield. There's an old saying: where there's muck there's brass, and my father was a self-made man. He worked, and made his fortune, and now he's long retired and I run the business.' He smiled then, cut a piece of lamb and put it into his mouth. 'We're all simple folk,' he said. 'We don't have airs and graces; we call a spade a spade. All this high-falutin living is very foreign to me.' Grinning broadly, he said, 'I don't fit the mould and they know it.' He chuckled. 'I don't mind that. What I do mind is they all think I'm a bloody fool.'

Bryony said, 'I would never make that mistake.'

'But you're not one of them, are you, love?'

'Oh dear, does it show that much?'

He laughed loudly. 'Don't get me wrong, you've obviously had a good education, but where the others carry an air of superiority, you don't. You're one of the real people, and that was meant as a compliment.'

'Thank you, George.'

'My pleasure,' he said, and picking up his glass of wine, he held it up to her. 'Down the hatch!'

Picking up hers, she said, '*Santé!*' And they both chuckled.

*   *   *

After lunch, Toby invited Bryony to accompany him to the stables to see Napoleon and the other horses that were in residence. She followed him eagerly.

The stable block was large and well stocked with thoroughbred horses trained for polo, Toby explained. Then there were four hunters, which belonged to his father.

'And here is your old friend,' said Toby, pausing in front of a stall.

Napoleon had whinnied as they approached, and Toby put out a hand, holding a carrot in the flat palm. Napoleon took it gratefully. Putting a hand in his jacket pocket, Toby pulled out another and, handing it to Bryony, said, 'Here, give it to him.' He showed her how to hold it.

She stiffened for a moment as the large head bent down and took it. She stroked his long nose as he chewed away and said, 'You really are a beauty.'

'Do you ride, Bryony?'

'Gracious, no.'

'Would you like to?'

'I've never thought about it. There are certainly no stables near us at home, not that I know about.'

'Jim!' Toby called to the groom, 'Saddle up Tansy, please.' Turning to Bryony, he said, 'I'll give you your first lesson.'

'Oh my God!' was all she could say.

Bryony was wearing boots, trousers and a light sweater, which was just as well, she thought, as the groom led a horse out of one of the stables and walked it over to a mounting block.

'Stand on there,' said Toby, 'and swing one leg over the horse's back.'

She did so and settled in the saddle. 'It seems a very long way to the ground,' she said nervously.

'Look straight ahead,' he said. 'Don't worry, Bryony. I won't let you fall.' He adjusted the stirrups and then showed her how to hold the reins. 'Now sit up and back a little . . . and relax.'

To her surprise she found that she felt comfortable.

Toby attached a lead rein to the horse and led her around the yard. 'There you are. You have a good seat, you know.'

'Do I?' Bryony wondered what that meant. Did it mean the size of her bottom? No. She didn't think so. It was horse talk.

'Grip the horse with your knees,' Toby advised. 'If you feel nervous, hold on to the pommel.' At her puzzled look he explained, 'The top of the saddle.' A while later he said, 'Now let's trot. Dig your heels into Tansy's flank, not too hard, but enough to let her feel it.'

She did so, and Tansy started to trot.

'Well done, Bryony! You're a natural.'

She felt exhilarated as they trotted round in a circle until, after a while, Toby called to the horse, and it slowed to a stop.

'That was excellent. You should think about having lessons. Now slip your feet out of the stirrups, lean forward over the saddle, hold on the horse's neck and bring your leg over the horse's back and I'll help you down.'

Once safely on terra firma, Bryony grinned broadly at her host. 'That was great.' She patted the horse, much to Toby's amusement.

'Not so scared of them now, are you?'

And she realised it was true. 'No, I'm not. I think they are such beautiful creatures.'

Toby stroked the long nose of the animal, then pulled her ear and said, 'Some people think a horse is a stupid animal, can you believe that?'

'How can something so majestic be stupid?' Bryony replied.

Handing the reins over to the groom, Toby put an arm around Bryony's shoulders and said, 'There! I knew you were a girl after my own heart. Come on, we'd best get back to the others.'

Afternoon tea had been served in the drawing room, and later, people started drifting away to their rooms.

'Take Bryony to the blue room next to yours, will you, James?' Toby asked.

'Of course,' he said, and led Bryony towards the stairs.

Opening her bedroom door, James said, 'I'll leave you to it in case you want to rest. Dinner is served about eight thirty, but we usually meet in the drawing room for an aperitif.' Kissing her cheek he said, 'See you later.' And closed the door.

The room seemed vast to Bryony. She thought her bedroom at home spacious, but it would have fitted into one corner of this room. Walking to the windows, she gazed out over the parkland, then, turning back, wondered where her suitcase was. She found it standing on a luggage rack beside the wardrobe. It was empty. Looking in the wardrobe, Bryony found her dress for the evening hanging with some of her other things. Opening a drawer of a splendid dressing table, she found her underwear and stockings. Of course she should have known that in such an establishment there would be servants to look after the guests.

She lay on the double bed and giggled to herself. Thank God she had packed her new stuff. How humiliating it would be for a servant to see tatty underwear! She tried to visualise her mother here, and couldn't. Wonderful as she was, Leila and her flamboyant way of dressing would look gaudy, though Bryony felt guilty at these thoughts. How very snobbish of her! Her mother was a wonderful, beautiful woman but, truth to tell, she would hate it here. She would think it all pretentious, whereas her daughter was lapping it up.

Taking advantage of Bryony's absence, Leila Travis put a few things in an overnight bag and, leaving a note for Dan, drove to Newbury where she knew the circus was performing for two weeks. As she drove through the entrance, she was filled with nostalgia. Before she'd married Dan, she'd spent a year with her sister, Rosa, performing nightly. It had been an exciting time, one filled with so many happy memories. Indeed, if Dan hadn't happened upon the scene, she would probably still be with them.

She parked the car and walked around. She watched as the elephants were getting their bath, swishing their long trunks, trying to catch the water from the hose, and spraying their trainer when they did so. They were such gentle creatures, despite their huge size, although she also knew a rogue elephant could be a killer.

She heard the roar of the lions before she saw them. There were three cages parked alongside each other. There were two lions in each cage, pacing up and down; the third held two magnificent tigers. In front of them stood Barney Norton, Leila's brother-in-law, watching the animals very carefully and frowning.

'Something wrong?' asked Leila.

'Hello, love. What on earth are you doing here?'

'Bryony's away and I thought I'd have a break.' She nodded towards the tigers. 'What's up? Only you looked worried.'

Scratching his mane of hair, Barney said, 'I'm damned if I know what it is, but Tara has been so moody lately. As far as I can tell, she's well enough, but she's really been playing up.'

'Where's Rosa?' asked Leila.

'Back in the trailer, over there,' he said, pointing. 'She'll be pleased to see you. I'll catch you later.'

Rosa greeted her sister warmly when Leila opened the door to the trailer. 'What a lovely surprise!' she said. 'Sit down. I'll make us some coffee.'

Leila looked around and smiled. 'This is a bit grander than the old days,' she remarked.

'Nice, isn't it? Lots of room and that does make a difference.'

The trailer was indeed luxurious. It was long and housed a kitchen with a small cooker and fridge, a sitting room that could be made up with spare beds, a toilet and, at the rear, a double bedroom.

As the sisters sat drinking their coffee, they reminisced about the old days.

'I really enjoyed working in the Big Top,' Leila said.

'You were good,' said Rosa. 'I expect you're a bit rusty now.'

With a slight hesitation, Leila asked, 'Do you still have my stuff?'

'Of course. I told you I did at Dan's birthday party. Your box is still here with your costumes and everything.'

'Is there somewhere I can practise, Rosa? Somewhere that doesn't interfere with anyone?'

With a look of puzzlement, her sister said, 'There's a field out the back you can use. It's only used for storage of spare equipment. Are you thinking of making a comeback?'

'Gracious me, no, but being here, the atmosphere, it makes me want to be a part of what's going on, and I thought it would be fun to see if I could still hack it.'

'When we've drunk this I'll take you to get it. Barney has stored your stuff with his.'

'I saw him outside the tigers' cage. He said that Tara is playing up.'

'Yes, he's been having a lot of trouble with her in the ring. It worries me to death. I make sure that there are plenty of the crew around when he performs and I have my rifle ready, just in case.'

Leila didn't like the sound of this but she made no comment. She would see what was going on for herself tonight, as she intended to watch the show.

Rosa took her to a cupboard beside the tigers' cage and ferreted around, eventually dragging out a small chest. 'Here you are, Leila. Have a good sort-through; I've got work to do. I'll see you at the cookhouse about five.'

Leila lifted the lid of the chest and started to remove her spangled costumes. 'Oh, my goodness, I'd forgotten that one,' she muttered to herself. She eventually found what she was seeking. Lifting out a long leather case, she closed the lid, pushed the chest back inside the cupboard and wandered off to the field.

Later, as the circus crew and performers gathered in the tent set up as a cookhouse, Leila returned in search of her sister and, sitting beside her, enjoyed the bangers and mash that were served.

'Nothing much has changed,' she laughed.

'Good nourishing stuff,' said Barney, 'and everyone's favourite.'

As Leila ate the tasty sausages and dark brown onion gravy, she could see why. It was simple food, but enjoyable.

'How did the practice go?' asked Rosa.

'Very well. I wasn't nearly as rusty as I thought, which did my ego a power of good,' laughed Leila.

'I'll give you a job if you want to come back,' teased Barney.

'I don't think Dan would approve,' she said.

That evening, Leila sat with the rest of the public to watch the show. There was a rustle of excitement when the ringmaster – resplendent in top hat and a red tail coat over black trousers – came into the ring to greet everyone. Then the band, heavy on the brass section, started to play the opening Sousa march and the parade of performers began. Leila looked around, observing the gleeful and expectant faces of the adults and children in the audience.

The trapeze artists, the Flying Kazamovs, thrilled everyone with their daring display, the tumblers enthralled, the clowns amused and teased the audience as they looked to be throwing buckets of water over them, when the contents were only confetti.

The Black Arabian Stallions looked magnificent with their plumed headdresses and the riders were daring as they galloped around the ring, doing their tricks. And the troupe of Romanian tumblers performed, followed by an act of trained poodles.

During the short interval, members of the circus circulated among the audience, selling souvenir programmes, drinks and balloons. Meanwhile, men were erecting a circular cage of steel that almost filled the ring, with a low tunnel leading from the cage.

The clowns opened the second half, followed by Rosa and her knife-throwing act, and then the aerialists performed on long ropes, hanging from the top of the tent. As they left the ring amid wild applause, there was a long drum roll before the ringmaster announced, 'Now, ladies and gentleman, hold your breath as you watch the amazing Orlando pit his will against the beautiful but dangerous big cats.'

A hush fell over the audience as first the four lions ran through the tunnel into the huge cage in the centre of the ring, closely followed by the tigers. The animals jumped up on their stands, all except Tara, who prowled around the ring, snarling. Leila held her breath as she watched.

She saw Barney, resplendent in an old military costume, enter the cage, cracking his whip in one hand, holding a chair in the other.

Rosa closed the gate behind him and picked up her rifle as several of the crew stood by the bars, watching.

Barney approached Tara, who backed away, still snarling. He continued to walk slowly towards her, jabbing the chair at her, defying her, calling his orders, as she argued with him, until she reared up on her hind legs and, with a final swipe of her paw in his direction, jumped up on her pedestal, to the loud applause of the crowd.

Leila found she was sitting forward on the edge of her seat as the performance progressed. All the time, Tara was showing her belligerence, which was unsettling the other big cats, and she knew that Barney was having a hard job to keep the act together and under control.

Suddenly Tara leaped from her pedestal and crouched low as if she were stalking her prey, and fixed Barney with her amber eyes, her lips curled, her teeth showing. Leila saw Rosa step forward and cock her rifle. The crew stiffened as they waited, but Barney had been doing this too long to be taken by surprise. He cracked the whip in the tiger's face. She flinched. He jabbed the chair at her, cracking the whip beside her ear, and she flinched again as it caught the tip of it, and then she started slowly backing off.

'Up, Tara!' he yelled, and cracked the whip again. Tara slunk away and reluctantly crawled back on to her pedestal.

Leila found she was perspiring.

Shortly after, Barney brought the act to a close, and the animals left the ring one by one, with Tara the last one. As she went past Barney, she stopped and pawed the air, before disappearing down the tunnel and out of the ring.

Leila couldn't stay a minute longer. She rushed outside and found Rosa and a very pale Barney standing by the cages.

'You've got to get rid of that cat!' Leila declared. 'She's far too dangerous to keep.'

'I've been telling him that the past two months!' said Rosa, who looked more than a little agitated. 'If he doesn't, one night she'll do for him!'

'I need a drink,' said Barney, and headed for the trailer.

'Let him be,' said Rosa. 'Tonight he was really in trouble, and he knows it. Now perhaps he'll listen to me.'

The two women walked over to a low brick wall and sat on it, smoking cigarettes. They could hear the laughter from the crowds as the clowns performed, and they watched the elephants line up to finish the show before the grand finale.

'Will he be back to parade?' asked Leila.

'He's never missed one yet,' Rosa said. 'You know my old man, a trouper to the end, but unless he gets rid of that bloody Tara it will be his end!'

The following morning, after breakfast, Leila took leave of her sister and brother-in-law.

'It was great to be back,' she said.

'Come anytime,' said Rosa as she hugged her. 'You take care now. Love to Dan and Bryony.'

Leila threw her bag in the boot of the car and the long leather case beside it.

Rosa looked at it and said, 'You be careful how you use that, my dear.'

'Don't you worry,' said Leila, 'I know exactly what I'm going to do with it.' And she drove away, waving and smiling.

'Oh yes,' she muttered. 'I know exactly what I'm going to do with it. And I will enjoy every minute.'

CHAPTER TWELVE

At Wallbourne Manor, the party was in full swing. Joining the half-dozen or so guests that were staying in the house, were others who arrived after dinner. All were resplendent in their finery, the men, handsome in their dinner jackets and the women wearing some very stylish creations. Bryony felt she looked as well turned out as the next girl.

The furniture in the drawing room had been moved back and the carpet rolled away to give the guests enough clear floor on which to dance to the records played on the gramophone.

'Come along, Bryony,' said James and, putting his arm around her, led her to the centre of the room. 'Are you enjoying yourself?' he asked as they moved around the floor.

'Yes, I am,' she said. 'This is such a beautiful house and Toby is a great host. Thank you for bringing me.'

He snuggled closer. 'I'm so glad you came.'

As she felt the warmth of his cheek against hers, Bryony wondered if her friendship with James would amount to anything. He obviously liked her, but being a gentleman, he'd gone no further than kissing her ardently. He hadn't tried to make a pass at her, and now she thought, after her father's warning, probably never would. She felt a little disappointed because she really liked him.

As the next number started, George approached, tapped James on the shoulder and asked, 'May I cut in?'

He was an excellent dancer, Bryony discovered, as he led her into a slow foxtrot, and surprisingly light on his feet.

'I don't suppose you know many people here,' Bryony remarked.

'Not many, but I know about a few of them.'

'Really? Tell me, please,' she urged, full of curiosity.

'Come and have a drink then, and we can sit and observe,' he said with a chuckle.

They sat beneath an indoor palm and looked around the room. Then George began, 'Over there, the girl with the red dress, she's the daughter of a prominent banker in the city. She works for Sotheby's, the big auction house. The blond young man beside her . . .'

'You mean Giles?'

'Yes, that's his name. His father is a High Court judge noted for his heavy sentencing and with a known dislike of queers.'

'Oh dear, he wouldn't have much time for those in the theatre then?'

'Not so. He enjoys a good play, but he abhors homosexuality with a vengeance.'

'The girl over there, the dark one with a big bust,' said Bryony, 'tell me about her.'

George burst out laughing. 'A very apt description, if I may say so. I do love a person who speaks their mind,' he said. 'She just swans around enjoying the Season, but her father has several race horses and is doing very well at the moment.'

'That's right! I heard her say her father won some big race at Royal Ascot.'

'Yes, Toby's father, Lord Havering, and he are good friends through their love of horses.'

'Lord Havering? You mean Toby's father has a title?' Bryony asked with surprise.

'Yes, Toby's father is the Earl of Havering. Our Toby is Viscount Beckford.'

Bryony was floored. 'I had no idea!'

'You are moving in very exclusive circles, my dear Bryony. Not that I think for one moment that would be very important to you.'

How could she tell him that it was? That this was what she'd dreamed of during her school days, reading *Tatler* magazine. She couldn't.

'No,' she said, 'not at all.'

Cassy wandered over. 'Here you are, George. Why are you hiding away?'

'That's the last thing I'm doing,' he remarked. 'I'm having a sensible conversation, for once, with someone who has some integrity.'

Bryony saw Cassandra bristle. 'What do you mean by that remark?'

138

Rising from his chair, he took her arm and said, 'You work it out, my dear.' To Bryony he said, 'Thank you for a delightful chat.' And he winked at her.

James came to sit beside her. 'So you got nobbled by old George?'

'I like him, he's very genuine,' Bryony declared rather sharply, 'so don't sound so condescending about him.'

Slightly taken aback by the fierceness of her remark, he said, 'Sorry, I didn't mean to sound condescending. Actually, I like him myself.'

'What's the story about him and Cassy?' she asked. 'Only they seem such an unlikely pair.'

'I've no idea. She says she met him through business about six months ago and they've been together ever since – well, when he's in London on business, anyway.'

'What sort of work does she do?'

'To be honest I don't really know. I know she works in London, something to do with public relations, I believe.'

Bryony watched Cassy from across the room. She couldn't imagine her being efficient, she was so . . . she pondered over a word that could describe the redhead and couldn't find one. Cassy was self-absorbed, always peering into a mirror at her reflection. She didn't just sit or stand, but poised herself, like a trophy to be admired at all times – unlike Davinia, who was languid, but funny, with a very dry wit. Now Bryony could imagine *her* in PR, but definitely not Cassy.

Imagine, she mused. She was in a home belonging to an earl, and his son, the viscount, had given her a riding lesson. Wait until she told her father about that! And about the maid who had unpacked her case after her arrival . . .

Towards midnight James suggested they go for a breath of air on to the terrace, which Bryony agreed to, as the room was warm and filling with cigarette smoke. Outside the night air was damp. James removed his jacket and put it around her shoulders and held her.

'Can't have my girl catching cold,' he said, brushing a stray hair away from her face.

'Is that how you see me, James . . . as your girl?'

He gathered her closer to him in his arms and said, 'I do. I hope that's all right with you, darling Bryony?'

She snuggled against him, brimming with happiness. 'That's perfectly fine with me.'

He kissed her longingly. 'If only your father hadn't made me promise to behave like a gentleman,' he murmured.

'Why?'

'Because I want to take you to bed and make passionate love to you, darling, that's why.'

'Oh, James,' was all she could say. In one way she wanted to be with him too, but in another, she wasn't sure if she was ready for a physical relationship. And she wondered if the other girls at the party would have turned him down had he invited them to bed. Cassy wouldn't, she felt sure, and Davinia? Was she a virgin? Had they all discovered the thrill of sex before her? Was she being parochial, or was she just a little too scared? So many uncertainties.

'Let's go back inside,' she suggested, as the damp air began to penetrate, despite James's jacket, 'or it will be you who will catch cold.'

They danced closely together for the rest of the night, Bryony secretly thrilled that she was now his girl.

Eventually, when the party ended, they all made their way upstairs, and Bryony saw Cassy and George enter the same room down the hallway. It seemed that Toby was very broad-minded, and Bryony wondered how many other bedrooms were being shared.

James took her into his arms and kissed her ardently. As she responded, he opened the door of her room behind her, lifted her off her feet and carried her inside.

All Bryony's good intentions were blown away as she felt the firmness of his body against hers.

'What your father doesn't know won't hurt him,' he said, kissing her again. At the same time, he slowly unzipped the back of her dress and slipped it off her shoulders until it fell at her feet.

The bedside lights were on and the bed turned back ready for its occupant. James led her towards it.

'I'm a little bit scared,' she said.

'Only a little bit?' he teased. 'That's better than being terrified. There's nothing to be frightened about, darling. Sex between two people in love is a wonderful thing.'

As he nuzzled her neck she asked, 'Are you saying you love me, James?'

'Of course. Come here and let me show you.'

They undressed and lay together, James kissing and

141

caressing her, murmuring tender words as his hands deftly explored her body.

Bryony was by now more relaxed, due to James's expertise, and she was grateful to be in the hands of someone who was obviously practised, as he led her through her first sexual experience, coaxing her, instructing her, exciting her – seducing her, until he was astride her. As his long fingers slipped beneath her thighs and discovered her most intimate places, she felt as if she were floating. Carried along on a wave of desire, she pleaded with him.

'Love me, James darling, please, love me . . . now.'

He was happy to oblige and entered her gently.

'Oh, darling, that feels wonderful,' she said.

After, they lay entwined, their warm naked flesh pressed together.

Kissing her forehead, James said, 'You've no need to worry, Bryony darling, I took precautions. I will always take care of you.'

She had been so carried away, she'd not noticed his thoughtfulness, but was grateful for it, as she realised she'd been quite wanton in her desire and could so easily have risked getting pregnant.

'You are wonderful,' she said as she clung to him.

As he pulled the bedcovers over them she said, 'What about the maid coming in, in the morning?'

'We'll send her for another cup,' he said. At the look of consternation on her face he chuckled. 'Don't worry, darling. She won't turn a hair.'

* * *

In Southampton, Dan Travis was remonstrating with his wife on her return. 'Why the hell didn't you tell me you were going away overnight?'

'I just decided to go on the spur of the moment. Anyway, I left you a note.'

'Which I didn't find for ages. And what's more, you didn't ask me about going.'

Leila turned on him. 'I don't need to get your permission. Who do you think you are?'

'Your husband.'

'Which you only remember when it suits you. I don't know what's got into you lately. Ever since Bryony has begun to spread her wings, you have become like a bloody gaoler.'

'What a load of rubbish!'

'I can understand it about your daughter – you're finding it difficult to accept that she's growing up – but please don't make the mistake of telling me what I can and can't do.'

She walked over to the sideboard and poured herself a drink. 'Do you want one?'

'Yes. A Scotch and soda, please. So how were Rosa and Barney?'

Leila sat in an armchair and told him about her visit and the trouble that Barney had had with Tara. 'I'm really worried about him, Dan.'

'Look, Leila, he's been in the business long enough to know when it's time to get rid of an animal. He won't put himself at risk, surely?'

'He damn well did last night. Tara really unsettled

143

the other cats. I was on the edge of my seat, I can tell you. He closed the act early, I know that.'

'Rosa will see that he does the right thing. What time are you expecting Bryony home?'

'When I see her.'

'She starts her new job in the morning, so I hope she's not too late.'

'I'm sure she'll bear that in mind. I'm going in the kitchen to see what we've got to eat.'

'Good. I'm hungry.'

After breakfast in the Cotswolds, Toby's guests, dressed in country clothes, made their way by car to a far part of the estate for the clay pigeon shooting. Giles, James and Bryony all piled in Sebastian's old Lagonda.

'Dan, my father, would love this car,' Bryony confided to Giles.

'Does he collect cars then?' he asked.

Laughing, she said, 'In a way. He has a huge car lot in Southampton, but he loves old cars.'

Giles froze. Of course! How stupid he was. In the Silver Dollar Club, Dan Travis had mentioned his daughter, Bryony, but here at Wallbourne Manor, among his society friends, he'd not even made a connection. He wondered if Bryony had ever met Sophie Johnson. It would be curtains for him if she had, because she might get to know of his own association with the man and then the cat would really be among the pigeons. If it got out that he was a homosexual, he would be finished with his family and most of his friends. He wondered if he would ever be invited to such a gathering as this again if his host knew his secret. It was time that he brought his friendship with Sophie to an end – but how? Sophie wouldn't like it and he was such a dangerous individual.

The shooting was underway and the noise of the guns was loud. Bryony stood, her hands over her ears most of the time. She hated every moment.

Davinia was a good shot and had joined the men. Of Cassy and George there was no sign, and Bryony wished that she had remained behind.

'All right, darling?' queried James as he emptied the cartridges from his gun and reloaded. She nodded, but made up her mind never to attend another shoot as long as she lived. She thought it was nerve-shattering.

A van arrived at lunchtime from the house, and two of the servants laid out food and drink for the party on folding tables. The men were chatting about their guns, and anticipating the pheasant season; the women standing listening and laughing at the banter, but as the van was about to leave, Bryony complained of a headache and asked to go back to the manor with them.

'Ask Jarvis to find a couple of aspirins,' James said as she departed, which she did, when she returned.

'Would you like anything else, madam?'

'A pot of coffee would be nice, thank you,' she said.

'I'll bring it to the drawing room,' the butler said as he departed.

Bryony heard raised voices as she approached the

door of the drawing room and recognised the northern tones of George Bamforth.

'Don't think you can treat me like an open bank account, lass,' he said. 'I pay only for services rendered, and if I feel like treating you to the odd gift, that's my prerogative, but as far as your ridiculous demands go, forget it, and the sooner you realise that and get it clear in your calculating little mind, the better! When will you realise I am not a stupid old fool?'

'But George, darling—'

'Enough, Cassandra. The answer is no! Go and pack our bags. I want to get back to Sheffield as soon as possible.'

A tearful Cassy opened the door and rushed past Bryony, who was at a loss to know what to do. She waited a few moments, then entered the room.

'Hello, George. I didn't know you were here.' She noticed how flushed and angry he looked, but he smiled at her.

'Hello, Bryony. How was the shooting?'

She grimaced and said, 'Very noisy. It was too much for me. I feigned a headache and came back in the van with the servants who brought the lunch.'

'It's all part of country living,' he said.

'Country living is wonderful, but there are just some things that I can't do with. All that noise! Thank goodness they weren't real birds being shot at.'

'Bet you don't think that when you eat them?'

'To be honest, George, I've never had pheasant, and I can't see myself ever eating it now!'

'Nothing beats a good old roast beef and Yorkshire pudding, in my book,' he said as he walked over to her. 'Well, Cassy and I are off now.' He kissed her cheek and added, 'Don't ever change, Bryony. You are like a breath of fresh air amidst this lot.' And he left the room.

Bryony stood at the casement window overlooking the grounds, drinking her coffee, and thought she'd never seen anything more magnificent and tranquil. What an absolute joy it must be to live here. She decided to investigate further.

Walking out of the door into the hall, she moved to the next room when she saw the door partially opened and, slowly pushing it wider, she went into what turned out to be the library. The room was very masculine, with its leather chairs and settees, she thought, but what took her breath away were the thousands of books that lined the walls. She walked slowly round, reading the titles. Many were about military campaigns, dating back through history. There were also classics, works by modern writers, books on art, architecture and English history. On a large table in the middle of the room were a vase of flowers and the Sunday papers.

Bryony wandered back into the hallway and studied the armour-clad figures, wondering how on earth a man was supposed to fight when he was weighed down so. The three banners in the corner that she'd noticed on her arrival still intrigued her.

'One is the family coat of arms, the other, my father's regimental flag.'

'Toby! What are you doing here?'

'I'm expecting an important phone call,' he explained, 'so I came back.'

'I just love this house,' said Bryony. 'How very fortunate you are to live here.'

He looked pleased. 'It's been in my family for five generations, but it is somewhat of a burden, trying to keep up the maintenance of such an old building. There is always something that needs doing.'

Bryony remembered her conversation with her father about the impoverished aristocracy, but she hadn't observed such hardship. How could Toby entertain on such a grand scale if he was hard up? It was all relative, she supposed. If she were broke, it would mean something quite different.

'It would be awful if such a wonderful house was to rot away.'

Laughing, he said, 'That's not liable to happen, Bryony. It would take centuries of neglect and we would never let it get to that state. My ancestors would all turn in their graves and haunt us for the rest of our lives.'

'Yes, I can see how such a beautiful place would make you feel that way. If it were mine, I'd fight tooth and nail to keep it.'

Putting an arm around her shoulders, Toby said, 'You really are a sweet girl to be so interested. Most of my friends never give it a second thought.'

'Ah well, that's because they're used to living in such surroundings. I'm not so I can appreciate its beauty. Sometimes someone on the outside can see things more clearly.'

He looked bemused. 'Where on earth did James find a girl like you?'

'His father bought him a car from my father, who has a car lot. I sold it to him and was there when James came to collect it.'

The butler interrupted their conversation. 'There is a call for you, sir.'

'I'll take it in the library. Sorry, Bryony, I'll have to go, but we must talk again.'

Unfortunately, neither had the opportunity before it was time for all the guests to leave.

Bryony thanked Toby for inviting her.

He smiled and kissed her on both cheeks. 'We didn't get a chance to chat, but another time. You must come for another riding lesson,' he said.

Driving home with James early that evening, Bryony mulled over her visit to the Cotswolds. It was true that this was all about gracious living, and it had indeed been an experience. But had it lived up to her expectations? In many ways it had: the beautiful building, with its vast parkland, the stables, the servants. But would she ever want to live like that, given the opportunity? She couldn't think of a nicer place. The people had all been very agreeable, but the conversation had all seemed a bit shallow. All of the guests came from wealthy families; the girls had probably never had to work to live, not like her father and mother. Except for Toby. He was a real gentleman. But glancing across at James, she knew that something wonderful had come out of it. She was in love and, what's more, she was loved in return. At least, that's what she'd been told. She suddenly remembered Jack Saunders' warning at the car lot when he saw James. Had he told her he loved her just to get her into bed?

James glanced over at her and reached out to squeeze her hand. 'Happy?' he asked.

She smiled back at him, her concerns melting away. 'Yes,' she said, 'very happy.'

'I'll call you in the week to see how the new job is going.'

'Oh yes, please do. I'm a bit nervous, I have to admit.'

'You'll be fine.'

'When will you be down again?' she asked.

'I don't know, darling. I have a lot of studying to do in the next few weeks as I have exams in the autumn. I'll call you.'

The next few weeks! Bryony's feeling of happiness plummeted. This all sounded a bit casual. This was the man who had declared his love for her, taken her to bed, made love to her. Had she made a terrible mistake?

'Right,' she said, her thoughts in turmoil. Which were no less confused as he unloaded her bag from the car when they arrived at her house, gave her a perfunctory kiss on the cheek, then drove away.

CHAPTER THIRTEEN

Feeling somewhat dejected, Bryony forced a smile as she put her key in the front door of her house and walked into the hallway. Leila rushed out from the living room.

'Hello, darling. Did you have a good time?'

'Oh, Mum. You should have seen the place. It was a huge manor house with acres of parkland. There were sheep grazing and, would you believe, a herd of deer! And there was a butler and servants to take care of you.'

'Bloody hell!' exclaimed her mother.

From the doorway of his study Dan said, 'And now no doubt you will find everything here a bit beneath you.'

'Don't be ridiculous, Dad, of course I won't.' She just couldn't resist adding, 'Toby's father is an earl, by the way, which makes him a viscount. He gave me my first riding lesson.'

'I suppose you'll be wanting to hunt with the hounds next?'

Bryony just glared at Dan. Turning to her mother she said, 'It was really interesting to see how the other half live, I have to say.'

'Of course it was. Don't take any notice of him,' Leila said, nodding in Dan's direction. 'A bit more gracious living in this house wouldn't go amiss!'

'You've got no bloody chance!' Dan snapped, and went back inside his study, slamming the door behind him.

Putting an arm around Bryony's shoulders, Leila said, 'Come into the kitchen and we'll have coffee and you can give me the details. I'm dying to hear all about it.'

As Bryony came to the end of her story of the weekend, Leila asked, 'And how was James?'

'Fine. He's studying these next few weeks for an exam, so I don't know when I'll be seeing him again.' She managed to keep the tone of her voice light.

'Well, he's got to do well, after all. Anyway, you'll be tied up with your new job. You'd better go and unpack and sort out your stuff for the morning. You don't want to be late on the first day.'

Picking up her suitcase, Bryony went to her room. She walked over to the window. Across the tree-lined road she could see the houses on the other side. It was a quiet road, and the front gardens were full of shrubs. It was peaceful, apart from the occasional car, but she couldn't help comparing it with the lovely rolling parklands of Wallbourne Manor. The view from her bedroom there had been so stunning. She had stood so often looking out at it that now it seemed engraved upon her soul.

*　　*　　*

The following morning, Bryony was up bright and early. She dressed carefully in a black dogtooth-check skirt and white blouse, comfortable black shoes with a small heel, and stockings. Looking at her reflection in the mirror, she thought she looked suitably attired for an office worker.

After a quick breakfast, Leila ran her to the office and, with a swift kiss on Bryony's cheek, wished her luck.

'What will you do about lunch?' she enquired.

'I don't know, Mum. But don't you worry, I can always slip out for a sandwich and coffee.'

'Good luck, darling,' said Leila, and she drove away.

Taking a deep breath, Bryony opened the door to Langdon and Associates.

The receptionist was standing at her desk, tidying some papers. She looked up and smiled. 'Bryony Travis, isn't it?'

Bryony nodded. 'Good morning,' she said.

'Please go into Richard's office; he's waiting for you.'

Richard Langdon was sitting at his desk, writing. He looked up and, getting to his feet, held out his hand. 'Hello, Bryony. Let's get the show on the road, shall we? Come with me.'

She followed him along the hallway to another office. It was quite spacious, with a drawing board in the corner near the light, and a large desk beside it. In the opposite corner of the room was a smaller desk with a typewriter and a chair.

'You will have to share with my son, Nick, who'll be in later. He's at a meeting with a client at the moment. I'll give you time to get settled. There're pens, pencils, pads, et cetera in the drawers. In fifteen minutes, come to my office. I need you to take some letters. All right?'

'Fine,' she said, hanging her coat up on the coat rack.

'Right, see you then. Must dash, only I've some calls to make.' And he rushed out of the room.

Sitting at her desk, Bryony sorted through the drawers, finding all the tools of her trade, placing them in an order that was good for her. Then walking over to the drawing board, she looked at a layout for an advertisement. It was for a builder's merchant. She studied the cartoon style of the presentation and smiled at the humour of it.

'I'm pleased to see that you find that amusing.'

She spun round to see who had spoken. The tall man was in his mid-twenties, wearing a smart business suit, carrying a large leather portfolio – no doubt containing drawings, she surmised. He was good-looking in a rugged sort of way, she thought.

'I think it's very funny,' Bryony said.

'Good. I'm Nick Langdon and you are the new dogsbody, I presume.'

'That's not a very flattering title,' she said.

'What would *you* suggest?' he asked as he sat in his chair and stared at her with piercing blue eyes.

'Well, let me see. General factotum; Jane of all trades; a necessary evil has a nice ring to it, or even a useful

154

member of the staff . . . something, anyway, with a little respect would not go amiss, Mr Langdon.'

His eyes twinkled. 'Feisty, aren't we?'

'Very! Now if you'll excuse me I have to take some letters for Mr Langdon . . . senior,' she added as she walked towards the door.

She could hear him laughing as she went down the hallway. Is that a good or a poor start, she wondered. Whatever it was, it was interesting. And she told herself if she could cope with the nuns at the convent and survive, she could certainly cope with Nick Langdon.

The first day went well. Richard Langdon, although giving the appearance of being eccentric, was a very clever and competent man, Bryony discovered, and they worked well together. He showed her the filing system in his office and explained how he would like her to use it.

Whilst she was typing up her letters, Nick was working at his drawing board and, though answering the occasional phone call, was mainly silent. He obviously liked to concentrate without interruption, which worked for her also.

At lunchtime, she went along the road to a small café and had a coffee and sandwich, looked around a few of the shops, and returned to her desk. Nick was not there and she had the space to herself for the rest of the day.

*   *   *

In the office of the car lot, Dan wondered how his daughter was getting on. As he sorted through his own paperwork, he dearly wished she were working for him. He'd have to think seriously of getting a woman in to help, as he was tired of taking work home. But if he did, he'd have to put her up in a different office, as there were too many dodgy deals discussed in his.

Jack, his right-hand man, entered. 'There's a man walking round the car lot, Dan, and I don't like the look of him. Is it anyone you know?'

Glancing out of the window, Dan saw Harry Burgess peering at the cars. 'Oh, yes, I know that bastard. Leave him to me.'

Walking up to the man, Dan said, 'I didn't know you had a driving licence.'

Burgess looked at Dan with undisguised hostility. 'What's it to you?'

Dan could smell the alcohol on his breath. 'Don't talk to me like that, especially on my own property, not if you know what's good for you.'

'I came here as a punter, so where's your pleasant sales talk, Travis?'

'I don't need money that badly. Now fuck off or I'll have you forcibly removed.'

'My money not good enough for you, is that it?'

'I couldn't have put it more concisely myself. Now do I have to escort you off the premises or will you go under your own steam?'

Seeing the threatening expression on Dan's face,

Harry Burgess began to walk away slowly. 'I wouldn't buy anything from you anyway.'

'Then why the bloody hell are you here? Perhaps you wandered in by mistake – your sense of direction let you down, did it?'

'Get knotted!' said Burgess, and walked towards the exit. Looking over his shoulder he called, 'Full of inflammable material, all these cars, aren't they?' And he grinned.

With just a few steps of his long legs, Dan caught up to him and grabbed him by the coat lapels. 'Don't even think about it. Anything happens here and you are a dead man, remember that.'

Burgess still smiled. In his eyes was a hint of madness as he said, 'I'll remember what you said. I wouldn't want to get my fingers burned, would I?'

'Don't think you can threaten me and get away with it, you mad bastard.'

The smile faded. With a sneer Burgess said, 'Mad? Not me, my friend. I'm perfectly sane.'

'I doubt that, otherwise you wouldn't have come here in the first place. Now, bugger off!' Dan let go and shoved Harry away from him. 'Just keep your nose out of my business, if you know what's good for you, and that is my final warning. If I find you within spitting distance, you'll pay.'

Harry Burgess shambled off, muttering expletives under his breath.

Jack walked towards Dan. 'What was that all about?'

'He's a mad bugger, and potentially very dangerous.

And he's drunk! I want a watch kept on this place at night for the foreseeable future. See to it!'

Back in his office, Dan lit a cigar. He pondered Burgess's hostile attitude towards him and wondered if it was because he'd warned him off young Giles when they were all in the Silver Dollar Club. Until then, they had hardly spoken. Dan was concerned. The man was a nutcase, of that there was no doubt, and such men were utterly unpredictable . . . and dangerous. Now he had to beg the question, should he be the one to strike first or wait to see if his threats were enough to frighten the man off? He had one or two deals coming off that necessitated him keeping a low profile at the moment, so perhaps it was wiser to tread carefully as far as Harry Burgess went – just for the time being. Perhaps it was just as well that Bryony wasn't here working. He wouldn't like her to be around if Burgess suddenly ran amok.

When Bryony arrived home after her first day, her mother asked her how it all went.

'Fine,' she said. 'Richard is really easy to work with and we got along very well. He was quite impressed with my shorthand speed, which was very satisfying, then there was his son, Nick.'

'What was he like?'

'Tall, good-looking and arrogant! But very talented, I would say.'

'Sounds interesting,' said Leila knowingly.

With a shrug, Bryony said, 'That remains to be seen. I'm going to have a wash and change, then I'll pop round to see Theresa. I want to tell her about my week-end in the lap of luxury.'

As her daughter left the room, Leila wondered how Theresa was faring with the chance of pregnancy hanging over her. She hoped that Bryony wouldn't sense anything wrong. That could be very awkward.

In fact, Theresa welcomed the chance to see her friend and listen to her adventures. She needed to take her mind off her problems. She listened eagerly to every word.

'My goodness, Bryony, it all sounds wonderful.'

'It was an experience.'

'And James – how did you get on with him?'

'Very well. He said I was his girl, but I'm not sure if he really meant it.'

'Why?'

'When he said goodbye, he was very casual, I thought.'

Remembering her own unhappy experience, Theresa said, 'Men! I wouldn't trust one of them.'

There was such venom in her voice that Bryony was surprised. 'Good gracious, that was a bit strong, especially as you've had no experience of them.'

'Well, you've only got to read the different agony columns in the women's magazines to know that men are not to be trusted,' Theresa said hurriedly, to cover her outburst.

'Maybe you're right,' remarked Bryony. 'Well, time alone will tell, I suppose.'

'How was your first day at work?' Theresa asked in an effort to change the subject.

Bryony told her all that had happened.

'It sounds interesting. Is this Nick married?'

'I've no idea, and frankly I don't much care as long as he keeps out of my hair. Well, best be off.'

'Give my love to your mother,' said Theresa as she showed Bryony out. 'I'll pop round to see you next week. As from tomorrow I'm on late duty.'

Bryony relayed her friend's message to her mother.

'And how is Theresa?' Leila asked.

'Fine. She said she'd come round next week as she's working late for the next while.'

Leila wondered if she was sending her a message. She really hoped that when Theresa did come round it was to tell her all was well.

But a week later, Leila found a weeping girl on her doorstep.

CHAPTER FOURTEEN

'Oh my God, Theresa! Come in.' Leila hustled the weeping girl into the kitchen, sat her down and, pushing a box of tissues towards her, put her arm around her shoulders.

'Bad news, I assume?' she said.

Theresa wiped her eyes and nodded. 'I'm late, Mrs Travis, and I'm always on time. What *am* I going to do?'

Leila put the kettle on and said, 'We need to think about this very carefully. Let me make us a cup of tea. I find it always helps me to concentrate.' It also gave Leila a bit of breathing space, knowing that the advice she gave the distressed girl would be vital to her future.

'Here, drink this,' she said, pouring a cup and pushed it towards her. Taking a deep breath, she said, 'I have to ask you several questions before we make any decisions. Firstly, do you want to have this child?'

The look of horror on the girl's face gave her the answer before she spoke. 'No I don't. I can't even bear the idea of carrying that man's baby.'

'Am I right in thinking you want this kept from your father?'

Grabbing Leila's hand, Theresa cried, 'He must never know. He'd kill me!'

'Come now, darling, no father would do that, but I can see it might be the last thing you'd want. What about your mother?'

'No. No one must know. You promised!'

'I did, but you know if this was Bryony and your mother was in my position and took it upon herself to do something without discussing it with me, I would be livid. After all, Theresa, you are her daughter, her own flesh and blood. Tell me about her – what sort of person is she?'

'She's a good mother, not as strict as Dad. She used to be a nurse and when I got tipsy at your party, she was great.'

'Is she any good at keeping secrets?'

'You mean from my father?'

'That's exactly what I mean.' Running her hand through her hair, Leila said, 'I have to tell her, darling; it's her right to know. And if she was a nurse, she might have a solution to your problem.'

'What if she makes me keep it? . . . I'll kill myself if she says I have to!'

'Now that's no way to talk,' said Leila sharply. 'There is nothing that can't be solved one way or another.'

'I don't know what to do . . . except I do know I won't have this baby.'

Seeing the desperation in her eyes, Leila said, 'I'll

make you a promise. If your mother won't agree, I'll see to it without her knowledge. All right? But if I do, we will have to tell a few fibs.'

Theresa threw her arms around Leila's neck. 'You are so good to me. I don't know what I would have done without you!'

As she patted the girl's back, she thought, I know what I'm afraid you would do. And her anger seethed inside her. I'll make that wicked bastard pay, she vowed as she thought of Lenny Marks. By the time I've finished with him, he'll never take advantage of another girl.

'Now listen to me, Theresa. I'll arrange to see your mother. I'll invite her round here tomorrow, and we'll talk.' Seeing the scared expression on the young girl's face, she said, 'Now I don't want you to worry. She is an intelligent woman, we are both mothers, and I'm sure we'll work it out between us.'

Blowing her nose, Theresa said, 'All right. I won't say anything to her.'

'No, leave it to me. Now go and rinse your face and go home. Keep busy, that's the best thing. What time is your father's surgery in the morning?'

'Nine until eleven.'

'Right. Who takes the telephone calls in the morning?'

'Mother, until the surgery opens, then the practice nurse takes over.'

The following morning at a quarter to nine, Leila rang the surgery. 'Mrs Kerrigan?'

'Speaking.'

163

'This is Leila Travis. I wonder if you could come round to my house this morning for a cup of coffee? Only I would like to talk to you about Theresa.'

Nuala Kerrigan was immediately alert. The call was so unexpected, but there was something in the tone of the other woman's voice. She didn't hesitate.

'What time, Mrs Travis?'

'How about ten thirty?'

'That will be fine. I'll see you then.' Replacing the receiver, Nuala walked slowly back into the kitchen.

'Who was that?' her husband enquired.

'Just someone from the Women's Institute,' she replied.

Now why on earth did I lie? she asked herself. It was an automatic response, but she had a gut feeling that all was not well. What on earth could it be? She and Leila Travis only saw each other very occasionally – they hardly knew one another – so why the call? And about Theresa, not about 'the girls'. Why specifically *her* daughter?

At ten thirty sharp, Nuala rang the bell of the front door of the Travis residence. Nice house, she thought as she waited.

When the door opened, Leila smiled at her and said, 'Thank you for coming. Please come in,' and led her into the living room. 'Please sit down. I'll go and get the coffee.'

Left alone, Nuala looked around the elegant room with its antique furniture, admiring some of the pieces. Very tasteful, she mused.

Leila carried in a tray set with coffee pot, cups and saucers and biscuits. She sat opposite Nuala and poured two cups, offered the plate of biscuits, which her guest refused.

'I'm sure you are puzzled as to why I asked you here,' Leila began, 'and to be honest, I don't quite know where to start.'

'How about the beginning?' Nuala suggested.

Taking a deep breath, Leila thought, well, there's no point in beating about the bush, and she told Theresa's mother everything, from beginning to end.

She was shocked. Putting her hand over her mouth, Nuala said, 'Oh, sweet Jesus. My poor girl. But why didn't she come to me? Why you?'

'Because she was terrified. That bastard raped her, then drove her home and pushed her out of the car. How could she come inside in the state she was in? And I was the nearest person.'

'But you say she consented to sex with him once before that? I find that hard to believe of my Theresa!'

'He flattered her and it was because she was a good girl and was so ashamed of having done so, she refused him the next time . . . and for this she was raped. I have to tell you, Mrs Kerrigan, I'm really worried about her mental state. She's terrified that her father will find out and that you may make her keep the child.' She paused. 'She said she would rather kill herself than have it!'

Tears filled Nuala's eyes. 'Oh my God!'

Leila poured her a brandy. 'Here, drink this. I'll join you.'

165

The two women sat in silence, Nuala trying to get her head around what she'd just been told, and Leila, watching her carefully, trying to gauge her reaction. Eventually she spoke.

'Mrs Kerrigan, I know this has come as a great shock to you, but we have to consider Theresa. I understand your Catholic upbringing, but that girl cannot have this child. It will destroy her!'

Nuala Kerrigan wiped her eyes, sat up straight and, looking at Leila, said, 'Bugger the Church! My child is more important to me.'

Leila looked admiringly at her. 'Now there's a woman after my own heart. How are we going to get her out of this mess? You were a nurse, I believe – do you know of anything other than an abortion, because I'm damned if I do.'

'Do you think I could have another brandy?' asked Nuala.

'Most certainly.' And Leila poured them each one.

'If we could get hold of some ergometrine, that might do it.'

'What's that?'

'A drug that will make the uterus contract. As she is just a little late, it might expel everything, but I obviously can't ask my husband for it.'

'Don't worry about that,' said Leila. 'I know a doctor who will give it to me, no questions asked. Just write it down for me.' She handed Nuala a pen and paper.

After writing, Nuala handed over the sheet of paper. 'Mrs Travis . . .'

166

'Leila, please.'

'Leila, I can't begin to thank you enough.'

'Please, Nuala, I'm a mother too, you know and, let's face it, we women are much better at coping in such emergencies. You won't tell your husband, I hope.'

'Of course not. This will be between you and me and my poor Theresa.'

'I'll not say a word to Bryony. That will be for Theresa to decide. But – and we do have to face this – what if this pill doesn't work, what then?'

'Then I'll take her to a proper doctor for an abortion.'

'Do you know of one?'

Shaking her head, Nuala said, 'No, but I bet you do.'

Leila started to laugh. 'You are really quite a woman. How on earth did you come to marry the doctor?'

'You may not believe it but he used to be a bit of a wild Irishman. He's just getting older. I have to give him a nudge occasionally to remind him.'

'I'll get on to my doctor friend today,' said Leila, 'and by tomorrow I'll have the pills. You will be gentle with Theresa, won't you?'

'Sure, what else would I be? Who is this man who did this to my girl?'

'Don't you worry about him, Nuala my dear. He'll pay for all this, you have my word. He won't put another girl through this. I'll see to that personally.'

'You won't do anything stupid, will you? I don't

want you to get into trouble because of my Theresa.'

'It's kind of you to be so concerned, but I'll be fine, honestly. When I get the pills, I'll call you. It's best I don't come to your house; it might raise a few questions.'

'I'll pop round here for them, if you like.'

'That will be fine.'

They walked to the door together. Nuala turned towards Leila and gave her a hug.

'You're a good woman, Leila Travis.'

Chuckling, she said, 'There are some who wouldn't agree with you.'

'Not ever in front of me they won't!'

As she watched her guest walking down the path, Leila smiled to herself. She would never have believed that the good doctor's wife had balls! 'Bugger the Church' – that was unexpected. What a woman! Theresa would have nothing to fear with a mother like that looking after her. Poor girl, she would come home in dread this evening wondering what she would have to face. She only hoped that these pills would do the trick. An operation to terminate the pregnancy would have a profound effect on the girl if she had to go through that ordeal.

Later that afternoon, Leila paid a visit to her doctor friend and left his surgery with a prescription in her hand, which she took to a pharmacy. Then she drove on to the warehouse where Dan's team of men were housed when not out on various jobs.

She opened the door and saw three of them, unpacking cases.

'Hello, Mrs Travis,' said one. 'What can we do for you?'

Lenny Marks staggered out of the Lord Roberts pub in Canal Walk and started to walk towards Union Street where his car was parked, unaware that he was being followed. Three men jumped him, put a sack over his head and bundled him into the back of a van. They drove away with him struggling, until one of the heavies thumped him, putting an end to his attempts at freeing himself.

He came to when a bucket of cold water was thrown in his face. Coughing and spluttering, he tried to move, only to discover that he was seated in a chair with his hands and feet tied to it.

'What the bloody hell is going on?' he demanded.

He was slapped across the face and told to shut up.

'That's no way to treat him, boys,' said a woman's voice.

He looked up to see Leila Travis standing away from him. 'That's right! Tell these bastards to undo me.'

'Undo him,' she said.

He grinned as two of the men cut the ropes that tied him. 'I should bloody well think so.'

'Strip him!' snapped Leila.

'What? Hey, you watch what you're doing—' he began.

'Shut up!' Leila looked at him with loathing and

watched whilst every vestige of clothing was removed.

'String him up,' she said.

Lenny found himself hanging by his wrists, from the rafter above, naked. 'What are you doing to me?'

'I'm going to teach you a lesson, Lenny. One you won't forget in a hurry.'

'Why, what have I ever done to you?' he asked, his voice trembling with fright.

'How about rape?'

'What?' He looked at her. 'What are you talking about?'

'You meet a nice young girl at my Dan's birthday party and you wheedle your way into her affections, and you rape her.'

He didn't answer as he was watching her as she took a long leather case off the table and, to his horror, removed a stock whip.

'I didn't rape her, I swear. She was asking for it, leading me on. She wanted it!'

The whip cracked loudly as it flew at him, cutting him across the chest, making him bleed. He screamed out.

Leila just stood staring at him. 'I used to do this as an act in a circus,' she told him. 'I was good. I could cut a cigarette in half, which was held in someone's mouth. Put one in his,' she told one of the men.

Lenny nearly threw up as the cigarette dangled.

'Hold it steady or you might get hurt,' Leila ordered.

He tried, but he was so scared it shook as he did.

With a flick of her wrist she took it off near his lips.

'I'm so pleased I haven't lost my touch,' she said, and laughed at him. Then staring at his genitals she said, 'Not much of a man, are you?' And cracked the whip again.

Lenny screamed as he felt the pain. He looked down and saw the blood on his penis.

'I could easily castrate you from here,' said Leila.

The men who were watching became a little restless and, to Leila's amusement, they automatically covered their genital areas with their hands. They blanched as she flicked her whip across Lenny's bottom, across his arms, and again as she aimed for his genitalia.

The pain was excruciating. 'No more, please, no more,' he screamed.

'Not such a brave man now, are you?' she said scathingly. 'You didn't care about that poor girl, did you, you little shit?'

'I'm sorry, I'm really sorry.'

'You bloody well will be!' And she whipped him again. Twice.

'Mrs Travis . . .' began one of the men nervously.

'Cut him down!' she snapped, 'and send him home.' She walked slowly over to the sobbing bloodied wreck of a man and said, 'If ever I hear about you treating any woman the same way, next time you won't survive – do I make myself clear?'

He could barely speak. 'Yes,' he whispered eventually.

'And don't think about going to the police or you'll be answering a charge of rape.' Leila picked up the leather case, wiped the blood from the whip, put it away and left the building. Outside she sat in her car and, with trembling fingers, lit a cigarette. She had no pity for the man she'd just left; he deserved everything he got. Her sympathy was for young Theresa, who would be marked by her experience for years to come.

Throwing her cigarette out of the window, Leila turned on the ignition and drove home.

CHAPTER FIFTEEN

Theresa arrived home in fear and trembling, wondering what reception she would receive from her mother, and what future plans were in store for her.

Hearing the key in the front door, Nuala walked into the hallway and, seeing the white face of her daughter, took her into her arms and said, 'It's going to be all right, darlin'.'

'Oh, Mammy.' She clung tightly to her mother for a moment and then declared, 'I won't have this baby. I won't!'

'Indeed you won't. Tomorrow I'll be giving you a pill which should start your period.'

'And if it doesn't?'

'Then we'll move on to plan B, but let's not think about that unless we have to.'

'I am so ashamed, Mammy.' And the tears welled in her eyes.

'I blame myself,' said Nuala. 'I've not prepared you for meeting young men.'

'How could you? I never meet any!'

'Now you're working you will, but, darlin', don't let a boy touch you in any other way than with respect. When you marry, well, that's different.'

'I'll never marry!'

With a soft smile Nuala said, 'Sure you will, one day when you meet the right person. But, Theresa, if you are worried about anything, please come and tell me. I am your mother, after all.'

'I'm really sorry, but that day, Dad was at home and I couldn't let either of you see me in such a state, and Mrs Travis was very kind.'

'Sure, and she's a good woman and I'll be forever grateful. Now away to your room and freshen up. Your father will be in for his dinner soon enough.' Putting a hand on Theresa's arm she added, 'We'll get through this, I promise.'

A little later, as the family sat at the dinner table, Sean Kerrigan glanced at his daughter and said, 'You look a bit peaky, Theresa. Are you not feeling well?'

With a startled look she said, 'No, Daddy, I'm fine, just a little tired. We were busy at the hotel.'

Nuala chipped in, 'And how was your day, dear?' Neatly changing the subject.

Theresa breathed a sigh of relief and tried to force her food down, having lost the taste for it.

Four days later, Theresa woke with a dragging pain in her stomach. With a heart full of fear and hope, she went to the toilet. When she realised that she was bleeding, the relief was overwhelming. She went into the kitchen and, sidling up to her mother, confided, 'Mammy, my period has started. Does it mean that I'm safe now?'

'Thanks be to God, you are, darlin'. We have been lucky. Make sure you thank Him in your prayers.'

'I will, oh, I will, but I'll not be going to confession for a while.'

'No, perhaps that's just as well kept between us.' Holding Theresa, Nuala said, 'You need to put this behind you now, my love. It'll take a bit of time, but if you don't that worthless article who raped you will have won, and we can't have that, can we?'

Tightening her mouth, Theresa said, 'I wouldn't give him the satisfaction.'

'That's my girl!'

Nuala was happy to be able to go to Leila Travis and tell her that Theresa was no longer pregnant.

'Thank God for that,' said Leila. 'We'll have a brandy to celebrate.'

When they were settled, Leila had a question. 'Forgive me for asking, Nuala, but, knowing you're a staunch Catholic, how do you salvage your conscience about what we've done?'

'Well, I look at it this way, if the Good Lord could forgive Mary Magdalene, I'm sure he could find it in his heart to forgive a mother for saving her daughter from that terrible sin done against her.'

'It makes good sense to me,' Leila agreed. 'How is Theresa?'

'Pretty subdued, which is not surprising, but we just have to give her time.'

Bryony had been working at Langdon and Associates for three weeks now and was enjoying it immensely. Her duties were varied. She took letters from Richard and typed them; sometimes she entertained clients whilst they waited, by making them coffee and talking to them. And she had even taken part in some research needed for a certain campaign. She was amazed at how much preparation was needed to set up a good advertising portfolio.

Nick she found very talented, infuriating, rather abrupt at times, and wholly cynical about almost everything.

'What a dreadful outlook you do have!' she remonstrated with him one morning.

'When you work in this business,' he said, 'you learn never to take anything on face value. When you grow up, you'll find out that I'm right.'

'I am grown up! I'll be nineteen soon.'

'You are an innocent virginal child,' he said, giving her a knowing smile.

Picking up some papers, she walked to the door, then paused and asked, 'How can you be sure of that?' And before he could answer she left the room.

He chuckled at her stand. He liked Bryony; she was a bright kid with an eye for a product. There had been times when he'd looked at his work and hadn't been able to put his finger on just what was missing. She'd pointed out the weakness immediately, and that took a certain talent. What made it all the more delightful was that she was totally unaware of it.

He considered her remark as she left the room. Was she serious? Had she given herself to someone? He found he was disappointed at the thought. She was far too young, in his opinion.

The one thing that blighted Bryony's happiness was the fact that apart from one phone call to see how she liked her job, James had not been in touch since. He had said he would be busy studying, but when she bought the latest edition of *Tatler* magazine, she saw a picture of him and a glamorous young blonde at an exhibition of paintings at the National Gallery. How could he do this if she was supposed to be his girl? She was very perturbed.

When the next day, he called her unexpectedly, she asked him about it.

'Oh, that,' he said dismissively. 'There was a crowd there – we just happened to be standing together when the photographer took the picture, that's all. You know, Bryony darling, that you're my girl.'

'That's what you told me at Toby's,' she retorted. 'Now I wonder.'

'Listen, darling, I wondered now that I've a short break from my studies if we can see each other this coming weekend?'

'Where?'

His voice softened as he coaxed her. 'Well, I know it's soon your birthday, so I thought we could spend time in London. I'll take you out to dinner and to a show, and then we could end up at a club somewhere. What do you say?'

She was thrilled that James had remembered. 'Won't that make it very late for me to get home?'

'Don't be a goose. We'll stay overnight. A friend of mine says I can use his flat as he's away.'

She so wanted to be strong, to say no, to teach him a lesson, but she was in love and couldn't wait to see James again.

'All right, that would be lovely.'

They arranged which train she would catch to Waterloo, where James would meet her.

'I can't wait to hold you,' he said. 'I've missed you so much.'

'I've missed you too.'

When she told Leila of her plans she told a white lie. 'We will be staying with a friend of James's who has a flat in town.'

Thinking of young Theresa, Leila said, 'You will take care, won't you, Bryony? Young, good-looking men can be very persuasive. I wouldn't like to think of you getting into any difficult situation you couldn't handle.'

'You don't have to worry, Mum. I'll be fine. James takes good care of me.' Bryony felt she wasn't being entirely untruthful, but if her mother knew in what context he was careful, she'd have a fit!

* * *

When Bryony arrived at Waterloo Station, she saw James waiting at the barrier for her. He swept her into his arms and kissed her enthusiastically.

'God, it's so good to see you,' he said. 'Come on, we'll get a taxi.'

He took her to a small French restaurant in Knightsbridge, where they sat and chatted over a delicious meal. Bryony studied his face, and was filled with happiness. James was indeed good-looking but there was more to him than that. He was intelligent, amusing . . . and in love with her; at least, he had told her he was when he first took her to bed at Wallbourne Manor.

'So how is the job going?' he asked.

She described her working day and the people in the office, and she told him about Richard and Nick.

'Richard is such a character,' she said. 'He wears flamboyant waistcoats and looks a bit like a crazy professor, whereas Nick is always immaculate in his dress. He's very talented, but a bit full of himself. He treats me like a child, which is infuriating.'

'Why, is Nick an older man?'

'Good heavens, no. He's in his mid-twenties, I would say. But I'm really enjoying it there.'

'Excellent! There is nothing worse than hating the idea of going to work every day. Come along, I thought we would take a look at the shops, pop into the Strand Palace for a drink before the show and dine after.'

'That would be lovely.'

*   *   *

By the time they arrived at the Strand Palace Hotel, both were exhausted and dying for a cup of tea, so they settled in the huge lounge area and ordered tea and sandwiches. As Bryony was looking around the sumptuous rooms she spied a familiar figure in the distance.

'Look! Isn't that Cassy?'

James said, 'Good heavens, so it is.'

Bryony was about to suggest they invite her over but as she watched, a gentleman approached Cassy, who after some discussion, rose to her feet and left with him. To Bryony's surprise, they walked up the stairs together.

'She must have a friend staying here,' James remarked as the waiter appeared with their tea. Cassy was then soon forgotten as they tucked into their food.

They both enjoyed *South Pacific*, and after dinner, James took Bryony to a club, where they drank and danced away what was left of the night.

As James put the key into the door of the flat, Bryony said, 'That was a lovely day, but I'm absolutely exhausted!'

James pulled her into his arms. 'Not too much, I hope?'

Entwining her arms around his neck, she said, 'Well, that will depend on you, darling.'

'I do like a challenge!' he said, sweeping her up in his arms. 'Come on, you minx. I promise you won't want to sleep.'

Sleep was the last thing on her mind as James's kisses

and fingers worked their magic on her body. All she wanted was to feel him inside her, loving her, desiring her as much as she desired him.

Dan Travis parked his car almost opposite the Albatross Club and watched. From what he could see, business was good. If this was the case, why were the takings down? He was the sleeping partner of this establishment, having put up most of the money to open it, leaving the running of it to one Terry Hart, a ship's barman, who had come to him with an idea that Dan had liked.

They had a contract that stated that Dan was the biggest shareholder and would be paid seventy-five per cent of the takings, and that laid out all the other rules and regulations. The club had taken a while to get established but then it had started to make real money. It was comfortably furnished and served bar food only, which saved the overheads and running expenses of operating a proper restaurant. Owing to its close proximity to the docks, it was convenient to ships' crews and locals. The membership fee was reasonable, and those who arrived on the doorstep wanting entry had to pay to join, but for the past month the takings had been dropping, and Dan was certain that Terry Hart was creaming money off the top.

Turning to Jack, his right-hand man at the car lot, Dan said, 'Right, let's go. I'll find a seat and you go to the bar for the drinks. I don't want that bastard Terry to see me for a while.'

They settled themselves quietly in a corner and

watched. There was another barman besides Terry, but it was his partner Dan watched closely. He noted that sometimes the 'no sale' showed when the till was opened, and he saw Terry slyly pocketing money, whereas the other barman was working honestly.

'I'll have that cheating bastard tonight,' Dan said to Jack. 'We'll go into the gents when he calls time, and come out as he locks up.'

'Right, guv,' said Jack.

Terry Hart locked the main door behind his last customer and after clearing the glasses he told the barman to go home. 'I'll finish up here.'

As the door closed behind the employee, Dan and Jack emerged from the gents' toilet.

'Hello, Terry.'

Startled, he said, 'Christ! You nearly gave me a heart attack.'

Dan stepped forward and, taking Terry's arms, he got Jack to hold them firmly behind his back.

'What the bloody hell are you doing?'

Dan didn't answer. He went through the man's pockets and then held up his hand, which was stuffed with notes, and waved them in front of Terry's nose.

'Well?' he asked menacingly.

'Oh, that,' he said as Jack released him. 'I never keep a full till in case anyone tries to knock us over.'

'Very commendable,' Dan said. 'Now let's go and total tonight's takings. If what you say is true, then the till will be short by this amount, won't it?'

Terry began to panic. 'You know what it's like on a busy night, Dan. There are always discrepancies.'

'Absolutely, but only by a bob or two.' He pushed him towards the counter, following behind. 'Let's see, shall we?'

Terry went through the motions, not knowing what else to do. The till was five shillings short.

Dan counted out the notes he'd taken from Hart on to the table. 'Fifty quid.' And he stared at Hart. 'You, my son, have just made the biggest mistake of your life. You've been creaming money off the top, and what's more, you cheating bastard, you've been doing it for fucking weeks!'

The man knew he was beaten. 'It was only a temporary measure. I was trying to clear my debts,' he cried. 'I was going to pay it all back, honest I was.'

'Of course you were,' Dan said amiably, but then he caught the man by the throat. 'Do you think I'm stupid? You got greedy, which is a sin, do you know that? But your biggest sin was trying to screw me!'

'What are you going to do to me?' Terry asked, terrified for his life.

Shaking his head, Dan said, 'I never understand people like you. You have a sure-fire business with someone behind you who was good enough to finance you and you shit in your own nest. That is stupid and when it involves me, it's dangerous.'

The man was trembling as he waited.

'As I see it, you have two choices. Pack your bags and leave Southampton quietly, or you disappear without trace – my way.'

'But I put money into this place!' Terry screamed at Dan.

'True, but not a lot. As far as I can see you have nearly covered your investment these past weeks. The rest I'll take as the goodwill of the place.'

'You can't do this to me!'

Dan caught him around the throat again and began to squeeze. 'I can do what I bloody well like to you. The choice is yours. The easy way or the other?'

'I'll go, I'll go,' Terry gasped.

'At last you have made a wise decision. Go upstairs with him, Jack, and pack his bags, then take him to the station and buy a ticket. Somewhere up north.' Glaring at the man, he threatened, 'If *ever* I set eyes on you again, you are dead. Do I make myself clear?'

Hart nodded. 'Yes,' he said.

'We'll put a manager in here tomorrow. I'll call one of the boys to collect you,' Dan told Jack. 'Put him on the train and watch it leave, I don't want any mistakes, understand?'

'No worries, guv. He isn't stupid enough to try anything, are you?' he asked, prodding the man in the back.

'Teach him a lesson first,' said Dan, 'but don't touch his face.'

Dan walked out of the building and, climbing into his vehicle, drove home. He was livid. That arrogant bastard, thinking he could mess with me, he fumed. Never mind, he's put a stop to it, and with a decent manager, the club would once again be profitable. And it was all legit.

CHAPTER SIXTEEN

Giles was finding it very difficult to bring to an end his relationship with Sophie Johnson. Sophie had insisted they meet in London before travelling to Southampton as he had dealings at Portobello Market with one of the stallholders, where, he discovered, the man he had sent up with some goods had cheated him.

'Good stuff that was, Soph,' said the stallholder. 'Really nice porcelain. My punters love it. I'll take any more you can get.'

'Good,' said Sophie. 'But to be honest I thought you were a bit harsh on the price.'

'Harsh? What the bloody hell are you talking about? I gave that bloke seventy-five quid!'

Giles saw Sophie's jaw tighten. 'Did you now? The little bleeder only gave me fifty.'

'You know I'm always fair with you, me old mucker,' protested the man.

'I know, Fred, that's why I'm here today to check.' He shook the other man by the hand. 'Thanks for the info. You won't be seeing that bloke again. I'll either come myself, or send young Giles here.'

As they walked away, Sophie fumed. 'When will people learn that I'm not a man to be crossed.'

'What are you going to do?' asked Giles nervously.

'Teach him a lesson. He'll be in the Silver Dollar Club tonight, and so will we.'

'I don't like going to the club,' said Giles. 'That dreadful man might be there.'

'Who, Harry Burgess? If he is, and is any trouble, I'll bloody well sort him too!' Glaring at Giles, Sophie said, 'No one mixes it with me, boy, and gets away with it, you might take note of that.'

'I don't know what you mean.'

'I mean that I've kept you in poncy clothes and pocket money for a while, so don't try and get smart, take me for a fool, or you too will find out what it's like to cross Sophie Johnson.'

His tone was so threatening, that Giles felt his blood run cold.

The club was almost full to capacity, as was usual on a Saturday night, when Giles and Sophie arrived. The air smelled of stale beer and tobacco. The smoke-filled atmosphere was like a London fog, and Sophie called to the barman, 'Can't you open a fucking window in here? I can't hardly breathe!'

Muttering under his breath, the barman did as he was asked.

'That's better,' said Sophie as he sat down at a table

that had just been vacated. 'Go and get us a couple of drinks, there's a good boy,' he said to Giles, and took a five-pound note from his wallet.

Giles went to the bar, quickly looking round for Harry, and was relieved that he wasn't there. I'm just a damned errand boy, he thought as he waited to get served. But he knew that in the present mood of his benefactor, it was safer and wiser to do as he was told.

Returning to the table, he sat beside Sophie and asked, 'Is the man you're looking for here?'

'Oh, yes. The little bleeder's sitting over in the corner with one of the local toms. She lives with him and I know for a fact he takes all her money. Why she doesn't move out I'll never know. If I were a woman, I wouldn't whore for anyone else. I'd want to keep my earnings.'

Giles looked across the room at the woman. She was tall and skinny, with peroxided hair, heavy make-up, tight-fitting clothes and hooped earrings. He suddenly felt demeaned. After all, he was no better. The only difference was that he was a man and he had one lover, but they were both selling themselves for sex.

Sophie waited until the man went to the gents' toilet. He rose from his seat and said to Giles, 'Come on.'

'What? You're not going to do anything foolish, are you?' Giles asked with a worried frown.

Sophie just smiled and winked.

Giles followed him into the gents. There were two men standing at the urinals and one of the cubicle doors was closed. Sophie undid his flies and spent a penny;

Giles washed his hands, wondering what on earth was going to happen.

When the two men left, Sophie whispered to Giles, 'Stand by the door and keep it shut.'

'But what if someone wants to come in?'

'Lock it from the inside. I don't want to be disturbed.' He walked to the basin to wash his hands just as his intended victim flushed the toilet and, leaving the cubicle, headed for the door.

'Don't you think you should wash your hands, you dirty bugger?' snapped Sophie.

The man turned and, when he saw who had spoken, said with a nervous smile, 'Yes, I was so deep in thought I forgot.' Turning on the tap, he soaped his hands.

'Like you forgot to give me all the money from Portobello, you mean?'

The man looked visibly shaken. 'I don't know what you're talking about.'

'You know bloody well what I mean, you sneaky bastard. You owe me twenty-five quid. I went up to the Smoke and saw Fred for myself. He paid you seventy-five smackers and you gave me fifty.'

As he started to protest, Sophie grabbed him by the wrist and said softly, 'In China, the Triads, if they catch someone thieving, have the perfect way to deal with them.'

'What? What?' protested the man, in a panic. 'Don't you touch me. I'll pay you the fucking money.'

'Indeed you will,' said Sophie, 'but now you owe me interest.' He took his cutthroat razor from his pocket and, with a quick flip, opened it and before the man realised what was happening, Sophie put the man's little finger on the worktop of the washing area and sliced the top half off with one quick swipe of the blade.

As the blood spread, Giles felt sick to his stomach. The man screamed and Sophie hit him, then he looked through the man's pockets and withdrew some notes.

'I'm taking my dosh,' he said. Then, tearing a bit of paper towel off the roll, he handed it to the man, saying, 'Here, put this round your finger. People outside might not like the sight of blood.' And with a nod to Giles to unlock the door, he left the toilet, walked over to his table and sat sipping his drink.

Giles was white-faced and trembling as he sat beside him. 'I feel sick,' he said.

'Don't you dare throw up!' warned Sophie.

'What if he goes to the police and reports you?'

'I can promise you he won't. He won't want them delving into his life . . . living off immoral earnings, for a start, and then if he shopped me he knows I'd get him later.'

They saw the man stagger out of the gents, his hand well wrapped. He quickly left the building, his girlfriend chasing after him.

Sophie sat smiling.

Giles rose quickly to his feet. 'I've got to get some fresh air,' he said.

Seeing the white countenance of the young man, Sophie nodded. 'I'll wait here for you.'

Outside, Giles was violently sick in the gutter. He

took a handkerchief from his pocket and wiped his forehead, which was wet with perspiration.

'Oh dear,' a voice behind him said, 'had too much to drink, have we, lovely boy?'

Turning, he looked into the leering face of Harry Burgess.

Giles felt his knees turn to jelly as Harry pushed him up against the wall.

'Now this *is* a bit of luck. I never thought I'd get you away from Sophie, and here you are, all alone.'

'Don't you dare lay a finger on me,' Giles said, his voice trembling.

'I love to hear you talk, pretty boy. So refined. It's nice to have a bit of class.' He ran his hand down the front of Giles's trousers. 'Oh dear, not up to it?'

'Get your filthy hands off me!'

Harry's coarse laughter rang. 'My filthy hands? Yet you let that old man touch you. Not that fussy, are you? Now you're coming home with me, and we'll have a really exciting time.'

'Sophie will kill you!'

Harry's laugh was chilling to hear. It was bordering on the hysterical and Giles knew that he was at the mercy of a madman. He started to struggle, and Harry hit him in the face with a blow that stunned him. Harry started to drag Giles away.

A car suddenly screeched to a stop beside him, and Dan Travis jumped out.

'Let go of him, you bastard!'

Harry turned to see who was challenging him and

was hit with a punch to the jaw so hard that it took him off his feet.

At the same time, Sophie Johnson came down the stairs. He looked at Harry Burgess sprawled on the pavement and at Giles, whose lip was bleeding and whose eye was swelling.

'Christ Almighty, what's going on?'

'Get in the car, both of you,' said Dan, opening the back door to the vehicle.

Bryony, who had been sitting in the front during the débâcle, stared in disbelief when she recognised Giles, but as she opened her mouth to speak to him, he shook his head, so she said nothing.

'I'll get you, Dan Travis,' screamed Burgess.

Dan ignored him and climbed into the driving seat. 'I was just passing,' he explained. 'I'd picked up Bryony from the cinema and was on my way home. I took it into my head to drive by the club, God knows why, and I saw that mad bugger set about Giles.' Looking at him through his driving mirror he asked, 'Are you all right, son?'

Giles was staring at the floor, as he couldn't look at Bryony. 'Yes. Thanks for coming to my rescue.'

'I'll drop you both home,' Dan said.

As the car came to a halt outside Sophie's house, Giles looked at Bryony and mouthed 'thanks', then got out.

As they drove home she asked her father, 'Who were those two men we just dropped off?'

'One is Sophie Johnson, a business associate of mine, and his boyfriend.'

Bryony was stunned. She'd never guessed that Giles was a queer. Whenever they had met at various gatherings, he'd flirted with the women, as any young man would have. What a revelation!

Giles was being fussed over by a worried Sophie. He soaked a cloth in cold water and placed it gently on the swollen eye of his young friend, cursing to himself as he did so.

'If that rotten nutter had got his hands on you, I'd have swung for him!' he stated.

But Giles was oblivious to his words; he was more concerned at Bryony discovering his secret life. He could be ruined! If his father found out about his sexual preference, he would disown him. At the same time, he was now terrified of Sophie. The coldness with which he'd chopped off the little finger of a man who had cheated him was chilling. What else was he capable of? Giles didn't want to know. How could he escape this man's clutches? The only way, as far as he could see, was to leave the country. But how on earth could he abandon his education? His father would never condone such a thing. He lay back on the settee and closed his eyes.

'Giles! You all right?' Sophie asked worriedly.

Opening his eyes, Giles said, 'Yes, I'm just feeling sore. I want to sleep.'

'Let me put you to bed,' suggested Sophie.

Giles balked at this. The thought of sharing his bed with this monster once more was beyond him. 'I'll just rest here, if you don't mind.'

'No, no, that's fine. I'll get a blanket and cover you,' said Sophie, full of concern. And he did so. Very gently smoothing Giles's forehead, he added softly, 'I would have killed that bugger if you had been harmed.'

'Thank you,' said Giles, closing his eyes. In his mind he was saying: please go away . . . leave me alone.

But Sophie wanted to make up for the unpleasant experience. 'Tomorrow, we'll go shopping.'

But when Sophie woke in the morning, Giles had left. There was a note on the side. 'I'll be in touch, love, Giles.

Sophie was overcome; tears welled in his eyes. He told himself that Giles had been so frightened in the toilet when he'd dealt with that cheating sod, and then, having been at the mercy of that bleeder Burgess, he'd taken fright and done a runner. But would he ever come back? He would give him time, and then he'd go look-ing for him.

Giles returned to London, and stayed with a friend, explaining his bruises away as an accidental fall. Then he rang Toby, knowing his family had a villa in the South of France. He said he was unwell, and needed a warmer climate than the damp autumn weather of London – could he possibly stay at the villa?

'Of course, old boy,' said Toby. 'The family won't be there until the spring. There is a maid and gardener there all the time – just ask for anything you want.' He gave Giles the address and told him, 'I'll let them know you are coming.'

'Thanks, Toby. I'll never forget you for this. You might well have saved my life!'

Toby laughed. 'Now don't exaggerate, Giles, just get better. I'll be in touch, there's a phone there, I'll give you a call to see that everything is fine.'

Giles could have cried with relief. When he was settled, he would write to his father, tell him he was recovering from influenza or something, and could he let his school know he wouldn't be there for the start of term. He would have to take a chance on Bryony keeping her mouth shut. But he would never return to Southampton and Sophie Johnson. Never.

CHAPTER SEVENTEEN

Bryony was busy at her typewriter when Nick's phone rang. 'Yes, please send him in,' he said.

The office door opened and looking up, Bryony was astonished to see Toby Beckford walk in. He was just as surprised to see her.

'Bryony! What on earth are you doing here?'

'Trying to earn an honest living.'

Laughing, he said, 'Well, that might be a problem as, I can assure you, you have fallen among thieves!' He shook Nick Langdon's hand. 'Hello, Nick. It's good to see you again.'

'Sit down, Toby. Bryony, would you get us some coffee, please?'

'Of course, I'd be delighted,' she said. 'You like yours black, don't you, Toby?'

It was Nick's turn to be surprised.

'You remember?' said Toby, pleased.

'How could I ever forget?' said Bryony with a provocative smile.

She chuckled as she went into the small kitchen. That

would give Nick something to think about. Innocent virgin indeed! A part of her purred like a cat to think this was the picture he had of her, but the minx in her wanted to show him she was a real woman!

After returning with the coffee, Bryony diplomatically left the two men to talk, but she was very curious as to how they knew one another.

She was talking to the receptionist when Toby left the office, Nick at his side to see him off.

Toby walked over to her, kissed her on the cheek and asked, 'Are you free this weekend, Bryony?'

'I've nothing planned,' she said.

'Good. Nick is coming down to Wallbourne Manor; he's offered to bring you with him. Pack an overnight bag. It's just us, nothing formal, slacks and sweaters,' he added. 'I'll give you another riding lesson.'

Her face lit up with excitement. 'Would you, really? That would be great.'

'You can ride out with Nick and me. We'll take it gently.'

'You can ride?' she asked Nick. Somehow she didn't equate him with horses, she didn't know why.

'Nick is a very good polo player when he has the time,' Toby told her. 'He's coming down to see a couple of horses I've bought.'

Nick was watching her reaction with a bemused expression. 'Bryony only sees me at a drawing board,' he said. 'I don't think she thinks I have anything else in my life.'

'It just goes to show the image we have of people

can be so very wrong,' she quipped. 'Thanks, Toby, I'll look forward to seeing you and Wallbourne Manor again . . . and Napoleon.'

He looked at her affectionately. 'This girl knows the way to a man's heart,' he said to Nick.

'Does she? That's interesting.'

Bryony returned to her desk, pleased to be going back to Toby's home for another visit, but not at all sure she wanted to make the journey with Nick. Oh, he was nice enough, even with his arrogance, but he was a bit of an enigma. Still, it could prove interesting.

It was a cold October morning when Nick collected Bryony. She saw the car arrive and hurried out, throwing her overnight bag on to the back seat. Sitting beside him she thought how different he looked. In the office he wore a smart business suit; today he was in a polo-neck sweater, slacks and a fawn sheepskin coat. It made him look very dashing and he was driving an MG sports model.

As Bryony started to enthuse to him about MGs and their engine capacity, he was astonished at her knowledge, and her enthusiasm.

'Where on earth did you learn all this, from your father?'

'Of course. We share a love of cars, but I'm a great disappointment to him, I'm afraid.'

'Why's that?'

'He wanted me to go into the business, run his office and, when he retired, to take over. I wasn't interested. Not as a career.'

'And what is your ambition in life, Bryony?'

'I'm not absolutely sure. I have a dream of a big house, horses, antique furniture, artwork, aesthetically pleasing things. I want to get away from the crude, the ugly, and commonplace. Wallbourne Manor is pretty much my ideal. I think it is the most beautiful house, and the grounds are magnificent. The wild life, the flora and the fauna. It's almost perfect to me.'

'Then you had better marry Toby Beckford!'

'Don't be silly, I hardly know him. He's a friend of . . . a friend.' She was going to say 'boyfriend', but James no longer seemed to fit into this category inasmuch as he wasn't constantly on the telephone to her, which was a great disappointment, making Bryony wonder how true were his declarations of love. But today she wouldn't think of that, she'd just enjoy her weekend.

'There's something wonderful about living in the country. The peace and quiet. The space to breathe, the smell of fresh air . . .' she said, as she settled for the journey.

Later, as they drove through the gates of the manor house, Bryony let out a sigh of contentment as she looked around. 'Isn't it beautiful?' she said.

'Indeed it is,' agreed Nick.

As she spoke there were sounds of shots being fired, which made her jump and Nick laugh. 'Peace and quiet, I think you said!'

'I wonder what's going on?'

'Toby is clay pigeon shooting, I would think.' He tooted the car horn as he parked the vehicle and soon after Toby emerged from the garden, a rifle draped over his shoulder.

'Hello, you two, just keeping my eye in.'

As the manservant took command of the luggage, Bryony and Nick followed Toby into the drawing room, where Bryony immediately walked over to the large window to look out over the woodland. To her great delight, the deer were in sight.

Nick came to stand beside her. 'Beautiful, isn't it?'

'How wonderful it must be to live here and look out on this every day of your life.'

'If you could do so, you would end up taking it for granted.'

'I could never do that,' she protested.

'That's because you were not born here.'

Toby joined them. 'You know, I never tire of looking out of this window.'

Bryony gave an I-told-you-so look in Nick's direction. He just grinned back at her and shrugged.

After drinking a welcome cup of coffee, they set off for the stables, and the men were soon deep in conversation as they inspected the two new horses, walking them up and down, feeling fetlocks, examining teeth and going over all the animals' muscles. Bryony eventually wandered off to the box that housed Napoleon. He whinnied as she stopped in front of him.

'Hello, you gorgeous creature,' she said, stroking his nose. 'Those two are talking horses,' she said quietly, 'but you are the most handsome horse here, and don't you believe anything else.' The horse nuzzled her as if he understood.

'Do you flatter your men friends in the same manner?'

Bryony turned around to see Nick leaning against the wall, with a bemused smile and eyes twinkling.

'According to you, I'm virginal so I wouldn't know any men,' she said.

'That's not strictly true,' he said. 'It's how well you know them, that's the point.'

At that moment Toby arrived and said, 'Come on, Bryony, the groom has saddled Tansy. It's time for another lesson.'

Bryony climbed into the saddle and was led by Toby to a practice ring where he attached a lead rein. She loved every moment of her lesson and felt very comfortable on horseback. She listened carefully to his instructions and followed them to the letter.

Toby let her ride back to the stable without the rein, as he walked beside her.

'You really are a natural,' he said. 'I've got a couple of Dad's hunters saddled for Nick and me so we'll go for a hack around the property. You can ride between us.'

Bryony was in heaven. The two men rode slowly at a walking pace, then at a slow trot. Toby instructed Bryony how to rise with the movement of the horse, but he wisely didn't canter.

'Next time,' he told her. Turning to Nick he asked, 'What do you think of my pupil?'

'She rides well. With further instruction, you could be very good,' he told Bryony. 'Perhaps I should take you myself when we are back in Southampton. It would be a pity not to continue. You obviously enjoy it.'

Her smile lit up her face. 'Would you really? That would be great. I'd love to be able to ride really well.'

'I'm trying to persuade Nick to ride for my polo team next season,' said Toby.

'Are you going to?' she asked.

'I might.'

His host grinned broadly. 'We'll go back to the stables and let Bryony off her mount, then she can come and watch us try out the new ponies.'

Bryony watched the two men as they put the ponies through their paces. She had seen Toby compete but she was bewitched as she watched Nick. His control of his horse was enviable and he rode with such daring he made Bryony catch her breath.

Laughing and breathless, the two men eventually pulled their horses up in front of Bryony. It was obvious to her that they were great friends.

After lunch, Toby loaned the pair of them some Wellingtons and took them to one of the farms on the edge of the estate. Whilst he was in conversation with the farmer, Nick and Bryony wandered around, looking at the hens and pigs, and the cows, which were being rounded up for milking.

'What a wonderful life this must be,' she sighed.

'It's very hard work, don't forget,' said Nick. 'Early mornings, and late nights if the cows are calving.'

'Yes, I know all that, but don't you see, it's all honest work. There's no wheeling and dealing here.'

He laughed and said, 'You should go to a cattle auction, Bryony.'

How could she explain? Her father wheeled and dealed every day of his life and she was no fool, she knew that much of his business was illegal. But here things were true, basic even, but clean, without menace. She recalled the scene outside the Silver Dollar Club . . . and she thought of Giles. No, it was a very different life, and she wished that she were part of it.

CHAPTER EIGHTEEN

Harry Burgess had bathed his bruised face each day after the débâcle outside the club, cursing Dan Travis and Sophie Johnson as he did so. Inside the man, the hatred for the two he saw as his enemies was building and he spent every moment plotting his revenge. He walked around the small, shabby, dirty house in the heart of the docklands, muttering to himself.

'Fucking Dan Travis, thinks he's bloody King Pin. Well, have I got some news for him. I wonder if he's heard the saying "the bigger they are, the harder they fall"? I intend to see to that fall!' But choosing how to go about it was the problem.

Burgess, for all his madness, was no fool. He carefully thought out each plot, calculating its success very carefully, before dismissing it for another. He intended to hurt both men where they were most vulnerable. With Johnson it was the young man whom Burgess lusted after, but he wasn't around at the moment, so he would bide his time until the kid showed up again. Travis, of course, had the car lot, which Burgess knew was now under guard during the night, after his visitation there when he was drunk. He deeply regretted that episode, as it had narrowed his opportunity. He would have to think of something else. He was a patient man, he thought, and there was a certain satisfaction to be gained in his twisted mind in the planning of it all.

In the office of Langdon and Associates, there was a slight change in the attitude between Bryony and Nick. She had seen a different side to him whilst they were at Wallbourne Manor. The weekend had been great fun, with the two men joshing with each other.

Not only had Toby given her a riding lesson, but he and Nick had also wanted to teach her the art of clay pigeon shooting. But she'd resisted.

'We'll have to get you trained to join us in the next shoot,' Toby had said when they were alone for a moment in the library.

'Oh no!' she had cried. 'I couldn't possibly shoot live birds.'

'It's part of country living,' he'd explained.

'I know, and I accept that, but I just don't want to take part in it,' she'd persisted. 'I hate the noise. When we were here in summer I made an excuse and left James to it.'

'Have you heard from him lately?' Toby had enquired.

Shaking her head, she'd said, 'No, I haven't.'

'Don't take James too seriously, Bryony,' he'd said quietly. 'I wouldn't like to see you get hurt.'

She hadn't been able to question him further as Nick had joined them, but it made her feel she'd been a fool to trust James in the first place. He had told her he loved her and stupidly she had believed him. Well, she wouldn't be so gullible in the future.

And now back in the office, there was no longer a *frisson* of tension between her and Nick, and when he suggested she accompany him this weekend to some riding stables that he knew to continue with her lessons, she jumped at the chance.

'Do you mind if we make it on Sunday?' she asked. 'Only I promised Dad I would help him out in the office on Saturday. He wants me to give him a hand with his paperwork.'

'That's not a problem. I'll pick you up at ten o'clock on Sunday morning. All right?'

'That'll be fine.'

Dan was relieved to have Bryony help out on the Saturday, as he was behind with his paperwork, and between them they would be able to catch up. He showed her what needed doing and they both set to, concentrating on the job in hand.

'Let's take a break, princess. How about a cup of coffee? My brain is becoming addled at this moment.'

They sat drinking the welcome brew and she told him of her visit to Wallbourne Manor, her riding lessons and the fact that Nick Langdon was taking her riding again on the morrow.

'What happened to young James?' Dan asked. 'I've not seen him around for a while.'

'I imagine he's busy with his studies,' she lied, having seen his picture in *Tatler* several times at various functions – always accompanied by a different débutante.

'Never mind, princess. It's better to have a good look round when you are young. It teaches you about human nature. Never an easy thing. If you have high expectations of everyone, it can be a difficult lesson when you discover that they don't always meet your standards.'

Bryony didn't answer and Dan wisely left his observations there and they continued to work until they had caught up with the backlog, congratulating themselves on the progress that had been made. So tired were they that when eventually, at the end of a long and tiring day, Dan drove out of the car lot with Bryony to go home, neither of them saw Harry Burgess hidden behind some trees across the road, quietly watching their every move.

The following morning, Nick took Bryony to a riding stable at Chilworth, where he was obviously known and where he had booked two horses for them. They walked through pinewoods and quiet roads until Bryony felt comfortable on her mount, then Nick took her back to the stables to a practice ring.

For the next hour he put her through intensive training, until her buttocks were tender, but she didn't complain. She was tired but elated.

When at last he told her to stop, she raised herself

from the saddle using the stirrups and said, 'I don't think I'll ever be able to sit down again!'

Grinning at her he said, 'You'll get used to it in time. Come on, we'll get the horses back, then I'll take you out for a beer and a sandwich.'

'Beer? Don't I at least warrant champagne after all that effort?'

With a sardonic smile he said, 'You've been spoiled by the upper crust, Bryony my dear. Beer and sandwiches or nothing. Take your pick!'

'I could eat a horse!' With eyes wide, she covered her mouth in horror with her hand, as she realised what she'd just said. Quickly patting her horse, she said, 'I didn't mean that, honestly!' Leaning forward she covered the horse's ears and whispered, 'Pretend you didn't hear, please.'

'It would serve you right if he threw you!' Nick protested, pretending to be upset, but the amusement mirrored in his eyes told a different story.

A short drive later found them settled near a log fire in a country pub, with a glass of beer each and cheese and pickle sandwiches.

'Now, Bryony, you must admit this is living!' Nick held up his glass and took a sip of the contents.

She had to agree, it was a good end to a great day. She looked at Nick speculatively. 'You and Toby are firm friends, yet I've never seen you at any of his social gatherings. You play polo, I would have thought you would be one of the in crowd.'

'Spare me from the in crowd, Bryony. I have better things to do with my time.'

There was a certain note of disdain in his voice, which she found hurtful as he was referring to people she liked. 'Yet you went to Wallbourne Manor! Was that a waste of time?'

'Don't get so defensive,' he told her. 'Toby and I were at school together; we're old friends. I just find that some of the in crowd, as you put it, are truly superficial. Rich kids with no real purpose in life.'

'And what is your purpose in life, Nick?'

'To be successful in my field and that is what I am working towards.'

'Not clay pigeon shooting, and polo?'

'Now you're being devious. Those pursuits have their place and I enjoy them, but they're not an integral part of my life. Fortunately, I am not heir to land and estate. That is not all a lot of fun, you know, Bryony. When Toby inherits, he will have enormous challenges ahead of him. I am only too thankful not to be in a situation like his.'

She had to agree. She had grown to love Wallbourne Manor already. The responsibility for its upkeep and the land around it would be a nightmare of enormous proportions.

Two days later, Bryony was working in the office when the receptionist told her there was someone to see her. She was extremely puzzled as to who would come to her place of work, and walked towards the door.

'Hello, Bryony darling.' James Hargeaves stood smiling with an arm full of flowers. 'Sorry I couldn't warn you I was coming. Here, these are for you.' He handed the flowers to her.

She took them with a quiet, 'Thank you, how nice,' and placed them on a nearby table. 'You had better take a seat,' she said.

The receptionist made an excuse and left the reception area, giving Bryony some privacy.

'Well, darling, I must say, you don't seem overly pleased to see me,' he said.

She raised her eyebrows and said, 'What on earth did you expect, James? That I would throw myself into your arms, delighted that at last you found the time to call?'

'I say, that's a bit harsh, isn't it?'

She ignored his remark and asked, 'Why are you here, anyway?'

'I'm free for a couple of days and had hoped we could spend it together somewhere.'

'In bed, you mean?'

He just smiled.

'All your little débutantes busy, are they?'

'I don't know what you mean.'

'According to *Tatler*, you have been doing a lot of socialising and with several different women. You photograph well, James.'

'You know how it is in our circle, Bryony. There is always some social occasion to attend.'

'But not with the woman you profess to love . . . or

209

do you tell all your women that? No doubt it makes them more malleable, more trusting. An easy lay!'

'What on earth has got into you, woman?' he spluttered. 'I've never seen you in this mood.'

'I'm not in a mood, as you put it, my dear James. For once I've come to my senses. I do not want to be just another of your conquests.' Picking up the flowers, she tossed them to him and said, 'Take these and give them to someone else. Someone who will appreciate them, someone who will spend their time with you, because I certainly won't. I have better things to do!'

He looked astonished at her outpourings and, getting to his feet, he said, 'I'm sorry you feel this way, Bryony. I thought we had something special between us.'

'So did I at first. But never mind, it wasn't wasted. I've learned a valuable lesson. Let me show you to the door.'

As she closed it behind him, Bryony was raging to herself about James. How dare he think he could just pick her up and drop her at will? But as she remembered his shocked expression as she threw him out, she grinned broadly and started to laugh. She felt great! And her heart wasn't broken – indeed, she felt strong. Vindicated. True, he had introduced her to the social circle she'd craved, but now she had friends of her own there. Toby and Nick had included her when they had discussed future events, so James, with all his charm, was superfluous to her anyway. It filled her with a certain satisfaction.

Nick, who, unseen by Bryony, was standing in the

doorway, said, 'Well, you sent him packing in no uncertain terms. You do realise he is one of the in crowd?'

'Now he's out!' And she laughed. But walking back to her desk she wondered just how much of the conversation Nick had overheard. If he'd heard enough, he would know she wasn't the virginal girl he had thought she was. This gave her a great deal of pleasure.

As she worked, she looked up from time to time and occasionally caught Nick gazing at her with a speculative expression. Maybe she'd given him something to think about after all.

CHAPTER NINETEEN

Theresa and Bryony were taking their lunch break together, poring over the newspapers, which were full of the news that Princess Margaret had decided not to wed Captain Peter Townsend.

'Well, I think it's a crying shame,' declared Bryony. 'Why shouldn't she be allowed to do so, if he's the man she wants?'

'She's royalty, that's why! When you move in those circles, the rules are different. You must have found that, Bryony, mixing with the toffs as you do.'

She thought for a moment and said, 'I have to be honest, they are different. Yet you see, when they're like Toby, they are somewhat special. He is such a gentleman. If only you could see Wallbourne Manor. It is so beautiful.'

'Is he married?'

'No, and, come to think of it, I'm not sure he has a girlfriend. One has never been mentioned.'

With a sly nudge, Theresa said, 'Well, here's your chance. He sounds as if he can supply everything you have ever wanted – and you like him.'

'Don't be daft! I don't come from the right kind of family. My background wouldn't be nearly good enough.'

'Oh, I don't know,' said Theresa thoughtfully. 'After all, in the twenties and thirties, lots of lords married actresses, or made them their mistresses. What about Lillie Langtry . . . or Nell Gwynn, even? She ended up with royalty!'

'Oh, for goodness' sake, we are living in the twentieth century, and I wouldn't be anyone's mistress. These things don't happen now.'

'You don't read the Sunday papers!'

'And I'm sure they don't have the Sunday scandals in your house,' laughed Bryony.

'But they have them in the hotel.'

'You best be careful then. Your father will have you down confessing to the priest if he hears that.'

Theresa was silent. It had taken her a long time before she was able to enter the confessional after being raped by Lenny Marks, and to this day she'd kept her secret, making her feel a hypocrite to her faith. She'd discussed it with her mother who told her the Lord would forgive her if she asked Him in her prayers, and that she didn't need a priest to do it for her, but it hadn't really solved the issue deep inside.

'What about Nick Langdon?' she asked.

'Yes, he's all right. Nice-looking, plays polo sometimes, but he's not into that world. He told me he thinks it's superficial . . . and I have to confess, he has a point. But at least these people have breeding, good manners, and I do like that.'

'But if they are insincere, what's the point?' asked her friend.

Bryony couldn't explain the difference between their world and hers without giving too much away about her father's unsavoury friends and Dan's somewhat suspect deals. 'Well, I suppose there isn't one!' was all she said.

As Christmas approached Giles's father demanded he return to join the family for the festive season. 'You must be recovered by now,' he declared over the telephone to the villa, 'and you've missed enough of your studies.'

Giles couldn't deny it. He'd lied to his father about his so-called illness and knew that his time in France was at an end. He would stay at home until next term started, when he really would have to work hard. There was no extra money coming from Sophie's generous pockets, so he really had no choice. As it was, he'd had to write to Hugo, his brother, and ask for funds to see him through his stay, although his food was supplied through the generosity of his host, but he did have to tip the two servants before he came home. It was the gentlemanly thing to do, after all. He did still have certain standards, which, when he thought about it, was ironic. He had not been averse to selling himself to fund his gambling, yet a certain decorum when it came to the staff was to be observed at all times. That was what breeding meant. What a world of double standards we live in, he mused.

* * *

Bryony was in high spirits. Her driving lessons had paid off and she had taken her test during her lunch hour one day, passing first time. She swept into the office, throwing her arms around a startled Nick, kissing his cheek, proclaiming, 'I can drive now. I've passed my test!'

He picked her up and swung her round. 'Well done, Bryony. Now what?'

'I want to buy a car, of course!'

'Won't your father do that for you?'

'Certainly not! He told me as much months ago. Besides, I want it to really be mine. I shall arrange monthly terms.' She smiled and, with a tilt of her head, said, 'I might look over a few at the car lot; see what's on offer. I certainly won't go anywhere else. At Dad's I know I won't be swindled.'

'I'll come with you, if you like, when we've finished here.'

'Would you? That would be fun.'

'I am doing it for the safety of the population of Southampton.'

'Whatever do you mean?'

'I don't want you tearing around town in a fast sports car, cutting a swath as you go, without you having a few more hours' practice under your belt.'

With a wide grin she said, 'Oh, ye of little faith!'

Later that afternoon, Nick drove her to the car lot. As he parked his MG, Dan walked out of the office.

Bryony introduced the two men. 'Dad, this is Nick Langdon.'

Shaking his hand, Dan looked at Nick, then at his car and asked, 'Thinking of a trade-in, are you?'

'Absolutely not. I am here to watch over your daughter. She's looking to buy a car.'

Dan turned to Bryony. 'You what?'

'I've passed my driving test, Dad.'

'I didn't even know you were taking it yet!'

'Ah well, you see you don't know everything. I passed today. I'm now a fully fledged driver.'

Looking at Nick, Dan shook his head and said, 'Women! Don't they drive you crazy?'

'All the time,' said Nick.

'Well, princess, I've got just the thing,' Dan began. 'A nice little Morris Minor, not too flash, not too fast.'

'Oh, for goodness' sake . . . you men!' And she walked away, searching among the line of vehicles. She looked at a Vauxhall Wyvern, then a Velox, before moving on to a Triumph TR3.

'You can forget that one,' called Dan. 'You haven't the skill yet to drive that model. She's headstrong, like her mother,' murmured Dan as he and Nick followed her. 'It would have been much simpler to have had a son, I'm sure.'

Nick found this highly amusing. 'My mother always thought the opposite. She would have loved a daughter.'

'What did I tell you? Women – they're never satisfied!'

The two men stood and watched as Bryony surveyed

216

what was on offer, opening doors, sitting in the driver's seat, moving on until she found one that really interested her. A silver Armstrong Siddeley. Turning on the ignition and then lifting the bonnet, she looked at the engine.

Nick said, 'Your daughter is an amazing girl. I've never met anyone quite like her.'

Beaming with pride, Dan said, 'I know. She's her father's daughter!'

'Just now, she took after her mother,' teased Nick.

'Only in some things,' Dan replied with a grin. 'If I'm really honest, my princess is her own woman and it scares the hell out of me.'

A head appeared around the bonnet. 'Dad! How much do you want for this old banger?'

'Banger my arse! You know a good car when you see it so don't try to kid a kidder. Besides, an Armstrong Siddeley is far too powerful for you. It has a two-litre engine!'

'Rubbish. I'm not an idiot; I know what power it has. I'll need to take it out for a run,' she said. 'Nick will come with me, won't you?'

'Of course,' he said, and walked round to the passenger seat of the vehicle.

Dan watched as Bryony drove out of the lot. Whatever next, he thought. My daughter grown up, driving her own vehicle. Where have the years gone? He walked back to his office shaking his head, wondering if he was getting old.

*　　*　　*

'Isn't this great?' asked Bryony with obvious excitement as she drove the car. 'Listen to the purr of the engine.' She quickly changed gear and slowly put her foot down on the accelerator.

Nick watched the speedometer go higher and higher. But Bryony was competent at the wheel so he let her have her head. She slowed down as they approached the brow of a hill, then when she'd driven down it; she went round a roundabout and headed back to the town.

'Well, what do you think?' she asked.

'Seems all right,' Nick conceded. 'I'll take a look at the engine when we get back and see if I agree with you.'

'I'll ask Dad's mechanics to service it for me.'

'You've decided then?'

'Oh, yes, this car has my name written all over it!'

'Are you always so impulsive?' he asked.

'Is that a bad thing?'

'Sometimes. Sometimes a little thought and time can save a lot of heartache.'

She immediately thought of James Hargreaves. She had tumbled headlong into an affair with him, but at least she wasn't heartbroken. But she did remember how awful she'd felt in the beginning when he didn't call her. He'd used her and she had been a willing partner. It was all part of growing up, she supposed. Thank God she hadn't got pregnant. James had seen to that. But of course he would, wouldn't he? With his string of women, the last thing he would want was one carrying a child. That would be the end to his philandering!

218

'Come back, Bryony!' Nick's sharp reminder brought her back to the present. 'If you're at the wheel of a car that is no time to go off into deep thoughts!' he chided. 'Keep your concentration on the road, if you don't mind, especially when I'm your passenger. This isn't a toy, you know!'

Laughing, she apologised. 'Sorry, I was miles away and you're right. Well, here we are. I'll park the car and go and bargain with my father.'

'That should be interesting. I'll look at the engine, then wait in the MG for you.' He watched as she walked to the office, her hair flowing in the wind, a bounce in her step. He thanked God he was not in her father's shoes because he bet that Bryony Travis had always been a handful to manage. As he thought about it, he found the idea very appealing and started chuckling to himself.

Somewhat later, she emerged beaming all over her face, with Dan behind her. They walked to Nick's car.

Getting out of the driver's seat, he said to Dan, 'Who won?'

With a grimace Dan said, 'If all my customers were like her I'd be broke!' But nevertheless he smiled affectionately at his daughter. 'I'll see to the insurance. You can take it tomorrow . . . but you be careful!' Turning to Nick, he asked, 'Do you think she's all right in this car, not too much for her?'

Nick shook his head. 'She handles it well.'

Kissing her father's cheek, she said, 'Now don't start. I'm a good driver.'

'She'll be fine,' Nick assured Dan. 'Let's face it, she understands more about a car's engine than most men!'

As they drove away, Dan thought to himself, now that is a real man. Someone who could handle Bryony, and that is exactly what she needs . . . but not yet. She is still so young.

He found this growing up very confusing and unsettling. He was learning that he had to let her have her head – but not too much.

CHAPTER TWENTY

Harry Burgess eventually hatched a plan. If he had his way he'd top Dan Travis, but he was no fool and didn't want to see himself at the end of a rope or serving a long prison sentence, so he had to be satisfied with getting his own back in any way he could.

He knew from keeping watch that the car lot was now patrolled at night, except for a certain time when the guard slipped across the road for a quick pint. Travis would go ballistic if he knew. The fact that big Dan was being tricked was a great joke as far as Harry was concerned, but it gave him a fifteen-minute break in the surveillance to get inside the area. Not long at all, but just long enough to slip a thin but strong trip wire across one of the top steps leading to Dan's office. Harry had devised a small contraption, which allowed him, from a hidden position behind the building, to tighten the wire when he wanted. From the shadows he waited until the watchman crossed the road to the pub, then he carried out his plan, leaving immediately and undetected.

* * *

The following late afternoon, when it was dark, Harry slipped into position behind the office, hidden in the undergrowth, awaiting his opportunity, after checking, making sure that Dan was working alone.

Harry held his breath as footsteps approached, but they passed by. He heard the office door open and Dan call out to one of his men.

'Did you get that rear axle fixed on that Ford?'

'I had a bit of a problem, guv,' called the man in reply.

Dan cursed to himself and as he descended the steps, Burgess pulled tight, and waited.

There was a loud yell from above, and a heavy clatter as Dan Travis fell all the way down the steps. His cries of pain brought members of his staff running.

Harry Burgess slipped away in all the confusion and watched from across the road.

'Oh, my bloody ankle,' moaned Dan.

'Can you move, guv?' asked one employee.

'I've done my bleeding ankle in and my arm feels odd. I think I've dislocated my shoulder. Call an ambulance, will you?'

Harry watched with glee as the ambulance arrived and big Dan was carted away, but when he saw Jack, the head salesman and Dan's right-hand man, slowly searching the area where he'd hidden, he thought it prudent to leave.

Jack picked up a piece of wire and saw it had been snapped off in the fall. He then found the other end and, seeing it was attached to something, started to investigate with the aid of a strong torch.

'He's been got at!' he muttered to himself, and started to sweep the area with the torchlight. He found the ground behind the office was flattened as if someone had been there. His eyes narrowed as he wondered just who it had been. Dan would not be a happy man when he was told of this.

But at that moment Dan Travis, being examined by a doctor in the casualty department of the hospital, was in too much pain to care about anything else.

Leila had been called and had rushed off to the hospital to see what was happening. When she was told her husband was having X-rays, she rang Bryony at the office to tell her.

Bryony was beside herself with worry, and Nick, in an effort to calm her, drove her to the hospital.

'Would you like me to come in with you?' he asked.

Her face was white and pinched. 'Oh, Nick, would you?' They made their way inside together and, after enquiring at the desk, found where Leila was waiting.

'What happened, Mum? How's Dad?'

'He fell down the steps outside the office; he said he tripped over something. The doctors are looking to see if his ankle is broken and his shoulder dislocated.'

'Oh my God!'

'I know it's a shock, ladies,' Nick chimed in, trying to be of comfort, 'but broken bones do heal. They are not necessarily life threatening. I've broken a few myself in my time.'

'This is Nick Langdon, Mum.'

Leila nodded in his direction. 'Let's hope you're right, Mr Langdon.'

And so, a few hours later, it was proved to be the case. Dan was to go into the theatre to have his shoulder reset and his ankle set and put in plaster of Paris.

'What about the business?' asked Dan. 'I'm liable to be out for weeks.'

'Oh, for heaven's sake, the business can take care of itself,' snapped Leila, still in shock.

'No it bloody well can't,' Dan insisted.

'I'll take over, Dad,' said Bryony firmly. 'I know how to keep your accounts and I know how to run the fore-court.'

'You can't do that!' he said, alarmed at the sugges-tion.

'I can and I will.'

The argument couldn't continue as the nurses came to take Dan to the theatre.

'I'll wait until he's had his operation, Mum,' said Bryony, 'and then I'll go and sort out the business. Don't you worry about a thing.'

'Come with me, Bryony, and we'll find some coffee for your mother,' Nick suggested. And as they walked away, he said, 'Are you sure you want to do this for your father?'

'What else can I do, Nick? He has always wanted me to run the business and I refused. Now I have to, for his sake.'

'What about your job with us?'

'I'll have to leave, unless you let me have this time free.'

'I'll have to get someone in your place, Bryony. You know how busy we are. I can't do without help for weeks on end.'

She was hurt by his remarks, even knowing that he spoke the truth, but hoping for some leeway.

'I am sorry, Bryony.'

'I understand, really I do. What happens when Dad is well enough to come back? What then, Nick?'

'We'll have to wait and see. There is no way of knowing how long this can take. When your dad is fit and well, we'll have to review the situation.'

Bryony suddenly realised how much she would miss the office, but, even more, seeing Nick, whom she liked and admired.

'We won't lose touch, will we?'

There was such a lost tone to her voice that Nick took her into his arms and held her close. 'No, of course not,' he said. 'I'll pop by to see you.' He tilted her chin and said, 'You are jumping into the deep end taking on the car lot. If you need me ever, just give me a call,' and he kissed her upturned mouth softly.

Bryony gazed into his eyes, not moving away from his hold. Indeed, at this moment she didn't want to be anywhere else. Within his arms she felt safe and secure. But the effect his kiss had on her was staggering. It was probably meant as a friendly gesture, she told herself, yet she wanted him to do it again and with passion.

She wanted to throw her arms around him and tell him how she felt! But she didn't, of course. She stepped back.

'Thanks, Nick. Let's go and find that coffee, shall we?'

When, a short time later, he returned to the office, Nick sat at his desk, lost in thought. He hoped that Bryony wasn't taking on more than she could handle. He admired her spirit, but he was concerned about the pressure she'd be under. Dan Travis was a formidable businessman; she would be pushed to maintain his standard. Apart from all this, he was going to miss her. She was an asset to him and his father; she fitted in so well, and had such a natural talented eye for a presentation. But it was more than that . . . and he'd not realised it until he'd kissed her. The girl had got under his skin. Christ! He was seven years her senior! What was he thinking of? He turned to his drawings and tried to concentrate, but all he could see were her tear-filled eyes, looking at him.

Leila and Bryony waited for Dan to come out of surgery and into the recovery room. It was suggested they return later when he had come round from the anaesthetic.

'He'll be a bit woozy for a while anyway,' said the surgeon.

'I'll go to the car lot,' said Bryony to her mother, 'and let them know what's happened. I'll come back later and meet you here.'

'Yes, I'll go home and freshen up,' said Leila. 'It has all been such a shock; it will give me time to sort myself out. I'll have to bring pyjamas and stuff in for your father. Towels, and things. You know how fussy he is.'

With a wry smile Bryony said, 'Yes. I don't envy the nursing staff when he feels a bit better.'

Bryony called a taxi to take her to collect her car, then made for the car lot. She took a deep breath, knowing that she was in for a difficult time, at least to begin with. Jack wouldn't take kindly to her being in charge. Well, he'd have to get used to it, as would all the others. She wasn't her father's daughter for nothing!

She called all the forecourt staff and Jack into her father's office. Sitting at his desk she faced them. 'My father has a broken ankle and a dislocated shoulder, which has been put back but, of course, he'll be in hospital for some time, and even after, he'll be out of action.'

There was a murmuring among the men.

'I will be taking his place until he is better.'

'There's no need to trouble yourself,' said Jack. 'We know what has to be done. Besides, you already have a job.'

'I quit this afternoon and I believe I do need to be here. Tomorrow I'll go through everything and I want each of you to give me your latest paperwork on sales and any other work in hand, and we'll go from there.'

She could see Jack about to speak.

'Thank you, gentlemen. That's all.' She rose to her

feet. 'I'm going back to the hospital to talk to my father – he should have come round by now. I'll see you all in the morning.'

As she walked down the steps she looked carefully at them and asked, 'What did my father trip over – did anyone find out?'

'Someone put a trip wire across the step,' said Jack, and he watched for her reaction.

'Are you telling me that this was a deliberate act and not an accident?' Her eyes flashed with anger.

'Yes.'

'Any idea who would do such a thing?'

'As a matter of fact I do, but I would suggest you don't tell your father.'

'I wouldn't dream of it! We'll talk about this tomorrow. But I suggest you check the security to make sure it is as stringent as it should be.'

'I'm looking into it.'

'Good, because I want that person found. I'll see you in the morning.' And she walked towards her car.

Jack Saunders watched her with mixed feelings. He couldn't help but admire her. She had the old man's spirit, all right, but he was not pleased the running of the place was not to be left to him. There were things going on here that Dan wouldn't want his daughter to know about, and how the hell were they to keep them from her?

CHAPTER TWENTY-ONE

When Bryony returned to the hospital, her father was in a small private room – alone and asleep. She looked down at the man who was usually a strong towering presence and was frightened to see how pale he was. Despite his build, there was now a sudden frailness about him. To see Dan so helpless, knowing it was at the hand of someone and not an accident, filled her with an overpowering anger. How dare anyone do this to him? He could have been killed! Who would hate him enough to do such a thing? But as she pondered over this, she knew that there were probably several who might welcome his downfall. Her father dealt with some very dangerous people; she'd seen this for herself, working for him. She frowned at the memory. She couldn't have this; no one was to be allowed to get away with such treachery.

A nurse entered the room and, seeing the look of anxiety on Bryony's face, said, 'He's come round from the anaesthetic and is sleeping, so just be patient. He'll wake later.'

'Is he going to be all right?'

Laying a hand on Bryony's shoulder, she assured her, 'He'll be fine. Your father is as strong as an ox.'

'He doesn't look it at the moment. I've never seen him so helpless.'

Chuckling softly, the nurse said, 'Then enjoy every minute, dear. Men are not good patients. He'll make himself heard all in good time.' And picking up a water jug, she left the room.

Smiling to herself, Bryony thought how well the nurse knew her job, as she was sure that Dan would be a headache as he recovered.

She took his hand in hers and whispered, 'Don't you worry, Dad, I'll take care of the business . . . and the bastard who did this – when I do find out who was responsible.'

Later in the evening, Bryony left her mother to sit beside Dan, saying she had business to attend to, and once inside her car, she sat deep in thought for several minutes before starting the engine, a look of grim determination on her face as she drove towards the docks. She was on a mission and knew just the place to start her search.

Bryony caused quite a stir when she stepped inside the Silver Dollar Club for the first time. She strode up to the bar, cast a glance around the room and asked the barman for a gin and tonic.

'You're big Dan's girl, ain't ya?' asked the man behind the counter.

'That's right.'

'I heard he's in the hospital. Sorry to hear that. He gonna be all right, love?'

'Yes, eventually. He broke his ankle but that will heal soon enough.'

'What you doing in here, my girl? This ain't the place for a lady like you.'

'I'm looking for any friends of my father.'

At that moment Sophie Johnson walked in. Bryony recognised him from the night of the fracas outside the club when her father gave Giles and this man a lift in his car. Johnson recognised her too, and walked over.

'Well, if it isn't Miss Travis herself. How's your father?'

After he'd been updated on Dan's condition, Sophie asked, 'What are you doing here? I imagine you have an ulterior motive for the visit.'

'What makes you say that?'

'Now, darling, don't treat me like a fool. This isn't your sort of place, but it is your father's, yet he's in hospital, so . . . there has to be something else to bring you here. What is it – information?'

Bryony laughed and said, 'Is it that obvious?'

Sophie just smiled at her and suggested they sit quietly in a corner. Once they were settled he stared intently at her and said, 'Look, darling, me and your dad are good mates. We trust one another, so what's your problem?'

'Dad's fall was no accident. Someone set up a trip wire. I want to know who it was, and why.'

'Does the why matter?'

'It might, it might not, but I would still like to know.'

231

'And if I find out the culprit, what are you going to do about it?'

Chewing on her bottom lip, Bryony said, 'I'm not sure at this moment, but I *will* pay him back, that is for certain.'

'What makes you so sure it was a man? It might have been a woman.'

Her eyes narrowed as she thought about it. Then, looking up at Sophie, she said, 'No, this person is definitely male. A woman would use other methods.'

'Well, young lady, how long have you been in the game to come to such conclusions? Studied psychology, have you?'

'Women are born psychologists, but no one hurts a member of my family and gets away it, male or female.'

'Now I don't want you doing something that might get you into trouble. Dan would do his nut if I let that happen, so I suggest when we find out who the bastard is – and we will – you let me deal with him.'

'Why? Dad isn't your relation!'

'True, Bryony, but I owe your father a couple of favours; it would be a pleasure to settle up with him. By the way, does he know he was set up?'

Shaking her head, she said, 'No, as yet no one has told him.'

'Best not, until it's all settled and he's out and about. No need to worry him any further. I'll ask around, and when I learn something I'll let you know.'

'Please, I would be grateful. But as far as dealing with the matter, I'll settle the score myself, thank you. You can contact me at the car lot. I'm running it until Dad is fit.'

'Are you indeed?' He gave a sly grin. 'What does Jack think of that?'

'Not a great deal,' laughed Bryony, 'but he'll get used to it.'

'Good for you! You put your foot down, my girl.'

Rising from the seat, Bryony held out her hand. 'Thank you . . . I'm sorry, I don't know your name.'

'Sophie, Sophie Johnson.' He took her hand and bent to kiss her fingers. 'You ever need me, darling, leave a message at the bar.'

'Thanks, I'll remember that.'

As she walked towards the door, a young man stepped forward and caught hold of her arm. 'Not leaving, darlin', are you?'

Looking at him coldly, she asked, 'What's it to do with you, may I ask?'

'Oh my, how very posh. I like that. Let me buy you a drink, love.'

She took hold of his hand and removed his hold. 'Thank you, but no thank you. I'm off to meet my father, Dan Travis. Do you know him?'

The man immediately backed off. 'Sorry, miss, no offence meant.'

'We all make mistakes, and that was yours,' she retorted. Then turning away, she left the bar.

Sophie, who had been ready to intervene, stayed quiet as he listened to her put the man in his place. That was Dan's girl all right!

*　　*　　*

When Dan eventually awoke it was to see his wife and daughter by his bedside. 'You don't have to look so worried,' he said. 'I haven't croaked yet!'

They both laughed, mostly with relief that their man seemed more like himself.

'How do you feel, darling?' asked Leila.

'As if I've been hit by a ten-ton truck. I ache everywhere.' He cast a glance towards the bottom of the bed where a cage had been placed to keep the weight off his foot. Shaking his head, he said, 'Who'd believe such a thing would happen to me! I damn well tripped. If I find one of the men left something on the stairs I'll have *his* bloody ankles!'

'Calm down, Dan,' said Leila sharply. 'There's nothing to be done about it, so just take the opportunity to rest. The sooner you do, the sooner you'll be up and about.'

'I need to see Jack about the business,' he fretted.

'No need, Dad. I've got leave from Langdon's and I've taken over the car lot. All the men know. I had them all in the office for a chat.' With a smile Bryony added, 'Just as well we got all the paperwork up to date – it will make it easier to start with.' As her father went to speak she said firmly, 'After all, you had wanted me to eventually run the business, so here I am.'

'But you enjoyed your work,' he said. 'Besides, what do they say at Langdon's about giving you time off?'

'When you are better I'll go back, but I'm free indefinitely.' She didn't tell him the prospect of going back to Langdon's was in doubt.

'But I still need to have a word with Jack,' Dan persisted. 'We have other business interests, you know.'

'And what are they?' Bryony asked.

'Those are not for you to know, princess; they're between Jack and me. We're partners in other concerns.'

Bryony left her parents together and went to the car lot. She decided to take a quiet walk around the cars and check what was in stock. It was a quiet weekday. Two of the salesmen were polishing a Humber Hawk, unaware of her presence nearby.

'Whoever did this to the boss is in the shit if big Dan ever finds him.'

'Or the missis. She taught that bleeder Lenny Marks a lesson.'

Bryony stopped to listen.

'What you talking about?' asked the other man.

'You haven't heard? Christ, it was the story of the month. I don't know what he did to upset her but she used a stock whip on him!'

'Bloody hell!'

'Not only that, she had him stripped naked before she started. She nearly bloody castrated the bugger!'

The man looked incredulous. 'What, Mrs Travis did that?'

Grinning broadly, the other man said, 'Yes, honest. I'd have paid money to see that. I can't stand that rotten little toad. Mind you, I've heard he's been pretty quiet lately.'

The men picked up their cleaning rags and moved away.

Leaning against one of the cars, Bryony went over the conversation again and again. And still she couldn't believe it – even later, sitting with her mother in the kitchen of their house, discussing Dan's condition.

'You do realise it was no accident, don't you, Mother?'

'I wondered, but how do you know that?'

'Jack found that someone had placed a trip wire across the stairs.'

Eyebrows raised, Leila said, 'Did they now? We really can't have that sort of thing happening. It's bad for the family name. Do you know who did it?'

'Not yet, but I have a few feelers out and I will find out.'

'And then what?' Leila looked at her daughter with interest. Her answer surprised her.

'I thought I would get a few hints from you, Mother dear. I hear you are pretty good with a stock whip!'

Leila tried to keep a straight face once she'd recovered from the surprise. 'Yes, I'm bloody good, I'll have you know. Where did you get your information from, might I ask?'

With a casual shrug of her shoulders, Bryony said, 'Local gossip. Whatever did the man do?'

'That is none of your business but, believe me, it warranted the punishment. The rest is confidential.'

Bryony sat looking at her mother, thinking: there is so much I really don't know about you.

Yes, as a mother she knew her well, remembering the cuddles when as a child she fell over or was unwell,

236

the domestic side, the cooking, cleaning, the support at school concerts, where Leila nearly always outshone the other mothers with her flamboyance, sometimes to Bryony's embarrassment, and she knew her in the role of the wife of her father . . . but now – who was this woman who could horsewhip a naked man and not bat an eye?

Under such scrutiny, Leila looked at her daughter and asked, 'What?'

'You are quite a surprise to me, Mother dear!'

Leila laughed uproariously until the tears ran down her cheeks. 'You should see the look on your face!' she said. 'Children are all the same,' she said. 'They look at their parents and they see just exactly what they want to. They never delve beneath the mother or father's skin to look for the real person.' Wiping away the tears of laughter, she added, 'Maybe that is just as well. They might not like what they find. As for this miscreant, whenever he's found, I don't want you involved.'

Bryony was furious. 'Why ever not?'

'Because your father wants you to be a lady. That's why he sent you to the convent, and that's why you will leave the other to me.'

'But you may get into trouble.'

Leila sat and stared at Bryony. 'You're old enough not to be a fool, darling. Your father and I have dealt with many things in the past – you know he's not whiter than white – but I don't want you involved. You run the car lot and keep that bastard Jack in line. The rest is mine. Understand?'

Bryony looked at her mother with admiration shining in her eyes. Everyone admired big Dan Travis, but Bryony was only just beginning to see the driving force behind the man.

That night, as she lay between the sheets, Bryony thought how strange that, because of her father's fall, she was beginning to see her family in an entirely different light. And she wondered what secrets she would discover during her time at the car lot, whilst her father was indisposed. Was she prepared to learn even more?

CHAPTER TWENTY-TWO

Dan Travis did his best to keep his daughter ignorant of his murky dealings by summoning Jack Saunders to the hospital, where the two of them planned the strategy of the immediate future, until Dan was back in charge of the business.

'How are you finding my girl?' Dan asked with a knowing smile.

Scratching his head, Jack reluctantly admitted, 'Well, she's got her head screwed on all right; I'll say that for her. The other day some bright spark thought he could pull a fast one on her when she was selling him a car. You know how men think: a girl knows nothing about cars. Well, honestly, Dan, it was lovely to watch. She took him apart, piece by piece. Firstly over the engine: she walked round him in circles with her knowledge – she blinded him with science. In the end he didn't know if he was coming or going. He paid over the odds too! And do you know what that minx did?'

Grinning from ear to ear, Dan said, 'No, what?'

'As she took his money she looked over his shoulder at me and winked! Cheeky little bitch.'

Dan roared with laughter. 'A chip off the old block, my boy, a chip off the old block.' Then, looking at his partner in crime, he said, 'Best not have any dodgy cars in for respraying whilst she's around. She's so enthusiastic about motors, she's always getting involved, trying to learn something new.'

'Well, she's keeping the men on their toes, I can tell you.'

'And how do you two get on?'

With a shrug, Dan's man said, 'We make do. I don't know why she took over; I could have handled things.'

'Of course you could, I know that, but she was hell-bent on stepping into my shoes and, to be honest, Jack, I was proud of her for doing so. She's even put her job on hold for me – how could I throw that back in her face?'

'Yes, I understand.' But he didn't inform Dan that his fall wasn't an accident. Bryony had made him swear not to let her father know.

'He'll only fret about it,' she'd said. 'I don't want that. When he's better is a different thing. Understand?'

'Perfectly. But God help whoever it was when Dan does find out.'

God help whoever when she and her mother found out, thought Bryony. But she kept this to herself.

Harry Burgess was keeping a low profile. He had done what he set out to, bringing the big man down . . . literally. Flat on his back! He chortled to himself. He was really pleased too. Dan Travis was so full of himself. Well, the bigger they are, the harder they fall. However, he knew that Jack Saunders had seen his little trap and he also knew that people would be sniffing around. It was common knowledge that he and Dan had crossed swords so he would have to be careful.

Sophie Johnson was not so easily fooled and from the first had Burgess down as the culprit, but at this moment he had more pressing things on his mind. He'd heard from his contacts in London that Giles had been seen around. It appeared he'd taken off to France for a while. Sophie decided to take the train to the city and find out more about his reluctant lover.

Sophie took a taxi from Waterloo Station to the fashion house run by his ex-boyfriend Tarquin, whom he had financed in the beginning of his career and who paid him a handsome yearly dividend on his investment.

'Darling!' Tarquin warmly greeted Sophie when he arrived at the salon. 'How lovely to see you. Come into the office and I'll send for some coffee.'

The two men sat and discussed, first of all, the yearly figures and success of the business, before getting down to the local gossip, which Sophie always loved.

'I had that bitch of a duchess in again last week. Well, who does she think she is? Her bust comes into the shop before she does and she wants me to dress her like a young girl. Really! I told her, please . . . let's be realistic!'

'And she still comes?'

'Of course! She wants to wear my clothes; frankly I wish she'd go back to Norman Hartnell. How long are you in town for, Sophie?'

'Why?'

'I'm having a cocktail party here tomorrow night. I'm introducing a new, prior-to-Christmas range. You should be here.'

'Who else is coming?'

'Some of my clients, a few members of the aristocracy . . .'

'Giles – will he be coming?'

'I don't know. I heard he was back in town. Would you like him to be here? Shall I invite him?'

'Yes,' said Sophie, 'but don't mention I'll be around.'

Raising his eyebrows, Tarquin asked, 'Had a row, have you?'

'Not exactly. He just took off.'

Staring hard at his benefactor, Tarquin said, 'And why would he do that, Soph? Did you scare him away? I know you, you old bugger. I won't bring him here if you mean to harm him. I won't be responsible for that.'

'Harm him? I love the little bleeder, why would I harm him?'

Tarquin's eyes narrowed as he looked at Sophie, trying to judge the man's state of mind. 'His mother, Lady Sinclair, is coming. I don't want her embarrassed!'

'Of course not. Would I do that to you?'

'It would not be wise, Sophie. I would have you removed discreetly from the premises and that would bring our partnership and friendship to an end.' Tarquin had dropped his usual camp demeanour and Sophie saw the steely side to his character, which his clients were not aware of but which made the young man the success he was. He knew his image was all part of the business, but he was astute and as ruthless as Sophie.

Placing his hand on Tarquin's arm, Sophie assured him, 'I will be dressed to the nines and my manners will be impeccable – I promise.'

'Have you got a dinner jacket at the flat, or do you need one of mine?'

Shaking his head, Sophie said, 'No, I'm all fixed up. What time tomorrow?'

'Seven o'clock.' Looking at his watch, Tarquin said, 'I must get on, darling, sorry.'

Sophie rose from his seat and kissed the young man on his cheek. 'I'm really proud of you, you know. You have come a long way since you were that long straggly-haired youth. When I look at you now it's hard to imagine that Bert Haines ever existed.'

Tarquin's hands covered his face in horror. 'I don't *ever* want to hear that name on your lips again. It would completely ruin my credibility!'

As Sophie Johnson left the building he smiled to himself. Scruffy little Bert Haines, who spent hours drawing frocks, suits and exquisite dinner gowns at his kitchen table. He felt proud to think he was the one to recognise his talent, but the boy had done really well. Far better than any expectation that Sophie had of him, so of course he would never put that success and hard work at risk by his jealous behaviour. But he knew that if Giles were at the fashion show, it would take all his willpower to play it cool. He also knew that unless he was very clever, he would lose Giles for good, and that would break his heart.

He made his way to his small flat near Portobello Road, which he used occasionally and where he kept a couple of suits, shirts, changes of underwear and a dinner jacket. It had only one bedroom, but it suited his needs if he had business in the city, and he'd bought it years ago at a good price. It was another good investment, he told himself as he walked around, opening a window here and there to air it.

At seven o'clock the following evening, people started to gather at the salon and partake of the champagne on offer before taking their seats to watch the fashion show. Sophie stood at the back of the room in the gloom of the lowered lights. The catwalk was well lit and Tarquin's models strutted down the red carpet, stopping, turning, twisting, and showing off the exquisite gowns, to the commentary of the compere, who was extolling their fashion points.

Sophie searched the rows of patrons until his gaze rested on two seats in the front row. He immediately recognised the blond head of his young lover and saw Giles speak to a very smartly dressed older woman, who Sophie assumed, from her stately bearing, was his mother. As she turned towards Giles, the likeness between mother and son was unmistakable and Sophie's breath caught in his throat as he watched them.

He ached with the need to rush forward and embrace the young man. God, how he had missed the young tyke! But he knew he had to be very careful. There was no way in which he could betray their relationship. Homosexuality was illegal so that it was dangerous to be perceived as homosexual, except for the likes of Tarquin, who was acceptable in the world of fashion and whose effeminate manner indeed added to his cachet.

When the show was ended, the chairs were removed, which allowed the patrons to move around the room, eat the canapés and drink more champagne and view the models.

Sophie moved forward, took a glass of bubbly from the waitress and strolled over towards Tarquin, who was speaking to Giles and his mother. Seeing Sophie approach, Tarquin beckoned him over and introduced him to Lady Sinclair.

'Mr Johnson is my sleeping partner, your ladyship. He was the man who helped get me started in the business.'

She smiled at Sophie and, holding out her hand, shook his. 'Then we should all be grateful to you, Mr Johnson. I love Tarquin's clothes. This is my son Giles.'

Giles was rigid with fright. The colour drained from his face as he looked at Sophie.

'How do you do, Giles?' said Sophie, shaking his trembling hand. 'It's easy to see where this young man inherited his good looks, madam,' he said smoothly.

Tarquin intervened. 'Lady Sinclair, if you come with

me, I have the most divine frock that would be perfect for you.'

Left together, Sophie said quietly, 'Hello, Giles my dear boy. How are you?'

Giles recovered quickly and, with eyes bright with both fear and anger, said, 'What the hell are you doing here?'

'That's not very polite, and you with such a good upbringing should know better. I am here as Tarquin's partner. Looking after my assets. I hear you have been staying in France.'

'Who have you been talking to?' asked Giles, a note of panic in his voice.

'I don't discuss my private life with anyone,' snapped Sophie. 'It was just mentioned in a normal conversation about people.' He paused. 'Why did you run away, Giles?'

'You damned well know why! What you did to that man . . . cutting off his finger, and then that dreadful fellow who tried to abduct me . . . what did you expect?'

Putting his hand on Giles's arm, Sophie said softly, 'I would never let anyone harm you, you should know that. I love you, Giles. You are very special to me.'

Shaking off his hold, the young man said, 'For God's sake, keep your voice down.' He looked furtively around.

'No one can hear me. Just relax. I won't give our secret away.'

At that moment Lady Sinclair and Tarquin returned. 'Come along, Giles. We have to meet your father.'

Turning to Sophie, she said, 'You must excuse us. It was nice meeting you.'

Watching them leave, Sophie said to Tarquin, 'Look at him! He can't get away quickly enough.'

With a sad expression his friend said, 'It's over, Soph. Can't you see? He doesn't want it to go on any longer.'

'But I do!' snapped Sophie, and he walked out of the salon.

It was the week before Christmas and Dan was allowed home. He used a walking stick to enable him to get about, but his foot and ankle were encased in plaster. His shoulder was still sore and he was receiving treatment from a physiotherapist. Frustrated at not being able to work, as the stairs to the office were more than he could manage, his temper was short. Bryony was relieved to be able to leave him to it as she drove to the car lot.

Sitting at her father's desk, she was surprised when there was a knock on her door and Nick Langdon came into the office.

'Nick! How lovely to see you. How are you?'

'Fine. More to the point, how are you?'

'Oh, you know, slogging away. Trying to keep out of Dad's way.'

'Is he getting better?'

'Yes, thanks, and he's itching to get back to work. But it will be a few more weeks yet until the plaster is removed and he can make the steps up here.'

'Never mind, it will soon be Christmas and at least you'll have a break. I don't suppose you are very busy at the moment, are you?'

Shaking her head she said, 'No. This is not the time of year to buy a car.'

'Have you made any plans for the Christmas festivities?'

'To be honest, I've not thought about it, except for flying around buying gifts for family and friends.'

'How about coming down to Wallbourne Manor for Christmas? Toby is having a few people round and he's asked if you will come.'

'Are you going?'

He smiled at her and said, 'Yes I am, as a matter of fact.'

With twinkling eyes she teased him. 'I thought you hated that sort of thing.'

He grinned at her. 'How well you remember. You are quite right, but there are to be only a few people and I want to join the hunt on Boxing Day. What do you say? I could take you down with me.'

As she looked at him, Bryony thought she couldn't think of anything she would like more. 'I'll have to ask my parents,' she said. 'You know what families are like about Christmas. I'll call you tomorrow – will that be all right?'

'Fine.' He walked to the door and paused. 'Try and come, Bryony. I've really missed you.'

She listened to his footsteps as he went down the outside stairs. She was stunned. Nick Langdon had missed her! She pictured his face, the way his mouth curved, and realised that she had missed him too. More than she had realised.

She'd been so busy keeping tabs on the car business, worrying about her father, she'd not had time to think, but after seeing Nick she realised that she was only filling in time, doing her duty as she thought. It would be awful if eventually she was unable to return to the office, and Nick Langdon.

CHAPTER TWENTY-THREE

When Bryony arrived home that evening, she approached her mother about going down to Wallbourne Manor for the Christmas holiday.

'Nick Langdon is going and he said he would take me with him. Would you and Dad mind if I went?'

'Of course not,' said Leila. 'You have been a brick, giving up your job to run the business. You've earned the break.'

'What about Dad – do you think he'll mind?'

'You leave your father to me.'

Dan couldn't argue with his wife's logic, and he was grateful to Bryony for working so hard during his stay in hospital, and so on the afternoon of Christmas Eve, Bryony was packed, suitcase in the hall, waiting for Nick to arrive.

As the front door bell rang Leila hugged her daughter. 'Have a lovely time,' she said. 'Don't worry about coming back to open up. Jack can take care of that. Business is slack, anyway.'

'Thanks, Mum.'

Dan hobbled into the hall and Bryony kissed him goodbye. 'Now don't try to run before you can walk, Dad,' she warned.

'If only,' said Dan. 'I have really appreciated what you've done, princess. Have a good time.'

He shook hands with Nick when Bryony opened the door. 'You take good care of my girl,' he said.

'I'll guard her with my life,' said Nick, smiling.

'Where's your white horse?' asked Bryony, chuckling softly, and at Nick's puzzled look she said, 'You sounded like a knight without his armour.'

As they walked down the path he said, 'Be happy I'm not the dragon in disguise!'

'Well, we who've worked with you in the office all know that you are capable of breathing fire!'

He looked mildly offended. 'How can you say that? You have never seen me in a temper!'

'True, but I have seen you get angry when things were not working.'

'That was my artistic temperament,' he retorted. But his eyes twinkled.

As they neared their destination, it began to snow. 'How wonderful!' said Bryony. 'A white Christmas.'

Nick started to take off Bing Crosby singing the famous song and he was very good at it, but when he started, 'Bub a bub boo . . .' in the manner of the crooner, Bryony collapsed in a fit of the giggles.

'Oh, for goodness' sake stop! My stomach is aching.'

251

She wiped away the tears of laughter with her hand-kerchief.

'That's not the attitude at all,' Nick remonstrated. 'You should be overcome with emotion. After all, in the films, Bing always gets the girl!'

'Then you must be doing something wrong!'

When eventually they arrived at their destination, the snow lay thickly over the ground. The barren trees against the white background were stark but with a beauty of their own. In the distance stood a herd of deer, the stag, with his huge antlers, looking proud and majestic.

Bryony let out a sigh of contentment. 'I just love this place. Whatever the season, it is absolutely splendid.'

Jarvis took their luggage and led them into the main hall. Bryony paused in front of the log fire and drank in every detail. The room was tastefully decorated with holly, ivy and coloured baubles, with a wonderful swag across the mantelpiece. Tall candlesticks were lit and cast dancing shadows on the high walls with its hanging tapestries and ancestral paintings. To her it was warm, inviting, elegant – and exquisite.

'Don't you just love it?' she asked Nick, her face aglow with delight.

'Not as much as you,' he teased. 'I have never seen anyone look so in love with a building as you.'

At that moment, Toby Beckford walked across the hall to meet them. 'You are wrong, Nick, my old friend. I too love this place and it thrills me to hear Bryony's sentiments. She really is the only one of my friends who sees the character of Wallbourne Manor. She sees behind the façade.' Putting his arm around her shoulders, he kissed her cheek and said, 'I am so very happy you are able to be here. Come into the drawing room. We are drinking mulled wine and roasting chestnuts.'

In the corner of the drawing room was the biggest Christmas tree Bryony had ever seen inside a house. It was heavy with decoration, and beneath were several gifts in Christmas wrapping, adorned with large bows of ribbon. She clapped her hands with joy. As she did so, the door opened and in walked Giles.

'I've—' He didn't finish as suddenly he met Bryony's gaze and dropped the glass he was holding. It fragmented as it hit the ground.

'I'm dreadfully sorry,' he blustered, bending down to pick up the pieces.

'Don't do that,' said Toby, clasping the bell pull to summon one of the servants. 'You could cut yourself.'

'Happy Christmas, Giles,' said Bryony, smiling at him.

'Happy Christmas to you,' he replied, 'I didn't realise you would be here.' But he looked around nervously and then went to sit on one of the sofas, taking another glass of wine from Toby.

'Come and sit by the fire,' Toby invited. 'We're roasting chestnuts.'

In the large open fire, logs crackled and flames danced as a round tin plate filled with chestnuts sat on top of the coals. Toby, using long-handled tongs, turned the nuts and the aroma filled the room.

There were two couples there whom Toby introduced. The men worked in the city with him and seemed amiable, as were their wives.

'My parents aren't here for the festivities,' Toby explained. 'Father hasn't been well so they are in the South of France, staying at the villa. The climate will suit him better at this time of year.'

'The South of France – how lovely,' Bryony said.

'Yes, it's a good place to escape to, isn't it, Giles? Giles stayed there for a few weeks recently.'

Looking at Bryony, Giles said, 'I wasn't very well myself. I really didn't want to come back. To live in France permanently must be great.'

Toby disagreed. 'It's nice for a break, but I couldn't bear to be away from here too long.'

'I can understand that,' said Bryony reflectively, looking around. 'If this was my home, neither could I.'

'We are being completely informal this evening,' Toby told his guests. 'There is no necessity to dress for dinner, but tomorrow there will be several people joining us in the evening when we'll have the traditional Christmas meal. Breakfast will be served in the dining room at nine o'clock, and there'll be a cold lunch as I want the staff to have a break with their families until the evening.'

'Sounds an excellent idea,' remarked Nick.

'We can go to the stables after breakfast,' Toby said to Nick and Bryony. 'You others can come with us if you like, or stay by the fire, go for a walk, whatever you wish. Just please yourselves.'

* * *

The evening was a great success. After a hearty warming meal and a few glasses of wine, they settled down and played charades, which made everyone relax with each other through the merriment it caused. The only person who was subdued was Giles. Bryony guessed it was because she'd seen him with Sophie Johnson and discovered he was a homosexual, and when later Giles found her in the library looking for a book to take to bed, this proved to be the case.

'Bryony!'

She turned away from the bookcase and saw him. He walked slowly towards her and she could see that anxious look on his face.

'Hello, Giles, are you looking for something to read too?'

Stuffing his hands in his trouser pockets to stop them shaking, he said, 'No. I need to talk to you. It's about that time in Southampton . . .'

She stopped him. 'Look, Giles, your private life is absolutely nothing to do with me – or anyone else, for that matter.'

The look of relief on his face was pitiful. 'You mean you won't mention our meeting?'

'Absolutely not!'

'Oh, Bryony! You have no idea what a weight has just been lifted from my shoulders. I would die if anyone found out . . . and besides, that relationship is finished.'

'You really don't have to explain to me, Giles, honestly, but please, do be careful.'

'If my father ever found out he would disinherit me,

and probably all my friends would abandon me.'

'Real friends wouldn't, I'm sure. Now, for goodness' sake, will you relax? You have been tighter than a spring all evening.'

He walked over to her and gave her a hug. 'Thanks, Bryony.'

At that moment, Nick walked into the room. 'Oh, here you are.' He eyed them without curiosity.

Giles stepped quickly away and left the room, muttering unintelligibly.

'There!' said Bryony, teasing him. 'Caught in the arms of my lover.'

'I don't think so,' declared Nick. 'I wouldn't think a female would appeal to him at all.'

Bryony was shocked at his remark. 'Whatever do you mean?'

'I would have thought his choice was more masculine.'

'What makes you say such a thing?'

'Being in advertising, I suppose I'm used to working with homosexuals. I can spot one a mile away.'

'But he doesn't act like one at all.'

'No, he doesn't, but you must admit, Bryony, for a young man he's very pretty.'

'Good-looking I would have said!' She tried hard to protect Giles.

With an enigmatic smile Nick said, 'Very well, if you insist.'

'You won't voice your suspicions, I hope?'

'What sort of a person do you take me for? I'm not

into gossiping, Bryony. I would have thought you knew me better than even to suggest such a thing.'

'I'm sorry, Nick. I didn't mean to offend you.'

He ruffled her hair playfully. 'Of course you didn't. Your friend's secret is safe with me, but I have to tell you it will all come out in the open one day. It always does.'

On Christmas morning all the guests met in the dining room for breakfast. Carols were being sung over the radio, which lent a festive air. When they had all eaten they retired to the living room, at Toby's request, and he handed out gifts to everyone. Bryony was delighted with her Jaeger scarf decorated with horses' heads and horseshoes. She had bought a book on polo ponies, which she had wrapped for him.

Toby was delighted and kissed her. 'Thank you so much. How very kind you are,' he said graciously.

Swirling her large scarf around her shoulders, she said, 'And so are you. This is really lovely.' For Nick, she had bought a pair of driving gloves, which he greatly admired.

He kissed her cheek and said, 'Thank you, Bryony.' From his pocket he produced a long box. 'This is for you.'

Like a small child, she rattled the box, then, her eyes shining with excitement, she unwrapped it. Inside the velvet case was an evening watch studded with marcasite. It was small but exquisite.

'Oh, Nick! It's lovely. Thank you so much.'

'Well, I know you've been through a lot lately and I think you deserve spoiling,' he said softly.

She looked at him with affection. How wonderful that he should know that her father's accident had affected her so.

'I don't know what to say,' she began.

'There is nothing to say.'

'Oh, but there is!' she suddenly exclaimed. 'You have to give me a coin of any value as long as it's silver.'

'Whatever for?'

'It's the gloves. An old superstition. If you give gloves it can mean a parting unless a silver coin is exchanged.'

He put his hand in his trouser pocket and took out some change. Handing her a florin he said quietly. 'Here. Us being apart is something I really don't want.'

The way he gazed at her as he said it made Bryony feel weak at the knees.

'Me neither,' she softly replied.

Toby walked over to them and asked, 'Fancy taking the horses for a hack? It's a bright morning and the exercise will do us good before the night's festivities. You can have the same mount as last time, Bryony.'

'I'd love to,' she said, looking at Nick, who readily agreed.

'Wrap up warm,' Toby warned. 'There is a bitter chill outside. We'll just walk the horses in case the ground is slippery.'

The two men saddled the mounts and they set off round the woods. There had been another fall of snow during the night and the only marks on the white blanket were the footprints of birds and deer. The air was crisp and cold, but exhilarating. A rabbit was seen scampering across a field nearby.

'Can you imagine a nicer way to spend Christmas morning?' asked Bryony, glowing with happiness, the cold bringing colour to her cheeks.

'Just look at her!' said a delighted Toby. 'The girl looks as if she was born in the country!'

Indeed she did. She was wearing ankle boots, trousers, a sheepskin jacket of Toby's mother's that he had found for her, and around her head, keeping out the cold, was her Christmas gift from her host.

Gazing at her, Nick Langdon thought she was beautiful . . . but then so did Toby Beckford.

CHAPTER TWENTY-FOUR

Christmas in the Travis household was quiet. Leila had invited Rosa and Barney to join them for the festive period. They arrived on Christmas Eve, in time for dinner.

'I hope you found a home for that troublesome tiger?' Leila said as they sat at the table.

'Yes, you could say that, I suppose,' said Rosa sharply.

'What do you mean?' asked Leila. Looking across at Barney she added, 'I hope you didn't work with her in the ring again, especially after the night that I was there?'

Rosa let out a snort of disgust and, glaring at her husband, said, 'Go on then, tell her!'

'I wouldn't take that pleasure away from you, my darling. I know you are dying to tell everyone all about it.'

'Don't you get sarky now. If it wasn't for me you wouldn't bloody well be here!'

Dan and Leila looked on expectantly.

Turning towards her sister, Rosa said, 'You remember how badly Tara behaved the night you came to see us?'

'Indeed I do! I told Barney the cat was dangerous.'

'Exactly!' snapped Rosa. 'And I have to say he did keep her out of the act for the rest of the week, but when we went on to the next town and set up the tent, he noticed that Sheba, one of the lionesses, had a sore foot. The vet advised us not to work her . . . so what did this stupid man do?'

'Don't tell me, let me guess. He used Tara,' said Leila.

'Precisely! Would he listen to sense? Would he hell. Well, I can tell you I was terrified of the consequences.'

'What did you do?'

'I had the men standing by. I also had the vet ready to dart her, if necessary, and I had a loaded rifle.'

There was an expectant silence.

Rosa felt her skin turn cold as she relived the episode.

The cage had been erected as usual during the interval and, as the drums rolled, everyone stood in readiness outside of the cage. The atmosphere was electric. The animals came rushing down the tunnel from outside and three of the lions obediently climbed on to their pedestals, as did the other tiger. Then Tara came into the tunnel. Slowly she moved forward, her teeth bared, as she snarled. There was absolute silence in the big top.

Barney waited until she was in the open and then, with his whip and a chair, forced her backwards towards her pedestal. She spat and snarled at him all the time. Eventually she reluctantly climbed up, swiping her enormous paw into the air as she did so.

Rosa's heart was pounding as she watched, and beads of sweat marked her upper lip as she cocked her rifle.

To begin with, all went well, although Barney had to

work hard to make Tara do his bidding. Rosa by now had entered the cage, standing just inside, by the door, her gaze fixed on her husband and the cats. Suddenly, without warning, Tara sprang, knocking Barney backwards. Flat on his back, he was helpless, but as the animal clawed at his shoulder, Barney tried to beat her off with the chair, which he grimly held on to, and which he used in one desperate swipe at the animal's head. She backed off for a moment from the force of the blow, but then she reared up on her hind legs, looming over him. It was then that two shots rang out, and the cat slumped to the floor beside the figure of her master.

There was mayhem. The crowd was screaming, then men outside the cage came in and with chairs in their hands they kept the other cats at bay. Rosa, rifle at the ready, moved quickly to her husband, who was dragged to his feet by one of the men.

Over the loudspeaker the crowd was urged not to panic, to stay in their seats and keep quiet.

Barney, blood dripping from his shoulder, picked up his whip and, with help, sent the other animals out of the cage. The vet walked slowly up to Tara, but Rosa was a good shot, and far quicker than he. Her bullets had entered the heart.

Clowns suddenly appeared, the band played loudly, women and children wept as Tara was dragged from the cage and out of the tent. There was chaos as the audience milled around, out of their seats, not knowing what to do. The show was eventually closed for the night.

After listening to the traumatic story, Leila, with a

look of horror on her face, gazed at Barney and asked, 'Were you badly hurt?'

'I had twelve stitches in my shoulder,' he said. 'I was lucky.'

'You were stupid!' snapped his wife.

'Yes, I was, I don't deny it. But now I've decided to retire from the ring.'

'What about your act?' asked Leila.

'I have found a younger man who's working with the cats now, and he's good.'

'Well, thank heavens for that!' said Dan, who had been mesmerised by the tale. 'Mind you, to me anyone who does your job has to be totally mad!'

Trying to change the subject and escape the wrath of his wife, Barney asked, 'Where is Bryony? I thought she'd be here.'

'No,' said Dan, 'she's staying with friends in the Cotswolds . . . at the manor house of a viscount,' he added with an air of pride.

'Bloody hell! Mixing with the toffs now, is she?'

'And why not?' asked Leila. 'She's as good as any of them!'

'Our Bryony could hold her own with anyone,' said her aunt. 'That girl is something special. We're really proud of her, aren't we, Barney?'

'Indeed we are. With the education she's had she could really go places. Not like us, eh, Dan?'

'That was the whole idea,' agreed her father, 'but I am a bit concerned.'

'Why?' asked Rosa.

'My princess has such high expectations. She sees the life that society lead and admires them, but we all know that whatever walk of life we are in, shit still happens.'

'It's all part of growing up, darling,' said Leila, 'and we have to let her get on with it. We can't protect her every minute.'

'More's the pity,' muttered Dan, taking another sip of his wine.

In the snow-covered Cotswolds, Nick, Toby and Bryony had returned from the ride, glowing from their exercise and, after removing their outdoor clothes, joined the others for lunch before spending the afternoon in comfort, reading and playing cards in the living room where the log fire burned and crackled, until it was time to get changed for the dinner party.

As she left her room an hour later, resplendent in a new black evening dress with a halter neckline and close-fitting bodice, the skirt flaring out at the hem, Bryony met Nick, looking very dashing in his dinner jacket.

'My, my,' he said, 'you look good enough to eat.'

'Steady now, you sound like one of the Three Bears, or is it that old dragon, rearing his head?'

'No, not at all . . . just a red-blooded male – and I know you've met them before.'

'You know nothing at all about me, Mr Langdon!' she retorted.

'You look absolutely ravishing and I know more about you, dear Bryony, than you could possibly imagine.'

She looked at him, trying to fathom his last remark, but he just met her gaze, the corners of his mouth twitching as he tried to suppress a smile. Bryony decided not to further this particular conversation.

Downstairs there was great activity as more guests arrived and were ushered into the drawing room, where drinks were served and introductions made. There were couples from neighbouring grand houses, and two young ladies who made up the numbers.

Toby came towards Bryony and said, 'Come and meet Captain Edward Collingham, the Master of Foxhounds. He's a good chap. You'll like him, Bryony. He has a good stable of horses too.'

Teddy Collingham was introduced and greeted her warmly. 'My word, Toby, what a very fine filly! How do you do, my dear? Are you riding with us tomorrow morning?'

'Oh, no,' Bryony answered quickly, 'I'm certainly not competent enough to join the hunt. I'm only just learning to ride.'

'Not yet, maybe,' agreed Toby, 'but you wait until next year. This girl is a natural in the saddle.'

'I'll look forward to the day,' smiled Teddy. 'Have you ever seen a hunt?'

'No, I must confess I haven't.'

'Then, my dear, you'll find it a sight to remember. We meet here first and partake of the stirrup cup, then we take off. Will you be following in a car?'

Before Bryony could answer, Toby said, 'Of course

she will.' To Bryony he explained, 'I've arranged a couple of cars for you and some of the others. I didn't want you to miss this as it is a great event here.'

'Thank you,' she said, 'that was very thoughtful of you. Is Nick going with you?'

'Of course. He wouldn't miss the opportunity of a good ride, would you?' he said, as Nick walked over to join him.

'Nick! Good to see you, old chap,' said Teddy. 'We don't see enough of you these days.'

'Ah, well,' said Nick with a chuckle, 'some of us have to earn a living, you know.'

'Cheeky devil!' retorted the man. 'I work very hard, I'll have you know!'

'Yes, I've seen your picture in the society pages.'

'There are different types of work, old boy. Mine happens to be of a more enjoyable nature.'

'So I've heard.'

'Now don't be naughty, Nick old boy. I don't want you to ruin my reputation in front of this beautiful young lady.'

Taking her arm, Nick said to Bryony, 'Don't go within an inch of this man, dear girl. He is a philanderer, the type your father always warned you about.'

'How fascinating,' said Bryony, which made Teddy roar with laughter.

Eventually dinner was announced and they all moved into the large dining room. Bryony wondered just how Toby was going to seat his twenty guests but the dining table had been extended.

The grandeur and elegance of the display made Bryony catch her breath. Along the length of the table were heavy silver candelabras. The silver cutlery was monogrammed, she noticed, and between the candles there were beautiful low-level floral displays. Besides each setting were crystal glasses, bright crackers, and a small gift box wrapped in silver paper, with a sprig of mistletoe slipped under the silver ties.

'How very beautiful,' she said softly to Toby, who had escorted her into the room.

'I'm glad you like it,' he said. 'You are sitting on my right.'

Bryony saw there were place cards on silver stands in front of the settings. Nick was sitting opposite her and he smiled across the table as they all took their seats.

The meal, which was beautifully cooked, tasted even better in such sumptuous surroundings, and although she loved being in such luxury, she found herself wondering if Toby ever sat and had beans on toast as she often did when she wasn't very hungry. And then she caught a mental picture of her host doing so at this long table, all alone. It amused her highly and she started to smile to herself. But she carefully hid her amusement behind her napkin.

The guests opened their gifts and were delighted with the contents – cufflinks for the men and earrings for the ladies.

There was smoked salmon mousse to start with, then roast turkey with all the usual trimmings. For dessert there was Christmas pudding, or peach melba for those who were too full to enjoy the richness of the pudding, which was served flamed with brandy. There were cheese and biscuits to finish. The coffee and liqueurs were to be taken in the drawing room after.

The conversation during dinner was both stimulating and varied. They discussed the fact that Kim Philby had been named as the third man, in the spy conspiracy, although Philby had denied being a communist. Several commented on Hugh Gaitskell winning the premiership of the Labour Party, but mainly the conversation was of country matters.

Bryony noted that the merchant banker colleagues of Toby kept fairly quiet on this subject. As one of them said, they were all city people. However, they all voiced their thoughts that living in the country had many advantages. The life was quieter without the ever-present rush of the city, of which they all longed to rid themselves.

'You will have to buy a second home around here,' suggested Teddy. 'Do any of you ride?' he enquired. None of them did, so he immediately lost interest, but he spent the evening charming the ladies.

'See what I mean?' mouthed Nick across the table.

Bryony just smiled and nodded, wondering who the young lady was who had accompanied the Captain. She'd been talking to someone else when Bryony had been introduced. She didn't seem to mind his flirting at all as she was in deep conversation with the gentleman beside her.

* * *

After dinner, they all retired to the drawing room and drank their coffee.

'That was really a splendid meal,' Bryony told her host. 'Thank you for the earrings. That was a lovely touch.'

'Well, it is Christmas, after all,' he said.

'You are the perfect host and lovely with it,' she said with a chuckle. 'I can't imagine why you are not married to some adoring woman. In fact, whenever I have seen you, you have been on your own.'

Laughing, he said, 'Don't get the wrong idea, Bryony. I like women and have been known to have a fling once in a while, but Wallbourne Manor takes up so much of my time when I'm not working in the city, that there is little time for romance.'

'Now that really is sad!'

Sipping his coffee, he said, 'This is my life's work, and will be even more so when my father dies. Then I will need a wife.'

Bryony sat up straight and looked askance at him. 'Toby! You say that as if it is the next thing on your shopping list. Feed for the horses, paint for the house and then a wife.'

He didn't laugh but said, 'I'm afraid it is a bit like that. I will need an heir.'

'But what about love?'

This did amuse him. 'It would be nice if love was part of the relationship. It would be a bonus.'

Remembering her father's words, she said, 'What you want is a brood mare!'

Smiling at her outraged tones he said, 'That is very crudely put, Bryony, my dear, but I suppose I do. Someone who is nice to look at and who loves the country life and Wallbourne Manor as I do, but if I am lucky it will be someone I really love.'

'And if you don't fall in love . . . ?'

'Why are we arguing about this, Bryony? One day I shall marry and have children and that's that!'

She couldn't let the matter rest. 'What happens if the first two children are girls?'

Now Toby was grinning broadly. 'I'll have to keep practising, won't I?'

'Oh, you are impossible!'

'No, darling Bryony, I will be the Lord of the Manor and with that there are responsibilities. What I want doesn't come into it very much. It's what is expected of me and, as a dutiful son, I will comply, as will my son and his after him.'

'It's like a job, I suppose, isn't it?' she reflected sadly.

'Yes, I suppose so . . . would you like to apply for the post?'

She wasn't at all sure if he was joking or not because he was looking at her with a very serious expression.

'Oh, my goodness, no,' she said lightly. 'I wouldn't do at all, Toby. I don't come from the proper background. My father is a car dealer and my mother is from gypsy stock. Just think how that would upset the family and the ancestors. They would turn in their graves!'

His hearty laughter filled the room, making others

turn to see what was so amusing. 'You are priceless!' he said. 'Some fresh blood in the family might be a great idea.'

'Now you're teasing me.'

He stared at her steadily. 'Am I?'

Bryony was greatly relieved when at that moment they were joined by Nick. 'You two seem to be enjoying yourselves,' he remarked.

Shaking his head, Toby said, 'This girl is so entertaining, life would never be dull with her around, I'm sure.' He rose from the sofa as some of his guests called to him to join them for a game of bridge.

Bryony wandered over to the French windows. From the light of the full moon she gazed out over the snow-laden park and stood, silently reflective.

Had Toby been hinting at marriage, or had he been joking? Could she imagine herself as Lady of the Manor? In many ways she could because she loved the place so much, and she was really fond of Toby Beckford, but all the trappings that went with it – being the wife of the Lord – meant so much more. This would be no cosy marriage with just a large house in the country to run. True, she would be part of the society she'd always craved, but deep down she knew that it would never work, not really. But as she watched a squirrel scamper along the parapet outside, she asked herself . . . could it work against all the odds? Was it possible?

Warm hands then held her shoulders and a head was pressed to hers. 'Looking at your favourite scene?'

But Bryony had her eyes closed. The feel of Nick's

firm body at her back, his hands on her, the scent of his cologne, made her tremble. Why did this man have such an effect on her, especially as she was wondering if she could ever marry Toby? It was almost too much. She couldn't answer.

'Bryony?'

'Oh, yes, yes, it's beautiful. Sorry, I was miles away. But would you look at that snow,' she said, grasping at anything to help sort her confused feelings. 'It's completely untouched. You know, Nick, I would really like to go out there and feel the snow beneath my feet, put my footprints on it, enjoy it, feel it . . . have a snowball fight!'

He gazed at the sudden childish excitement and said, 'Why not? Go and put some sensible shoes on and a warm coat. I won't be responsible for you catching pneumonia.'

Bryony hurried from the room. On her return she found several of the others all muffled up, waiting to join in – and when the French doors were opened, they all ran outside with cries of delight.

Like children, they made snowballs and threw them at each other. Screams and cries filled the air, and Bryony didn't know when she'd had so much fun. Eventually, breathless, she leaned against an enormous urn, one of a pair, which stood at the top of some steps, and watched the others until she was hit forcibly on the side of her head.

When she saw Nick laughing uproariously, she yelled at him, 'Right, you devil, just you wait!' But he was too quick for her. Catching her by the revers of her coat, he hauled her towards him.

'And what exactly are you going to do, Miss Travis?'

'How about murder?'

Nick pinned her arms to her side as he encompassed her within his and asked, 'What can you do now?'

'I could destroy your manhood with my knee, but seeing as I know you are a friend of the host, I'll spare you!'

'You cheeky tyke. I believe you would too!'

Raising her eyebrows she said, 'Let's hope you never have to find out!'

'I should put you across my knee and tan your hide, but I know you are a friend of the host . . .' They both laughed uproariously together.

'I have a much better idea,' said Nick as he suddenly stopped laughing and gazed into her eyes. He drew her closer and leaning forward, he kissed her.

Bryony was no longer aware of her surroundings as Nick's mouth explored hers, his sensuous lips demanding a response, which she was only too willing to give as his hands slipped inside the coat and she felt the warmth of them in the small of her back, gently stroking her spine. She put her arms around Nick's neck and lost herself to the wonderful sensations sweeping over her until an onslaught of snowballs broke the spell.

Through the windows of the drawing room, Toby Beckford watched them.

CHAPTER TWENTY-FIVE

The weather on the Boxing Day morning was bright but cold. Everyone was urged to eat a good breakfast to keep out the chill and to dress warmly. Toby, resplendent in his hunting pink, again produced his mother's sheepskin coat for Bryony to wear.

'It suits you,' he remarked. 'The hunt will meet here in an hour for their stirrup cup, and the cars will be waiting to drive you and the others so you can follow and take part in some way. I do hope you enjoy it, Bryony.'

'It'll certainly be a new experience,' she said as they helped themselves to the breakfast from the silver dishes on the sideboard.

'You eat all that and you'll go pop!'

Bryony looked behind her into Nick's smiling eyes. 'My word,' she said as she looked him up and down and admired his outfit, which was similar to Toby's, 'you look typical of the country gent. Very dashing, I must say.'

'Thank you, but as we both know I am no country

gent and have no wish to be, but an occasional outing, following country pursuits, can be really enjoyable.'

'He wants the best of both worlds!' teased Toby.

'That's hardly fair,' Nick retorted. 'You spend time in the city, visiting the fleshpots.'

'*Touché!*' laughed his host. 'And why not? Life is to be lived whilst we are able.'

The morning was quite an education for Bryony and for the guests from the city, who were driven along country roads, keeping up with the hounds and horses. Bryony looked very concerned as she watched Toby and the others jump fences and ditches in pursuit of the fox, which, to Bryony's delight, escaped them all and went to ground. She found the whole morning exciting and admired the skill of most of the riders, and watched in horror when one or two of them fell from their mounts whilst jumping various obstacles. But apart from a few harsh words and curses amidst the bruises, no one was badly hurt.

She listened with some amusement when, after the event, they all met in the drawing room of Wallbourne Manor, to quaff champagne and discuss the meeting.

Nick wandered over to her.

'Did you have a good ride?' she asked.

'It was great. I can't tell you how exhilarating the chase is. Flying over hedges and unforeseen barriers. It's a challenge for rider and horse.'

'But no good for the poor fox!'

'It may seem cruel to you, Bryony, but foxes are the

scourge of farmers. They don't kill to eat, you see. They just kill and leave their victims, to great cost and upset to the owners.' Seeing she didn't look convinced, he added, 'They have to be culled one way or another. Either by the hounds, or by the gun. It's part of living in the country.'

'It seems whatever part of life you come from, there is a down side,' she lamented.

Putting an arm around her, he said, 'Poor Bryony. Life is full of cruelty; you are too soft-hearted; yet you eat meat. You don't mind doing that.'

'That's different,' she argued.

Toby joined them at this moment. 'Good hunt, wasn't it, Nick?'

'Excellent. I'm trying to inform Bryony about the country laws; she's not convinced.'

'You would be if you became part of it,' Toby said quietly.

Bryony was confused. Was he making a point here, or was she imagining it?

'But I'm not,' she said, 'so I'll have to take Nick's word for the way it has to be.'

She was saved from further conversation as lunch was served.

Whilst Bryony was enjoying the high life, the Silver Dollar Club, a rather seedier establishment than Wallbourne Manor, was doing a roaring business. Many of its clients were nursing Christmas hangovers, especially Sophie Johnson, who had spent Christmas Day in an alcoholic haze. He hated Christmas! It was a family occasion and he was without any such ties at all. He had spent most of the day bemoaning the fact that young Giles was no longer interested in continuing their relationship. Sophie went through all the emotion: grief for the loss of the boy he loved, anger at the way that Giles had used him, and, eventually, a determination to get him back.

Sophie sat at a table chatting to various local criminals, all with some gripe or other. They commiserated with each other over one drink and then another until the small gathering was well on the way to another hangover. Then Sophie saw Harry Burgess enter the bar. It was obvious that he'd been doing the round of the pubs from the way he swayed on his feet as he ordered a beer.

Sophie's eyes narrowed as he watched the man. Burgess was always a little loose-tongued when he'd had a few and Sophie waited.

Burgess gazed around the room and then said to the barman, 'I see Dan Travis isn't here. I heard he had an accident. How's he doing, do you know?'

Sophie listened intently.

'I believe he's on the mend,' the barman told him. 'It would take a lot to get him down.'

'Not as much as you might imagine,' leered Burgess. 'The bigger they are, the harder they fall, is the old saying, and Travis found that out, didn't he? He shouldn't go around throwing his weight about, upsetting people!'

Sensing the belligerence in the tone, the barman ignored him and turned to serve another customer.

Getting to his feet, Sophie strolled over to Harry.

'You would know something about that, wouldn't you, you little bleeder?'

With a sudden watchful expression Burgess said, 'I don't know what you mean!'

Fingering the cutthroat razor in his pocket, Sophie said, 'Oh, I think you do. Dan's fall was down to you, wasn't it?'

'Don't be bloody ridiculous! I had nothing to do with it.'

'We both know you're lying, don't we? Just watch your back, Burgess, because one night when you least expect it, I'll be there. Dan Travis is a good friend of mine and I don't like to see my friends got at, so be warned.'

Burgess drank up and said, 'You can't prove nothing!'

Sophie's laughter rang out. 'Prove? Only the police need proof! I know and I'll get you, so enjoy yourself whilst you can because your days are numbered, mate!'

Burgess hurriedly left the bar.

The landlord looked over and said to Sophie, 'Are you trying to ruin my business, frightening my customers away?'

'You are well rid of that one,' Sophie snapped. 'He's more trouble than he's worth.'

Outside the club, Burgess stopped to light a cigarette.

His fingers were trembling as he held a match. Sophie Johnson was a dangerous bugger and Harry wondered just how he knew that Dan Travis's so-called accident was down to him. It was all guesswork, he concluded, as there was no proof. Yes, the wire was found, but so what? That didn't mean anything. But it would be wise to keep away from the club for a while.

He ambled away, muttering to himself.

CHAPTER TWENTY-SIX

After Boxing Day lunch, all the guests at Wallbourne Manor prepared for the journey home. In the baronial hall, Bryony took one final look around. As she and Nick were about to leave, Toby walked her to the door.

'Thank you so much for coming. I do hope you had a good time.'

'Oh, my goodness, Toby, how could anyone not enjoy such fine hospitality in such wonderful surroundings?' She hugged him and kissed his cheek. 'It was the best Christmas ever.'

'I have to go to a ball in London in January, Bryony, I would very much like you to come with me.'

She was stunned.

'It will be a rather grand affair at the Dorchester Hotel. We'll stay overnight ... in separate rooms of course,' he added as he saw her consternation. 'Please say you'll come.'

'I'd be delighted,' she said.

'Good. I'll be in touch later. I can always find you at Nick's office.'

'I'm not there any more, Toby. You see, I'm running my father's business at the moment. But I'll write to you and give you my home address and number.'

'That's fine. I'll probably have to send a car to take you to London, as I will already be in the city. You can bring your ball gown and change at the hotel.'

She didn't know what to say. A chauffeur-driven car? Whatever next?

As she sat in the passenger seat of Nick's car, Giles popped his head in the window and said, 'I heard Toby's invitation, if you need something really special to wear, go to my friend in London, he's a designer, here's his address. You won't be disappointed.'

'Thanks, Giles. Take care.'

'What was all that about?' asked Nick as he put the car into gear and pulled away.

Waving to their host who was standing at the top of the steps, she said, 'Toby has invited me to a ball in London at the Dorchester in January and Giles knows a dress designer. As Toby said it was a grand affair, I will need something very special to wear.'

'Indeed you will, Bryony. It is an annual charity event. All who are high and mighty will be there. You will be very much with the in crowd.'

'Are you going?'

'No,' he said shortly.

She sensed the hostility in his manner, but she didn't know why. After kissing her on the terrace, Nick hadn't made any other move, which, if she was honest, did disappoint her as she'd enjoyed being in his arms, so why did it seem to matter to him that Toby had asked her out? Could it be that he was jealous? She glanced at him. His glowering countenance made her think he was. How perfectly splendid, she thought!

As they drove home, the atmosphere between them seemed a little tense and to break this, she asked, 'How is business?'

'We're really busy closing one account and I'm about to start working on another.'

'Did you find someone to take my place?'

'Yes. Great girl, very efficient.'

The rest of the journey was made in silence broken only by the music playing on the car radio.

When they eventually reached Bryony's home, Nick retrieved her suitcase from the boot and, walking her to the door, said, 'Thanks for coming. It was a good time, wasn't it, Bryony?'

He looked into her eyes and she wondered just what was behind the intensity of his gaze. 'I had a great time, the best. And thank you, Nick, for taking me.'

'My pleasure. Take care,' he said and walked to the car, then drove away without a backward glance. No mention of seeing her again. Nothing.

Men! Bryony thought as she put her key in the door.

The following morning, she drove to the car lot, pleased to have something to do, as Nick's behaviour had unsettled her. Jack, she noted, didn't seem too pleased to see her.

'I thought you might have taken a few days off as we are not very busy,' he said.

'It gives me a chance to tidy the office and catch up on the little things,' said Bryony. She looked out of the office window and said, 'The men don't seem to be too anxious to work. Get them cleaning the cars, will you, and turn the engines over.'

'I was just about to,' he snapped.

'Did you have a nice Christmas?' she asked.

'It was all right. I ate and drank too much, as did most people. When is your father coming back?'

'Don't worry, Jack, he'll be here just as soon as he can.'

As she spoke a man drove an American car, a Buick, into the forecourt. 'Now that's what I call a car,' Bryony said, as she walked to the steps outside and went down to speak to the driver.

'Nice car.' Looking inside she admired the cream upholstery, which was in excellent condition. 'What can we do for you?'

'I want to sell it, are you interested?'

Jack was now beside her and he said, 'No, I'm sorry, but we can't help you.'

'Just a minute, Jack,' Bryony interrupted. 'Don't be in such a hurry.' To the customer she asked, 'Can I take a look at the engine?'

Getting the man to rev the engine after she'd opened the bonnet, she inspected the workings of it and asked, 'Can I test-drive it?'

'Certainly. But it's a left-hand drive.'

'Yes, so I see.' To Jack she said, 'I won't be long.' She ignored his thunderous expression.

Sitting at the controls with the owner beside her, she drove the vehicle carefully out on to the road. It was a joy to drive once she'd mastered the steerage on the wrong side, and after half an hour she reluctantly returned to the office where she made some coffee for them both, and started to haggle over the price he was asking.

Outside, Jack was fuming. An American car with a left-hand drive – they would never shift it! The boss will be furious when he finds out, he thought to himself. In any case, the price is probably too much for us. But when he saw Bryony emerge from the office holding the car keys, his heart sank.

'Will you drive Mr Hunter into town, Jack? He hasn't any transport.'

As Jack drove away, Bryony had the men clean the car. 'I want it polished and gleaming,' she said. 'Get some cream leather cleaner. I want it to smell expensive!'

Whilst they were carrying out her orders, she made a couple of phone calls, then left the office, saying, 'I'll be away only about half an hour.'

When she returned, from her car she took out two flags, a Union Jack and the Stars and Stripes, with two long narrow poles on which to mount them. Then when the car was clean and ready, she drove it into a central position where she had the men mount the flags, one either side of the vehicle. Displayed this way, people were stopping to look at the car, a fact that Jack Saunders couldn't fail to notice on his return from taking the owner of the car to his destination. Neither could Dan, who arrived shortly after, driven to the car lot by Leila.

As Dan cautiously stepped from the car, aided by his wife, he saw the vehicle that was making such an impression on the passers-by and cursed under his breath.

Seeing her father, Bryony rushed towards him. 'Well, Dad, how do you like the Buick?'

'What on earth were you thinking of, buying a left-hand drive? We'll be stuck with it for ever . . . and how much did you pay for it?'

Bryony saw the smile of triumph creeping across Jack's features as Dan berated her and she was furious. 'Do you think you can manage the steps to the office? We can discuss business there rather than on the forecourt. Jack will help you.'

She walked ahead of him and deliberately sat in her father's chair behind the desk. She was in charge for the moment and he had better accept the fact. He would not browbeat her. She wouldn't allow it!

As Jack helped Dan into the office, followed by Leila, Bryony looked at her father's right-hand man and said, 'Thanks, Jack, that'll be all for now.'

He looked across at Dan, who nodded for him to leave, which he did, very reluctantly.

Glaring at Dan, Bryony said, 'Don't you dare tell me off in front of any member of staff ever again!'

He was taken aback, but Leila hid a smile as she saw the anger boiling inside her daughter.

'It demeans me, and destroys any authority I may have. Do you understand, Dad?'

'Well, yes, I see what you mean, but, Bryony! For God's sake, a Yankee car! Who the hell is going to buy it?'

'You haven't even looked at it properly. The car is a beauty! The interior is all but perfect and the engine is in good nick. What red-blooded man wouldn't want it? Don't you realise that all the girls in town would give their eye teeth to be seen in it, because it is so different?'

'Well,' he conceded, 'I suppose you do have a point there.'

'By the time I've finished, Dad, you will certainly sell it *and* make a profit.'

'Why, what have you up your sleeve?'

'My few months working in advertising have taught me a lot. I'm going to run a publicity campaign and then I'm going to auction it!'

'You what?'

'Yes, Dad. A Dutch auction. You start each day with a price which is clearly displayed, then every day the price drops. The public will be intrigued!'

'Are you mad, princess?'

'Not at all. We start way above the retail price but as the days pass, and there is no sale, and the price is going down, those who really want to buy will be so worried that it will go, they will make a bid.' She pushed a piece of paper across the desk towards Dan. 'This is what I paid for it.'

He looked at the slip of paper and asked, 'How did you manage this?'

With a broad grin she said, 'I asked him how the devil did he think I'd be able to sell a left-hand drive, that if I bought the car it would probably sit on my forecourt for months waiting for a buyer, and every week it stood there would cost me money and the vehicle would deteriorate.'

Dan started laughing. 'I couldn't have done better myself.'

'Besides, before I thought of the auction, I knew that Uncle Barney would buy it. You know how he loves all things American.'

'You crafty little minx! Now why don't you and your mother go and do a bit of shopping? I'll look after the office.'

'No, I'm sorry, Dad, that's not convenient. I have work to do.' And as he started to argue, Bryony said, 'There you go, you're doing it again!'

'Doing what?'

'Dismissing me! Be a good girl and go shopping! I am running this business until you return to take over. Then I will relinquish my post. Until then this is *my* office!'

'She's absolutely right, Dan!' said Leila. 'You cannot come in here and undermine her like this.'

'Sorry, princess,' said her father, 'but I'm itching to get back. Staying at home is doing my head in!'

287

'Just let me know when you're ready, and I'll leave.'

'Don't you want to stay on and work with me?'

'No, Dad. You know how I feel about working here full time. Besides I have a job to go back to,' she lied. But even if Nick didn't want her back in the office of Langdon's she would find work elsewhere.

Dan rose from the chair and, with the aid of his walking stick, walked to the door. 'I'll just have a wander around . . . if you have no objections,' he said, looking at his daughter.

'Of course not. Don't be silly.'

Once again Jack assisted him down the steps. 'Did you ever find out what I tripped over?' Dan asked.

'Yes, guv. It was a trip wire.' Jack had promised Bryony he'd keep quiet about this, but he was mad at her over the Buick and not inclined to keep the promise.

'A trip wire? Whatever do you mean?'

'Someone set you up. There was a device which they used to pull the wire tight when you came down the steps.'

'Where were they when this happened?'

'Hidden in the shrubs on the ground behind the office. You could see where they'd been.'

'Who on earth would do that and how could they get in? There was supposed to be a night watchman.'

'Yes, I fired him after we found the trip wire. It seemed that at the same time every night he used to slip across the road for a pint. He was away about fifteen minutes.'

'Bastard!' stormed Dan. 'Because of his neglect I've

spent weeks in great discomfort. Have you any idea who did this?'

'I can only think of one person mad enough to try.'

Dan scratched his chin in quiet contemplation. 'Mm, I can only think of one person too, and that's Harry Burgess.'

'My thought exactly!' agreed Saunders.

'Right! I want you to pick me up at eight o'clock tonight and we'll go to the Silver Dollar and see what we can find out about this rotten bugger.'

'I'll collect you . . . and, by the way, any idea when you'll be back in the office?'

'Doesn't sit easy with you, Jack, does it, my girl being in charge?'

'No, I can't say I enjoy being told what to do by a slip of a girl.'

Patting Jack on the arm, Dan said, 'Never mind, it won't be for long. But you must admit, she does a good job, doesn't she?'

'I'll not take that away from her, she does, although I'll reserve my judgement over the Buick.'

'Yes, that will be interesting,' agreed Dan, 'but it will be great publicity. She's right there.'

'I've got a couple of cars that want a respray and doctoring but I'm a bit reluctant to get them in with Bryony here. However, I need to turn them out quickly now. I can't hang about any longer or I'll have the law breathing down our necks.'

'Bring them in,' said Dan. 'There is no way that she'll know they are hot. The owners simply want a change of colour if she asks, that's all. Just be careful. I'll see you later then.' And he called for Leila to take him home.

Giles Sinclair, the object of Sophie Johnson's lust, was having as miserable a time now he'd returned home from Wallbourne Manor as his rejected lover had over Christmas. Giles's father, the illustrious judge, was harping on about his stay in France and how behind it must have made Giles in his studies.

'I was ill, Father. For goodness' sake, I couldn't help being sick!'

'No moral fibre – that's your trouble, my boy. Not like your brother.'

Giles stormed from the room.

His mother came to his defence. 'Really, Douglas, leave the boy alone! He's not like Hugo in any way – when will you realise that?'

'And that is a great shame,' snapped the judge.

'If you showed a little more patience with him, encouraged him instead of berating him all the time, he'd do much better.'

'The boy is weak. God knows who he takes after!'

'That will do, Douglas!' Lady Sinclair rose from her chair. 'You are impossible! I can't talk to you in this mood.' And she too left the room in search of her son.

Giles was in the library, where he helped himself to a stiff brandy from the decanter on the side. He looked up as his mother entered the room.

'Try not to let your father upset you, Giles,' she said.

'Whatever I did would never be enough, Mother. For two pins I'd quit my studies and push off somewhere and do what I want.'

'Now you're being ridiculous.'

Flinging himself down on one of the leather settees, Giles said, 'Why? I hate it at school. I'll never be as successful as Hugo; I'm not academically clever like he is.'

'How would you make a living if you gave up your studies?'

'Oh, there are ways and means, believe me,' he said aggressively.

'Like Tarquin, you mean?'

Suddenly watchful, Giles asked, 'What do you mean?'

'Of course, Tarquin is talented, but he wouldn't have made it without his partner's help. Mr Johnson, I believe his name was.'

Giles froze.

'How do you know such a man?' asked his mother.

'I don't know him,' Giles lied. 'I met him for the first time when you did, at the fashion show.'

'Don't take me for a fool, please,' she snapped. 'Don't you know I am aware that my own son is a homosexual?'

Giles choked on his drink.

She carried on. 'I have known for some time. I also know that you spend time at the bookies and various racetracks. I can only surmise where you get the money to do so.'

'Oh my God!' Giles felt the blood drain from his face. 'Are you going to tell Father?'

'Don't be stupid! You know how he feels about queers.'

The terminology sounded cruel to her son. 'He must never know,' he said.

'That depends on you, Giles dear. If you continue with your studies and are discriminating in your private life, he should never have to. It would destroy him, you know that.'

'Oh yes, the good name of the judge must be protected at all times!' he said angrily.

'Not only his name, Giles, but Hugo's and mine too. You seem to forget that we would all be involved in any scandal.'

He was contrite. 'I'm really sorry, Mother. I can't help the way I am. I wish I was different, and of course if my preference became public knowledge I too would be finished. My friends would all drop me. My social life would be non-existent.'

'All the more reason to be careful, and I would suggest you keep away from that dreadful man Johnson.'

'Believe me, you have no worries there. I can't stand him.' Gazing at the stately figure sitting opposite him he said, 'You are amazing to have kept this to yourself.'

'I am your mother,' she stated as she rose from her seat. 'Now then, whilst you are at home, please keep out of your father's way. It will save us all a lot of aggravation.'

Left alone, Giles poured himself another drink. Well, that was a revelation, he thought. His mother had shocked him to the core, but never had he admired her so much. He resolved to get his life together, knowing that she would be watching him carefully, but he did need to find a way to make extra money as he was still in debt to a couple of bookmakers and they were beginning to push for payment. Fortunately for him, Giles's problem was solved the following morning when he received a call from London.

'Giles, darling!' It was Tarquin, the fashion designer. 'I have a proposition to put to you.'

'Now don't be naughty,' teased Giles.

'Ha, funny boy! Look, I am holding a huge fashion show in February and I want to show men's fashions as well as ladies' and, darling, as you are so pretty, I thought you might be ideal for one of my models.'

'Sounds great, Tarquin. I've heard this is quite a lucrative business – perhaps I could do this professionally, what do you think?'

'Why ever not? I can put the word around, but you need to have a portfolio of photographs to take to agencies.'

'But that's expensive, isn't it?'

'Look,' said Tarquin, 'do the show for me and I'll pay for your portfolio and give you some cash as well. I'll be your Svengali – or fairy godmother if you prefer?' He started laughing as he said, 'It's probably a more fitting description, don't you think?'

'That would be wonderful, Tarquin. Thanks, you'll never know how much I appreciate it.'

'Good, because in the future you owe me a favour and one day I may call it in. OK?'

'Of course. When do you want me to come to London . . . ?'

After arranging an appointment, Giles put down the receiver and, grinning from ear to ear, he walked into the dining room for his breakfast, where he found his brother alone.

'Good news?' asked Hugo.

'The best. I may well have sorted out my future.'

'Excellent. Are you going to share it with me?'

'Not at the moment. When it's all settled I'll let you know.'

'I'm sure Father will be pleased to know you have something solid in mind.'

Giles thought this was hilarious. The judge whose son was a male model. How wonderful! His father would hate it. 'Don't say anything, Hugo, not at this stage.'

'All right, old chap, whatever you say.' And he buried his head into the paper he was reading.

Giles was happy to be left to his own thoughts and plans.

CHAPTER TWENTY-SEVEN

The owner and punters of the Silver Dollar Club greeted Dan Travis warmly that evening when Jack Saunders helped him in. He had been unable to make the stairs until now and had felt very out of things. The club was like another office to him and an important place to pick up information. Those who were beyond the law knew that here they were safe in their dealings with each other. Sophie Johnson was particularly delighted to see him.

'Come on over here, Dan my old mucker! What'll it be? How about a large brandy?'

'Sounds good to me,' said Dan as he sat down, smiling at all and sundry. When his friend returned, Dan wasted no time in asking, 'Have you seen Harry Burgess recently?'

'I saw him on Boxing Day, in here, drunk as a skunk. Why are you asking?'

'I think he was the one who set me up to take a tumble.'

'Did you know your girl was in here asking questions?'

'My Bryony?'

Johnson nodded.

'What the hell was she doing in here?'

'Gutsy kid, that, Dan. She was looking for information. She said someone had tried to nobble you, and wondered if I had any ideas.'

Frowning, Dan turned to Jack and said, 'If she knew about this, why wasn't I told?'

'She said she didn't want you worried.'

'Bloody hell! I don't want her mixed up in anything like this.'

'I told her that. I said we were mates and I'd sort out the bastard when I found out who it was,' Sophie informed him. 'Do you know what she told me?'

'No, what?'

'She thanked me most politely but told me she would keep it in the family. I told her I'd be in touch if I found out.'

'I hope you were not serious?' Dan growled.

'Don't be bloody silly! Of course I wouldn't tell her. In fact, I warned Burgess I'd have him before long. He nearly shit himself!'

'But we don't know for sure it was him.'

'I'm sure. I went in the shops opposite your place and asked if they had seen anyone hanging around at the time, and one rather nosy old girl who owns the sweet shop described him to me. She was ready to call the police as she thought he was acting suspiciously, when he stopped coming. And guess when that was?'

'After I fell?'

'Exactly. I'm surprised that you didn't go over to the shops and do a bit of delving yourself, Jack.'

Saunders looked uncomfortable, knowing that he had let his boss down.

'So where is this bastard hiding now?' demanded Dan.

Shrugging, Sophie said, 'Who knows? He's not been seen since I confronted him here. Mind you, I've not gone into it any more than that. He may be holed up in his shabby room. I don't know.'

'Thanks, Sophie. I owe you. I'll sort it. So how have you been?'

'Bloody miserable, if you want to know. Young Giles took off to France for a while. I saw him in London with his mother at a fashion show. He doesn't want to know me any more. Ungrateful pup!'

'Well, Sophie, I'm afraid if you will fall for young lads, this will always happen. Can't you find a boyfriend nearer your own age and settle down?'

'Queers my own age don't appeal, darling. Who wants to share a bed with another old fart?'

'Never mind, you'll soon find a replacement.'

'You don't understand, Dan. I don't want anyone else. I want Giles.'

'You're not going to do anything daft, are you?' a worried Dan asked.

'I don't know what I'm going to do, to tell you the truth, but come on, let's forget about my troubles and drink to your return to health.'

* * *

Later that evening, as Jack drove Dan home, he was told, 'Get the boys together and go and sort out Harry Burgess.'

'How far shall we go?'

'Frankly, I'd sooner he was permanently removed, but we can't stick our necks out that far. Put the frighteners on him. Hurt him but don't kill the bugger. But be careful, we don't want him going to the old Bill, so make sure that he can't identify anyone.'

'What are you going to do about your daughter asking questions?'

'I'll get Sophie to tell her it's sorted. She'll think he had something to do with it.'

'She's no fool, guv.'

'No, that's true, but if she's told it's been taken care of, she won't pursue it, will she?'

'I hope not.'

Two nights later, Harry Burgess was taken by surprise as three men wearing balaclavas burst into his house and beat him severely. Whilst they pummelled him, no one spoke a word, but as they left him, writhing and bloody on the floor, he knew why they had called. In his twisted mind, however, he thought it had been worth it to bring Dan Travis to his knees.

It was a further week before Dan returned to the office to take over. Jack had called him because Bryony had begun to question the two cars being resprayed.

'Where's the paperwork for all this?' she asked Jack.

'I haven't had time to do it, I've been too busy,' he told her, but when she discovered the engineer changing the chassis numbers she had blown a gasket!

'What you are doing is illegal!' she fumed at Jack. 'Wait until Dad knows about this. You'll get him into all sorts of trouble if the law finds out.'

Jack had lost his temper. He'd had enough of this young girl running the place, and all the frustration that had been building in him since she took over came to the fore.

'Your father is well aware of what is going on, you stupid bitch! You think you're so bloody smart – well, you know nothing about running such a place. You have no idea how your father makes his money. It isn't all about selling cars off the forecourt!'

She paled at his words. 'What on earth do you mean?'

Knowing he'd gone too far, he said, 'Ask your father!' and stormed out of the office.

Bryony got into her car immediately and drove home. She burst through the front door of her house and confronted Dan.

'You are selling stolen cars! How could you?'

His worst fears were realised. He'd carefully hidden such transactions from her when they had sorted out the paperwork and he'd thought he'd covered his tracks. He knew there was no point in denying things.

'Yes, that's right.'

She was floored by his confession. 'I realised you dealt with some unsavoury characters, but I had no idea my father was a criminal!'

Dan remained calm. 'I would hardly call myself that. Every trade has its grey side, princess. All businesses have their fiddle, even if it is just lying to the taxman. I make good money this way and I have several other business deals in lots of areas, all legal. Besides, I'm very careful.'

'But if you were caught, you could go to prison.'

Lighting a cigarette he said, 'I have no intention of getting caught.'

'Well, I hope you realise that I can no longer work for you?'

'Don't get all high and mighty on me, girl. My work paid for your education, this house and the clothes you wear, and don't you forget it!'

Leila, hearing the commotion, walked into the room. 'What's going on?'

'Dad is selling stolen cars. He resprays them, changes the chassis numbers and sells them on.'

'So?'

'You knew this?'

'I don't question your father as to how he makes his money. Have you ever gone without?'

'No. But that's not the point!'

'That is exactly the point. He's a shrewd man, he works hard, not all his business is beyond the law, so why all the yelling?'

'I don't believe you two. Well, as far as I'm concerned I no longer work for you,' she said glaring at her father.

'Fine! I'll go back to the car lot tomorrow and you can go back to Langdon's. You don't intend going to the police with this knowledge, I hope?'

'What? And shop my own father? How could you even ask such a thing?'

'Good. But before you storm out feeling all sanctimonious, remember that makes you an accessory!'

'You are impossible!'

Her parents heard the front door slam and Bryony's car drive away.

'What happens now?' asked Leila.

'Absolutely nothing. She'll get over it.'

'I'm not sure that she will.'

'Then we'll have to wait and see, won't we?'

Bryony drove in a rage down Westwood Road. How could her father take such chances, and how could she have been so blind? When she first worked at the weekends in the car lot, she'd seen the sort of men who had visited her father in the office and she remembered the number of times she'd been sent on an errand to get her out of the way. She recalled the jewellery she'd seen for a fleeting moment on one such occasion. Now she was terrified, wondering just what other illegal deals her father was involved with.

She found herself near Langdon's and parked her car. She now needed a job. Was there any point in asking for her job back? Nick had said the girl who took her place was efficient. Nothing ventured nothing gained, she told herself as she walked towards the office.

The receptionist greeted her warmly.

'Bryony! How lovely to see you. How is your father?'

'Better in health than temper!'

With a broad grin the woman said, 'Well, that sounds a step in the right direction.'

'Is Nick in his office?' asked Bryony.

'Yes, go in. I'm sure he'll be pleased to see you.'

With a sinking heart, Bryony knocked on the door and entered the office she used to share with Nick Langdon. He was sitting at his drawing board, a pencil held between his teeth, studying his drawings. He looked up as she entered.

'Bryony! This is a surprise.'

The girl sitting at the desk that was once Bryony's domain looked up from her work.

'You haven't met Lucy,' said Nick.

'Hello,' Bryony said. She walked over to Nick's work and studied it. 'Something wrong?' she asked.

'Why do you say that?'

'You seemed a bit perturbed when I came in, that's all.'

'Take a look at it and tell me what you think. What I'm trying to convey is . . .' and he explained his ideas to her.

Bryony studied the layout carefully. It was sleek and snappy, conveying the message of the goods to sell the product to the customer, but it lacked a certain something.

She suddenly saw how it could be improved and suggested a couple of subtle changes.

He was delighted with her idea. 'You are absolutely right! Why on earth couldn't I have seen that?' He took his pencil and improved the layout.

'There you are,' she said, pleased with the result.

'Come on, Bryony,' he said, 'I'll buy you lunch. I have been sweating over that for an hour.'

Turning to Lucy, he said, 'I'll be back by two o'clock, if anyone wants me.'

They walked to the Court Royal Hotel. As they entered, Bryony saw Theresa at the reception desk.

'How are you?' she asked her friend.

'Fine. I've not seen you since your father had his accident. How is he?'

'Better now, thanks. I've been running the business for him.'

'Goodness me. I thought you had a job.'

'I did, but I had no choice. I'll come round and see you soon.' And she followed Nick into the restaurant.

'The receptionist a friend of yours?' Nick asked.

'Yes, and I feel really guilty. I've not been in touch with her for ages.'

'You've been busy,' he said.

They studied the menu and ordered. Then Nick looked at Bryony and asked, 'Did you come to see me for a reason or was it just a friendly call?'

'My father is taking over the business again so I'm out of work.'

'You're not staying on then?'

'Definitely not!'

'Oh dear, do I detect a note of defiance in your voice?'

What could she say? She couldn't tell him the real reason.

303

'You know I never intended to work with him; it was only circumstances that put me there these past weeks. I had no choice. I was hoping to come back and work for you, but I know that you have someone in my place.'

The waiter served them their soup.

Nick sensed that Bryony was unhappy and asked, 'Is there something wrong?'

'No, of course not. What could there be?'

Whatever it was, she wasn't telling him, so he dropped the subject. 'Lucy is very efficient, and therefore I can't dismiss her just like that,' he said, and saw Bryony's disappointment in her expression. 'However,' he continued, 'you have a certain gift for picking the weak points in our presentations and this is a talent that shouldn't be wasted. How about coming back and being my personal assistant?'

The relief that she felt was enormous. 'And what would that entail?'

'Coming with me when I meet a client to discuss exactly what they want, working with me on my ideas, researching the market . . . Are you interested?'

'Oh, Nick, that sounds really interesting. I'd love to do that.'

'Good.' As the waiter cleared their soup plates and served the main course he said softly, 'I've missed you being around.'

Looking into the soft expression in his blue eyes, Bryony felt her heart miss a beat. 'I've missed being around,' she said.

'When can you start?' he asked.

'How about tomorrow?'

Laughing, he said, 'I do love enthusiasm. Tomorrow it is.'

After the meal he walked her back to her car. 'I'll see you in the morning, Bryony.' And he kissed her softly on the mouth.

As she drove home, Bryony was fighting her mixed emotions. So much was happening suddenly and she wasn't prepared for any of it. Her father was a criminal. Somehow it surprised her. Before, she'd only imagined he was doing some kind of dicey deals, but faced with facts, that was something quite different. The consequences were frightening . . . and now there was Nick Langdon. Again, he was playing with her. Why did he have to kiss her? Not that she minded, but it was infuriating. Did it mean anything, or was it just a friendly gesture? As she pulled into her driveway she decided to see what happened when she started working for him. Then she would find out if his kiss meant anything at all.

CHAPTER TWENTY-EIGHT

As Bryony drove home, she was singing softly to herself she felt so happy. She would tell her father she had her job back. There was nothing she could do about the way he ran his life, she decided; she would just have to get on with hers. But when she got home and saw Dan, he had something to say about her sudden departure.

'I shall be back at Langdon's in the morning,' she told him.

'Fine! But what about the Buick? You bought the bloody thing. What about the publicity campaign, and selling it in this Dutch auction you had planned?'

She'd forgotten all about it in her anger.

'Don't worry about it,' she said sharply. 'I'll still see to it, if only to prove you and Jack wrong about the purchase! I'll write out the adverts for the *Southern Daily Echo*. And the notices of the falling price to be put on the car every day. After that all you'll have to do is wait for a buyer.'

'And if it doesn't sell?'

'Oh, it will. I'd put money on it.'

'You had better hope so, princess, because if it doesn't, you'll have to pay for it yourself.'

'Fine!' And she left the room and went upstairs.

'That's a bit harsh, Dan, isn't it?' said Leila.

'Rubbish! She has to learn about business and to put her money where her mouth is. Now will you run me to the car lot? I'd better go and see what's happening. Jack will bring me home later.'

Bryony heard them leave. She only hoped her plan worked because to cover the cost of the Buick would take her all of her wages for a long time. But then there was always Uncle Barney if she was desperate. She really wanted to prove to her father she knew a good deal when she saw one, though. She started to work on the advertisement.

Whilst Bryony was making her plans, young Giles Sinclair was making his. He was seated in a photographer's studio with Tarquin in attendance, having photographs taken for his portfolio.

Tarquin had sorted some clothes from Giles's wardrobe for his protégé to wear.

'Nice clobber,' he said. 'Sophie always was a generous queen. He did like his boys to be well turned out.'

'I bloody well earned every stitch on my back,' grumbled the young man.

'Of course you did, dearie, but you must admit he is a generous man, and I won't hear a word against him.'

'Of course you won't. After all, he did set you up in business.'

'For which I am eternally grateful. A little gratitude wouldn't come amiss from you, Giles.'

'He was good to me,' Giles admitted, 'but he scares me to death,' he added. 'Do you know he carries a cutthroat razor in his pocket?'

'He always did.'

'That didn't ever bother you?'

'No, why should it? After all, I never saw him use it.'

'Well, I did. It made me sick to my stomach.'

Holding up his hand, Tarquin said, 'I don't want to hear about it.'

A couple of hours later they left the studio and returned to the fashion house where Giles was taught how to parade up and down the catwalk dressed in some of the finest menswear he'd seen.

'You'll do very well,' said Tarquin. 'You have a natual elegance, and an aptitude for showing off. My clients will adore you.'

Which proved to be true. The fashion show was a great success and earned a lot of press interest in the tabloids. The headlines praised the new find in the field of fashion for Tarquin and his clothes, especially his menswear. There was a large photograph of him receiving the applause of his audience, with another picture of Giles, his new male model, who had taken the catwalk by storm.

* * *

The eminent Sir Douglas Sinclair choked on his breakfast when he saw the coverage.

'What in hell's name is that stupid boy up to now? A model! How very demeaning. Can you begin to imagine what my colleagues in chambers will say when they see this?' he stormed to his wife.

'For heaven's sake, Douglas. At last he's doing something with his life. You are always complaining that he has no future; it seems now he may have found his forte.'

'What about his studies? Is he going to continue with them?'

'I have no idea,' said Lady Sinclair as she calmly buttered another slice of toast. 'You know he's not suited to academia. As you keep saying, he is unlike his brother. Can't you be happy for his success?'

Glaring at his wife, Douglas said scathingly, 'You really can't be serious? You know perfectly well the sort of people who are mixed up in the world of fashion. It is full of poofs. Do we want our son mixing with their like?'

'Tarquin is a very talented designer; I wear a lot of his clothes, as do many of my friends. Surely that speaks for itself. Success comes in many guises.'

'In my book he may as well be a male ballet dancer!'

Putting down her napkin, Lady Sinclair rose from her seat. 'You, Douglas, are committing a crime far worse than any homosexual . . . you are a bigot! This is not a good thing for one of Her Majesty's judges, a man who is supposed to be upheld by the nation as fair-minded and impartial. Perhaps *you* are in the wrong job, not your son!'

Her husband was speechless as she swept from the room.

The judge wasn't the only person to be surprised by the article in the papers. Sophie Johnson was taken aback when he saw the pictures of Giles. He was also angry that Tarquin had kept this piece of information to himself when he knew of the relationship between Sophie and the young beautiful man smiling at him from the printed page. But at least he'd learned now where young Giles was to be found. He picked up some scissors to cut out the picture, which he placed on the mantelpiece, where he could see it clearly. He'd maybe buy a frame for it, he thought as he lovingly ran a finger over the face.

'You are so beautiful, my boy, but you are a little bleeder nevertheless,' he murmured, 'and you will come back to me.'

Bryony read the article with great interest when she saw it. She recognised the name of the fashion house, which Giles had told her was a good place to shop for a special gown. And she would need to wear such a dress to the Dorchester Hotel, with Toby.

She had settled into her new job with Nick and found it both challenging and interesting, yet totally frustrating. She and Nick worked well together, but he had slipped into a strictly business mode when they were together, which, as they were extremely busy, wasn't totally unexpected. Their time together was absolutely hectic, organising an advertising campaign for a very important client. They had worked late on several evenings, and there had been no time to spare for familiarities other than working ones, and by the end of each day they were both exhausted.

But this coming Saturday, she was off to London to hunt for the dress. Her first call would be at Tarquin's salon.

As she travelled by train to London, Bryony contemplated her life. Her father was back in his office, so was a happy man, especially as the Buick had sold at a profit, as Bryony had predicted. The advertising she had planned had created such an interest that it brought in more business as well, so it had been a success. She was pleased to be working, and earlier in the week Toby had called her at home to make plans for their trip to London.

Bryony was to be collected by car in the afternoon and taken to the Dorchester where a room was booked for her, and then Toby would collect her at seven thirty, when they would go for cocktails before the dinner. Leila had been all of a twitter at the arrangements and had wanted to come to London with her, but Bryony preferred to do this by herself. Nevertheless, she had happily accepted the sum of money her mother had insisted she take to buy her gown.

A taxi took her to the salon and after she'd paid the

driver, Bryony took a deep breath and opened the door. As she entered, who should come out of the back room but Giles with Tarquin, whom she recognised from the newspaper article.

'Bryony!' Giles greeted her warmly and kissed her. He introduced her to Tarquin.

'This is a great friend of mine,' he said, 'and I do believe she's looking for a ball gown?' He looked questioningly at her.

'Yes, I am!'

'She's going to the charity ball at the Dorchester this month with Viscount Beckford.'

'Several of my clients are going,' Tarquin told her, 'but, darling, none of them has your looks! I'm going to find you something really stunning.'

The next two hours flew by in clouds of net, satin, brocade and velvet, as Bryony was dressed in a variety of beautiful gowns. She pranced and flounced in front of the mirror, as did both the men who were helping her. At last they had the choice down to two, and they paused for a glass of champagne to discuss this dilemma.

'Well, darling,' said Tarquin, 'both look gorgeous on you. It depends on what message you want to send.'

'What do you mean?' asked Bryony.

'Take the red one. That, with its tight bodice and bustle at the back, is definitely Scarlett O'Hara, without a doubt, whereas the ivory satin, with the sweetheart neckline and fitted waist, is more Jane Eyre, demure and innocent.'

Bryony looked full of mischief as she said, 'How very

boring. I definitely feel Scarlett would be just right. I would like to live a little more dangerously.'

'You take care that your words don't come true, whilst mixing with the aristocracy.'

'What do you mean?' she asked.

'Listen, darling, they may come from the highest in the land and there are many who deserve their position in life, but there are a lot of arrogant types who think they can say and do as they wish and their family name will protect them . . . and the women are the worst offenders. If anyone offers you cocaine, make sure you refuse.'

'Cocaine?' Bryony was horrified.

'Oh yes, my dear. So watch yourself in the ladies' powder room. That's where it will be, mark my words.'

She turned towards Giles and raised her eyebrows in question.

'Tarquin is speaking the truth, Bryony.'

'Do you take drugs?' she asked him.

'My God, no,' said Giles. 'I have enough problems of my own to cope with.'

'Surely Toby doesn't take anything like that?'

'Good gracious, no! Toby is one of the good guys of the world. He is a true blue aristocrat, with a strong sense of duty to his name and to his country. He is pure gold. If I was a woman I'd marry him!' Giles laughed.

'Once he sees Bryony in her Scarlett O'Hara outfit,' said Tarquin, 'maybe he'll pop the question. How about that, Bryony? Would being the Lady of the Manor appeal to you?'

'No, I don't think so. I like gracious living and

country estates, but to be a member of the aristocracy, no. Besides, I don't have the right pedigree.'

'You can have all that without marrying a title,' said Tarquin. 'Just make sure your man has money. There is nothing wrong with a self-made man. Look at me.' And he struck a very camp pose besides a balustrade. 'See?'

Both she and Giles burst into guffaws.

'What? What?'

'Not exactly Rhett Butler, are you?' teased Giles.

'No, more like Ashley Wilkes. You know I thought that Leslie Howard played him rather effeminately and I did wonder . . . ?'

'You are outrageous!' Bryony gasped as her laughter subsided. 'But thank you so much for a great time. And I love my dress.'

'Instead of you taking it back to Southampton and having to cart it back up to London, I could have it delivered to your hotel, all pressed and ready to wear on the night.'

'That would be wonderful.'

'Where are you staying?'

'The Dorchester.'

'Of course, where else? I'll call in the morning of the ball to get your room number.'

'Thank you so much, Tarquin.'

Kissing her hand, he said, 'It was my pleasure, darling. You will look stunning and if anyone asks you where you bought your gown, you will of course tell them.'

'Absolutely!'

* * *

On the morning of the ball, Bryony went to the hairdressers where she had her hair fashioned into the style of Scarlett O'Hara in *Gone With the Wind*, with the aid of a hairpiece of ringlets. When the stylist had finished and Bryony saw her reflection in the mirror, she gasped with amazement. She looked very much the Southern belle, and, she thought, when she was in the dress the final picture should surprise Toby as much as it did her. Turning her head first one way and then the other, she tried to look provocative, living the role she had created. This evening she hoped would be fun, living up to such a character. But then, she told herself, she mustn't embarrass Toby when he was among his peers.

When the chauffeur-driven Bentley arrived to collect Bryony, her mother saw her off, trying not to show how impressed she was.

'Have a lovely time,' she said. 'I can't wait to hear all about it.'

Bryony sat back among the plush leather of the seats and thought, now this I could get used to. But as she reflected a little more, she knew she would rather be at the wheel of her own car. However, once in a while this luxury was really no hardship!

When she arrived at the hotel, she was given a letter at the reception desk and shown to a sumptuous bedroom, where, to her delight, her ball gown was hanging in the wardrobe waiting, as Tarquin had promised. Seeing Toby's family crest on the envelope, she opened it.

He had written: 'I do hope you like the room. Do order a tray of tea and sandwiches if you are hungry. I'll pick you up at seven thirty. Love, Toby.'

Bryony walked over to the window and looked out over the park. She was a little apprehensive about the evening, not quite sure about the proceedings, but determined to enjoy it. She ordered tea and sandwiches, and when they were delivered she ran a bath, pouring in the complimentary bath crystals and wallowing in the scented water, careful not to wet her hair, until it was time to dress.

When later, she opened the door to Toby she gave him a little curtsy. He stood before her in his dinner jacket, looking elegant and important.

'Oh, Toby, how smart you look!'

He kissed her cheek and then held her away from him. 'And you look absolutely beautiful! I will be the envy of every man in the ballroom this evening.' He stepped inside and, taking a long box from inside his jacket, he said, 'I wondered if you would like to wear these this evening,' and opened the box.

Bryony let out a cry of surprise. Inside were a diamond and ruby necklace with matching earrings.

'Oh, Toby!' was all she could say.

'These are a family heirloom and I took them out of the bank vault for the evening.'

'How fortunate that I am wearing red,' she said.

'Well, not quite. To be honest I rang your mother to ask her if she knew what colour the gown was.'

'Still, had I been wearing green, they would still have looked wonderful.'

'Had you been wearing green, I would have brought the emeralds.'

'And a blue gown would have been the sapphires, I suppose,' she said cheekily.

'No, Bryony, we have never liked sapphires much. It would have been the diamonds.'

'Are you serious?'

He chuckled softly. 'I'm afraid I am. The ladies of my family have all had a love affair with jewels over the centuries. Here, let me put them on for you.'

Bryony felt them against her neck, and when the clasp was closed, she rushed to a mirror to admire them. Putting on the earrings with pear-shaped drop, she said, 'Toby, they are exquisite. I hope I do them justice.'

'You have no idea how much,' he said and, leaning forward, he kissed her softly on the mouth. 'Shall we go?'

The cocktail bar was full of elegant women in a variety of sumptuous gowns and jewellery, and men in their dinner jackets. Bryony stood proud and tall. She knew she looked as good as all of them and better than many, and the family heirlooms gave her an air of confidence, which was not dented a bit when, at the far end of the bar, she saw James with a blonde girl. He looked across the room and did a double take as he recognised her. She gave a half-smile in his direction, then turned away.

Handing her a glass of champagne, Toby said, 'This should be a very good night. The food is usually

317

excellent. Then, after dinner, an auction is held, with the money raised going to charity.'

'How wonderful. I'm really looking forward to it.'

Toby introduced her to several people who approached them; he reeled off their names. Lord this, Lady that, the Earl of somewhere else and eventually Sir Douglas and Lady Sinclair, Giles's parents.

Bryony didn't like the judge on sight. To her he seemed dour, pedantic and overbearing, but his wife, she thought, was charming.

'You know Giles?' Lady Sinclair asked.

'Yes I do. In fact he helped me to choose my gown.'

'Tarquin designed it then?'

'Yes. His clothes are quite beautiful.'

'I do so agree, and, my dear, you look absolutely stunning.'

'Thank you.' Bryony was not going to mention Giles again, thinking it safer not to do so, but his mother did.

'You probably know that Giles is now modelling Tarquin's menswear?'

'I saw the article in the paper,' said Bryony, 'and I'm delighted that he did so well. Giles always looks elegant anyway. I think he has a natural feel for fashion.'

A smile swept the woman's features. 'How kind of you to say so. I heartily agree . . . unfortunately my husband doesn't.'

Glancing towards the judge, now deep in conversation elsewhere, with slightly hunched shoulders and a scowl, Bryony said, 'I can see that he wouldn't understand . . . but I bet he passes judgment beautifully!'

Lady Sinclair burst into peals of laughter. 'How perceptive an observation! You, my dear, are a delight!'

As Lady Sinclair excused herself and joined her husband, George Bamforth came over. 'Hello, Bryony, remember me?'

As soon as she heard his northern accent, she placed him immediately.

'George! You were at Toby's house party with . . . Cassandra, that's it.'

'How lovely of you to remember, my dear. How are you? By the way, you are the most glamorous woman in the bar.'

She felt the colour rush to her cheeks at the compliment. 'Thank you, George. Are you alone?'

'No, Cassy is around somewhere. Now I do like this kind of do,' he confided, 'because it does some good. Charities need all the help they can get and for once I can do something about it.' He winked at her. 'My brass is as good as anyone else's. Here I am on equal terms!'

Toby, having greeted George, said to Bryony, 'We will soon be going in to dinner. If you need the powder room, I would suggest this is a good time.' And he told her where it was situated.

As she opened the door of the ladies, the smell of expensive perfume almost took her breath away. But what almost stopped her breathing altogether was the shock of seeing Cassandra, sitting on a low stool in the corner, opening a small box, dipping in what looked like a salt spoon, and then sniffing the substance she had removed from the box. Beside her were two young women, cutting lines of a white powder, which she surmised was cocaine, sniffing it with rolled banknotes.

CHAPTER TWENTY-NINE

Bryony returned to the bar, shaken by what she'd seen, even though she'd been previously warned. Cassandra, intent on what she'd been doing, had been oblivious of the others around her, and therefore had not seen her.

'Are you ready to eat?' asked Toby as she stood beside him. 'Only we are about to go into the dining room.'

'Yes, I'm really quite hungry.' As she spoke, she saw Cassandra walk up to George and put her arm through his.

The room was filled with circular tables, which seated twelve, beneath crystal chandeliers, and with rich velvet drapes at the window. At one end was a small stage with a lectern placed in the centre from where, Bryony assumed, the auction would be conducted later. Sebastian Wallace was at their table with Davinia, as were George and Cassandra, who was looking very bored with the whole thing.

Whilst she waited for the first course to be served,

Bryony cast a glance around the room. She spotted several stars of the silver screen. Diana Dors' blonde hair shone out like a beacon. Michael Wilding, Anna Neagle and Herbert Wilcox were seated elsewhere, and she saw Giles and Tarquin, sporting flamboyant waistcoats beneath their jackets, at another table, but was unable to catch their eyes.

After the sumptuous meal was over, coffee and liqueurs were served, and then the auction – and the fun – began. The prizes on offer took Bryony's breath away: a weekend in Paris; a day at Royal Ascot; a trip to New York on the *Queen Mary*, another a cruise on the *Caronia*; dinner for two at the Ritz Hotel; tickets to a London show; beauty treatments and appointments with West End hairdressers who styled the hair of the rich and famous; and so on.

The comedian Tommy Trinder was the auctioneer. His non-stop patter and one-line jokes kept everyone in stitches as he urged them all to put their hands in their pockets.

'Do come along, ladies and gentlemen, it's no good rattling the family jewels and shaking your diamond tiaras, it's your money we want – unless you want another Peasants' Revolt!'

The bidding was spirited, among much laughter and friendly joshing. Tarquin outbid everyone for a weekend in Nice, and was volubly enthusiastic when he was successful.

George was determined to be the winner of the return trip to New York. As there were several people also interested, the fervour increased as the price rose. Bryony, watching him, was impressed at his calmness. His face was impassive. He just nodded and upped the bid until the trip was his. There was loud applause because the price he paid was way above the actual real cost of the voyage. He just smiled and puffed on his cigar.

Toby bid for several items but was overtaken, but when Bryony sympathised he said, 'I was only driving the price up until something comes along that I really want.' Then a polo pony was brought on to the stage, causing great excitement, and Toby became genuinely enthusiastic.

Trinder read out the pedigree of the horse as it was written on the page before him, then said, 'Well, there you are, you lucky people, that's what it says. Frankly, I don't understand a word. All I know about horses is you feed it at one end and it comes out the other, usually paid for by the money I lost on it at the races. Now, who will start me?'

'A hundred pounds!' someone called.

'You're havin' a laugh!' snorted Trinder. 'Blimey, I'm surrounded by the richest people in the land who talk money in telephone numbers and who now quote me a price more suited to a bloomin' rocking horse! Let's start again, shall we? What is your bid, gentlemen?'

'Five hundred pounds!' called Toby.

Trinder beamed. 'At last, a real gent. Do I hear six?'

'Six!' called a voice from the back of the room.

'Seven hundred,' yelled another.

Bryony looked at Toby and waited to see if he would join in. 'One thousand pounds!' he said loudly.

There were enthusiastic cheers all round and, much as he tried, Trinder could find no higher bidder. 'Very well, sold to Viscount Beckford!' And he smacked the gavel down with great gusto.

'Good heavens, Toby,' Bryony remarked, 'that's a lot of money.'

'Ah, well, you see, I know the pedigree and after the horse has finished its days on the polo field, it will make a lot of money at stud. Philanthropic I may be, but I am also practical.'

Tarquin, who was by now quite carried away with the whole event, approached the lectern and, after a whispered conversation, the comedian made an announcement.

'Ladies and gentlemen, Mr Tarquin the designer has just made a very generous offer. A gown for a lady or a suit for a gent from his salon, combined with an evening spent with Giles, his famous new young model. Now ladies, how does that appeal to you?'

There was a lot of chattering as the ladies implored their husbands to bid on their behalf, and among lots of laughter and humour from the auctioneer, the bids came in thick and fast, until eventually Tommy Trinder, holding the gavel, ready to let it fall, said, 'Right, four hundred and fifty pounds! Is that your final bid?' There was silence. 'Going once, going twice,'

'Five hundred pounds!'

Heads turned, everyone wondering who the bidder was.

'Five hundred!' announced Trinder. 'Are we all done?' As there was no response, he banged down the gavel. 'The prize is yours, sir. Can I please have your name?'

'Derek Johnson!'

Bryony turned in her chair and saw Sophie sitting smiling as he looked across at Giles and Tarquin. She followed his gaze and saw how pale Giles looked. She suddenly felt apprehensive, although she didn't know why. Perhaps it was the expression of fear she'd seen on Giles's face.

Others, though, seemed to have found the auction great fun and were pleased with their purchases. Sebastian had successfully bid for a hair appointment for Davinia, which delighted her, and even Cassandra had at last shown some interest in the proceedings when George had bought the crossing on the *Queen Mary*.

'Well done, George,' said Bryony, as they started to leave the dining room for the bar. 'You were very determined to win.'

Looking pleased, he said, 'I was. I know I paid well over the odds but that's why I'm here. It's all for charity, after all, and I've never been to the States. I really want to see New York.'

'When are we going?' Cassandra asked.

'Oh, you're not coming, my dear. I shall take the wife!'

Her face flushed with anger. 'You bastard!' she said, and she stormed from the room.

Bryony was at a loss for words.

'Sorry you had to see that,' he apologised.

'I didn't know you were married, George.'

'But Cassandra does. She is my mistress, my dear. I keep her in a nice flat in London, and she is there to entertain me when I come down from Yorkshire. Oh my, I feel I've shocked you.'

'Not shocked, but surprised me, George, but I have to say that tonight has been full of surprises. Perhaps I ought to see if Cassandra is all right.'

'You must please yourself, but I'm going to the bar.' And he walked away, completely unconcerned.

Toby caught hold of her arm. 'Come into the bar for a nightcap.' As they went together he said, 'I do hope you had a good time, Bryony?'

'I did, thank you so much. The food was excellent and the auction was really exciting.' But she couldn't get Cassandra out of her mind. 'Toby, excuse me for a moment, only I want to go to the ladies' room.'

'Certainly. I'll be here when you come back.'

Bryony pushed open the door to the ladies, and looked around. It was pretty full, and for a moment she - couldn't see Cassandra anywhere, but then she emerged from a cubicle, wiping her nose with the back of her hand. She walked to the line of plush basins and started washing her hands.

Going over to her, Bryony asked, 'Are you all right?' But she was taken aback by the vitriolic look cast from the girl.

'Why the hell should you care? You're all cosy these days with Toby, playing your cards right, by the look of you.'

'Whatever do you mean?'

'Well, you're wearing some of the famous Beckford jewels, aren't you?'

'Yes, Toby lent them to me to wear this evening. Famous? I didn't know they were. But as for playing my cards right, Toby and I are just friends, that's all.'

'Do you take me for a fool?'

Bryony felt her hackles rise. 'I hadn't thought about it, to be honest, Cassy, but now you ask, I think you must be.'

'What?'

'You, who come from a good family, have had a good education, and with the looks that you have, I ask myself what are you doing with your life? Snorting coke and being an old man's mistress – which one of us is the fool, would you say?'

'Who the bloody hell do you think you are to judge?'

'I'm not being judgemental, merely stating facts. It just seems so much to throw away.'

Cassandra started to laugh. 'You know nothing! I have a beautiful flat in the West End, and money to spend, and I use the flat for my own purposes when George is with his wife. Men are happy to pay plenty of money to go to bed with me.'

'I'm sure they are. Is George aware of this?'

'Don't be stupid!'

'I would be very careful in that case, because George

is a canny northerner. If he thinks he's being used, you will be out on your ear, so for your own sake, I would take great care.'

Cassandra just sneered at her. 'You think you know it all. Do you think I'm foolish enough to use the flat all the time? Of course I don't. I work in hotels – only the best ones, of course. I don't sleep with just anyone, only men with money. And I make plenty!'

'I saw you in the Strand Palace one evening,' said Bryony, suddenly remembering.

'You probably did. Now just mind your own business and leave me alone.'

Bryony was happy to do so. As she stepped through the door into the room outside, she bumped into Sophie Johnson.

'Mr Johnson! Hello, I saw you bid and win one of the prizes earlier.'

'Why, Miss Travis, how beautiful you do look, and so very elegant. Yes, I did. I'm really looking forward to collecting it. By the way,' he lowered his voice, 'that little business of your father's accident. It's been taken care of.'

'What do you mean, "taken care of"?'

'The person was identified and dealt with.' As he saw Bryony's look of concern he said, 'The man was punished severely and I'm sure he will not make the same mistake again.'

'Who was this person?'

'You don't need to know, my dear. Just forget about it . . . It's over!'

328

There was just a hint of menace in his voice that stopped her asking further questions.

'Well, thank you, Mr Johnson.'

'Happy to oblige. Now I'll not keep you from your friends,' he said as he espied Giles and Tarquin about to leave.

'Hello, Giles, my dear boy. How very well and smart you do look. I must congratulate you on you recent success.'

Tarquin stepped forward and quietly said, 'You are not about to cause a scene are you, Sophie?'

'Of course not. Why would I? I'll be in touch about the prize.' Looking at Giles, he said, 'I'll look forward to our evening together. It will be like old times.'

There was such a crush in the bar that Toby suggested ordering coffee and brandy to be sent to his room, where he and Bryony could sit in comfort. 'Is that all right with you, Bryony?'

'Of course. It will be nice to have a bit of breathing space,' she said.

Toby's room was next to hers, she realised. They both entered with a sigh of relief.

'It's nice to find a peaceful spot after all the noise of the evening, isn't it?' he asked.

Bryony collapsed on a sofa and heartily agreed. 'You had better take off the necklace before we forget,' she suggested. 'I really loved wearing the jewels, Toby. Thank you.'

'It was my great pleasure.'

Just then a waiter arrived with a tray of coffee and the brandy, which was poured for them.

As the waiter left, Bryony said, 'Do you do this sort of thing often?'

'What sort of thing?'

'Important functions like tonight.'

'More than I like, to be honest,' he said. 'I have a certain position to maintain in my father's absence, and even when he's around.' He sipped his coffee. 'I'm not saying I don't enjoy them but I could do with a few less.'

'You prefer to be at the manor?'

Laughing he said, 'How well you know me, Bryony, you dear girl.' He came to sit beside her. 'Do you think you could settle to the kind of life that I lead?'

Her heart missed a beat. 'Only some of it, I'm afraid. I'm not one for functions. I like to dine out, but to be on parade before your peers, no thanks. I would be so tempted to do something shocking, just to liven up the place.'

Toby started to laugh. 'Oh my, how often have I wanted to do just that but didn't dare.'

'Besides,' she added, 'I'm really too selfish. I have a duty towards my parents, of course, but otherwise, I like to do what I want, and how I want, not to have to consider letting the family name down. My father can do that all on his own!'

'Whatever do you mean?'

'It's better you don't ask, Toby.'

330

He rose from the sofa. 'I had better let you get your beauty sleep.'

Bryony stood up. 'Please take the jewels off me, or I might be tempted to abscond with them.' She removed the earrings and held them out, then turned around so Toby could undo the necklace.

He did so, then he turned her round until she was facing him. 'You were such delightful company tonight, and one of the most beautiful women there. I was so proud of you.' He leaned forward and kissed her, gathering her closer to him as his kisses became more ardent. And eventually he released her.

'I could easily fall in love with you, you know that, don't you?'

'Please don't. You know any future for us is impossible.'

'Would it really matter? We could have so much fun together.'

'Oh, Toby, I'm sure sharing your life would offer even more than that, but you have a duty to your heritage. I'm not sure I would be able to comply. I'm a bit of a rebel and would surely let you down, and then you would be disappointed in me. I wouldn't like that.'

'I don't think you could ever disappoint me, dear Bryony.'

She smiled at him as she said, 'It is wonderful of you to have so much faith in me, Toby, but I can't be what you expect to have in any woman who is to share your life.'

'If only things could be different between us, Bryony.'

'But they can't be, Toby. We don't love each other. But we can be really good friends, can't we?'

'Of course.' He walked towards the door. 'What time do you want the car tomorrow?'

'I could go home by train,' she suggested.

'Rubbish! I won't even consider it. Besides, you would crease your dress. How about ten thirty? I'll have them send you some breakfast an hour earlier.'

'That will be fine,' she said.

Toby walked her to her room. 'Good night, Bryony,' he said as he kissed her softly. 'Some man is going to be very lucky one day.'

'Good night, Toby, and thank you for a wonderful evening.'

Once inside her room, Bryony went over the night's events in her mind. It had been quite an evening, one way and another. She'd really been given the taste of the high life, but in all honesty, it wasn't quite what she thought it would be, and that was a disappointment. But the experience was one she would not have missed. She felt she had the best of both worlds. Toby was a dear friend and she was sure they would see each other again as friends, so she would still enjoy mixing with the social circle she used to crave, but at the same time, her feet were firmly on the ground.

CHAPTER THIRTY

When Bryony walked into the office on Monday morning, it was to find Nick in a foul mood. He was impatient with everything and everyone. He seemed to snap at her whenever she spoke and eventually she reached the end of her tether and suggested to Lucy that she go and make some coffee so that they could be alone.

'Right, Mr Langdon, that's enough! If something is annoying you, why don't you spit it out instead of putting us all through the wringer?'

'What are you talking about?'

'Your attitude. Poor Lucy has almost been reduced to tears by you, and I'm sick of you jumping down my throat.'

'What nonsense! Spending time with the in people has made you forget that work can be demanding. There is no easy option here, you know!'

Bryony was furious. Hands on hips she glared at him. 'So that's what all this is about! You didn't like me going to the Dorchester as Toby's guest. I've never

333

heard anything so very juvenile. And I thought you were so sophisticated and grown up.'

He flushed with anger, but remained controlled. 'Why should I mind where you go?'

'I have no idea. None at all.'

'Good time, was it?'

'Yes, brilliant. I don't know when I've been happier!' It was now she who was behaving like a child, baiting him. But she was so angry, she didn't care.

'When are we to read about the happy event then?'

'What?'

'Your forthcoming engagement. I know Toby Beckford is in love with you.'

'I'm afraid I can't tell you that, and now I'm off to do some research. Perhaps by the time I get back you will be a bit more civilised.'

Well, she hadn't exactly lied, she told herself. She couldn't tell him about any engagement, because there wasn't going to be one. Meantime, he could just stew in his own juice! But as her own anger cooled, in true female fashion, she was delighted that Nick was so angry at the prospect. He wouldn't give a fig if he didn't have some sort of feelings for her. But why the hell didn't he say something instead of blowing hot and cold?

She took herself off to the Court Royal Hotel and arranged to share a lunch break with Theresa.

They sat in a small café and exchanged news over a sandwich and cup of coffee.

'It seems ages since we spent time together,' said Bryony. 'I just don't seem to have had a minute to myself.'

'Well, you had your father to consider and before that your new job. How is James?' Theresa asked. 'The last time we spoke you were very taken with him, it seemed to me.'

'I dumped him when I discovered I was one of several,' Bryony told her bluntly. 'The more I see of men, the less I understand them. How about you, any boyfriends?'

Shyly Theresa told her about Michael, who worked for the council. 'He's in the Administrations Office. He's just a clerk at the moment, but he's hoping for promotion.' It had taken Theresa a long time to trust another man after her dreadful experience with Lenny Marks, but now she was happy.

'Is this serious?' Bryony asked, seeing her friend's look of contentment.

'Maybe . . . probably. I don't want to make a mistake, so we'll see how it goes. What about you?'

Shaking her head, Bryony said, 'No, nothing but an irritating boss, I'm afraid. Lots of friends, but nothing serious. Have your parents met Michael?'

'Yes, he comes home to tea sometimes.'

'What does your father have to say about him?'

'They seem to get on, but in the end, Bryony, it is my choice, not my father's.'

'My goodness, I never thought I'd hear you say such a thing. Your father used to rule you with an iron hand, as I recall.'

'I've grown up at last, I suppose. But Mother likes him and that's more important to me.'

'How is your mum?'

'Fine. She's great.'

Bryony sensed that there was an underlying meaning behind the words of her friend. As far as she could remember, Theresa hadn't been especially close to her mother and she wondered what had brought about the change.

Looking at her watch, Bryony said, 'I must fly. I left my boss in a bad mood earlier. Better go and face the music, I suppose.' As they left the café she said, 'Don't forget to invite me to the wedding.'

Theresa smiled broadly. 'As if I would!'

Nick was sitting at his drawing board, concentrating on something intricate when Bryony returned to the office. She glanced at Lucy, who just pulled a face as she looked over at her boss, but at least the office was now quiet. And so it remained for the rest of the afternoon.

As they left together at the end of the day, Nick caught Bryony by the arm. 'I'm sorry about earlier. I know I was a bit of a pig.'

'A whole bloody porker, I would say! Now do tell me tomorrow will be better or I may call in sick!'

A smile flicked the corners of his mouth. 'Tomorrow we have a lot to do, so don't you dare. I need you.'

She stared straight into his eyes. 'Do you really need me, Nick? I wonder.' She turned on her heel and walked to her car. As she drove away, she saw that he was staring after her and she wondered what was going through his mind.

*　　*　　*

In the great metropolis, Giles was ranting and raving to Tarquin about having to meet up with Sophie Johnson. He strode up and down the office, unable to settle.

'I don't want to be on my own with him,' he cried. 'The man terrifies me. Why the hell did you have to suddenly make such a ridiculous offer?'

'I thought it would be great publicity for both of us. You have certainly made the grade; I have several fashion houses wanting you for their shows. By the end of the year, you will be a very rich young man, and, of course, as your agent, I'll be taking my ten per cent.'

'What ten per cent?'

'Oh, come now, Giles. Who paid for your portfolio and gave you some training? I did, and for that I expect to be repaid.'

'I have no problem with that,' Giles said hastily. 'I just wish you'd told me.'

There was a sudden coldness in Tarquin's voice as he said, 'I didn't think I would have to.'

'Look, I'm sorry, all right? I'm just on edge.'

'We have to honour the pledge I made at the Dorchester whether you like it or not. Just make sure you spend time with Sophie in a public place. Make him take you out to dinner where there are a lot of people. He can't do anything then.'

Giles sat down and tried to explain his feelings to his friend.

'You see, for the first time I am absolutely free as a bird. I can now tell my father I don't care if he disinherits me; I don't need his money.' Smiling softly, he said, 'I no longer need to continue with my studies – I hated it anyway – and I don't need Sophie.' A deep frown creased his forehead. 'The only thing is, he doesn't want to let me go. I ran away to France to escape his clutches; I can't do that now.' His voice was filled with anguish as he appealed to Tarquin. 'Please don't let him spoil everything for me.'

'I certainly won't if I can help it. After all, Giles, dear boy, you are an integral part of my success at the moment. You are hot! Sophie will not be allowed to ruin that.' He sat and pondered the situation. 'When he takes you out for the evening, I'll come too! Of course, that's the answer. We'll both go! In fact, it gives me a great idea.'

Giles looked concerned; he knew that the designer could be a madcap at times.

'I'll use the evening to give us added publicity. I'll get him up here for his new outfit, which was part of the prize, and we'll meet in Southampton at the best hotel, invite other guests, and the press, and make a splash in all the newspapers – the locals and the nationals. He won't dare do anything wrong in the glare of all that. What do you think?'

'There is safety in numbers, is that it?'

'Exactly! We'll invite Bryony, wearing my gown, Sophie will wear his new outfit and you will wear another of mine. I'll take along a couple of my mannequins and I'll hire a room. We'll make it a really splendid occasion, a mini fashion show. After that, he has no call on you.'

'Tarquin, I am forever in your debt!' The relief that Giles felt was overwhelming. He so wanted to be successful, using his own skills. He had been given back his pride and no one was going to take that away. Certainly not his father or Sophie. He was free now to be himself, to stand on his own two feet. It was a wonderful feeling.

Sophie Johnson was not at all pleased when he received a phone call from Tarquin, outlining his plan. This was definitely not what he had envisaged. He'd planned a cosy evening with Giles in his London flat where they could be alone, where he and Giles could renew their relationship. He'd even purchased new bedding for the occasion. But when he tried to argue with Tarquin, he got absolutely nowhere.

'Sorry, Sophie, but as you must realise, the offer at the Dorchester was a publicity stunt and I must make the most of it. You're a businessman, you can see that I'm right . . . and, after all, you will gain financially in the long run as my partner. It's a great opportunity to spread the word, especially as I am a Southampton boy made good. That's great local interest.'

There was no way that Sophie could argue. He made an appointment to visit the London salon. 'Will Giles be there?' he asked.

'No. Giles is on a photo shoot for a magazine, in Tunisia,' he was told.

*   *   *

When Bryony received a call about the event from Tarquin she was thrilled.

'Of course I'll come,' she told him. 'It will give me a valid excuse to wear that beautiful gown again.'

'I've hired the ballroom of the Polygon Hotel,' he said. 'I'm bringing a couple of my girls but I thought it a good idea to dress some of the local ladies in my gowns to add a bit of interest. Do you know any that are slim and good looking?'

She immediately thought of her mother and Theresa. 'I know two.' And she told him who they were.

'Excellent. A young girl and an older woman. Couldn't be better. Better ask your father along, and bring a boyfriend. It's going to be a great night and we'll have a party after. I'll put a couple of invitations in the mail,' he said.

Bryony didn't think Leila would mind being a model, but she was doubtful about Theresa, who was a little shy, but when she rang her and put the proposition to her, she agreed without hesitation.

'Oh, Bryony, how wonderful. To be dressed by Tarquin. I've been reading about him in the papers. I'd love to do it.'

By the same token, her mother was very enthusiastic. Dan had been less than attentive of late, which meant he had some totty somewhere. This would be good for her ego, and maybe make him sit up and take notice of her again. She knew he'd soon get bored with his new interest, as he always did, but every time he wandered, she worried.

* * *

When the invitations arrived in the post, Bryony took hers along to the office and asked Nick if he was free on the night of the show. Then she told him what was planned.

'Would you like to come with me?' she asked.

'I would be delighted. Full evening dress?'

'I'm afraid so.'

'Don't apologise,' he said. 'It's nice to dress up for such an occasion, but I'm surprised you haven't asked Toby to escort you.'

'I'm sure he is far too busy. Besides . . . I have no prior call on his free time.'

'You don't?' He looked surprised. 'Have I read the situation between you two wrongly?'

'We are great friends, that's all. How you thought we could be anything else, with our differing backgrounds, I really don't know!' And she walked away before he could say more.

When Giles returned from his work in Tunisia, he found he had some free time, so he went home. The photo shoot had been very successful, which gave him the confidence to face up to his father, once and for all.

His mother was pleased to see him and was interested to hear about his work. He sat in the drawing room and told her all his news.

'You have done very well, Giles,' she said. 'I'm really proud of you. I do hope that now you'll get your life together.'

'Don't you see,' he said earnestly, 'now that I have

found my niche in life, I can be a real success. I no longer have to suffer the taunts about not being as good as my brother, because we live and work in different worlds. He will do well – there was never any doubt about that – but so will I! And that is what counts. I am someone in my own right, no longer in Hugo's shadow.'

'I'm not sure that's how your father sees it,' she warned him.

'But don't you see, Mother, that doesn't matter any more? I don't need Father's approval. In fact, I really don't want it.'

'Be very careful how you handle him this evening. He'll be home for dinner later.'

'Good. It's time to get all this settled.' He left her and went to his room to pack some of his clothes. He was moving into a small flat in London, which he could now afford, and was anxious to take most of his things with him. As he did so, he remembered the misery he'd endured during his teens, through his father's constant haranguing. How his life was changing. His penchant for racing was a means of escape, he realised, and now he was able to pay off his debts without having to rely on the likes of Sophie Johnson, which still filled him with some shame when he considered what he'd allowed himself to become. That was all behind him. He could start afresh with his head held high, moving on from his chequered past . . . if only he could shake off his ex-lover.

* * *

Giles and his mother were sitting talking over a glass of sherry when his father came home. His mother shot him a warning glance as Sir Douglas came into the room.

'Hello, Father.'

With a look of surprise his father said, 'Giles. I didn't know you were coming home.'

'I've just returned from Tunisia, and came to pick up my things.'

'What on earth were you doing there?'

'Working. I was doing a photo shoot for a fashion magazine.'

The judge poured himself a sherry, then sat down. 'A fashion shoot? What does that mean?'

'I was modelling some clothes for them.'

Sir Douglas frowned. 'Yes, I saw the spread in the papers about you. I'd like you to know you caused me some embarrassment in chambers afterwards.'

'Really? I can't imagine why,' Giles said coldly.

'Oh, come now, you can't mean that? A male model, for goodness' sake. When is this nonsense going to stop? I really can't allow it.'

'It has absolutely nothing to do with you. You may as well accept the fact that this is now my chosen career, and I'm very successful at it. I'm booked up for every month during this year.'

'And what about your studies?'

'I've dropped out of school. I don't need it any more. I'm managing very well as I am.'

The judge's face was puce. 'If you continue to defy

me in this way, then I'm afraid I cannot continue to support you financially any longer.'

'Douglas!' Lady Sinclair tried to intervene.

'No, Mother. Don't say anything.' Giles rose to his feet. 'I no longer need your financial backing, Father. I am making enough money to pay for myself. I have a new life ahead of me, and I'm afraid you will be seeing much more of me in the papers. Try not to be too embarrassed. You could try to be proud of me for a change.'

'Proud? In the fashion industry? It is run mainly by homosexuals. This is not a world I want my younger son mixing in.'

'Why ever not? Your younger son is also a homosexual, so I suppose you could say it is more than fitting!'

'Giles!' his mother cried.

Sir Douglas looked shattered. 'Tell me this is a lie, just to annoy me.'

'Why would I lie about such a thing? I am surrounded by very talented people who make a great contribution to society, and I am proud to be part of it. I, of course, will be discreet, not for your sake but for Mother and Hugo's.'

The judge looked at him with undisguised disgust. 'Not only will I disinherit you, but from this moment, you are no longer welcome in my house.'

'That's fine with me as I never felt I belonged here anyway.' Walking over to his mother, he said, 'I'll get my case and call a taxi to take me to the station. You and I will meet often in London.'

'I am so sorry, my dear boy,' she said. And rising to her feet she added, 'I'll put a few things in a case and come with you.' Turning to her husband she said, 'I will be staying in our London flat for the foreseeable future.'

'I absolutely forbid you to leave,' he declared.

'I am your wife, Douglas, not a prisoner in the dock!' She put her arm through her son's and left the room.

CHAPTER THIRTY-ONE

In the latest edition of *Tatler* magazine was a large centre-page spread of the charity event at the Dorchester, with several pictures including a splendid one of Bryony and Toby, headlined: 'Viscount Beckford with Miss Bryony Travis of Southampton'. Leila was poring over the pictures of the many members of the aristocracy and VIPs, with great glee and pride.

'My word, Bryony, who would have thought it – our daughter mixing with the likes? You have certainly come up in the world.'

'But it's not my world, Mum. The life they lead is far away from the one that I want. Yes, these events are wonderful occasionally, but Toby has so many responsibilities. When his father dies and he inherits his estate, he will have one hell of a job to keep things going. It will be his duty and he is very aware of what is expected of him. He will need a wife to help him in his work.'

With a smile, Leila said, 'You wouldn't like to be in that position?'

'I love Wallbourne Manor. It is so perfect and I really

can't tell you how I feel about it, except to say that to me it is very special, but I am not from the right stock. His family has such a history and a great lineage, which has to be maintained. Besides, even if I was from the upper classes, fond as I am of Toby, I'm not in love with him. I'm just so happy to have him as a friend.'

'Does he feel the same?' her mother asked with a knowing look.

'He told me he could easily fall in love with me, but we both know it wasn't possible for us to be anything but friends.'

'That seems sad because you really like him, don't you?'

'He's one of the nicest men I know, but I need to love a man deeply to want to spend the rest of my life with him. But I will see Toby again, and that will be great.'

'Life is strange, isn't it?' remarked her mother. 'I am from gypsy stock, yet my daughter mixes with the high-est in the land. That's progress for you.'

'At least, as I am, I'm not being traded in for a title!' Bryony exclaimed. 'I am free to marry whom I choose.'

'The main thing is that you are happy. Nothing else matters.'

'Are you happy, Mum?'

Leila thought for a moment before she answered. 'I'm not as happy as some, but happier than many. Your father has many faults, but you see, darling, I love him. I don't want anyone else.'

*　　*　　*

When she was alone, Bryony thought about her mother's words. She knew that her father didn't always treat Leila as he should, and she was aware of his roving eye and wondered just how her mother managed to cope with it. But what worried her more was the fact that much of his business was suspect. If ever he were caught, what would happen then? It was a constant concern to her, but she knew that nothing would change him. He knew the risks he was taking. She only hoped that he didn't push his luck too far.

Tarquin's plans for the mini fashion parade had grown out of all proportion. He had now turned it into a big event. There was to be a full-blown fashion show. He had taken over a large bedroom suite in the Polygon Hotel where make-up artists and hairdressers would do their stuff.

The local papers were full of the forthcoming show: the mayor and mayoress would be present, and local dignitaries. Tickets were selling as fast as they were printed, with a percentage of the profits going to charity.

Tarquin was thrilled with the thought, Giles less so as he would still have to see Sophie Johnson. But at least he would be surrounded by people, and that was a relief.

For Sophie's part, the more advertising he read about the forthcoming fashion show, the angrier he became. He rang Tarquin at his London salon to complain.

'You are making a circus out of my prize!' he yelled down the phone. 'I was supposed to be spending an evening with Giles. That was the prize, apart from the clothes.'

Unfazed by his anger, Tarquin remained calm and collected. 'Now don't be an old grump! You should be pleased. Think about all the extra business we will draw, the money to be made.'

'I'm not interested in the fucking money!' Sophie stormed.

'No! You're more interested in fucking Giles!' Tarquin had dropped his soft approach. 'Now you listen to me, Soph. Giles is very important to my – our – business at the moment and I will *not* have you jeopardise that in any way. He has a great future before him in the fashion world, and you need to let go.' He tried a different tack. 'Listen to me, Sophie, you helped me to get on my feet; do the same for Giles, please.'

Sophie slammed the phone down and walked around his room, fuming and cursing.

He knew that his need for Giles was bordering on the obsessive, but he couldn't control his feelings. The fact that Giles didn't want him was hard enough to swallow, but what he couldn't bear was the certainty that Giles would start a new relationship in the future, and this he couldn't accept.

On the afternoon of the show, Leila, Bryony and Theresa were to go to the Polygon Hotel to be made up and have their hair done, and Leila was to have her clothes chosen for her. But when they arrived, Tarquin eyed Bryony's mother with some dismay. Here was this woman with a great figure and looks that had been spoiled by her own style, which was flamboyant and bordering on the tacky. Being the professional he was, he could see beneath the dreadful permed hair and the loud clothing.

After they had been introduced, he took her aside.

'Do you trust me, Leila?'

With a certain suspicion she said, 'Why do you ask?'

Sitting her down he took her hands in his. 'You have a great figure and looks, but, darling, you are certainly not making the most of them. Will you trust me to bring out the best in you?'

She saw his earnest expression and for no reason that she could give, she did trust him. 'Yes, do as you wish,' she said.

He kissed her on the forehead. 'Great! The first thing we must do is change your hair.' He took her upstairs to the bedroom and introduced her to his stylist. He and Tarquin wandered off into a corner and Tarquin gave his orders.

Leila waited with some anxiety, but she did know that she didn't make the best of herself – she wasn't a fool – and this was a godsend of an opportunity. It would make Dan sit up and take notice and that was no bad thing at this moment.

Theresa, who was excited at the prospect of being dressed by the designer, was taken aside also to have her wardrobe picked out and her hair dressed.

'This is so exciting,' she said to Bryony. 'I can't wait to see what I look like in Tarquin's clothes.'

* * *

Dan and Nick had decided to meet in the American bar at the hotel before the show and have a drink together. As Dan had said, 'I need some support this evening with both my women being made into stars.'

The two men got on well together, each appreciating the business acumen of the other. Nick was explaining what he did in the advertising world, which was foreign to Dan, and he found it most interesting.

'I had no idea that so much went into any production,' he said.

Laughing, Nick said, 'Neither have most people. Bryony has a special talent in this field. She can immediately pick out the weak point of any advertisement. It's a sort of a sixth sense. I'm good at what I do, but I wish I had this instinct of hers.'

'You like my girl, don't you?'

'Yes, Dan, I like her very much. Is that a problem?'

'Not at all, as far as I can see,' he replied. He had taken to this young fellow. He seemed a man of the world, one that Bryony could look up to and, knowing his daughter, Dan knew that any male she could manipulate would not appeal to her. This Nick was very much his own man: a strong character, presentable, sophisticated, and he liked that. He wondered what Bryony really thought of him.

Eventually it was time for them to leave the bar and take their seats. They were placed in the front row, and Dan wondered if he was going to be bored. Further along the row sat Sophie Johnson, a thunderous look on his face. Knowing that young Giles was part of the show, Dan hoped Sophie wasn't going to cause any friction. Well, he wouldn't allow it. Bryony and Leila were part of this evening and he knew how excited they both were, especially his wife, and he wouldn't have the likes of Johnson spoiling it!

Tarquin took his place at the lectern at the side of the stage, and made his opening speech. He welcomed everyone and hoped they would enjoy the evening. Then, as he announced them, the models came on one by one.

The gowns were magnificent, described by the designer as the models walked the length of the catwalk, turning, flouncing, showing their wares. The audience was captivated, as was Dan, to his surprise.

Halfway through, Giles and two other male models showed the menswear. Dan was impressed as to how professional Giles was and he admired the clothes. He and Nick remarked on the suits and waistcoats, some of which were flamboyant, but beautifully cut.

Glancing along towards Sophie, he was perturbed at his expression every time Giles stepped on to the catwalk. This was not healthy and he was relieved when at last the female models replaced the men.

Towards the end of the show, Tarquin made an announcement.

'Ladies and gentlemen, so far you have seen my professional models. Now you will see three of your own. From Southampton, mother and daughter, Bryony and Leila Travis and Miss Theresa Kerrigan, a friend of Bryony's. You will see that everyone can wear my clothes.'

Bryony was the first down the catwalk, wearing a flowing floral summer dress and a broad-brimmed straw hat. She looked the perfect English rose.

As she left the stage, Leila appeared, wearing a smart suit and sophisticated hat. She looked very classy.

Dan couldn't believe his eyes.

Theresa followed, wearing a floating afternoon dress in pale blue, which was just right with her fair colouring. When eventually she left the stage, Bryony stepped out wearing her ball gown. She looked beautiful. With a confident air and a smile, she seemed to glide down the catwalk, head held high as she paused, turned and walked around. Her hair was dressed on top in an elegant style with the aid of hairpieces. Both Dan and Nick were surprised and bewitched. The applause was loud and enthusiastic, as she swept out behind the curtains.

Theresa stepped out next, wearing a cerise evening gown with a scooped neckline and full skirt. She walked confidently down the catwalk, smiling, swishing the skirt as she turned. She grinned across at her young man and her mother, who were watching, then walked back, turning once again before disappearing behind the curtains.

Leila was announced again.

Dan was speechless! Without a hat, she looked amazing! Gone was the harsh look. Her hair, which had been coloured by an expert, was smooth and shiny, now a rich dark brown with auburn tints, which was more of a natural colour than the darker dye she had used before.

Her make-up was softer, bringing out her lovely amber eyes. The elegant evening gown, in a heavy maroon silk, was simply but cleverly cut, showing the natural curves of her body. As she stopped opposite Dan, she looked at him and smiled. He didn't know when she'd been more beautiful.

'Your wife looks stunning,' said Nick softly.

'Yes, doesn't she?'

Finally, Tarquin called Bryony, Leila and Theresa out from behind the curtains and the three women again trod the catwalk, but this time together, holding hands and laughing.

The applause was deafening. Dan and Nick clapped as loud as anyone.

The three women left the stage and one of Tarquin's models walked on to close the show, wearing the most exquisite bridal gown, which caused many a gasp from the ladies in the audience.

As all the models, plus Bryony, Theresa and Leila, paraded together, Tarquin stepped forward and took his bow. When the applause died down he addressed the packed ballroom.

'Thank you so much, ladies and gentlemen, for your support tonight. I don't have the figures as yet, but we will be able to make a handsome contribution to tonight's charity because of you. This fashion show came about from a charity dinner held at the Dorchester in London last month. One of your residents, Mr Derek Johnson, made a bid for a prize I offered, which was a new gent's outfit from my range, and an evening with

Giles, my male model. And from there the idea for tonight grew. I would like Mr Johnson to stand and take a bow, because without his generosity, tonight would not have happened.' He pointed to Sophie. 'Please stand up, Mr Johnson.'

Sophie had no choice.

'As you can see, gentlemen, he is wearing one of my outfits and I'm sure you will all agree, he looks splendid.' And then cheekily he added, 'Please, sir, give us a twirl.'

Seething inside, Sophie did as he was asked, then quickly sat down, glaring at Tarquin, defying him to do more.

As the audience started to filter out of the ballroom, Dan, Nick and Sophie stepped up on to the stage.

'You look beautiful,' Nick told Bryony, gazing admiringly at her.

'Thank you,' she said, feeling pleased at the compliment but slightly flustered by it.

Dan held his wife in his arms and said, 'I cannot believe I am married to this new and wonderful woman. What have they done to you?'

'Tarquin took me in hand,' she told him. 'Do you like me like this?'

'You remind me of the first time I saw you – of course I like it.'

'Good,' she said. 'Tarquin has offered to be my adviser; so I'm afraid my new look could be costly! Although he has kindly given this gown to me.'

Dan kissed her and said, 'It will be worth every penny.'

Sophie went up to Giles and said, 'Right! We can go now, can we?'

Tarquin intervened. 'Go? Go where?'

'I have the rest of my prize to collect, an evening with Giles, although most of it has gone with this bloody floor show!'

'We are all having dinner here together!' said the designer crisply. 'Your prize didn't state where you were to spend the evening, and as I am the sponsor, I've arranged a table for the Travises and us. Come along, everyone!'

As they started to walk towards the dining room, Nuala Kerrigan came up to Leila. 'You look amazing,' she said.

'Thanks. I must say, I am surprised myself at the transformation.' Speaking softly she said, 'I am so pleased to see that Theresa has met a nice young man.'

'Thanks to you, my dear,' said Nuala. 'I will always be in your debt.'

'You would have done the same,' Leila said. And kissed her on the cheek.

The seven of them were seated at a round table in the dining room, Giles next to Sophie. As Tarquin had told him, 'This you can't escape, so you'll just have to suck your teeth and get on with it. After all, what can happen with all of us there? Be polite to the man – after all, he's been a brick to you in the past. Remember that.'

Champagne was opened as they all ordered from the menu.

Giles, trying to carry out his instructions, turned to Sophie and said, 'That suit looks good on you. How have you been?'

'I've been very lonely, Giles, as a matter of fact. I miss you.'

Giles felt his hands begin to shake and he drank deeply from his glass. 'I'm sorry about that but, as you can see, my life has taken a sudden change. Thanks to Tarquin I have a career that I really enjoy. Surely you don't begrudge me that?'

'Of course not! But I don't see that it has to change anything between us.'

Doing his best to try to make the older man understand, Giles quietly explained, 'I want to be free to follow my dream. I am going to be really busy this coming year and I just don't want any kind of relationship, with anyone. It's not just you, Sophie. I suppose it is selfish of me, but I don't want to have to consider another person. It will only complicate things. But we can still remain friends.'

Sophie didn't get annoyed as Giles feared he might, but his words chilled the blood in Giles's veins.

'That's all very well for you, dear boy. But, you see, I don't feel the same way. In fact, I find it unacceptable. By all means, follow your career; I want that for you, I'm not that selfish. However . . . I own you lock, stock and barrel. There isn't a stitch of clothing you have that I haven't paid for; I covered your debts, more than once. You owe me and, believe me, I intend to collect.'

Dan noticed the sudden pallor on Giles's face and wondered what Sophie had just said to him. He felt sorry for the lad. He knew Sophie Johnson of old. He'd seen many a young man pass through his hands, but never had the relationship been so intense on Sophie's part as this one. And that spelled danger for young Giles.

The meal progressed and, apart from Sophie and Giles, who remained silent, everyone was happy. But Bryony too was aware that all was not well as she watched. Giles gave her a beseeching look at one time, but there was nothing she could do.

Towards the end of the meal, the young man made his excuses and left the table to go to the gents. A minute or so later, so did Sophie.

Watching him go, Dan said, 'Oh dear,' and pushed his chair back.

Nick asked, 'Is there something wrong?'

'I feel there may be trouble brewing,' Dan answered.

'Want any help?'

'I might well do.'

Nick rose from his seat and the two men left the dining room together.

Giles was washing his hands when the door to the gents opened. His heart sank when Sophie Johnson walked in.

'At last,' the older man said, 'we have a minute alone together.'

'You're not going to make any trouble, are you?' Giles asked nervously.

'That all depends on you, darling boy.' His hand went into his pocket where he kept his razor.

The door swung open as Dan and Nick entered. 'My God, I had to get out for a minute's peace and quiet,' Dan said.

'And I am bursting to spend a penny,' added Nick as he walked over to the urinal.

'Good show tonight,' said Dan, patting Giles on the shoulder. 'I thought you did very well. Congratulations on your success. I read about it in the paper. By the way, Tarquin was asking for you.'

Giles quickly made for the door. 'Thanks, I'd better go,' he said.

'What are you playing at, Dan?' asked Sophie angrily.

'Now you listen to me,' said Dan. 'Tonight has been a great evening. My wife and daughter have been a part of it and no one is going to put the kibosh on it, Sophie. Not even you.'

'This is none of your business. It is between me and Giles.'

'Not when it involves my family; then it becomes my business! Now stop being a stupid old queen and pull yourself together. Sort out your differences privately, not in such a public place.'

'I don't have any choice now, do I?'

'Afraid not,' said Dan. 'Now come on back. The evening is almost over.'

Sophie was so upset by the whole evening he really wanted to walk out, but Giles was still here, so he said, 'All right, but don't think this is over. It isn't.'

Nick had washed his hands and was waiting to see what happened next. Then, as Sophie walked out of the gents, he said, 'I'll follow him to see where he goes.'

'Thanks,' said Dan. 'I desperately need a slash.'

Once they were all settled again, coffee and liqueurs were served. After which Tarquin said, 'Well, folks, that's it, I'm afraid. Giles and I are being driven back to London as I have clients in the morning. A van will collect the gowns and the models. Thank you, Bryony and Leila. You made a valuable contribution to the success of the evening.'

Leaving the dining room, they all walked towards the foyer and out of the hotel, where a car was waiting.

It was Dan who spotted Sophie putting his hand in his pocket as he walked towards Giles. Taking the razor out, Sophie flicked it open and as he lunged at his young lover, he screamed, 'If I can't have you, no other bugger will!'

Nick, alerted by the sudden movement, reacted in a second, sending Giles flying to the ground with a rugby tackle. At the same time, Dan caught hold of Sophie's arm as he slashed the air, and struggled with him, sustaining a cut as he did so. But he grappled the man to the ground. The razor was sent spinning across the entrance.

Bryony stifled a scream and went towards Giles, but Leila grabbed hold of her, keeping her out of harm's way.

Tarquin picked up the weapon and yelled at Sophie, 'You stupid bastard, what the hell did you do that for?'

Helping Giles to his feet, Nick sent him over to where Bryony and Leila were standing. Bryony held the young man, who was trembling from head to foot, in her arms.

'It's all right, Giles,' she said. 'It's all over.'

'He was going to kill me!' Giles cried. 'He's crazy.'

The management, seeing the skirmish, called the police.

CHAPTER THIRTY-TWO

Having been informed that the police were on their way, Dan took control of the situation. Hauling Sophie Johnson to his feet, he glared at him.

'Do you want to go inside, you stupid old fart?'

Sophie, somewhat more docile than before, said, 'Of course I don't.'

'The least you could be charged with would be GBH; at the worst, attempted murder! Then it would come out that you were queer and that would give you plenty of hassle with the cons.'

'What's your point, Dan?' Sophie snapped.

'That we say this was all a misunderstanding after a few bevies, and apologise. With a bit of luck you'll get away with a warning.'

'Do you think so?'

'There is one more thing, Soph. You have to let young Giles go. The boy is on the brink of great things – don't spoil it for him. This obsession of yours isn't healthy. Look at tonight – you could have been facing a murder charge if we hadn't stopped you.'

Johnson looked drained and weary as he gazed across at Giles, who was being comforted by Bryony. To Dan he said, 'There is no fool like an old one. I love that boy ... but you're right, I do have to let him go, or he'd end up hating me, right?'

'Absolutely.'

'I don't know what came over me just now. I lost it. You'd think I'd have more sense, wouldn't you?'

Taking a cigarette case out of his pocket, Dan offered one to Sophie. 'Here, puff on this. I'm going to send the girls home, and I'm also telling Tarquin and Giles to go before the police come. We certainly don't want any scandal. After all, tonight was for charity so we don't want a good deed smeared in the press.'

When Dan went over to the others with his suggestions, Nick offered to take the ladies home. Giles and Tarquin were only too happy to leave the scene and climbed into the waiting vehicle. Consequently, when the police arrived, there was just Dan and Sophie, smoking and chatting.

Dan explained to the two officers that there had been a heated argument, but it was over and finished. 'As you can see, everyone has gone home.'

The police officers grumbled on about people wasting valuable police time, but eventually they left.

'Come on, Sophie, I'll drive you home. I don't know about you, but I've had enough excitement for one night.'

*   *   *

Alone in his flat, Sophie took his razor, that had been returned to him, out of his jacket, placing it on the table. Wandering over to the mantelpiece he picked up the picture of Giles he'd cut out of the paper. As he gazed lovingly at it, tears trickled down his cheeks. He knew he would never see him again and the pain of his great loss was more than he could bear.

When Nick arrived with his two passengers at their home in Westwood Road, Leila invited him inside.

'Come on in, Nick. I don't know about you, but I could do with a stiff brandy to settle my nerves after all that kerfuffle.'

'Thanks. I won't say no.'

'You were very quick off the mark outside the hotel,' she remarked. 'That was some flying tackle.'

'Well, I was sort of on the alert. There had been a little bit of a situation earlier, which Dan and I managed to defuse, but I could feel the anger brewing in the old chap.'

'I'm really sorry you had to be mixed up in all this,' said Bryony, embarrassed that Nick had become involved. 'It was a dreadful experience. I keep thinking of what might have happened. It kind of takes the shine off the evening.'

'What rubbish! As it happened, a drama was avoided. Apart from that incident, the evening was most enjoyable, and you two ladies look amazing.'

They settled in the living room and chatted until Dan returned.

'Was everything all right?' Leila asked.

'Thankfully. I managed to talk some sense into Sophie, then I took him home.' He looked over to Nick. 'Thanks for your help tonight. It really could have been very nasty but for your quick intervention.'

'You did pretty well yourself,' Nick answered.

Eventually Dan and Leila excused themselves and went to bed. Bryony suggested she make some coffee.

'That would be very acceptable,' said Nick, following her into the kitchen. 'Nice place your parents have,' he said. 'Your father has a good eye for antiques, or is that your mother's choice?'

'No, it's Dad's. He loves old things and he's really very knowledgeable.'

'He's quite a man,' remarked Nick.

'He takes too many chances,' she said, 'and it worries me.'

'You can't live other people's lives for them, Bryony. Adults have to be answerable for their own actions. You just have to get on with your own life.' He held her shoulders and said, 'You must stop worrying so much about other people.'

'What do you mean?'

'Your father for one, Giles for another. And maybe Toby.'

'I don't worry about Toby Beckford. His future is mapped out for him, and now Giles seems to have settled to a career that will keep him out of trouble. But I do wonder where mine will lead.'

Tipping her chin upwards, he looked into her eyes and said softly, 'The future has a way of sorting itself out, but I might like to have something to do with your present.'

'You would?' she said shyly.

'Would the idea appeal to you?'

'I would like it very much,' she said, putting her arms around his neck as he leaned forward to kiss her.

When he eventually released her reluctantly, he said, 'Well, I must say, it has been quite an evening, and more interesting than many I've had. However, much as I'd like to stay, I'd better go.'

She walked with him to the door, where he kissed her again, softly and lingeringly. 'I'll see you tomorrow,' he said.

Bryony watched him drive away, then went to her room. She removed her dress and sat on the bed, happily reliving the past few minutes. She was in love with Nick, she knew that, and if she was honest with herself, she had been attracted to him from the first moment. Would their relationship last? She fervently hoped so. She remembered how hurt she'd been over James, but surely Nick was different. But how well did she really know him? Not that well, really . . . but did it matter?

With all these happy yet uncertain thoughts, she climbed into bed.

Two days later, the body of Sophie Johnson was found by a neighbour, who noticed the milk bottles still on the doorstep and reported the fact to the police. When they arrived, they broke in when they looked through the window and saw him sitting in a chair. He'd used his razor on himself. Beside him was a note, which said he had nothing left to live for.

When Dan told Bryony, she did feel sorry for the man. He had been kind to her when she'd visited the club looking for a clue to the identity of the person who'd caused her father to fall, and she remembered he had later told her the situation had been sorted.

Feeling that she owed the man some respect, Bryony accompanied her father to Sophie's funeral, which was well attended by his friends and many local criminals. Tarquin too attended. He owed Sophie Johnson a great deal and he was fond of the man. It saddened him to know that Sophie had been so unhappy he'd taken his own life.

Giles Sinclair did not go. He was just too relieved not to have to worry about his benefactor and lover. He said as much to Tarquin, who turned on him in a fury.

'He was good enough when you needed money! You didn't mind using him then.'

'No I didn't, and I can't deny the fact, but you had no reason to fear him. I did! Christ, he tried to cut me after the fashion show. He wanted to kill me!'

Unable to deny the fact, Tarquin quietly said, 'Just don't ever decry him in my hearing, that's all.'

Giles was consumed with guilt when later he received a solicitor's letter informing him that Sophie Johnson's estate was to be divided between him, and Bert Haines, known as Tarquin, the fashion designer.

* * *

Harry Burgess listened to the news of Sophie's passing with glee. He'd never liked the man and wondered if he were behind the severe beating he'd received. If it wasn't him, then it had to be men who worked for Dan Travis. Although his wounds had healed, the burning dislike for the car dealer still festered deeply inside him. And he felt he still had a score to settle.

He'd seen the spread in the local papers with the many photographs taken at the fashion show. It had shown Dan's wife and daughter together in fancy gowns. There had also been a picture of Dan and Sophie together. They were as thick as thieves, he thought, which didn't sit well with him.

Unaware of Harry Burgess's building hatred, Dan, now fully recovered, carried on business as normal, and Bryony was working happily with Nick.

Although they were working hard, Bryony and Nick found time to spend together, their new relationship blossoming.

By now it was early summer and they were looking forward to attending a polo match at the weekend.

When they arrived, they went in search of Toby, whose team was playing. He was delighted to see them.

'Bryony, Nick! How lovely to see you!' He put an arm around Bryony and kissed her on the cheek. 'My goodness, are you are still working for this reprobate?'

'I'm afraid so.'

'There, and I thought you were a sensible girl!'

Grinning at his friend, he said, 'How the devil are you?'

'Fine, and you?'

'I have some great news,' Toby told them, with a broad grin. 'I am about to announce my engagement.'

'Oh, Toby, how wonderful!' cried Bryony. 'I'm so happy for you. Who is the lucky girl?'

'Lady Helena de Lisle Bush.' With a wicked glint in his eye he looked at Bryony and said, 'And I really am in love with her.'

Knowingly, Bryony said, 'That's great news. Is she here?'

'Sadly not. She's abroad with her parents at this moment, but I certainly hope you'll both meet her in the near future.'

After the match, when they were driving home, Bryony turned to Nick and said, 'I am so happy that Toby is marrying for love.'

'Whatever do you mean?'

'We once had a conversation about him finding a bride. He made it quite clear this was on his agenda, as he would have to produce an heir to carry on the name, whatever the circumstances. At least she isn't just a brood mare!'

'Bryony! What a dreadful thing to say.'

'No, it isn't. I'm speaking the truth,' she said stubbornly.

'But do you have to be quite so blunt about it?'

'Why beat about the bush . . . or the de Lisle Bush?'

'You are incorrigible!'

* * *

369

The following Monday, Bryony was the last to leave the office, as she had been doing some extra work on the latest project. Her car was parked near the office in a private car park used by her, Nick and his father.

She was feeling particularly happy as the project was going well, and life couldn't be better. She was in love with a wonderful man, her father was well and, since the fashion show, her parents seemed to be getting along without any arguments.

Putting the key into the door, she was surprised to find it already unlocked. She mused that she must have forgotten to lock it when she'd parked this morning. She had been a bit late and was rushed, so perhaps that was why. She turned the ignition and started the engine. As she slowly backed out of the car park and on to the road, a voice came from behind her, which made her gasp in fright.

'Do as you're told, and you won't get hurt.' There was a sharp jab in her shoulder. 'I am holding a knife here. Try anything clever and it will be the last thing you do.'

Bryony looked in the rear-view mirror and saw the head of her unwelcome passenger whose face was covered by a scarf.

'Who the hell are you and what do you want?' she demanded.

'Just shut your mouth and do as you are told. Drive towards the docks. I'll tell you where to go.'

The blood in her veins ran ice cold and her fingers, gripping the wheel, were shaking. I mustn't panic, she thought. I must not panic. As she followed the intruder's instructions, subtly slowing her speed to give her time to think, she tried to sound calm as she asked, 'Why are you doing this?'

'Your father would understand.'

'My father? What has he to do with this?'

She could hear the anger in the man's voice. 'Fucking Dan Travis. Thinks he owns the world and everybody in it. Well, he doesn't bloody well own me! I taught him one lesson he won't forget. How's his ankle?'

Bryony caught on at once. 'It was you that set the trip wire?'

The man's wild laughter chilled her even further. 'Yes, that was me. I put him out of action, didn't I?'

'He'll kill you if anything happens to me,' she said angrily.

'He sent his men to beat me up, I reckon he owes me for that. He'll pay handsomely to get you back. He's got plenty.'

At this stage, Bryony thought it wise to stop any further conversation. Her mind was working overtime, trying to think of a way out of her dangerous situation.

As if able to read her thoughts, the man dug her further with his knife.

She gave a cry of pain as the knife penetrated her skin.

'That's just to show you I mean business, missy, so don't try and be smart. If you are good, you may come out of this unscathed, but don't push your luck!'

She had no choice but to do as she was told.

*   *   *

Eventually she was told to park the car inside an old broken-down garage. She was then forced out of the vehicle and pushed inside a shabby empty house, where she was made to sit on a rickety chair. The man bound her hands and feet and put a gag in her mouth, tying it at the back of her head. She still couldn't see his face because of the scarf, but the wild shining eyes terrified her.

The man stood back and looked at her whilst he laughed at her poor attempts to struggle free.

'You can spend the night here. You won't be lonely – the rats will keep you company.'

As he walked towards the door, she tried to call out, but could only make noises behind the gag.

'Sleep well, girl. Tomorrow I'll call your father.' He closed and locked the door.

As she heard the key turn, tears filled Bryony's eyes. What the hell could she do? She struggled with the bonds tying her hands, but the rope cut into her wrists when she tried, and those binding her ankles were just as tight. She looked around for inspiration. The room was empty except for a table and the chair she was sitting on and, in the corner, a grimy sink. The dirt and dust on the bare floorboards had been there for some time. Torn paper littered the floor. The small window was covered with cardboard. She started as she heard a rustling in the corner. A mouse scuttled across, disappearing down a hole. She smothered a scream. Rodents terrified her! She was now frightened of rocking the chair too much, in case it tipped over and the mice ran over her prostrate body.

Oh, Nick, where are you when I need you? she thought.

When Bryony didn't return from work by nine thirty, Leila turned to Dan and remarked on her lateness.

'Maybe she's stayed behind extra late at the office.' Which at times, when they were on an important deal, wasn't unusual. But when it got to eleven o'clock, her parents began to worry. If Bryony was going to be this late and wasn't out with Nick, she always rang to tell them.

Dan got up from his chair and, walking over to the telephone, he looked up Nick's number. 'Is Bryony with you?' he asked.

Leila saw him frown. 'No, she's not here either. I'll give Theresa a call and get back to you.'

'Dan?' said Leila, looking worried.

But Dan was already dialling another number. 'Is Bryony there?' he asked. 'Right, thanks.' He put the receiver down. 'I don't like this,' he said, ringing Nick again.

When he told him she wasn't anywhere to be found, Nick said he would be right over. In the meantime, Dan called the police. There was a heated exchange before he slammed down the receiver.

'Bloody useless, they are!' he cursed. 'They said she would probably turn up. If she wasn't home by the morning, they would take details.'

They heard the screech of tyres outside and then a hammering on the door.

Leila went to let Nick in. He rushed into the room. 'Have you found her?'

Shaking his head, Dan said, 'No. What time did she leave the office?'

'I don't know. I had an appointment and left early. Dad said he went at six thirty and Bryony said she would be another half an hour and would lock up. I drove there just now, but her car wasn't there. What's happened to her, Dan?'

Running his hands through his hair, he said, 'Christ knows. This isn't like Bryony at all. She always lets us know if she'll be late. It is an unbroken rule in the house to save her mother worrying. She's always done it.'

'Then what has happened?'

'I asked the police if there were any accidents reported, they said no. I'll ring round the hospitals.'

Whilst he was doing this, Leila poured them each a brandy.

Eventually, Dan put down the phone. 'That's all of them,' he said, 'and she isn't in any of them.'

'That's something to be grateful for, anyway, but what could have happened to her?' He looked at Dan and asked, 'Is there anybody, anybody at all, who has a score to settle with you?'

'There is only one man,' said Dan. Picking up his car keys he said, 'I'm going out.'

'I'll come with you,' said Nick.

'You stay here, Leila, in case Bryony calls,' Dan said. The two men left.

Dan drove to Harry Burgess's home. After getting no

response he kicked down the door and entered, yelling at the top of his voice, 'Burgess! Burgess, are you there?' He searched downstairs, then, taking the stairs two at a time, he searched the bedroom.

'He's not here,' he told Nick. 'Come on, we'll see if he's in the club.'

But the barman at the Silver Dollar told him Burgess hadn't been in for quite a while.

They returned to Dan's house. There had been no messages.

'I'll wait, if you don't mind,' said Nick.

'Of course not,' said Dan.

The three of them kept an all-night vigil, dozing on easy chairs and the settee, waiting for the phone to ring.

CHAPTER THIRTY-THREE

When the telephone rang at eight o'clock the following morning, Dan, sitting beside it, picked it up immediately. 'Yes?' he barked into the receiver.

'You sound a bit worried, Mr Travis. Didn't your daughter come home last night?'

'Who is that?' he demanded.

'You need to speak nicely to me, you ignorant bastard!'

'Burgess, is that you?' Dan asked, recognising the voice.

'Mr Burgess, if you please.'

'Don't you bloody mess with me, you wild bugger!'

'Dan!' Leila pleaded.

Taking notice of his wife, Dan took a deep breath and said, 'Mr Burgess. What is it you want from me?'

'That's better.' With a childish giggle, Burgess continued, 'Pretty girl, your daughter, wouldn't you say?'

Dan felt sick. This man was crazy. Had he harmed his princess? He spoke very carefully. 'What do you want from me, Harry? I'm sure we can come to some mutual agreement.'

'Oh, all friendly now, aren't we? That's the first time you have ever spoken a civil word to me. Hard for you, was it?'

'Look, Harry,' said Dan, doing his best to calm the situation, 'you and I may have had our differences in the past but I'm sure we can put this behind us. My daughter has nothing to do with this. Let her go. Please.'

'Yes, you'd like that, wouldn't you?' There was a long pause, then he said, 'I'll let her go, for a price.'

'Name your figure!'

Nick and Leila exchanged glances.

'Now, let me see,' said Burgess, playing with Dan, 'she must be worth a fortune to you.'

'How much?' Dan demanded.

'Five grand.'

'All right, but I need a little time to get the cash together, and I want to speak to my daughter.'

'No can do, I'm afraid. There isn't a telephone where she is. You'll have to trust me.'

Dan Travis, worried though he was, was no fool. 'I don't talk to my girl, you don't get the money!'

'Dan, for God's sake,' cried Leila.

Nick caught hold of her hand. 'Dan is right, Leila. If he insists on hearing Bryony, we will know at least that she is alive.'

'Oh, my God!' she moaned.

On the other end of the line, Harry Burgess was ruminating about this last demand. He wanted the money badly. He needed it to get away from Dan Travis because he knew when this was over, he had to make good his escape or he was a dead man.

'All right, Travis. You get the money together and tonight, I'll get your girl to a telephone.' He slammed down the receiver.

'Well, she's still alive,' said Dan, with a sigh of relief. 'He's bringing her to a telephone tonight.'

'What can I do to help?' asked Nick.

'At this moment, nothing. Go home, freshen up, have a sleep. I have to get the money and I've some favours to call in. We have to find Bryony. There will be lots of men out scouring the town for her who know Burgess. I'll give them the number of her car – it has to be somewhere. They will smoke him out.'

'What about the police?' asked Nick.

'I can manage this situation better without their interference.'

'Are you sure about that?' Nick protested.

'I am sure. Look, do you think I would put my girl's life at risk?'

'No, of course not. I'll go home, but I'll come back this afternoon. Meantime, I need to go to the office and organise a few things.' He kissed Leila on the cheek. 'Try not to worry,' he said. 'We'll find her somehow.'

Dan made numerous calls to people, arranging for them all to meet within the hour at his warehouse. Putting on his coat, he said, 'I have to go to the bank before I go to the meeting.'

'I'm coming with you,' Leila said.

*   *   *

An hour later, many of the town's villains were gathered to listen to Dan outline his plan.

'Let's make a list of any of the places that bastard may have my girl. And don't forget, he'd have to stash the car somewhere.' He gave them the registration number. 'Any ideas?'

Several of the men named various hangouts that Burgess was known to frequent, and a few empty garages they knew of. A plan was then formed and the men sent off with the addresses they were to try.

'We'll gather again here in a couple of hours,' Dan said. 'I have a couple of places to cover myself.'

Leila looked around the warehouse; the last time she was here was to teach Lenny Marks a lesson. This time it was for her own daughter she was there and she was fearful of the outcome.

Dan insisted she go home. Putting his arm around her, he said, 'There is nothing you can do here. If we hear anything, I'll call you immediately.'

Burgess had returned to the run-down house and, having removed his scarf, which he now considered unnecessary, crowed to Bryony about her father.

'I made him call me Mr!' he said, beaming from ear to ear. 'This time he had to show me respect. I like that.' He walked over to Bryony and said, 'I'm going to take this gag off you, but if you make a sound it will be your last. Understand?'

She nodded.

When the gag was removed, she coughed and

spluttered. 'I need some water,' she said between parched lips.

Picking up a dirty metal cup, Burgess barely rinsed it under the tap, before filling it. He held it to her mouth and made her drink from it.

Bryony was so thirsty, she didn't care that the receptacle was dirty. The water poured down her front as Burgess held it higher, making the water flow quicker than she could drink. Her wrists were sore and she felt as if they had swollen beneath the bonds.

'Tonight, when it's dark, you and me are going to the phone box along the road to call your father. You are going to tell him you are all right. And that's all you will tell him. Understand, do you?'

'Yes, I understand.' But Bryony's brain was racing. She would have to be very careful, but she wondered how she could give her father some sort of clue as to where she was. Her car was in the lock-up garage, which she had recognised as part of an old storehouse that used to belong to Timothy Whites, the chemist. How could she impart this news?

'I need the toilet,' she said. She was anxious to have her ankles untied. If she could stand maybe she could make a run for it.

Burgess hesitated. The girl probably did need to take a piss; she'd been tied up all night. As he kneeled down to untie her he said, 'You behave, girl. One false move and I promise you, you'll be sorry.'

Her ankles were stiff where the bonds had hampered her circulation, and as Bryony tried to stand, she staggered, her legs felt so weak. She knew that at this moment, she couldn't run. Burgess dragged her up the rickety stairs to a toilet that hadn't been cleaned for many a month and stank of urine.

'Untie my hands or how do you think I can manage?' she demanded.

'I don't like your tone, missy.' But there was little else he could do.

She rubbed her swollen wrists and cursed beneath her breath, as the ropes were undone.

'I'll be outside waiting so don't try and be clever.'

Bryony had no choice. She was desperate to use the toilet, and God knows when she would be able to do so again. She looked around desperately. The window was small and high. There was no escape there.

'Hurry up, damn you!' called her captor.

Opening the door, when she'd finished; she was grabbed by the hair.

'You're hurting me!' she cried, but Burgess took no notice, pulling her down the stairs and back into the room, where he pushed her towards the chair.

Desperation made her take a swing at him, but he was ready for her and hit her across the face, sending her staggering. He threw her on to the chair, and grabbed her hands behind her back to tie them.

'You are as bad as your old man. You think I'm stupid – well, I was ready for you.'

Her struggles as he tied her ankles brought forth another heavy blow and she felt her senses reel. Now she was even more frightened and began to wonder if she would ever get out of this situation alive! This man was crazy, hellbent on revenge. He wouldn't let her go. How could he? She tried to keep such thoughts to the back of her mind or she would panic, and that would only make matters worse. She started to pray.

Dan Travis and his men met up again, but no one heard anything or found the missing girl. They had searched every place they thought she might be.

Dan was frantic. 'Right! We'll start a systematic search, taking an area each. Now, where would you take someone if you were Burgess?'

'Knowing him, it would be somewhere seedy. The docks, Chapel, Northam maybe,' said Jack Saunders. 'There are still some old places around those areas suffering from bomb damage from the war. That sounds more the sort of place.'

They all agreed. With a map of the local area, they set out to cover it all between them.

'I want that bastard alive!' Dan shouted. 'He's mine when he's found.'

'If we don't find him, what will you do when he calls tonight?' asked Nick.

'We'll have to play it by ear. It all depends where the drop is. He's a crazy man, but he's very cunning. All right, let's go.'

Harry Burgess had put a board across the front door of the house where Bryony was prisoner. From the outside it looked solid, so although a couple of Dan's men looked at the war-damaged building, they took it for granted that the house was unoccupied because of the boarding. They had been within calling distance of Bryony Travis, and hadn't known it. The garage, though old and dilapidated, was locked, so they couldn't see Bryony's car, hidden inside.

As it grew towards the evening, they returned and were told to wait until Dan received his call from Burgess and then they would make further plans.

At the house, Leila made some sandwiches and coffee for Nick and Dan. No one felt able to eat, but they sat drinking the coffee and waited for the telephone to ring.

When it did, Dan let it ring a few times before answering it. He didn't want Burgess to feel his anxiety.

'Dan Travis,' he said into the receiver.

'Have you got the money?' Burgess demanded.

'I have. Have you got my daughter?'

'She's here, but don't try and get smart with me or I'll hurt her.'

'Don't you dare touch her, you bastard! Put her on.'

Burgess removed the gag and said menacingly, 'Just tell him you're all right.'

Speaking as loud as she could, she asked, 'Can I ask Dad to collect some pills I need from Timothy Whites?'

'No you bloody well can't. Now just say you're fine.'

Dan heard what Bryony had said and wondered what on earth she was talking about, but the relief at hearing her voice took all other thoughts from his mind.

'Dad, are you there?'

'Princess! Are you all right?'

She felt the tears well, but fought to control them. 'I'm fine, Dad. Just get me out of here.'

Burgess snatched the phone away. 'Right, you've heard your precious daughter. I'll call back and tell you where to take the money.' He slammed down the phone.

'Burgess!' called Dan down the dead line. 'Burgess, talk to me.'

'What happened?' asked Leila. 'Did you speak to Bryony?'

'Yes. She sounded terrified.'

'What's happening, Dan?' asked Nick.

Lighting a cigarette with trembling fingers, Dan said, 'He's going to call back.'

'Sit down,' said Nick, 'and tell us word for word what happened.'

Scratching his chin, Dan thought for a moment and then he said, 'I could hear them talking. Bryony asked if she could ask me to get her some pills she needed from Timothy Whites.'

'Pills? What pills?' asked Leila. 'That doesn't make sense. She's not taking any kind of pills.'

'What else happened?' Nick persisted.

'She said she was fine, but to get her out of there.' His voice trembled.

Nick Langdon was deep in thought. 'She was trying to give us a clue,' he said. 'But why Timothy Whites? Think, Dan, for God's sake. She was trying to tell us something.'

'Timothy Whites is a chemist in Above Bar. He wouldn't take her there. He couldn't get inside.'

'Where else would they have any kind of building? A storage or something?'

'As far as I know, they use their present building for deliveries. They used to have a place near the docks, but it was bombed.'

'That's got to be it!' Nick cried. 'Show me on a map where it is.'

Dan produced a map of the area and they pored over it.

As he studied the map, Nick began to get excited. 'That's what she was trying to tell us. That's where she is – it has to be. My God, she's using her brain. What do we do now?'

'I have to wait for his call, but I'll get on to my men. I'll send them mob-handed.'

'Think about this, Dan,' Nick urged. 'You send them in like the cavalry, they could spook him. We have to think of Bryony's safety.'

'You're right, you're right. I'll pick my best men. They can creep around until they find the place. When I know where I've to leave the money, we'll have him followed in case the others haven't found her.'

'I'd like to go with the men to the old storage place, if you don't mind,' said Nick.

'Of course. I'll just call and arrange things.'

And so the plan was set. Nick was to drive near to the old Timothy Whites storehouse near the docks and meet the men there. Dan would see him later.

*　　*　　*

The streets around the dock area were lit but not very brightly, and the gloom helped to cover the presence of the men. Cars were parked quietly around some of the side streets and six of Dan's men met up with Nick Langdon.

'Show me where this place is,' he said.

When he saw the building, his heart sank. It was dilapidated and damaged by the bombing. There was only half a roof, and the rafters open to the sky looked unsafe. Dear God, he hoped Bryony was all right. One false move here and the building looked ready to collapse.

He and the men silently entered the building, searching what was left of the rooms. There was no sign of anyone having been there since the place had been bombed, and no sign of Bryony. Outside they gathered again and whispered to each other.

Nick's mind was working overtime. Why would she send them here? This had to be the right place. He walked along the pavement, studying the other buildings until he spotted the lock-up garage and the boarded-up house. One of Dan's men came along and said, 'I searched this area earlier today.'

'What about this house?'

The man shook his head. 'No. Well, you can see it's boarded up.'

Nick studied the board, then putting out his hands, tried to move it. To his surprise it wasn't nailed down. The two men looked at each other. Carefully removing the barrier, they pushed open the door. Inside was dark, but, armed with torches, they crept carefully inside, followed by the others.

The building was obviously unsafe, with crumbling, cracked walls. Ceilings had fallen down.

'Be careful,' warned Nick quietly.

They walked carefully to the front room, but it was empty. It was evident from the litter that it hadn't been occupied for a very long time. The next room was also empty. When they came to the kitchen they slowly pushed open the door and shone the torch inside. In the beam of light they saw a black hole in the ceiling and rotted timbers precariously holding up what was left of the ceiling.

Flashing the torch, Nick saw the back of a figure, drooped from the shoulders, sitting on a chair.

'Bryony,' Nick called softly. 'It's me, Nick.'

The head went up.

'Be careful,' one of the men warned Nick. 'The rest of the ceiling looks about to cave in.'

'Look around upstairs,' he whispered, as he went forward towards the chair. As he shone his light, he was horrified at what he saw. Bryony was bound and gagged. Her eyes were full of tears, her face swollen and bruised.

He untied her as quickly as he could, holding her close. In her ear he whispered, 'Whatever you do don't make a noise.'

At that moment, movement from above brought the rest of the ceiling plummeting down upon them. Both were showered in dust and plaster and an old beam fell across them, causing Bryony to cry out in pain. Nick winced as it caught his arm. When all was still, he carefully moved the beam and, picking Bryony up, made his way towards the door, holding his breath as more rubble began to rain down on them.

One of the men came out and said, 'The place is a death trap. Take the girl home. We'll wait here in case Burgess comes back.'

Once in the safety of his car, Nick held her tightly. 'Oh, my darling,' was all he was capable of saying.

Bryony clung to him, unable to stop sobbing.

When eventually she controlled her tears, he wrapped her in his car rug, trying to warm her as she was trembling all over. Putting the car into gear, he turned up the heating and said, 'I'm taking you to the hospital.'

'No, Nick, please take me home. I want my mother.'

'All right, if that's what you really want.'

'Oh, Nick, I thought he was going to kill me.'

He patted her knee and said, 'But now you're safe, you're with me.' He found his emotions were so shattered, he couldn't say any more.

When he turned his car into the front drive of Bryony's home, Leila rushed out. 'Have you found her?'

Getting out of the car, Nick said, 'She's safe, but she's badly shaken.'

Dan came running out just behind Leila. Rushing round to the passenger side of the car, he lifted Bryony out and carried her into the living room. Kissing her, he said, 'I can't stop, princess. I have to meet Burgess.

I'm going to kill him for doing this.' And he ran out to his car.

'Stop him, Nick, please,' begged Bryony.

'Go! I'll look after her,' said Leila. 'Please stop Dan, if you can.'

Nick chased after him and climbed into the passenger's seat just as Dan was about to drive away.

'Right, tell me what's happened,' he demanded.

'That fucking bastard wants me to leave a shopping bag with the money in a rubbish bin in Mayflower Park. I'll leave him something, all right! I'll wait for him and then I'll bloody well have him!'

'No, Dan, you won't. This time you'll let the police handle it. By all means catch him, but then we call the police.'

'No bloody way!'

'Don't you think Bryony has been through enough?'

'What do you mean?'

'She's going to take some time to recover from all this – does she have to worry about her father being had up for murder as well? You'll destroy her, and what about your wife?'

Dan clenched his hands on the wheel. 'I just want to get my hands round his throat and squeeze. Did you see my girl's face, all bruised and swollen?'

'Of course I did. I found her and, believe me, murder isn't far from my heart at the moment because I love her! But, because I love her I won't let you do this!'

Dan was silent. He inwardly digested Nick's words. 'What do you suggest?' he asked.

'Are your men going to be hidden nearby?'

'Yes. They have their orders.'

'Right. When you have Burgess and the bag, that's when you call in the police. Let's do this legally. All right?'

'It's not my way, son. We usually sort out our own problems, but what you say makes sense. All right, we'll do it your way. But this is because of Bryony.'

'Of course,' agreed Nick, quietly breathing a sigh of relief.

The park was dark. A winding path went from one side to another, along which were benches, and an occasional rubbish bin. Burgess had been specific about which one Dan was to put the money in.

In the well-established shrubberies men were hiding, waiting.

Dan drove up to the park entrance, climbed out of his vehicle and walking to the designated bin, put in a shopping bag, which was filled with cut-up newspapers. He walked back slowly, climbed into the car, drove a couple of roads away, and parked again.

Hidden in the dark of the entrance to the South Western Hotel, Harry Burgess waited. He recognised Dan's car as he pulled up. He saw him go to the rubbish bin and place a bag there. Then he watched him drive away. He lit a cigarette and waited. It was his first mistake.

One of the men in hiding saw the light from the match and he watched the spot closely, wondering if it could be Burgess. He nudged the man hiding with him and warned him to be ready.

When eventually Burgess decided it was safe to come out into the park, he was being closely observed. As he went over the bin to collect what he thought was his ill-gotten gains, the men jumped him. There was a tussle, blows were exchanged, there was a lot of shouting and cursing, but Burgess was outnumbered.

Dan sauntered over to the small gathering. 'Hello, Harry,' he said quietly.

'You hurt me and you'll never find your daughter,' Burgess threatened.

'You're wrong there, you rotten little scumbag. My Bryony is safe at home.'

'I don't believe you!'

Dan laughed. 'My girl is very bright. She gave me a clue over the telephone.'

'You're a liar! She only told you she was fine and to get her out.'

'Yes, but before that she mentioned Timothy Whites.'

'So what? She wanted some bloody pills. That's all.'

'You really are as stupid as I thought,' mocked Travis. 'She had recognised the old chemist's storehouse. We soon worked it out. And you thought you were so bloody clever.'

'But you got the money! You was scared enough to do that!' Burgess was furious to think he'd been fooled by a slip of a girl.

'Show him, boys.'

One of the men grabbed a handful of the cut-up

newspaper from the bag and shoved it under Burgess's face, letting the pieces flutter to the ground.

With a cry of anger, Burgess tried to hit out. Dan punched him in the stomach, making him double up with pain.

Catching hold of Dan's arm, Nick said firmly, 'That's enough! Send one of your men to the telephone and call the police. This is now over, Dan.'

Reluctantly, he agreed.

Within a short space of time, several police cars screamed to a halt beside the park and after a heated conversation with Dan, they took Burgess away under arrest.

As the last officer got into his car he said, 'You should have let us handle this from the beginning, Travis.'

Dan turned on him angrily. 'When I rang you, you didn't want to do anything until the morning. You didn't believe my girl was missing. I've done your bloody job for you!' And he stormed away.

When the two men returned to Westwood Road, Leila met them at the door. 'I want everything quiet and peaceful,' she said. 'I've had the doctor to Bryony. He's given her a sedative, and she's asleep in her room.

'Can I go up to see her?' asked Nick. 'I promise not to waken her. I'll just sit with her, if you don't mind.'

'You go,' she said, and put out her hand to stop Dan following. 'Leave them,' she said.

*　　*　　*

Nick climbed the stairs. The door to Bryony's room was open. A small bedside light was on, showing the sleeping figure. Nick pulled up a chair and sat beside her. His anger mounted when he saw her bruised cheek. He was not a violent man, but he knew then that he too was capable of murder. For the first time, he was able to understand Dan Travis.

Leila brought him a cup of tea. She stood looking at her daughter, tears streaming down her face.

Nick squeezed her hand. 'She's alive, Leila. Keep telling yourself that; don't let yourself think of what might have been. It will drive you crazy.'

'You really love her, Nick, don't you?'

'Yes,' he said, gazing at the sleeping figure. 'I really do.'

'I'm glad,' she said. 'I'll leave you here. I must take care of Dan. He's very shaken. Thank you for stopping him doing something stupid tonight.'

'I know how he felt. I wanted to kill the man myself.'

'But that's not your style, and I'm grateful for that. Bryony has seen enough of the other side of life. I don't want it for her now she's an adult.'

'I can promise you, all the time she's with me, she won't.'

Left alone with the sleeping and bruised Bryony, Nick gently stroked her face. He felt so sad that such a bright young thing had had to experience the horror of being held by such a violent man and he wondered just how she was going to cope with the aftermath.

CHAPTER THIRTY-FOUR

When Bryony woke in the morning, it was to find Nick wrapped in a blanket, sleeping in a chair beside her bed. As she stirred, he woke.

'Bryony?'

'Nick! I am so pleased to see you.' Tears filled her eyes as she started to cry. He lay on the bed beside her and held her in his arms.

'There, darling, you let it all out. Tears are a great safety valve.'

When she eventually stopped, Nick found the bathroom and soaked a hand towel in cold water, and brought it to place over her swollen face. 'Here, this will help. Would you like me to make you a cup of tea or something?'

'No, just hold me. I feel safe in your arms.'

Nick climbed on the bed and held her close.

'You have no idea how I felt when you went missing. I thought I would go out of my mind,' he told her.

'I didn't mean to be such a worry,'

He tipped her chin up and, looking into her eyes, he

said, 'I knew then just how much I loved you. If I had lost you, I don't know what I'd have done.'

'Oh, Nick. You do know how to make a girl feel good. Hold me tighter.'

He did and they snuggled down together and fell asleep.

When Dan and Leila woke, they put on dressing gowns and went to see how Bryony was.

'Just look at them,' said Leila, as she saw the two sleeping figures.

For once, Dan wasn't jealous of another male paying attention to his girl. 'He's a good man,' he said. 'He'll take care of her. Come on, let's cook them some breakfast.'

Later, they all sat round the table together as Bryony had insisted on getting up. She drank several cups of tea.

'I am so thirsty,' she said. 'I didn't have much to drink in that dreadful place.'

'Do you feel you can tell us what happened?' Dan asked.

She related the story of her abduction. 'He said he was the man who set a trip wire at your office,' she told her father.

'I know that. I thought he'd been taught a lesson.'

Bryony just looked at him, knowing what the inference was. 'Well, it didn't work, did it? He said he owed you for a beating, and if you hadn't tried to teach him a lesson, maybe I wouldn't be in the state that I am.' She was so angry.

For once her father was at a loss for words. It hadn't occurred to him that it might have been his fault that all this had happened. It devastated him. His look of anguish was painful to see.

'It's time to change, Dan,' Leila remarked. 'The old ways have to go. You have a successful business and other interests that bring in a decent income; you don't need to deal with dodgy people any more. You could make a good living without all this hassle. Besides, you are getting older. It's time to bring a little restraint into your life. We don't need aggro any more. I certainly don't – I've had enough. A quiet life sounds good to me.'

'Bloody hell, woman! Are you telling me to go straight?'

'That's exactly what I'm asking. Wheeling and dealing is part of your life, I know that, but be choosy.'

Nick, who had been silent, said, 'Why don't you go into the antiques business? You definitely have the knowledge, I believe, and it's something you really like. Besides, it is an interesting business, and if done properly, very profitable.'

Dan grinned broadly. 'I like this young man of yours,' he said to Bryony. To Nick he said, 'It's an idea I've toyed with many a time.'

'We could go to auctions together,' suggested Leila. 'I could help you. We could open an antiques shop!'

'Dad?' Bryony looked expectantly at him. 'Please think about it.'

'I will, princess, I really will, I promise. Your mother's right. It's time to take stock of my life.'

Two weeks later, Bryony returned to work, at her own insistence. Her bruises had all but faded, and although she still had nightmares about her abduction, she said she needed to get back to normal, otherwise Burgess would have achieved something, and she wouldn't let that happen.

The man had been up before the court and charged with her abduction. The case was to be tried three months hence. Meantime, Burgess was to be examined by a panel of psychiatrists. Bryony would be called as a witness, and although she didn't relish the idea, she had recovered her spirit and was determined to give her story and do her utmost to get Burgess sent down for a long stretch.

Meantime, life went on. Toby had set a date for his wedding and had asked Nick to be his best man. It was to be a very grand affair with the ceremony taking place at Westminster Abbey, and the reception at the Dorchester.

'Oh, my goodness,' said Bryony. 'I'll have to have something splendid to wear.'

'Why don't you go and see Tarquin?' suggested Nick.

'Mum paid last time but I can't afford his prices!'

'No, but I can. You deserve a treat. Give him a call and we'll go this weekend. Let's make a night of it. We'll book into a hotel and see a show.'

'I'd love that,' she said, and picked up the phone.

* * *

Tarquin was delighted to see them both. 'My dears, this is the wedding of the year,' he said, 'and I'll be thrilled to see you wearing one of my frocks, Bryony.'

'How's Giles?' she asked.

'Giles is absolutely fine. He hasn't a moment to call his own these days he's so busy.'

'I'm really pleased everything worked out for him,' said Bryony.

'Sophie Johnson left his estate to be shared between us, you know.'

'No, I didn't.'

Smiling, Tarquin said, 'He was most generous. It was just at the right moment for Giles. It gave him a nice nest egg. He was able to hold up two fingers to his father, who had disowned him anyway. Old bugger! Now let's find you something splendid to wear, darling.'

And he did: a beautiful chiffon dress in the palest green, with a broad-brimmed straw hat, in lemon, trimmed with small flowers.

Bryony stepped from the cubicle and twirled for Nick's benefit.

'What do you think?'

'I think you look wonderful.' He walked over to her and said, 'Do you think whilst we are here, we ought to see if Tarquin has a bridal gown that would suit you?'

'What?' Bryony was dumbfounded.

Taking her hand, Nick said, 'I love you, Bryony, and I want to marry you. I don't have any other title than Mrs to offer you, unlike Toby. But I would be honoured if you would accept it and become Mrs Langdon.'

Tarquin held his breath.

'Oh, Nick!' She flung her arms around his neck. 'Mrs Langdon sounds wonderful.'

'How exciting,' Tarquin cried, brushing tears away. 'I'm sorry but I'm such an emotional being.' He clasped Bryony and kissed her on both cheeks and, to Nick's consternation, did the same to him.

'But, Nick, my dear! You can't possibly see your bride-to-be in her gown! Whatever next!'

'He's right,' she said.

Laughing with happiness, Nick said, 'All right, we'll make another appointment, but I can take her to buy a ring.'

That evening in the Grill Room of the Savoy Hotel, Bryony sat, her hand outstretched, looking at the large square-cut diamond on her finger. 'Oh, Nick,' she said, 'it is lovely and I'm so happy.'

Taking her hand in his, he said, 'And so am I. We'll buy a nice house in Southampton, your father can find us some decent furniture, and in time, we'll start our own dynasty. We'll have a good life together, Bryony darling, I can promise you that.'

'You don't have to promise me anything,' she said. 'The day that we are married, I'll have it all.' And she leaned forward and kissed him.

'We had better call your folks and tell them the good news.'

'Let's do it in the privacy of our room,' Bryony suggested.

'Our room? What are you suggesting?' His eyes twinkled as he asked her.

'Darling, we are engaged, after all. You certainly don't imagine that we are going to sleep in separate rooms . . . do you?'

Chuckling softly, he said, 'Are you trying to seduce me, you minx?'

'Absolutely!'

'I can see that living with you is going to be quite an experience.'

'I do hope so,' she said as she stood up. Holding out her hand, she said, 'Let's go and ring Dad and Mum.'

In the luxurious bedroom, they rang Bryony's parents and told them their news. Both Dan and Leila were delighted, as was Nick's father when Nick rang him.

As Nick replaced the receiver, he leaned over and, catching Bryony by the hand, said, 'Come here.'

Gathering her into his arms he kissed her. 'I do love you, Bryony darling,' he murmured as he nuzzled her neck.

'And I love you too.' Winding her arms around his neck, she returned his kisses with an urgency that left them both breathless.

He undid the buttons at the back of her dress and as he slipped it off her shoulders he said, 'You are so beautiful.'

'You are a lucky man, Mr Langdon,' she whispered as she undid his tie and then his shirt front.

Picking her up in his arms, Nick carried her over to

the bed. They lay entwined in each other's arms, loving one another, enjoying the exploration of each other as their caresses became more intimate.

As Nick moved above her, his voice husky with desire, he said, 'I'm going to love you as long as I live.'

She smiled softly at him and said, 'We have longevity in our family – can you stand the pace?'

Laughing, he said, 'Toby was right. Life will never be dull with you around.'

Kissing him again, she said, 'You talk too much.'

Caressing her breast, he said, 'You're absolutely right.'

Nick's caresses took Bryony into a world of sexual enjoyment she never knew existed. As he helped her to the zenith of her passion, she knew that with him she would really be loved by a man who would care for her and satisfy her beyond her wildest dreams.

Toby Beckford's wedding was indeed a grand affair. Nick played his part as best man with grace and good humour. When he told Toby of his own impending marriage, he was thrilled.

'Bryony is an exceptional woman,' Toby said. 'I hope that I'll get an invitation?'

'I expect you to do as good a job as my best man as I have done for you,' said Nick, grinning from ear to ear.

'I'll be very honoured to do so. How would you like to spend your honeymoon in the villa in the South of France?'

'That would be perfect, Toby. Thanks.'

'I'll lay everything on for you. The staff will take good care of you and I'll have a car there for your use. It will be my wedding present to you both.'

And so, three months later, on the day of the wedding at Highfield Church in Southampton, Toby stood beside Nick, waiting for the bride, who was the traditional ten minutes late.

'Stop worrying,' said Toby as Nick became more nervous with every minute.

The first notes of Mendelssohn's Wedding March started and Nick sighed with relief. Turning, he saw Bryony smiling proudly, walking towards him on the arm of her father, who was resplendent in his tails.

As his bride stopped beside him, he saw her smile as she pushed back the froth of veil from her face.

'You look wonderful, darling,' he said as he took her hand.

'And you are unbelievably handsome,' she said with a smile that lit her face.

They exchanged their vows solemnly and, having signed the register, left the church with more beaming smiles. After the photographs they were showered with confetti.

The reception was held at the Polygon Hotel, as Dan had promised. None of his old business colleagues were there. This was a family wedding, with the people attending who were important to him, his wife and daughter.

Theresa was there, wearing an engagement ring. She introduced her fiancé proudly to her friend.

'Who would have thought it?' she said to Bryony. 'I wonder if the nuns would have guessed that we'd both turn out quite as well as we have?'

Laughing, Bryony said, 'In my case they would be surprised, I'm sure.'

'Well, you did get to the Savoy and all those posh places you always wanted, and Nick had a viscount as best man, to boot.'

'True, said Bryony, 'but I have to tell you, the high life was a bit of a disappointment and I wouldn't change the way things are for anything. To be a lady is one thing, but to be married to a man you love, and who loves you in return, is much better!'

As she and Nick climbed into Toby's chauffeur-driven Bentley to take them to the station, she thought how strange life was. Her father was now intent on being an honest citizen. He and her mother seemed happier because of it, and she herself was the luckiest girl in the world. Her world, not the one she had once craved.

'Are you happy, Mrs Langdon?' asked her new and handsome husband.

'Deliriously!' she replied as she kissed him. And she was.

Every Time
You Say Goodbye

June Tate

It's 1943 and, despite the threat of German bombers, Southampton is alive and kicking. American GIs have swept into town, bringing glamour, swing music and even chocolate to local girls hungry for excitement.

One of these is Kitty Freeman. Married for only eighteen months, she's miserable. Brian Freeman wants nothing more than a quiet life, a tidy home and a wife to make his dinner. But when he receives his call-up papers and is sent to France, Kitty feels like a bird set free from its cage.

Will she be able to resist the charms of local villain Gerry Stubbs? Does the handsome American lieutenant Jeff Ryder want more than just friendship? One thing's for sure: the war holds more for Kitty than she could ever have imagined . . .

Praise for June Tate's passionate and popular sagas:

'A heart-rending tale of the life and loves of a brave and compassionate woman' Gilda O'Neill

'Displays June's customary flair for keeping the reader glued to the page' *Coventry Evening Telegraph*

'Excellent and gripping' *Sussex Life*

'Compulsive reading' *Woman's Weekly*

0 7553 2109 X

headline

For Love Or Money

June Tate

Connie Ryan has always wanted to be a star. She has a voice like nectar and the looks to go with it but, coming from a working-class family, there seems little hope of her achieving her ambition. Then the chance of a lifetime arrives when bookmaker Les Baxter, a rich and powerful older man with friends in all the right (and wrong) places, offers to become her benefactor and manager.

As Connie climbs the ladder of success, and her friendship with pianist Ben Stanton blossoms into something more serious, Les's attitude towards her begins to change. Just as her dream is finally within her sights, Connie is forced to make a choice that will change her life for ever – fame and fortune, or lasting love.

Praise for June Tate's novels:

'This gritty saga [is] compulsive reading' *Woman's Weekly*

'Her debut book caused a stir among Cookson and Cox devotees, and they'll love this' *Peterborough Evening Telegraph*

'A heart-rending tale of the life and loves of a brave and compassionate woman' Gilda O'Neill

0 7472 6550 X

headline

Now you can buy any of these other bestselling
books by **June Tate** from your bookshop
or *direct from her publisher*.

FREE P&P AND UK DELIVERY
(Overseas and Ireland £3.50 per book)

Riches Of The Heart	£6.99
No One Promised Me Tomorrow	£5.99
For The Love Of A Soldier	£6.99
Better Days	£6.99
Nothing Is Forever	£5.99
For Love Or Money	£6.99
Every Time You Say Goodbye	£5.99

TO ORDER SIMPLY CALL THIS NUMBER

01235 400 414

or visit our website: www.madaboutbooks.com

Prices and availability subject to change without notice.

News & Natter is a newsletter full of everyone's favourite storytellers
and their latest news and views as well as opportunities to win some
fabulous prizes and write to your favourite authors. Just send a post-
card with your name and address to: *News & Natter*, Kadocourt Ltd,
The Gateway, Gatehouse Road, Aylesbury, Bucks HP19 8ED. Then
sit back and look forward to your first issue.